The 48

DONNA HOSIE

HOLIDAY HOUSE  NEW YORK

For me!

HOLIDAY HOUSE is registered in the U.S. Patent and Trademark Office.
Printed and bound in July 2018 at Maple Press, York, PA, USA.
www.holidayhouse.com
First Edition
1 3 5 7 9 10 8 6 4 2
Library of Congress Cataloging-in-Publication Data

Names: Hosie, Donna, author.
Title: The Forty-Eight / by Donna Hosie.
Description: First edition. | New York : Holiday House, [2018]
Summary: "A secret government organization sends two brothers back
in time on a perilous mission to Tudor England to rewrite the history
of King Henry VIII's court"— Provided by publisher.
Identifiers: LCCN 2017024827 | ISBN 9780823438563 (hardcover)
Subjects: | CYAC: Time travel—Fiction. | Brothers—Fiction.
Twins—Fiction. | Secret societies—Fiction. | Jane Seymour, Queen,
consort of Henry VIII, King of England, 1509?-1537—Fiction.
Henry VIII, King of England, 1491-1547—Fiction. | Great Britain—
History—Henry VIII, 1509-1547—Fiction. | Science fiction.
Classification: LCC PZ7.H79325 For 2018 | DDC [Fic]—dc23
LC record available at https://lccn.loc.gov/2017024827

one

Margaret

Mother didn't approve of my wearing the light blue gown at court; she said it made me look pale and uninteresting.

Thomas once said it matched my eyes. He smiled when he said it. Thomas didn't find me pale and uninteresting. Thomas said I was a joy to behold. A delicate violet in a tangle of Tudor roses.

I didn't have to be a delicate violet, as far as my father was concerned, or even a rose, so long as I acted the part of a flower. I had six and ten years. I was a maid of honor in the court of Queen Anne. Ready to be plucked.

I knew the type of plucking my mother and father intended for me. It was my duty, as a highborn daughter, to comply with it. Recently, word had reached me that a match was being sought with an earl from Moray, in Scotland. I had not even seen the man, but one of the ladies at court said he was a horror to behold: fat as a toad and covered in warts. Worse, he was so old his youngest son was thrice my age. The earl had already buried two wives. I prayed my future did not lie with him—not with someone who already repulsed me by reputation alone.

Yet I knew better than to voice my wishes to my father, devoted as he was to the king.

My future was now in the hands of His Majesty, who would approve a match for me that enhanced the security of his reign.

The king didn't find me pale and uninteresting either, though I wished he would. Twice since the feast of Christmas he had made lustful eyes at me in the presence of the queen, for which I later suffered her humiliated ire. At least I wasn't alone in this injustice. My friend Jane Seymour bore the brunt of the queen's fits of jealousy. But she took it better than I.

Jane was like that—she had a placid temperament. She had no preference as to whom she would marry. She was happy to be a possession of her father and elder brother, content with the knowledge that the king would decide her fate too. It was an honor, she said.

Perchance it was because she was older than I—wiser, some would say—that she felt this way, but I could not come round to her way of thinking.

I was a maid of honor, yet I found no honor in the position. Instead, I felt only fear.

This court of Tudors, with its contradictions and violence, was terrifying.

***

So I wore the blue gown. I wore it as often as I could. Not because Thomas had said it matched my eyes, but because I *wanted* to be pale and uninteresting.

I did not want to be noticed by anyone.

***

I was dressed in blue on the clear March morning I'd spent in the palace gardens, walking and sitting with the other ladies of the court. On a sunny day, those gardens were my favorite place in the world to be. Nothing in God's kingdom could be as beautiful as the blackthorn trees in full bloom, and it was a rare moment when my court companions and I found ourselves liberated from the tension that constantly pulsed around the queen.

That particular morning, Her Majesty had taken to her bed with a head pain that could only be eased by quiet and darkness. Many of us fretted that a different sort of quiet and darkness was coming for her, but we rarely spoke this fear aloud. And on that March day, especially, in all its loveliness, no one wished to be reminded that the end of the queen could also mean the end of us all.

"Lady Margaret! Lady Margaret!"

I turned on my bench to see a young chambermaid running toward me. Her round face was flushed with exertion. I stole a deep breath and composed myself, trying not to let her panicked expression affect me. A lady was to display decorum and an air of detachment, and too many of the queen's maids of honor were giggling children. Such behavior was frowned upon by Her Majesty.

"Yes, child?" I asked, with as superior a countenance as I could muster. Inside, I was filled with dread.

The chambermaid tried to catch her breath.

"Lady Margaret, Her Majesty...Queen—"

"I know who Her Majesty is, child, now out with it," I said quickly. If the queen had commanded my presence, it would not do to keep her waiting.

"She—she was resting and the physician said she was not to be...be disturbed. But she has been...disturbed...Lady Margaret," gasped the maid. "Lady Jane said...to find you. The queen is much distressed—"

I crossed myself, stood, and picked up the hem of my dress, not waiting to hear the rest.

Another maid of honor, Lady Cecily, followed as I set off down the path toward the castle. I glanced back at her and nodded gratefully. It was not wise for a young lady of the court to travel the grounds unaccompanied.

We reached the end of the garden and heard male laughter coming from behind a large topiary. Our pace dropped to a brisk walk. I arranged my hood and lowered my eyes as Sir Edward Seymour and a companion rounded the corner.

They walked as if steered by someone who had drunk too much mead. Men of this nature, and in this state, were to be engaged with as little as possible, yet Lady Cecily and I nevertheless dropped to a curtsy, and the gentlemen bowed. Formalities performed, I made to take my leave.

"That gown brings out the color of your eyes, my dear," said Sir Edward's friend, grabbing my arm. "Lady Margaret, isn't it?"

"Yes, sir," I replied, trying not to show my discomfort. "Forgive my haste, sir. I have been summoned to the queen."

"A summons will be coming for *her* soon, with any luck," muttered Edward Seymour. "A summons to the Tower."

"Run along then, Lady Margaret," said the companion, his bony fingers releasing my arm. "Better not keep the queen waiting."

"They despise her," whispered Lady Cecily as we reached the stone steps of the castle. "What will become of us if—"

"Hush," I interrupted.

"I'm frightened, Lady Margaret."

I clasped Lady Cecily's hand in mine. I wanted to reassure her; I wanted to tell her that all would be well, that we would soon be married off to men who could protect us from this court. Perhaps even love us.

Yet if I didn't believe it myself, how could I, in good faith, try to convince her of the untruth? There was no pretending the queen wasn't losing the king's favor. And if she was taken to the Tower, and the court continued to whisper, our lives could be in danger too. We were inexorably linked to her. We were Her Majesty's near-constant companions. We sewed clothes for the household at her bidding, read the verses she requested, made music when she demanded it, and played host to lords from foreign lands at her command. We were hers. With such a close association with Her Majesty, the queen's enemies might become our enemies too.

A few of the maids of honor hoped that salvation could be found in marriage abroad. The king, however, was loath to make unions with men in Spain and Prussia. He needed us here to maintain ties to the lords of England and Scotland. *For peace and prosperity,* intoned his closest advisor. And when the all-powerful Cromwell spoke, the king listened.

⁓

Suddenly a cascade of noise broke through the silence. Lady Cecily and I both jumped.

The bell in the palace tower was tolling.

two

Alexander

That's the bell in the palace tower ringing! Why do you suppose—?"

"I don't care, Charlie," I said. I was too engrossed in the psaltery that Mark Smeaton had lent me to pay attention to much else. The instrument was somewhat like a harp but small enough to be placed on the lap and plucked.

I wasn't having much luck playing it. My strumming wasn't tuneful; it sounded more like a cat being tortured. If I played this at court I'd be tossed into the Thames with stones tied to my feet.

"The tolling could be important," said Charlie, ever the worrier. "Possibly a sign of danger."

"Or it could be a couple of fools swinging on the pull rope," I replied. I winked at him and laughed. My brother laughed too, but grimly. We were both thinking the same thing: *We'd* been the last couple of fools to swing on that pull rope. And we were almost skewered by yeomen because of it.

"You are enjoying life here far too much, Alex."

"And you aren't enjoying it nearly enough," I replied. "Must I remind you that we return home tomorrow evening? You should make the most of the time left. There are plenty of pretty maids of honor here just waiting for a handsome son of the land of Cleves to sweep them off their feet. Think of the swooning and pining they'll do while you're away!"

Charlie gave me a look.

"I can hardly concern myself with pretty maids when I'm worrying about your safety, Alex."

"I assume you're referring to Marlon. I'm simply doing my part for diplomacy between our great houses," I replied, placing the psaltery on the bed. I knew a lost cause when I saw one. "The Tudors and the Cleves will go down in history."

"I'm sure he's a lovely person. But we're not at home and you need to take care at court, for your sake *and* his." He glanced at the door. "Especially tomorrow morning."

In the morning we would be formally introduced to His Majesty, an occasion I was looking forward to with nerves and pride.

"I will," I said, standing up and stretching. "And *you* bear in mind that I'm better-looking than you, so don't be jealous when I get all His Majesty's attention."

"We're twins," said my brother, sighing. "We're identical."

"I'm still handsomer," I replied, digging him in the ribs with my elbow. "It has to do with scars. I have more scars than you, and scars are marks of bravery."

"And sometimes lunacy."

"I'll ignore that, brother, because I need your forgiveness. I'm deserting you now to meet Marlon. He's promised to show me a wing of the court I haven't seen yet."

"Great," replied Charlie. "But remember—"

"I know, I know. This court is dangerous."

<hr />

My brother was not mistaken. We'd only arrived a few days ago, but I truly *was* enjoying life in this court. And I would enjoy it even more when we returned for the real reason we had come calling on King Henry VIII.

three

Margaret

The bell had ceased clanging by the time I reached the queen's apartments, and no mention of it was made by the other ladies, two of whom were openly weeping. Queen Anne, Lady Jane told me, had raised herself from her bed long enough to rage at everyone in her rooms before retreating to her chamber. The physicians were treating her now with an infusion of lavender, rose, and sage, which I suspected would do no good.

Jane had sent for me, I understood, because mild-mannered as she was, she would have liked a friend by her side in the face of the queen's wrath. Some measure of me was sorry that I'd not been there to aid her. Even so, I gave silent thanks that I had been in the gardens when Her Majesty had lashed out.

This was not a happy court. I had no allegiance or loyalty to Queen Anne—her treatment of Queen Catherine, the queen before her, had been cruel, and few in the court felt sympathy with Anne's predicament now.

And yet this court was where I was, and where I would remain until my future was decided. My father had no other children— none he accepted as legitimate, that is—and so being born a female, I had been a source of great consternation to him. Serving in the court of the queen had been the best I could do for him, as a daughter. I had been brought here at the age of one and ten years, when it was Queen Catherine who sat beside the king on the throne. My mother had been a lady-in-waiting to Her

Majesty, but Mother, like Queen Catherine, had failed to produce sons and was similarly discarded by my father for being a disappointment. King Henry's desire for Anne Boleyn had never been a secret, and he had humiliated Queen Catherine with divorce. My father came to court and ordered my mother back to our cold ancestral home in Hampshire. It was a home I could never hope to inherit by virtue of my sex and visited only when summoned by my mother to deliver news and receive instruction on how to advance at court. My value to my parents and king lay in a beneficial marriage, and nothing more.

For five years, I had lived my life in the Tudor court in quiet observation of the ways of men and women, and the desperate desire by both sexes to do just enough to gain favor with the king without courting death in the process.

'Twas a fine line between those fates.

My father, Sir Richard Montague of Hampshire, now served the king in his navy. His fighting prowess and uncanny ability to foresee the enemy's advances at sea had ensured the king's approval—and my continued place in the court of the queen.

"Another turn outside, Lady Margaret?" asked Lady Cecily, shaking me from my thoughts. "It seems we are not needed here after all, and it would be a shame to waste such a beautiful day. The weather in March can be so..."

"Temperamental?" I suggested, glancing pointedly at the thick paneled doors that led to the queen's inner sanctum.

Lady Cecily flushed a pink so bright she could have been mistaken for a rose.

"You are wicked, Lady Margaret," she whispered, smiling.

"Wait!" exclaimed a voice, high and harsh. We turned to see Lady Rochford approaching. A sister to the queen by marriage, and despised by most.

"Lady Rochford." I acknowledged her with a nod and the briefest of curtsies, despite her elevated rank amongst the ladies of the court. Lady Cecily trembled beside me, obviously afraid her jovial words about wickedness had been overheard. *Wicked* was not a word used in civilized conversation. It inspired thoughts of witchcraft—and none among us wanted to be accused of that.

"A piece of text that the queen had been sewing was removed to the library for comparison by the biblical scholars," said Lady Rochford, barely returning our curtsies. "It has been deemed acceptable, and thus Her Majesty wishes to have it back. It brings her comfort."

The text was scripture, and every lady in the room knew who had removed it for comparison to ensure that the words were not blasphemous: Lady Rochford herself.

"Then we will go there and return with it," I replied.

I took Lady Cecily's arm, and without a word to the others, we left for the open air once more. Walking outside with the cool breeze gently caressing my face reminded me of Thomas's touch. It was a sensation I could no longer seek out or encourage.

I tried to push the memory, and all thoughts of Thomas, out of my head. But he sprang right back to mind when Lady Cecily and I entered the corridors and encountered his friend and fellow yeoman, Marlon. Marlon was with one of the new faces at court, Alexander of Cleves, who had only recently arrived with his brother, Charles, and their father, the Duke of Cleves.

Both sons had come from the womb at the same time. Their

likeness was a novelty, and they had already proven themselves popular at court, especially the gregarious Alexander, who appeared to find joy in everything from music to the artwork that hung in the Great Hall.

Not that I had approached him to confirm his appreciation for such things. I had merely observed him from afar.

The men bowed as we approached; we replied with a small curtsy. My deepest drop was reserved for the king and queen only.

"Alexander of Cleves," offered the newcomer. "A pleasure to finally make your acquaintance."

"The pleasure is ours," I replied formally. "I am Lady Margaret, and this is Lady Cecily. We are maids of honor to Queen Anne."

"I have seen you about," said Alexander of Cleves.

"As we have seen you," I replied. "You appear to have charmed the court already."

"I am the life and soul of this court," he said, his gray-blue eyes twinkling as if they had caught the stars. His voice was unusual. I knew Cleves was in the northern Rhineland, but the tone and pitch of his words seemed to suggest he was attempting to be more civilized in the English way.

"How long is it that you have been at court now, Alexander of Cleves?" I asked. The young man smiled. He was tall, with the physique of someone who excelled at sport. He and his brother both possessed a head of fiery red hair that had led more than one courtier to wonder whether two more of His Grace's bastard sons had been accepted into court life.

"My brother, Charles, and I arrived just four days past, milady," he replied. "We journey to our homeland tomorrow to attend to other matters, but we will return for a much longer period in due course."

"Do you have far to travel?" I knew the answer; unlike many of the other ladies and maids of the court, I was somewhat learned, having had a sympathetic tutor in my father's household as the only child. But I was interested to hear his reply.

"Yes, milady," he replied after a long pause. "And it is not a journey I am looking forward to repeating." His voice was becoming ever more pleasant to my ears. Melodic, almost. The voice of a singer. I wanted to ask more of him, but to show a keen interest in any man would have been improper in the open. Cromwell's spies were always on the lookout for impropriety. And Cromwell's spies were everywhere.

"Is Thomas guarding the apartments?" I asked Marlon, changing the subject.

"N-nay, Lady Margaret. He is...he is..." Marlon trailed off, his cheeks flushing.

A sharp pain rose in my stomach and pierced my chest. Marlon's chivalrous hesitation explained very well what Thomas was likely doing.

It was what *all* men did, whether they were married or not, highborn or lowly. Whether or not they'd once felt affection for a maid of honor, or someone else of virtue.

"You mean to say he is *not* on watch, and is making merry with the loose women of London outside the castle walls," I said testily.

"Lady Margaret," scolded Lady Cecily. "You should not speak of such things. It is not for a lady to know of them."

"To know things, even *these* things, is to have power," I replied.

"The king is the only one with power," she said. "And his

knowledge and word are all that matters. You should care not what a lowly yeoman like Ladman attends to. He is beneath you."

"I care nothing for Thomas Ladman," I lied. "I was merely stating that knowledge is powerful, if you wield it wisely."

"I happen to agree with you, Lady Margaret," said Alexander of Cleves. "Knowledge is a gift. Tell me, do you like to read? Perchance there is a library nearby? In my few days here, I have yet to find it."

"I love to read," I replied. "And indeed there is a library. It is not as large or handsome as the library in Richmond, but it is still impressive. In fact, I've just been ordered there to retrieve a verse the queen has been sewing. It was removed from her rooms."

"And you have been sent to reclaim it from the person who stole it away?" asked Alexander of Cleves, smiling. "A task for a brave person."

"I am not afraid," I said, resisting the urge to smile back.

I wondered just how deep the vaults of gold ran in the House of Cleves. The king could decide my fate any day, but perhaps he would not marry me off to an English lord or that warty, lecherous old Scotsman if a suitor from elsewhere were rich enough. I could feign affection; I had seen courtiers proclaim love after a simple walk around the gardens. Love was declared every day here. It was done for survival. And if a son of the House of Cleves was made to believe that he could love me, then an immediate match could be made. I already liked this Alexander well enough; he spoke to me as if I was worth speaking to. His questioning was sincere. I noticed that his pale skin, even lighter than mine, was free from the effects of pox and other illness. He wasn't powdered like many of the men in the court, or sour-smelling. He had an almost divine odor about his person: perfumed, but not heavy.

I wanted to send him a sign. I gently brushed myself against the handsome stranger as we walked, but lowered my lashes as I did so. This was bold, to be sure, and my actions felt somehow disloyal to Thomas. But at that very moment, Thomas was off philandering—and I had long known that my love for him was childish. This was a risk I had to take. I had no future with a yeoman, but there could be a future here. One of my own making.

At my touch, Alexander of Cleves's throat bobbed like an apple dunking in water and he seemed to catch Marlon's eye.

"Would you still like me to accompany you, Alexander of Cleves?" said Marlon. He spoke slowly, deliberately—almost as if he was questioning more than our destination.

"Do not leave me," replied Alexander of Cleves with great haste. "Not for one moment."

They nodded in silent agreement, about what I could not tell. It was very peculiar behavior.

In the library, Lady Cecily and I recovered the queen's property after a good deal of pleading with the scholar on duty.

Then Mark Smeaton, a musician in the household of the queen, arrived to inform us that the queen was not to be disturbed for the remainder of the day or evening. The needlework could wait. I forced a smile to hide my exasperation. Queen Anne's whims were becoming exhausting. Lady Cecily and I took to a window seat, where we were offered wine by a cupbearer to the king's scribe. Alexander of Cleves looked about the busy room.

"Well, shall we amuse ourselves in the library, then, since we've come all this way?" he asked. I nodded, and Lady Cecily's breathing steadied enough to show that she was not totally averse to this idea.

I made a show of studying a set of Latin texts but observed as two chambermaids entered and began making eyes and more at the handsome son of Cleves, who soon abandoned the volume he had opened. He had not yet been corrupted by court life, but I would not have long before he was. It was my good fortune that Marlon interrupted the chambermaids' advances on at least two occasions; yet as the minutes passed and the wine kept flowing, the foursome's laughter became louder.

I wondered for a moment what it was like to live with such abandon. A closer inspection of the chambermaids, however, reminded me that it was really only the men who could truly be at ease. Both girls had bruises. One was wearing a dress that was too large for her, despite her ample charms. Her bruises lay around her neckline and looked like green fingers stretching across her skin.

"It is time we took our leave, Lady Cecily," I announced loudly.

Alexander of Cleves was suddenly on his feet. "Do allow me to escort you to your rooms, Lady Margaret."

His chivalrous offer heartened me. "That would be most kind," I replied. I avoided eye contact with the chambermaids, and with Marlon, who had risen unsteadily to his friend's side. I could not acknowledge a yeoman who was clearly the worse for wine, and on duty as well.

"Please accept my apologies, Lady Margaret," said Alexander of Cleves, slurring his words slightly as we walked. "Just now I was neglectful of our—our newfound friendship. Can you forgive me?

I give you my word that I will be more attentive when I return to court after my travels."

"There is nothing to forgive, sir," I replied. "I pray that this is the first of many meetings between our houses. I long to tell you of my father, Sir Richard Montague, and his lands in Hampshire, and I would be most pleased to hear more of the House of Cleves."

I hoped my words were of interest to the son of Cleves. I wanted him to know that my father was a Knight of the Realm and I would be a rich reward for any courtier.

Alexander did not seem to find my daring untoward. When we reached the queen's apartments, he bowed deeply. Lady Cecily and I curtsied. As she and I slipped through the doors, I turned back to see Alexander of Cleves pat Marlon on the shoulder.

What a beguiling gentleman, I thought once more.

Yet I could not fathom what was in that wine that would have caused him to lose the Saxon intonation in his voice.

four

Alexander

"Hunt, sing, and dance,
My heart is set!
All goodly sport,
For my comfort,
Who shall me let?"

What on earth are you doing?" moaned my brother from his bed.

"Singing," I replied. "It's one of the king's compositions."

"Butcher his songs like that and they'll hang, draw, and quarter you."

"You're only saying that because I woke you up. Really, you're jealous because you can't sing like me."

"That's true," muttered Charlie, and his obvious admiration almost made me blush.

I pulled back the heavy, dusty drapes. A gray, gloomy light filtered through the windows, and rain pelted the glass. It was so noisy it was probably hail. I could feel the damp spreading into the room. We had been warned about the English weather. Rightfully so.

"What time is it?" asked Charlie, sitting up groggily.

"I've no idea anymore," I replied. "It is whatever time the king says it is."

Charlie buried his face back in the pillow.

"Everything feels so wet," he mumbled. "And there's a musty smell coming from those drapes."

"I'll make sure to see a few peasant washerwomen are hanged, just for you," I replied, smiling. "You look like death, brother."

"I feel like death. After you deserted me yesterday for Marlon, I ended up drinking with one of the keepers of the keys."

"Keeper of the keys to what?"

"The wine cellar, apparently. I can't move yet. Leave me here until later. I need to sleep," said Charlie, his voice muffled by the pillow.

"Questionable behavior from the brother who told *me* to be careful?" I said. I was genuinely surprised, and secretly pleased. On any other day, I'd have plied him for more details. But we had important matters to attend to. "You don't have time to sleep. Or have you forgotten? We're being introduced to the king this morning. Aramis was just here, and he said he doesn't care if you're actually dying. He'll have our heads if we're not ready soon. And he recommends dressing warmly. Apparently the king wants to go riding, even though it's the type of weather that'll drown ducks."

"The king!" Charlie groaned.

"Yes! The king!" I replied. "Big man, red hair? Likes to behead people?"

I pulled back my brother's sheets and he howled. I couldn't blame him; the room was freezing. The fire had run its course during the night and no one had been in to stoke it.

"Are you going to die quietly or die making a fuss?" I asked. "Because I could collect a crowd to cheer you on." Charlie dragged his legs out of bed and placed his bare feet on the cold stone floor.

"You're in a good mood," he said. "You're always in a good mood. It's very annoying, Alex."

"Of course I'm in a good mood. I've had a bath, I've been fed, and I've made several new friends over the last few days," I replied. "This short reconnaissance to England has been a success. I could actually get used to this way of living."

"Well, don't." Charlie stood up and winced as his back cracked.

"Have something to eat and drink, you'll feel better," I said, determined to keep up a cheerful appearance for my brother's sake. "What about some wine?"

"I'm going to kill you if you don't stop talking. And did you really mean it when you said the king wants to go riding? I thought Henry was still recovering from the jousting accident a few months ago."

"He is. Aramis thinks it's just bravado, but do you want to volunteer to be the one to tell the king he can't get on a horse?"

"Don't cock your eyebrows at me," said Charlie with a groan as he tried to move. "You look like you have two red caterpillars doing the Almain over your eyes."

The door suddenly flew open.

"Are you *still* not dressed, Charles?" yelled Aramis, storming into the room. Two young boys, no older than ten, scuttled in after him.

"I've only just woken, *Father*," he replied.

"The king wants to go riding," said Aramis.

"So I've heard," Charlie said miserably.

"Well, a poor impression you'll make if he is curtailed because you couldn't find your pants!"

Charlie dressed with haste and ran with me down the corridor after Aramis. We drew looks from everyone. Two redheaded, six-foot-tall marionettes here for their amusement.

Aramis stopped suddenly as we reached two huge doors, guarded by four armed soldiers on each side. He beckoned us over to a tall window that was stained with blue, green, yellow, and red glass.

"Charles, Alexander," he said in a low voice. "It's all down to you and the choices you make from now on. I have spent months gaining the trust of the court and king to enable you to take over from here. The future is in your hands. Remember that the king will look at you both and see a mirror image of himself. His vanity and pride are to be used to your advantage. So is your age. Recall that half of those alive in England are no older than eighteen years. This court is filled with people younger than you. Your age makes you superior in the eyes of the young court, and appealing to a king who wishes to maintain an appearance of virility. So if Henry wishes to hunt, you hunt until your hides are numb. If he wishes to feast, you stuff your stomachs until you cannot move. He will ask for your counsel because you are new and he likes to be flattered. Make the king adore you and he will listen to the House of Cleves when you work it into his head that he is *not* to marry Jane Seymour when he goes looking for another wife. And why not Seymour?" Aramis looked severely at me.

"Because he is to marry a Protestant," I answered automatically.

"And why is that?" He turned to Charlie.

"Because the Catholic faith is dying in England. Marrying another Protestant after Queen Anne will be its death blow."

"Correct. Now, make an impression this morning, and when you return to the court, your task will be easier. You've done well in a short period, do not fail today."

"I don't think we should keep the king waiting any longer," I whispered, flicking imaginary dust off my clothes.

Aramis nodded. This was it.

Aramis nodded to the guards, who opened the two doors outward in perfect synchronization. I was expecting an announcement of our names, but there was nothing. Following Aramis like two faithful puppies, my brother and I walked into a long room filled with circular pillars and lined on both sides by more stained-glass windows.

"Cleves," said a low voice to our left. A large man in black robes lined with brown fur seemed to slide out from behind a pillar. He had a round face, a bulbous nose, and black hair that fell like curtains around his face. I knew immediately that this was Thomas Cromwell, the king's chief minister.

"What is it, Cromwell?" replied Aramis. His Rhineland accent was much thicker than the one Charlie and I spoke with.

I looked around as Cromwell bent his head low and started muttering to Aramis. I could only catch every fifth word, and if I had moved closer it would have been obvious I was listening.

Eyes were flickering around the room. It must have been populated by at least twenty people. There were several men—both young and old—costumed as Charlie and I were, but in more colorful doublets. There were also a number of women—some of whom didn't seem older than twelve years—dressed in long gowns with tight bodices and flared skirts that made them look like stacked triangles. All of the women had their hair swept back beneath French hoods.

The queen was absent.

The king was not.

He was sitting on a dais, dressed in dark purple. His tunic was fastened—only just. Even from my position at the back of the hall I could see the buttons straining across his expansive chest. He was wearing a fur gilet and chunky brown boots.

We locked eyes and my stomach tried to escape via my mouth. I had never felt so intimidated in my life. The king wasn't smiling; he was grimacing, as if he was in pain.

All of my training in proper behavior in the inner sanctum of the king flew out of the stained-glass windows as I looked at him. I couldn't remember if I was to nod, bow, get on my knees and crawl—

"Shut your mouth, Alexander," hissed my brother. "You look like a fish. Now bow...bow."

I did as my brother instructed, just as the king's barking voice echoed above all others in the room.

"Cleves...come here, man."

"Follow me and do not speak unless spoken to," said Aramis. The Duke of Cleves walked confidently up to the dais and bowed deeply. Charlie and I did the same.

"So these are the sons of Cleves," said the king, leaning back. He was rubbing his thigh. "Which is the heir, and which is the spare?"

The court burst into spontaneous—and very fake—laughter. The king either didn't notice or didn't care. He was the center of attention and that was all that mattered.

"Alexander, Your Grace," I said, going down on bended knee. "By virtue of a few moments, I am the spare."

The king snorted his approval at his own joke being repeated.

"Which means you can have a lot more amusement," he said. "I was in that position—once."

The tension in the court was so heavy it was as if the stormy elements from outside had crashed into the palace. Not a breath could be heard.

"And I am Charles, Your Grace," said Charlie, sinking to a knee and filling the silence. "My brother and I are honored to have been afforded a place in your court."

"Do you both ride, heir and spare?" asked the king.

"We do, Your Grace," replied Charlie.

"And what say you to riding today?" asked the king. "My advisors say it is no weather to be hunting outside. The cowards are scared of getting wet."

"I think they are correct, Your Grace," said Charlie.

Now the collective intake of breath from those closest to the dais was completely audible. I half expected to see my brother's head fly in an arc across the hall. Had Charlie lost his mind?

"You believe I am frightened of getting wet?" asked the king in a low, menacing voice.

"No, Your Grace," replied Charlie. I clenched every muscle I possessed as he rose to full height to look the king in the eye. "I believe it will be the animals you wish to hunt that will be scared of getting wet. The deer in the parks will not be running freely. Their wish to cower from the elements will curtail your enjoyment. How can a king truly hunt to his full potential when the animals do not run to theirs?"

The king sat back and raised his chin, as if he was appraising us. His body language had gone from taut and uncomfortable to more relaxed. Charlie had made the greatest first impression ever. With his left elbow resting on the arm of his throne, Henry clicked his jeweled fingers, and a golden goblet was handed to him.

"I have affairs of state to attend to with my advisors," said the king. "But I will have your company, heir and spare, this afternoon. Do you play archery?"

"We do, Your Grace," I replied, standing. "I am more skilled than my brother. In my experience, second sons usually have the lion's share of the talent."

That comment raised a smile. It wasn't one that showed a set of teeth, but the king's lips definitely curled at the edges. He nodded to Aramis, and we were dismissed without further comment or question.

We took several steps back to show deference and then turned as the dais was surrounded by men with papers and quills.

"Seymour," called Aramis to a thin-faced man with a long black beard. "My sons, Charles and Alexander."

"Your offspring saved us all from a soaking this morn," replied the man. "The court will be grateful."

"This is Edward Seymour, first Earl of Hertford," said Aramis. "The Seymours' residence is Wulfhall, a favorite of the king's." Seymour smirked at that comment. "Sir Edward's sister, Lady Jane, is a maid of honor to Queen Anne."

The introduction was strategic. When we returned to the court, we would have to make the king turn away from Seymour's influence.

"It's an honor to meet with you," said Charlie.

"Cleves here speaks of you both often," said Seymour. "I would wager he is angling for earldoms already."

"Only if the king is prepared to throw in some pretty girls," I said, forcing a laugh.

Seymour laughed too; it was high and squeaky.

"Then we will see what we can do," he said, placing a hand on my shoulder. "I would introduce you to my sister, but more and more it seems she is spoken for."

His mud-colored eyes flicked to the king, whose voice was getting louder and louder with impatience.

"It would still be an honor to make her acquaintance," Charlie said with a bow.

As my brother straightened and stood by my side, Seymour seemed to be taking the measure of our long frames. "I have a request concerning your archery contest, sons of Cleves," he whispered. "A personal favor in deference to our new friendship. Don't let him win."

"Why doesn't Seymour want us to let the king win?" I asked softly as we left the room. "I would have thought his opponents would sabotage their own bows rather than defeat Henry."

"Because if the king loses, then Jane can be sent for to make him feel better," replied Charlie. "It's all strategic."

"Not for us it isn't, if we beat the king," I said grimly. "And I have such a pretty head."

five

Charles

I expected Aramis to scold Alex for making light of the king's bloodlust. But when we entered the corridor, the man instead stopped short, listening. For a split second his eyes widened. What had I missed? Rain was still pelting against the glass, and now rumbles of thunder echoed in the eaves. Then, somewhere underneath it all, I heard footsteps.

"Your Majesty," said Aramis, suddenly bowing deeply.

I turned to see a woman walking down the center of the corridor, followed by two young ladies. Her long green gown swept the ground as she held her head high. A small leather-bound book was clasped tightly between her hands.

The woman stopped directly in front of Alex and me. Aramis had stepped back into the shadows. My brother bowed, but I was paralyzed, hypnotized by the woman's eyes. They were as black as night.

"The sons of Cleves," she said in a throaty French accent. "Just what this court needs. More men to make foolish decisions for us all."

It was Anne Boleyn.

I was very good at holding my breath, but it was only when I heard the slow beat of my pulse in my temples that I realized I was doing it. It was hard to stay calm. The union of King Henry and Anne Boleyn only a few short years ago had split not only England, but seemingly all of Europe. It pitted religion against religion, as Aramis was fond of saying. Monarch against monarch.

"Your Grace," I said with a bow. "Miladies."

"You have seen the king?" asked the queen, staring directly at me.

"My brother and I were only just introduced to His Grace by our father," I replied.

"And how was my husband?"

"Eager to get outside."

Anne touched a small gold cross at the base of her neck; her skin was pale and flawless.

"Who was with him?"

"People of the court," I replied, trying to remember names. "I do not know many of them yet. I believe Cromwell was there... and Seymour."

"Lady Jane?" snapped Anne.

"No... no," I replied quickly. "Sir Edward."

"Likely you merely overlooked her. I have no doubt that English mouse was waiting to scuttle out of the darkness," said Anne, her eyes narrowing. "She has not appeared in my chambers for three days now."

I didn't know what to say. I wasn't prepared for the queen's openness about the disintegration of her own court, although it was all anyone else here talked about.

Anne cocked her head at me like a quizzical dog.

"But then you have only been at court for a few days at most, son of Cleves," she said. "You would not yet be acquainted with the whisperings of witches and sorcerers. And I understand you are leaving again."

"My sons will return to the court shortly," said Aramis, stepping forward. "We have some affairs to attend to at home first."

"Why?" demanded the queen. "Why would you return here?"

"We are to be of service to the king and our father," I replied. "To be friends and allies."

"Fresh meat for the slaughter," said Anne, walking over to a rain-splattered window. "Watch your backs, Charles and Alexander of Cleves. The knives are being sharpened everywhere, but Cromwell, Seymour, and Norfolk have the longest blades." Her face had become stony and harsh, like one of the stone carvings on the façade of the palace.

The queen then swept past us without so much as a backward glance. But one of her attendants let her gaze linger on Alex as she passed. My pulse quickened as I started breathing again.

"Who were the ladies with her?" asked Aramis quietly.

"Lady Margaret and Lady Cecily," replied Alex immediately. "Lady Margaret is the only child of Sir Richard Montague of Hampshire. He's in the king's navy. According to Marlon of the yeoman guard, she's in love with Thomas Ladman, the bastard son of some earl or duke, and has been since they were children. They have no future and they both know it. He's recently taken to seeking the comfort of women outside the palace. She's sixteen years old and will be married before the year is out, probably to a Scottish earl or northern lord. Lady Cecily is fifteen. Her mother has already made overtures about marriage to one of the sons of the Duke of Somerset. The king is considering it."

"Excellent work, Alexander," said Aramis. "Did you see how Lady Margaret was looking at you?"

"Unfortunately," replied my brother.

"Exploit that if you have to."

Aramis didn't say a word to me. I knew it was because I had

disappointed him. This was a reconnaissance. I, too, was supposed to be gathering information that could be used strategically to advance our cause when we returned.

⸻

"Don't be hard on yourself," said my brother as we walked back to our rooms.

"I'm not."

"Yes, you are. You can't lie to me. And the only reason I knew who the ladies were was because I met them yesterday when I was with Marlon."

"You're better with people than I am," I said quietly. "You could get information out of a corpse."

"Yes, I am," replied Alex. "And yes, I could. But think of all the ways you're better than me."

"Like?"

"I would bet a stable of horses that you're already prepared for the journey back."

"Yes."

"And I'm not prepared at all."

"You don't need to be," I said. "I've already checked everything for you."

Alex clapped his hand on my shoulder.

"I would be lost without you, brother of mine. And don't you ever forget it."

I wouldn't. Alex and I were a team. We had come into this world together, and we would leave it together.

And unlike most people, we had a good idea of when our demise would come.

six

Margaret

It appeared that the fates were conspiring to acquaint me with both sons of Cleves now. I took the crossing of our paths as a sign. Lady Cecily had been quivering beside me as the brothers spoke with the queen, afraid, as she always was, that words would be uttered that could somehow be twisted and used against us.

I, however, had held my composure. If Alexander had showed overfamiliarity toward us during our interaction, I would have kept a mask of indifference. Who were the sons of Cleves to me in the presence of the queen?

Other than my possible salvation away from this murderous den of snakes?

Thankfully, the queen had been in no mood for idle chatter, not even with distinguished guests from abroad. Perchance if the sons of Cleves had been from France, where Her Majesty had spent much of her childhood, she might have tarried longer. Queen Anne still believed herself to have allies there who could somehow protect her. The truth was she did not have allies anywhere, and even her family members at court were openly rebelling against her. In her position, I would have stolen away on a ship for distant shores and never returned.

"I see what they are doing better than they see themselves," Her Majesty hissed when we were some way down the corridor. Lady

Cecily and I exchanged glances. To which of us was the queen speaking? Were we meant to acknowledge her utterance? Queen Anne would often speak aloud and then rebuke a person for answering her. Yet her wrath was fearsome if she believed she was being ignored.

"What do *you* see, Lady Cecily?" asked the queen.

"Your . . . Your Grace?" stammered Lady Cecily.

"Open your eyes and tell me what you see," demanded the queen. She was walking at such a pace it was as if the hounds of Hell were snapping at her feet.

"I do not understand, Your Grace." Lady Cecily had gone the color of sour milk.

"Foolish child," snapped the queen. "Lady Margaret, tell me. What do *you* see in the arrival of the sons of Cleves at court?"

"I see His Grace allying himself and strengthening the bonds of friendship between the houses of the Saxon lands and England. His Grace has a gift for seeing the advancement in friendships between countries."

"Exactly," replied Queen Anne. "At least I am blessed with one maid of honor who is not a simpering mess or a disloyal wench.".

We knew to whom she was referring with that latter insult. I stayed silent, for I would not condemn Lady Jane Seymour. Recently, my friend had been moved to more spacious, luxurious apartments closer to the king—and the mystery of her whereabouts at night rankled Her Majesty no end. Yet Lady Jane was even more loyal to her family of Wulfhall. The king was sending her gifts. The queen knew this, and there was nothing she could say or do to stop it.

It wasn't just the king who needed to advance friendship between countries.

I needed to get away from this life.

And I believed I had found a way.

"Lady Margaret," said Queen Anne, as if reading my thoughts. "I want you to find out what has become of that treacherous witch."

"Yes, Your Grace." There was no heart to my reply. I would not forsake Lady Jane, either. I would lie if I had to.

"And I command you to get acquainted with the sons of Cleves upon their return to court. I want to know when they see the king, how often, and what is being said."

"Yes, Your Grace." This I could agree to in good conscience.

"You saw their resemblance to the king?" asked the queen.

"There are similarities, Your Grace."

"I have neither the time nor the patience for more bastards in this court. When I have a son in my belly, my husband will forget these usurpers. And I will make them rue the day they believed they could discard me like a commoner."

It was an understandable obsession with her now: providing the king with a son and heir would almost certainly turn His Majesty's attention back to her.

But it was never going to happen. The sole child the queen had borne was female, and since then she had lost too many, too early. The king's patience was spent. He was virile. He had bastard sons. In his eyes, it was the queen's fault he had no heir.

I prayed for Lady Jane's sake that if her time came, she wasn't barren.

For my sake, I prayed that one of the sons of Cleves was amenable to being acquainted with a potential bride.

seven

Alexander

With the rain continuing to do its best to drown England and everything in it, the court decamped to another, much larger, hall in the palace for an afternoon of archery. While Charlie and I despised our toxophilite instructor back home, I had to grudgingly admit that Piermont had turned me into a great bowman. It was the law of King Henry's land that any fit man over the age of twenty-four should be able to shoot a target from two hundred and twenty yards, which was around the length of ten tennis courts.

I was seventeen years old and had been able to hit that target outdoors since the age of thirteen.

***

No one was allowed to touch the bows until His Majesty arrived. When he did, he was accompanied by the large-nosed Thomas Cromwell on his left and the thin-faced Edward Seymour on his right. The large king was hobbling, and Seymour appeared to be limping so as not to outstride Henry. It was quite the sycophantic spectacle, and it took a lot of effort not to laugh out loud.

Yet another learning experience in how far men would go to curry favor with the king.

"That must be Lady Jane," I whispered to Charlie, nudging him with my left elbow. "Behind Edward and next to Lady Margaret."

Lady Jane had a plain freckled face, with an angular nose and a weak chin that disappeared into her neck. She also had small eyes and thin lips. It was the kind of face that disappeared from memory the second you looked away.

"And the king has chosen her over Anne?" whispered back my brother, incredulously.

"Apparently, but we're here to make sure he *doesn't* choose her. Or more importantly, her religion," I replied. "Besides, I don't think it's her face he's interested in."

"Their son *would* be a redhead," quipped Charlie.

"I'm sure there are some redheaded Protestants around," I whispered, running my fingers through my own bright hair. I couldn't resist smiling at Marlon, my new friend, who was standing near the archery targets. I'd made his acquaintance only a few days ago. He was a yeoman, and according to the laws of this court, beneath me. But he was kind. Unassuming, but self-respecting. And yes, handsome. I'd felt drawn to him immediately. I didn't see the harm in at least being amicable.

"Will you stop being so obvious?" hissed my brother.

"Nothing wrong with being friendly." It felt good to say aloud. "When in England, as they say—"

"Right now in England, even friendly can get you hanged, drawn, and quartered," interrupted Charlie.

With an exaggerated sigh, I went back to looking at Jane Seymour. Her covered head was bent; she was staring straight at the floor. It was the antithesis of what most of the younger girls were doing; they *wanted* to be seen. Lady Jane wouldn't stand out in a crowd of one, let alone drown out the vivaciousness of the current queen.

But it was also a lesson in self-preservation. It was a tactic that my brother, too, used brilliantly, but that I could never quite master myself. If no one notices you, then you don't become a target. Lady Jane wasn't meek and mild. She was playing the game and winning.

And I admired her on the spot for it.

"I'll concentrate on flattering the king. You concentrate on flattering Jane," Charlie whispered. "We need to start drawing her away from him. If we can report that we've already made headway when we return, our positions will be strengthened."

"I like the sound of that," I replied.

"Cleves, come here," barked the king, beckoning with his fingers without looking at either of us. I immediately walked forward, as did Charlie.

"Come as a package, do you?" said Edward Seymour, smirking.

"All great things come in twos," I replied, bowing. The king laughed. The courtiers laughed too. Edward gritted his teeth and smirked.

"Pick a bow, man," ordered the king.

Two were offered to me by a yeoman guard. Both were made of yew with hemp strings strung tightly together. At six feet tall, I had a long reach. I flexed both bows before deciding to take the one that was a little more rigid. Harder to fire for an amateur, but accurate in the hands of someone who knew what he was doing.

Charlie got the second bow by default; he didn't look happy. Then I remembered he was the one who was supposed to be impressing the king. Time to push down the pride and get in the shadows. I passed my bow to my brother, knowing he would do well with it.

I was handed a brown leather quiver filled with birch arrows, tipped with tiny gray goose feathers. The king's fur-lined coat was stripped from his shoulders by an aide and he immediately took aim with an elongated, fluid movement. Henry was an incredibly large man, and when his chest was exposed, he looked very intimidating. In that moment, I completely understood why people were terrified of him.

Henry's arrow flew through the air and landed. The target wasn't the colorful board I was used to practicing on, but was instead a black outer circle with a smaller white bull's-eye. The king's arrow had just made the white. The courtiers clapped enthusiastically.

Edward Seymour caught my eye as Charlie stepped up next. He wanted one of us to win so his sister could console the king. I needed to be average, to disappear into the crowd and get to know Jane, so today, Charlie's prowess with a bow needed to elicit a memory in the king that reminded him of . . . him.

Charlie's arrow wobbled slightly off course as it sailed in a straight line. He was better over the curve with a longer distance, but this wasn't the length of ten tennis courts. His arrow just made the white like Henry's. There was polite clapping.

I then hit the black—on purpose. I practiced archery back home more than anyone. Not because I liked it, but because I was terrified of Piermont placing an orange on my head and practicing on me as punishment for poor performance.

Courtiers, male and female, all had a shot, except Jane, who stayed behind her brother and close to Lady Margaret, who had been the most enthusiastic of clappers at my shot, even though it was a miss. The younger courtiers didn't struggle as much as I thought they would. There were a few who were good enough to deserve a respectful nod. One earl, who stood out because he was almost as tall as me, asked me for some tips, which gave me an introduction into his group of friends.

I caught Jane Seymour's eye several times. She seemed to be impressed that my brother was actually trying to beat the king; I was even sure he got half a smile from her at one point, but Jane showed no interest in taking up a bow herself.

The king was a very talented archer, and after several rounds, he and Charlie were well placed ahead of the rest of the court. I pretended to get very annoyed at my game, blaming everything from the bow to the strings to my fingers. Then the daughter of one duke took a particular shine to my ineptitude and started *assisting* me, which simply seemed to involve a lot of sighing and chest-heaving.

I tolerated it, as her attentions had inadvertently drawn me closer to where Lady Jane and Lady Margaret stood. My new friend, Marlon, was also nearby.

When the duke's daughter finally tired of helping, Edward Seymour approached. "The fair Lady Agnes seems enamored of you," he said with a smirk. When I made no reply, he asked, "Her feelings are not reciprocated?"

"Women are a mystery to me," I replied.

"You hope to be a man of the cloth, then?"

It took all my willpower not to laugh at his question.

"I do not see you presiding over a church, Alexander," said Marlon, stepping closer to the small group. "You are too—"

"Foreign?" interrupted Edward Seymour spitefully.

"I was going to say *honest*," said Marlon, smiling.

"What would a yeoman know?" replied Edward Seymour, barely keeping the sneer from his face. "Cleves, in this court, yeomen know their place, and it isn't to converse with nobility. You would do well to remember that, sir."

"I'm not certain of my future," I said, deciding to intercede quickly before matters took a turn for the worse. "Especially the Church's role in it."

"All men should be certain of their future," boomed an angry voice behind me. It was the king. "For every man's future should have God, riches, and heirs."

"My brother reads the core theological teachings," said Charlie, rescuing me from the king's ire and incredibly bad breath. "And yet I believe he is right to question the future. We both have concerns about the wealth of the Church, for one."

"Explain."

"We believe in the divine right of the king. A man of the cloth has no requirement of jewels and gold, because a divine man should be a penitent man. The wealth should come to the king. It is he who governs the people," said Charlie, taking his last arrow from the quiver. "And it is the king who should provide, for he knows his people best."

I had no idea where my brother pulled these lines from, but they were brilliant. And the king clearly agreed.

"A chief ministership I see in your future with rhetoric like that," said Henry.

"Or shall I be a poet?" replied Charlie. "Both are talented with words."

"Ha!" barked Henry. "Cromwell, you have your match here." The chief minister dipped his head in deferential reply. He and

Edward Seymour took several steps back and started conversing quietly, occasionally pausing to look up at the king and those around him.

"Your brother is a fine archer, Alexander of Cleves," said a quiet, calm voice behind me.

"Lady Jane." I bowed. "I am honored to make your acquaintance. Lady Margaret, a delight to see you again."

"You and your brother are looking well, Alexander of Cleves," said Lady Margaret boldly. "I had hoped to see you..."

Lady Margaret suddenly trailed off. Her pale blue eyes were transfixed by my wrist. Damn. I pulled my sleeve down, hoping no one else had seen—hoping I'd been fast enough that she'd simply rationalize it away.

A trick of the light, she might say. That was all it was.

"Is this your first time at court, sir?" asked Lady Jane.

"It is indeed. My brother and I leave for home this night, but we will return shortly. The king informed our father on our second day here that we have been afforded the honor of a place in the court until the summer and possibly beyond."

Not that we'll need to stay that long, I thought, watching Lady Margaret carefully.

"Will you require assistance in removing your belongings to a carriage?" asked Marlon quietly, barely moving his lips. He was taking a risk in continuing to converse with me, but I was glad he did. "I could speak to the groomsman to ensure that the best horses are made available to you."

"All arrangements have been taken care of," I replied. "As we are to return, most of our possessions will remain. But I thank you for your attentiveness."

Marlon nodded and stepped back in deference to my status, but his dark green eyes remained locked with mine.

"When *will* you return?" asked Lady Margaret.

"As soon as we possibly can. It is a great honor for us to be of service to His Majesty."

"As it is for all of us," said Lady Jane, lowering her head. I looked over at her brother, who was now glaring at me.

The atmosphere in the room was getting heavy with the condensed breath of so many people. The king suddenly ordered the game over, and a welcome blast of frigid air swept through the hall as the main doors were opened. Everyone congratulated Henry as if he had won. The king inhaled and stood up straight to receive his heavy coat once more, and he grimaced as his legs took his full weight.

"Well played, Cleves," called the king. "You will practice with me daily on your return to the court."

"It would be an honor, Your Majesty," replied Charlie.

"Just you."

Henry pushed past me and offered his hand to Jane Seymour, and she placed hers on his. He dwarfed her in every sense. The room chilled quickly as everyone departed.

"I think I was just dismissed," I said as Charlie sidled up to me.

"Henry saw Jane talking to you," he replied. "What did you expect?"

"Is that going to be our strategy? I'll flirt with Jane and get the king jealous, and you'll stop him from chopping my head off by kissing his ass?"

"It's one of my strategies," Charlie replied. "If only because watching you flirt with women is hilarious."

We made our way back to our rooms. We would be traveling light, and Aramis had already spoken to the head of the household to keep our clothes in storage while we were gone.

"Is everything arranged?" I asked my brother.

"The painting is still exactly where it was this morning, and yesterday, and the day before…"

"So the nighttime departure is on," I replied. "How very… clandestine."

"Story of our lives," muttered my brother. "Story of our lives."

eight

Margaret

"You appeared rather enamored of Alexander of Cleves," whispered Lady Jane, slipping her arm through the crook of mine as we left the Great Hall after dinner.

"It—it is a highborn lady's role to welcome visitors to the court of His Grace, is it not?" I replied, staring straight ahead as we made our way to the queen's chambers.

"Ah, so you were just being welcoming?" she teased.

"I am here to serve His Grace—nothing more, nothing less. Charles and Alexander of Cleves are here by the king's favor."

"Mm. But did you notice? He is very handsome, and such a good archer."

"The king. Of course. He is—"

"Not the king, you goose," whispered Lady Jane, pulling on my arm. "Charles of Cleves."

"I had not noticed."

She feigned shock by gasping dramatically. "I never thought I would live to see the day when my dear friend Lady Margaret Montague would utter a falsehood to me. Oh, Margaret, I would so dearly love to see you matched with a handsome young man from a great house. I want you to be happy."

"And what of you and the king? He made eyes at you in the same way Mark Smeaton makes eyes at the queen."

"No one makes eyes like Smeaton," she replied sadly. "If he continues to fawn over Her Grace with such abandon, the day will come when they are plucked from their sockets by the crows."

"Please, Lady Jane. Do not speak of it," I said.

"Then let us speak more of the sons of Cleves. You cannot fool me, Lady Margaret. I saw you staring."

I looked around, my eyes sweeping every doorway, every corner, for hidden courtiers who could be listening in. Then I took Lady Jane's hand and pulled her toward a stained-glass window that showed a bright green-and-yellow fish leaping from a pool of water.

"Very well, Lady Jane. I admit your eyes did not deceive you." At this, Lady Jane smiled. "You must have heard the whispers already, that the sons of Cleves are the bastards of the king, and I have been thinking on this. What if they are to receive his grace and favor? What if they are both here for wives? They could be our salvation."

"You cannot mean—"

"Yes. We could leave this poisonous place forever and never return, my dear friend. We could forget the cruelty of our fathers and the lecherous, fumbling old men here at court. Charles and Alexander of Cleves seem kind men. Strange, perchance, but that is simply the foreign way. We could learn to love them."

"My family would never allow it," whispered Lady Jane.

"If the king agreed to it, they would have no voice to object."

"You do not understand, Lady Margaret."

"If you become the next chattel of His Grace, you will be living under the sentence of death forever more," I said urgently. "Let His Grace down now, before it is too late. These are dangerous times, my dearest Lady Jane. You have been a friend to me, protected me, for years. Let me do the same for you now."

"Never speak to me of this again, Lady Margaret," said Lady Jane, pulling away from me. She straightened her hood and stared into my eyes. "It is too late for me."

———

I watched her walk ahead of me to the queen's rooms. Lady Jane's back was straight, yet her steps were slow and heavy, as if the weight of the world were upon her shoulders.

Perchance it *was* too late for her.

Yet I would not, could not, let it be too late for me. I was going to claim one of the Cleves brothers. I would use any means necessary to see that it was done.

And this night, I would make my move.

nine

Charles

The entire palace was asleep and the only light was from the crescent moon streaming in through one of the windows of the Great Hall.

Alex and I stood in front of the life-sized oil painting of Henry by Hans Holbein the Younger. It was so new, I could still smell the pungent pigments that had been used to create it.

We had seen this painting a hundred times in the past six months, and I knew every brushstroke. It showed Henry posing in front of a golden brocade drape. He was wearing a silver tunic that fell just above his knees, with a red-and-gold embroidered short-sleeved cloak over it that was just a little longer. A black beret studded with pearls, and enough jewelry to sink the *Mary Rose* covered the rest of him. Cream tights and golden slippers completed the look.

"Do I have to wear something like that?" had been my first question when I was shown a replica of the painting.

Alex had laughed so hard he'd almost peed his pants.

<hr/>

"Ready?" I asked.

"Let's go home," replied Alex.

ten

Margaret

Three knocks on my chamber door had been the signal. A boy from the kitchens had been more than willing to aid a queen's maid of honor in return for a coin that would feed his family for a week.

Lady Cecily made to protest—to leave our chamber was reckless, foolish—but I would not hear her. I wanted to follow the sons of Cleves. To bid them farewell in person. To ensure that I was seared in their brains as the last person they saw at Hampton Court. And, perchance, we could speak just a little.

The sons of Cleves were deep in conversation as I tiptoed behind them, but the words were all being spoken by Charles, the more serious of the two. He appeared to be giving instruction to Alexander. I felt my brow furrow when I saw they had no one and nothing with them. No servants, no belongings.

And they were heading for the Great Hall. Why did they not make for the stables?

I loitered by the door and watched from the shadows as the tall redheaded bastards of His Majesty gazed at a portrait of the king. Charles kept looking at his wrist. I had seen a strange mark on Alexander in the same place earlier in the day. I thought it a birthmark. *They are of the same womb, it stands to reason that they have the same feature,* I told myself.

Alexander spoke of home. There was longing in his voice that warmed my soul.

And then my breath caught in my chest. If I had been able, I would have screamed.

Charles and Alexander of Cleves disappeared. Body and spirit gone in the blink of an eye. It could not be, and yet I knew what I had seen.

They were sorcerers.

I shrank back in the shadows, breathing hard, willing myself not to whimper. My thoughts came as fast as my breath. Whom could I tell without implicating myself? I was out of bed and unaccompanied. That alone would bring me trouble. And there was hardly any wisdom in telling anyone regardless. No one spoke of witchcraft without bringing suspicion upon themselves. I could see the blade of the axe falling on my neck for merely sounding the alarm.

No, I dared not tell a soul what I'd just seen. And yet...

Witchcraft could still save you, whispered a voice in my head.

My breath slowed as the thought wended its way through my brain. Perhaps. Perhaps this was so. Perhaps the mere threat of exposure would persuade the sons of Cleves to help me—to see that I got out of this court. And if I was going to burn in the fiery pits of Hell, I would not be alone in that eternal torment. I had been raised not only to love God, but to fear Him too. The king was now the Supreme Head of the new Church, and those of us who adhered to his word became followers too, but old ways, old fears, do not die on the words of a king driven by lust.

My eternal soul clawed at me. Would the Devil himself want me if I turned to dark ways? If so, I would take the brothers of Cleves with me, from this life into the next, if they refused to aid me now.

Curse them.

Curse them all.

eleven

Charles

Excerpt from *The Forty-Eight Tenets*

Through your Director, you will receive orders from the Termination Order Directorate (TOD), a top secret, multinational scientific unit established shortly after the United States bombed Hiroshima and Nagasaki, Japan, in August 1945. TOD's formation was, in a sense, a "fortunate" by-product of the Manhattan Project, born of the very science that had so recently led to the development of an atomic weapon of mass destruction.

As with many scientific endeavors that chart new territory, experimentation has revealed applications for nuclear fission. As certain implications of nuclear fission became clearer, TOD was formed and funded by a clandestine group of forty-eight like-minded and well-funded citizens from around the globe whose objective it was to bypass the corrupt morals of governments to sustain mankind into the future, with the understanding that some human collateral damage is necessary for the preservation of the masses. This objective was, and is, to be achieved through a series of missions carried out by human Assets over time—and through it. Assets are trained to be time writers—weapons of historical manipulation—whose successful travel relies both on the reconfiguration of human anatomy on an atomic level through space and time, and on the use of carefully harnessed cosmic strings. Over several decades, TOD's finest physicists have perfected the time travel technique, pinpointing precise dates using the radiation emitted by objects created at the source of the time destination.

You are now in The 48.

Director Asix surveyed the small group of Asset trainees with eyes so dark they were almost black. Exhausted tension rippled through the students. They had been awake for two days.

This was their final test before selection—a process Alex and I had already been through. Now we were observers in the gallery, glorying in the knowledge that we would never have to face the preselection test again. The Asset trainees on the floor knew better than to make eye contact with us, but they were aware we were there. And they knew our presence meant we had just returned safely from our first reconnaissance mission. Meaning we had officially joined the only gods that mattered: The 48.

<hr>

"Ready stance!" barked Asix.

In one fluid movement, the group stepped left, leaving their legs apart. As one, they raised their hands to their sternums, closed them into fists, and lowered them to their navels.

"On my count...Taebaek Dan...three...two...one..."

Tiger Stance, Low Knifehand Opening Block, Right Front Kick, Right Front Stance, Double Punch.

"Death Tenet!" shouted the director.

"Do not fear death!" they all cried.

Front Stance, Swallowform Knifehand Strike, Right Front Stance, Left Punch, Left Front Stance, Right Punch, Right Front Stance, Left Punch.

They completed the next movements in the tae kwon do black belt form in perfect synchronization.

"But do not make death your friend!"

The air in the windowless room vibrated as every trainee's voice became one. Alex and I watched transfixed. It was beautiful, almost like a dance.

Six steps later, Mason Isaacs screwed up. Asix's cane whacked Mason's legs, and he collapsed. He didn't make a sound. When he got to his feet, he limped to the side of the room, overtightening his black belt in his fury at himself. He would have to repeat the sequence until he got it right.

I didn't sympathize with his pain or his humiliation. He was weak.

"Death is your master and your servant!" continued the remaining ten voices. Only eight would recite the next line of the Tenet after another two exhausted trainees failed to complete the next movements to Director Asix's satisfaction.

"There is no escape!"

Tiger Stance, Scissors Block, Right Front Kick, Right Front Stance, Double Punch, Tiger Stance—with the right foot, with the right foot—*Scissors Block, Left Front Kick, Left Front Stance, Double Punch.*

"For it comes to all in *the end*!"

<hr>

The final two words—screamed by the six remaining—hung in air so ripe with carbon dioxide I felt light-headed just watching.

The trainees returned to the ready position. My heart was thumping in my chest for them. Had they passed? Would they get to experience what Alex and I had?

The door opened and Piermont walked in. I felt Alex flinch. Piermont had that effect on people. It wasn't just his appearance, which was large, menacing, and severely scarred from the many altercations he'd weathered over and through time.

It was more than that. Of all the Senior Asset Instructors, he was the most exacting. The most ruthless. And as Alex and people like Jack McConnell knew especially well, he was the most sadistic.

I didn't want to think about Jack McConnell right now.

"*They* need to repeat," Asix told Piermont, gesturing to the trainees still gasping on the side of the room. "The rest are dismissed. Charles Douglas, Alexander Douglas—follow me."

As Asix turned to leave, the faint smell of mint wafted through the air. It was a scent all senior Assets had about them, and I would too one day. If I was fortunate enough to live that long.

Alex and I swapped the briefest of glances as Piermont passed us without comment.

"Did you hear me, sons of Cleves?" Asix asked sarcastically. "Physics lab, now." He walked out without a word of congratulation to the trainees who had passed, but they all looked too exhausted to care. The 48 could have thrown a party and they wouldn't have had the energy to go.

Not that we ever had parties at The 48.

I looked back at Mason and the other failures as we left the room. I wished I hadn't. For Mason Isaacs, the threat of Piermont now overseeing his retesting had done what a cane to the back of the legs hadn't. His face was a picture of fear.

———

The signal for the end of trainee lessons was sounding as Alex and I hustled after Asix. The physics lab was in the outer block, well away from the institute's dormitories, living quarters, and Asset training areas. From a distance, the entire institute looked like a prison. Each building was ten stories high. There were bars on the windows, and the doors were usually locked. The buildings were painted ocher, but in the winter—which seemed to begin in September and last all the way to May—it would get so cold the snow would stick to the walls.

It wasn't for camouflage. We didn't need it. No one knew we were here.

The lab was the newest building, even though physics was the cornerstone of TOD and The 48. It was the oldest Imperative lesson, and arguably the most important.

The last building had been gutted by fire. An electrical fault, apparently. Alice whispered that it might have been sabotage.

Alice whispered a lot.

———

Director Asix had outdistanced us and was waiting for us in the new building's main corridor when we entered. It was so white and clean and clinical in there that the faint shadow of a figure in the far corner of the hallway wasn't hard to detect. But Asix had his back to it, so unless he had eyes in the back of his head, the eavesdropper was safe.

My stomach tightened and I tried not to flush. I should have been angry with Alice for listening in. I should have reported her to Director Asix. This wasn't *her* time. And we weren't together anymore. There was no reason for her to be here.

But this was an important day for my brother and me. And if Asix was about to do what I hoped he would, then a minuscule part of me was glad Alice was witnessing it.

"Aramis has informed us that you did well on your reconnaissance," said Director Asix. "I have a note here for you that came with his observations. Deputy Director Grinch and I have evaluated your report, and you are authorized for the full RE assignment."

I tried not to grin. Before now, RE missions had only been assigned to highly experienced Assets. Our hard work had paid off.

"Cryostorage is in room two." Asix gestured to the door at his right. "The code to enter is eight-six-three. From there, you are to access the storage drawers. The pills for the forty-eight-day assignments are stored in the first drawer in the center console. Take only one each. Do it now."

Alex and I turned to the door. I input the code. The sound of decompressing air hissed as the door opened.

"This is a test," I whispered as we entered. "To make sure we follow instructions."

"Yeah, which means they're probably listening in. So for the record, please don't make me out to be an idiot." Alex smiled at me. "I'm already capable of doing that by myself."

We reached the center console. I felt no itching desire to go pawing through any of the other drawers lining the wall, even though there were at least twelve of them and thin wisps of cold vapor were lazily drifting out of the edges of one. We retrieved our pills as instructed. Each was contained in a small, clear protective packet.

"Back to your dormitory," instructed Director Asix when we returned. He handed me the letter from Aramis; it was sealed. "Doors are still locked at seventeen hundred hours. If you're late, you sleep outside. No exceptions. Even if you are Assets now." My stomach dropped as he glanced toward the area where Alice had been hiding, but she was gone. "I should not have to reiterate that the cryostorage code is for official Assets only. You are now part of something that is bigger than either of you. Take care to remember that."

His polished shoes tapped on the white-tiled floor as he left us. I looked down at the letter. My hands were shaking.

"Director Asix shouldn't have to reiterate…but he did anyway!" said Alex.

"No turning back now, brother."

"Why would we turn back?" replied Alex. "I can't wait to get back to the Tudor court."

"Okay, show me," called a voice from the shadows. Alice slipped out from behind a pillar and walked over to us. She was wearing skinny olive-colored jeans and a thick white sweater, which was three sizes too big.

I wanted to hug her.

I didn't.

"We've been given the go-ahead," said Alex, shaking his little bag with a bright blue oval pill inside it. "We're officially Assets."

"How was it?" asked Alice. "How was the Tudor court?"

"Amazing," I replied. "The adrenaline rush is something that training just can't prepare you for."

"And we're already a big hit with the ladies," said Alex, laughing. He stopped quickly when he saw the look on my face.

Alice kept her face neutral as she looked at my pill bag. "Why did you only take one? Asix didn't check. Seems like it might be smart to take a couple of extras, just in case."

"We took one each because that's what we're supposed to do," I replied, still fighting the urge to hug her. "These are the forty-eight-day pills, and we only need one because we're only going to the one destination. He didn't check because he trusts us."

"Is that it?" asked Alice. "Or is it that *you* trust *him*?"

"Would *you* have taken more than one?" asked Alex.

Alice smiled. "I guess I'll have to see when it's *my* time. Now, are you going to open that letter?"

I looked at Alex, who shrugged. He had no problem with Alice seeing the contents, and neither did I.

I thought it would be an evaluation, but it wasn't. It was a single piece of ocher-colored parchment.

C/A:

I commend you on a solid reconnaissance.

By now you've received word that you are to continue with the full assignment.

Before you depart, be advised that while you work exceptionally well together, it was over my protests that Asix and Grinch permitted this Asset pairing. Assets must be prepared to put themselves first, and as yet I am not convinced a pair of brothers will be capable of that should the need arise.

Prove me wrong, sons of Cleves.

Until we next meet at Hampton court, good luck.

A

twelve

Alexander

Death is the only constant in life. The majority of lives end without notice or legacy, and memories fade into the same dust as the bones to which they once belonged. We of The 48 are charged with ensuring that certain lives either assume, maintain, or are removed from a path of historical significance. As we do, we recall these instructions: Do not fear death. But do not make death your friend. Death is your master and your servant. There is no escape. For it comes to all in the end.

Those were the words written on the three Post-it notes I found affixed to my forehead when I woke up. It took me a split second to remember where I was, and to realize that I still *really* wanted to be sleeping.

"Why'd you write all this down?" I asked, furious but trying not to sound pissed.

"Because I figured Paris was as good a place as any to remind you about the Death Tenet," replied Charlie. "All you've done is sleep since we left Toronto."

"Yeah. Because sleep is good for the body, mind, and soul," I replied. "You should try it, because you look like hell."

"You slept the entire flight to Charles de Gaulle," retorted my brother. "You slept in the taxi to the hotel—"

"That wasn't sleeping," I interrupted. "Parisian drivers have a death wish and I didn't feel like watching death coming for me in a Citroën 2CV. So I closed my eyes."

My brother was stressed. I had learned a long time ago that sometimes it was best to just let Charlie be...Charlie. But when I was sleep-deprived I was less inclined to be charitable. Besides, I *hadn't* slept the entire flight. Mostly, I had shut my eyes so I could concentrate on what was about to happen on the ground.

My brother and I were finally heading off on the real deal.

<hr />

I dozed off again. When I awoke, Charlie was inspecting our kit bags. I wondered how many times he had done that since we had checked into the hotel. He had an obsessive need to make sure everything was exactly right. Mostly, I was grateful for it. Detail wasn't my forte.

The 48 had provided us with two bags that we'd strap to our bodies when we traveled back to the Tudor court. We would be taking more stuff with us this time, like the dossier and small vials of medicine, and Charlie was being extra-meticulous.

If I asked him why he was checking my bag for the millionth time, he'd say nothing must be allowed to interfere with the success of our mission.

If anyone asked me, I'd say my brother was looking out for me.

<hr />

Loud voices were drifting up from the street below. Our small hotel stood on a side alley that was barely big enough for two cars to pass each other—although that didn't seem to bother the drivers in Paris, who had no qualms about mounting the sidewalk when necessary. I wasn't joking about greeting death via a Citroën. From our fifth-floor, front-view window, I had witnessed several fights already over road territory. This sounded just like another argument.

I levered myself off the bed, pulled back the net curtain that covered the grimy glass, and looked down. A silver van with blacked-out windows was parked across from the hotel. Two of its four wheels had mounted the curb, almost blocking the entrance to the pâtisserie opposite.

"What's going on down there?" Charlie asked, zipping up my kit bag.

"Another fight," I said. "Go throw some water over them, Charlie. Or go the Middle Ages route and throw a bucket of piss out the window. We could say we're getting into character again."

My brother joined me at the window, listening. After a few seconds he turned to me with three fingers raised on one hand and one on the other. I nodded. There were four distinct voices: three sounded male, one seemed female. It occurred to me that something about the female voice was familiar.

Then it cried out three words that were unmistakable above the rest of the shouting.

"Screw The 48!"

"That's Katie," I gasped.

"I think one of the other voices is Willem's," said Charlie. "He was her Asset contact for the Beijing assignment forty-eight days ago."

"What the hell are they doing here? Should we go help?"

"No," replied Charlie sharply. "There was nothing in our briefing about meeting up with other Assets. And it's not like they have to keep us informed of every mission TOD's running. This could be a test."

"A test? For *us*? Out in broad daylight? That's insane! The 48 is as covert as it gets."

"I know," replied Charlie, biting his lip.

We listened in silence for another twenty seconds or so. Some-one was going to be in serious trouble back at The 48 for making this so public. But Charlie was right; we couldn't allow it to become our problem.

Then Katie started screaming and the side doors of the silver van were suddenly pulled back.

"What are they *doing*?" asked Charlie.

"I don't know," I replied. "But I don't like it." Several Tenets were running through my head, but it wasn't my voice reciting them. It was the voice of Piermont, the one senior Asset who terrified me above all others.

Then we saw our colleagues.

Willem, portly and bald on top, was being dragged toward the van; he was trying to fight off two other men who weren't saying a word, despite the altercation. They were dressed in gray sweatpants and black T-shirts, and another two people had Katie by the arms and legs as well.

I dropped the curtain before anyone looked up and saw us. Then I grabbed the TV remote. I would block out the noise with a French soap opera if I had to.

But I couldn't quiet my mind. I knew how things were supposed to be done in our world. If this was a disposal of an aging Asset, then it would still have been covert. One day they were there, the next day they weren't. It definitely wasn't done on a public street—in the daylight. Piermont's voice practically sang the section in the Tenets about disposal in my head.

No Asset will continue with The 48 once their forty-eighth year comes to an end. At that age, an Asset's health, like any person's, will have begun its terminal decline. Impaired eyesight, fitness, and mental capacity are liabilities that can result in both the death of other Assets and assignment failure. Thus all Assets must operate at full capacity at all times. Those Assets incapacitated by incurable illness/disease before their forty-eighth year will also be terminated. There are no exceptions.

"I don't like this, Charlie," I repeated.

"It doesn't matter, Alex," said Charlie. "If we don't move fast we're going to miss *our* assignment. Shut off the TV and get ready."

I caught my reflection in a grimy mirror near the door as I obeyed. The blood had drained from my face. I looked like a ghost.

Charlie softened. "Look, we'll find out what happened as soon as we get back."

"Do we have a backup plan?" I asked quietly. "Just in case."

"Of course not." Then Charlie glanced at the window. "But it probably wouldn't hurt..."

My brother was always one step ahead of me. So I didn't question him as he pulled out a wad of hundred-euro notes and taped them to the underside of a large lamp with a rectangular base.

"Even if it's moved for dusting, no one will find it unless they physically pick up the lamp and look underneath it," he explained.

"Good idea," I replied. "Now, what about—"

I didn't have to finish my sentence. Both of us always instinctively knew what the other was thinking. We were supposed to leave our passports in a PIN-protected locker near the Louvre.

The number had been provided by The 48, which meant they could access it at any time.

"I think we should leave the passports here too—just in case we fail and forget the number to the locker," I said. "Judging by the dust in this place, no one has cleaned it since 1973."

"We won't fail," said Charlie reassuringly. "Not at any of this. We've already assimilated into the court. We'll just be picking up where we left off. Everything's going to be fine."

But he left the passports with the money anyway.

Fifteen minutes later, my brother and I were in a taxi, heading for the Louvre, and forcing whatever the hell had just happened with Willem and Katie to the periphery of our minds.

Our assignment was on.

thirteen

Charles

We of The 48 do not become Assets until we possess an appreciation of special relativity and general relativity. Physics is an Imperative area of study. The works of Albert Einstein are required reading. To Outsiders, time travel is a subject of fiction. To The 48, it is real, present, and the means to our success.

Reciting Tenet excerpts calmed me down. So I said them in my head the entire way to the museum. I focused on elements of the time travel Tenet, which had always made me feel good. Special. Like I was part of something important.

I glanced at my brother as I did my recitations. Trainee Assets sometimes asked me if looking at Alex was like looking in a mirror. We weren't the only set of twins at The 48, but we were probably the most obvious on account of our height and hair color.

Most of the time I replied yes, just to be polite, before excusing myself from the conversation. But in truth, finding Alex wasn't like finding my reflection, because when I looked at my brother I saw not only his features, but also his personality. And we were different. Alex rarely excused himself from anything. He reveled in being noticed. In that very important way, Alex and I were nothing alike, and secretly I envied him—just a little.

Alex and I had been born on a Sunday. For Outsiders, Sunday tended to be convenient for things like births—or funerals, or grocery shopping—because Sunday wasn't a workday.

The day of our birth was neither convenient nor inconvenient for our parents, because they weren't Outsiders. Every day was a workday for them, including the Sunday—three years after our birth—when our father was terminated.

Just like his father before him.

Our mother followed our father into oblivion two years later.

Just like her mother before her.

I didn't want to follow in their footsteps, but I'd always known my chances of reaching middle age were nonexistent.

I was one of The 48. We didn't live to see the age of forty-nine.

<hr />

We'd flown to France from Toronto. The 48's compound was in Canada, not because of any allegiance to that country's government, but simply because of geographical convenience. It had huge swaths of land that were remote enough for us to operate discreetly, but still close enough to civilization to quickly access what we needed to exist in relative comfort. And to do training in the midst of Outsiders. Interaction with the outside world was necessary for our education, of course, and growing up, we were often taken into the field.

The field never came to us, though. Outsiders were forbidden at The 48. Our leaders were happiest when we were running as insularly and self-sufficiently as possible, so when it came to things like meals, or maintenance, or making babies, we looked no further than our own walls.

As for TOD, we had no idea where it was headquartered. Alice told me she'd once heard a rumor that it operated secretly under the very noses of the UN delegates in New York. What we did know for sure was that the time writers who became the founding fathers and mothers of The 48 were from many different nations.

Our cabdriver had gotten us to the Louvre in record time—so early that Alex and I had a few minutes to kill before our meetup. We opted to meld with the huge crowd swarming the *Mona Lisa*. Hundreds of tourists with camera phones were trying to take photos above one another's heads. Most of them would end up getting the surrounding walls or a reflected flash, as the painting was sealed behind thick, bulletproof glass.

"This is ridiculous," said Alex. "And boring. Entertain me, Charlie."

I ignored him and concentrated on the painting. Personally, I didn't see the appeal. It was small. Colorless. Nondescript.

It was also a fake. The 48 had the real one hidden in a safe house in Italy. Assets couldn't use historic artifacts if they were covered in protective glass.

My brother nudged me again, harder than the first time, nearly propelling me into the thick red rope that had been placed in front of the painting. I glared at him.

"Knock it off, Alex," I growled. "Are you *trying* to draw attention?"

"Lighten up. I'm just eager to get this thing started."

"Do us both a favor and shut up," I whispered. "It's not time yet. Let's move."

Alex smiled and followed me obediently. I was the older twin by four minutes, but I knew I sometimes acted like I was four years older. Or maybe it was that Alex acted four years younger. Either way, I felt responsible for him, despite what Aramis had written about the importance of looking out for number one. What a pointless piece of paper. Alex and I had been so annoyed by it that we'd tossed it the second we left the physics block.

In the relative quiet of the adjacent gallery, I checked my watch.

"We have ten minutes," I said, placing my hand on my brother's upper arm. He was rippling with tension and excitement. "We can head up to the second floor now—but only if you calm down. We can't stand out."

My brother gave me a look. *The* look. The look that said *We're six feet tall, redheads, and twins. Of course we'll stand out.*

Then he smiled and squeezed my shoulder, just long enough to ease some of my tension, before darting past *The Coronation of Napoleon* to the stairs.

When I reached the second floor, Alex was waiting.

"Where are we meeting Grinch again?" he asked. "I know they moved the painting."

"Outside room twelve. It was in the paperwork, remember?" I said, wondering just how seriously Alex was taking all this. But as we walked toward room 12, I noticed that he seemed to shrink a little. His movements were slower, more deliberate. He was breathing in through his nose, doing the calming exercises The 48 drilled into us on a daily basis.

It was hitting him, just as it was hitting me, that this was it.

<hr />

Grinch was waiting. Naturally. She was so timely she would arrive early for her own funeral, not that she'd ever have one. The 48 didn't do funerals.

Grinch wasn't her real name, of course. The Deputy Director of The 48 had earned the moniker because she had a slight green tinge to her skin: a side effect of the radiation that was worse in the older Assets because of the amount of time traveling they had done. The nickname stuck only because Grinch wanted it to. Some people said she never shut it down because she was secretly fond of it, which in itself was remarkable because Grinch was the least sentimental person on the planet.

There were rumors about a lot of things at The 48, but I tried not to pay attention. Tenets, Imperatives, and my training were all that mattered. Gossip sure as hell wouldn't keep me alive.

⸻

Grinch's sickly coloring looked even more pronounced under the artificial lights of the museum. She was reading a floor map. It was totally for show. Grinch knew every nook, every cranny of the Louvre. She had been coming here since she was seventeen. This would be her last year. She was forty-seven years old.

⸻

"Bonjour, Charles. Bonjour, Alexandre," said Grinch in flawless French.

"Bonjour, Madame," we replied in unison. Our French was perfect too. Authentic. We had been students of the world, past and present, since we could crawl.

"You have four minutes left, gentlemen," said Grinch, switching quietly to English. "Room twelve is clear and the cameras have been disabled. The collection of Tudor artwork is in place. It will remain that way until forty-eight days have passed."

Alex inhaled sharply. It was suddenly all too real. We had been gone from the Tudor court for two weeks. This time we would not return to the present day until our time had run out and we were pulled back through the cosmic string.

"You have everything," said Grinch. It wasn't a question, but I nodded anyway. Of course I had everything. Since arriving in Paris two days earlier, I'd been on near-constant inventory patrol. I had triple-checked our packs the night before, and double-checked that morning to make sure Alex hadn't switched anything around or taken anything out as a joke.

"Very well. Then I suggest you take the next half minute to visit the bathroom," said Grinch, indicating the restroom in the hall next to us. "You do not want to arrive at your destination in wet pants."

Grinch had no sense of humor, so we knew she wasn't joking.

"I'm okay," I replied. I glanced at Alex. He was chewing on the inside of his cheek. He shook his head.

"Fine. Then I'll leave you with a few reminders. As before, concentrate on the vanishing point," said Grinch. "Do not take the pill until you are fixed on it. This is a portrait, not a landscape, so the vanishing point is harder to find. Recall that your arrival on your reconnaissance mission did not go according to plan. This time your thread will take you to Wolsey's apartments, so you won't be tempted to misbehave again. Your timer will activate when you arrive. You've been given forty-eight-day pills, and you will be brought back to the present after forty-eight days have elapsed. Remember that at that time, you must be fixed on the vanishing point of a painting in the Tudor court that still exists in the present day."

We knew all this, but as I glanced at my brother, I was finally seeing the mirror-me. His face was pale; his pupils were so large it was as if someone had blotted black ink over his blue irises.

He looked how I felt.

Grinch lifted the sleeve of her cream-colored blouse to check her watch. "It's time. Please enter room twelve. You know the painting: *Portrait of Henry VIII*. Look beyond the image and concentrate on your intended time destination."

"Time destination," we repeated.

"Take the blue pill once you are fixed," said Grinch.

"Will you be here when we get back?" asked Alex, securing his backpack over both shoulders.

"No," replied Grinch. She nodded once, turned, and walked away. No goodbyes. No good lucks. Nothing.

"Did you notice how green she looked?" muttered Alex. "I swear she's actually morphing into an amphibian."

"She doesn't have long left," I replied as we entered room 12 and a riot of color assaulted my senses. The paintings on loan to the Louvre there were larger than life—literally.

"Do you think we'll turn green if we get to her age?"

"If I reach her age, I'll be happy to be green with blue spots."

"We're gonna be okay," said Alex. "I've read through the archives like a hundred times. Only three Assets have ever died on their first assignment."

"Don't look through the archives for deaths," I snapped. "Why the hell would you do that?"

"Because I wanted to know what the odds were of us reaching our eighteenth birthday," replied my brother.

I sensed that Alex, at least, was cautiously optimistic about our chances. Our assignment was to prevent Henry VIII from marrying Jane Seymour. She was a devout Catholic, and her death as queen would see a resurgence in the Catholic faith in England as people mourned for the "sainted" wife who gave them hope after the toxic years of Anne Boleyn's reign.

Our assignment was a small piece of a large puzzle. The 48 had been ordered by TOD to start working to eradicate religion from history throughout the ages. The process had to be implemented in stages and was so expansive we knew it wouldn't be finished within our short lifetimes. TOD believed that all religions had—or eventually would—become a catalyst for conflict among people. For humankind to endure, we were told, the religious past had to be changed. That meant TOD needed Assets from The 48 deployed around the world, in every country, through time. My brother and I were but two of hundreds. In our case, we'd been sent to ensure the continuation of the Reformation ushered in by Henry VIII's marriage to Anne Boleyn.

Alex and I had authorization to kill Jane if necessary, but it wouldn't come to that. Not only because my brother and I enjoyed a psychological challenge, but also because it wouldn't be much of a challenge to begin with. The king didn't love Jane. To his disgusting way of thinking, she was just a walking incubator, like all of his other wives. We would be able to change his mind easily. And we'd be doing Jane Seymour the biggest favor she'd ever get.

***

I checked my watch, then unstrapped it and left it on the floor. I wouldn't need it where we were going.

One minute to go. Alex and I quickly wound our kit bags to our torsos and took our places in front of the life-sized painting of Henry VIII by Hans Holbein the Younger. TOD physicists had worked out the exact spot at which cosmic strings were most stable, and the timings of our departures from the present and past were calculated to ensure that we arrived in one piece. I was thinking of none of that, though, as I stood in front of the painting. If this calculation was not correct to the microsecond, violent oscillations in the loops would split the natural atomic radiation in our bodies into a million fragments.

The brass plaque next to the painting stated that it was a replica, as the original had been destroyed in a fire in 1698.

False. Unlike the *Mona Lisa*, this was, in fact, the original. The 48 were very good at going back in time, swapping original artwork for fakes. If for any reason the fake was destroyed, the art world, then and now, would mourn the loss of the original, not realizing that the original was safe and sound—and hidden in plain sight. This subterfuge meant that precious artwork wasn't targeted by thieves, because no one went after something they thought was a copy.

Next to the painting of Henry VIII was another face I recognized: Thomas Cromwell. This was another original, yet again swapped and carried off as a copy to deter thieves. Grinch herself had gone back to the Tudor court after Cromwell's arrest and taken it. It was much smaller than Holbein's painting of Henry.

But there was something about it...something unnatural. It was pulling me toward it.

"Charlie," prompted Alex. "It's time."

"Blue pill," I said to Alex, snapping myself away from Cromwell's small portrait. My brother held up his left hand. The oval tablet was already in his pincerlike grip.

My senses were in overdrive. The bitterness of adrenaline was coating my tongue. I could feel the grains of the pill beneath my fingertips. The red cloak in the painting of Henry was starting to bleed outward...

I placed the pill on my tongue.

I could smell blood.

I could hear screaming.

"What the hell is that?" yelled Alex, turning as the screams echoed like a bell through the deserted gallery. "Is that *Grinch*?"

"If it is, we can't help her!" I cried. "We only have seconds, Alex. Concentrate on the vanishing point!"

"Charlie, if that's Grinch we can't just leave her!"

"We have no choice!" I yelled. "Alex—for God's sake, the painting. Look at the vanishing point in the painting!"

I could hear the second hand on my watch vibrating on the hard floor.

10

9

8

My head started spinning. I reached out for my brother. He reached out for me.

7

6

5

In my peripheral vision I saw a figure appear in the entrance to the gallery. Was it Grinch? I tried to open my mouth to speak, but my tongue was swollen. I couldn't breathe. The air around me was distorting. Stretching and pulling my body through the ages.

4

3

2

I could smell burning wood and the stench of open sewers. I could hear bells tolling . . .

1

We had forty-eight days left.

fourteen

Alexander

There were four stages to time travel. The first was a heightened awareness of the five senses—not just in the time you were departing from, but also in the new time you were invading. It was disconcerting to the extreme—almost like a sixth sense. For time travelers, atoms in the air had a corporeal mass that could be felt.

The second stage of time travel was the sensation of one's body stretching through space. It hurt. A lot. Like someone tying your four limbs and your head to separate pieces of rope and then pulling you through fire.

The third stage was the worst. It was also the one that lasted the longest. The firelike heat dissipated and was replaced by biting cold that felt like it was snapping at your skin. Some Assets with real-life experience said the sensation was like being flayed.

The first three stages only lasted for as long as you fought them. It was perverse, but if you accepted the pain—totally gave yourself to it—then you recovered to a new normal a lot faster than if you tried to fight it off.

⁘

The new normal for Charlie and me was the year 1536.

Our time destination was Hampton Court Palace in England. I could hear my brother groaning. I hated to hear him in pain, but the guttural noises he was making reassured me that we had come through together. That had been my biggest fear: being separated by time, especially after what had happened in the Louvre before we left. Distractions during the time travel process could be deadly; I had read about that in the archives.

I couldn't help Charlie until I helped myself. I needed to fully come to. I could tell that my left cheek was lying against stone. Everything was dark and freezing cold. *Open your eyes,* I thought. *Just open your eyes. It isn't as bad as it feels. It really isn't as bad as it feels.*

But aside from feeling like I was encased in ice, my head was pounding. I recognized the metallic taste of blood right away. I had bitten the inside of my cheek. My throat was constricting.

Don't fight the third stage. Don't fight the third stage.

My old senses of the Louvre and the modern world were fading, although those screams were still echoing in my ears.

"Alex," groaned my brother. "Don't fight it. The pins and needles don't last for long."

I found my voice. "Pins and needles? I'm being stabbed by steak knives here."

I took a deep breath. With my eyes still closed, I pulled myself up onto all fours like a dog. My balance was okay. I felt around with numb fingers. I still had all my limbs. A head. Hair. The relief I felt over that was ridiculous, but I was kind of attached to my hair. It wasn't vain to not want to be bald at the age of seventeen.

My eyes were swollen. I leaned back on my calves and pried open my eyelids with a thumb and forefinger. I had to blink several times before they stopped watering. Eventually they started to focus.

Get a grip, Alex, I thought. *This is the third time you've done this time distance. You should be used to it by now.*

We were in a small, circular room constructed of neatly stacked pale gray stone flecked with dark flint. Directly above us was a large, copper-colored bell, which was rusting around the rim. It was attached to a sturdy-looking wooden pulley. A long piece of frayed rope dropped from the mechanism through a large hole in the center of the stone floor. The area around the hole was fenced off by a rotting wooden railing. I peered over the edge. We appeared to be about eight stories high.

Our surroundings were all too familiar. "Not again," I said, groaning. "We've arrived in the same place as last time. Grinch is going to kill us."

"Only if you insist on ringing the bell again like an idiot."

He had a point. The last time, I hadn't been able to restrain myself. But I wasn't expecting to come face-to-face with temptation again. We were supposed to arrive in Thomas Wolsey's rooms, which had been left empty after his death.

I shook my head and crawled gingerly to a window five feet to my left. The landscape before me took my breath away. "We're really back, Charlie," I whispered. "Wrong arrival point, but we're back."

The enormous brick palace of Hampton Court was straight ahead. To my right was the river Thames, pea-green and foamy. Small wooden sailboats jostled for position near the embankment walls. Beyond the palace were the gardens, beautifully manicured and connected like pieces of a jigsaw puzzle. Black smoke rose in thin tendrils from various chimneys around the palace. The smell of burning wood rent the air.

"We need to change," said Charlie. He hadn't joined me at the window, but he was finally compos mentis.

Our backpacks were lying on the ground next to us. Charlie had been obsessive about checking their contents earlier, but it wasn't as if I wasn't aware of the inventory. Together they contained a change of clothes, a small explosive charge—one that our scientists had configured to ensure that it didn't set off sensitive alarms at the Louvre—for burning our twenty-first-century clothes, and a pocket-sized dossier on the assignment itself.

"Can you hear anyone?" I asked, crawling to another gap in the floor. It led down to a set of narrow wooden stairs.

"No," replied my brother. He propelled himself forward and sat for a moment with his head between his knees.

I had to say something about our departure. "Charlie, that screaming back in the Louvre. What if it was Grinch?"

"Alex, just—just don't. Please don't. That stuff with Katie and Willem, and now the Louvre, it's all distraction. We *can't* make it our problem because we can't *do* anything about it right now. The mission is all that matters for the next forty-eight days, and we have to *focus*."

We remained silent for a few seconds, staring at each other. Finally, I nodded. My brother nodded too. Then we started to get dressed. Quickly. We had to hurry because the fourth and final stage would soon be upon us.

The fourth stage was the reason Assets continued to time travel without complaint, even as their assignments became more dangerous and their bodies started to experience the painful side effects of radiation. Older, seasoned Assets called it the Quickening. Younger recruits like us called it the best high you would ever have. It made you fearless. It made you feel stronger. Everything around you was more pronounced, from the color of the sky to the intonation of your vowels. You didn't fear death. You felt like you could rip its mangy head off.

It was amazing. But it was a dangerous state to be in, because it could make you lose control. And Assets were always supposed to be in control. Assets had gotten themselves killed during the Quickening before acclimatizing to their new surroundings. So the sooner we were dressed in proper clothing and away from heights, the better.

White shirts with pearl buttons, long black pants, and knee-high leather boots were the outfits we had been given to change into. We even had to wear sixteenth-century underwear, which essentially meant boxers the size of board shorts. The pants were made of thick cotton and were high-waisted, with lots of buttons. The sleeves on our shirts were fashioned from enough fabric to make bedsheets—a fact I'd found most convenient when packing. The boots were comfortable, but we could only pull them on while we were lying down because they were so long.

I had missed several things about the Tudor court, but the clothes weren't one of them.

"Do you have the dossier?" I asked Charlie. He was having a fight with his right boot. The boot was winning. Charlie's face was getting redder and redder, and his eyes were growing wide.

Damn. The Quickening had already started for him. Which meant I wouldn't be far behind.

"Yes," he replied, panting. "I have it. Alex, it's starting."

"I know."

I did know. My lungs were filling with glorious oxygen. My skin was tingling, but it wasn't unpleasant; it was as if all the hairs on my body were rising like feathers. I could swoop out of here if I wanted to and fly across London.

"Great!" I shouted. "If you've got the dossier, then I'm detonating the charge." I jumped up. My whole body was shaking like a dog drying itself after a bath.

"I think we should get downstairs before we do anything else."

I grinned. An evil, *I can do anything* grin. All teeth and no lips.

"Don't do anything stupid, Alex," warned Charlie.

"Define *stupid*."

"Alex..."

"It's coming, Charlie-boy!" I cried. "Race you to the bottom!"

I flicked a round charge, the size of a dollar coin, onto our discarded pile of twenty-first-century clothes. Without waiting to see if it combusted, I straddled the wooden railing and grabbed the rope.

This was déjà vu, medieval style. We had done this the first time we arrived, and I had been feeling reckless. This time, caught up as I was in the fourth stage, reckless didn't even begin to cover it. I laughed maniacally as I slid down. Charlie followed me and the bell pealed our arrival to every living soul in the surrounding countryside. Who cared about arriving quietly? We were otherworldly. Ecstatic. Invincible. Omnipotent. Gods. I was fire and wind and the sky and the earth and everyone would see me and love me, and—

—And suddenly, the godlike feeling started to fade. Five feet from the ground, Charlie let go of the rope and dropped. I didn't drop so much as fall.

By the time I picked myself up, the fourth stage was over and my hands were killing me. I looked them over and saw that my palms had thick red welts from rope burns.

"You freaking moron," groaned Charlie, kneeling on the dusty, straw-strewn ground. "What made you jump down the rope—again?"

"What the hell made you follow me—again?" I groaned back, shaking out my stinging hands.

Charlie snorted. I started laughing. I knew damn well he found it almost impossible to stay mad at me most of the time. Though it was a fact I often took for granted.

"I suppose I should be thankful you didn't try to fly out of the window," said Charlie.

"An Asset did that once! I read about it in the archives."

"What is wrong with you, sicko? Is that all you do, read the archives for death stats? Why can't you stick to Tenets and Imperatives like the rest of us?"

"I read the archives for lots of things. Not just Asset deaths. Tenets and Imperatives only teach you so much. The archives are where you get the real information—which is why I've brought several of them with me." I patted my sleeve.

"*What?* When did you sneak archives in there? I've been watching you. I checked our inventory before we left!"

"Yeah, well, you didn't check my Tudor shirtsleeves, obviously. They're big enough to hide a whale." My brother looked royally pissed, so I smiled and said, "Come on, Charlie. It's not illegal to copy archives, and I've had them on me the whole time. You just weren't watching me hard enough. I didn't *sneak* anything— except this knife."

"What the...how did you get that through the Louvre security?" exclaimed Charlie.

"Ask me no questions, I'll tell you no lies," I replied, winking.

"I'm going to watch you like a hawk from now on." My brother sighed and took a good look around. "We should probably start up with Charles and Alexander again. Right now."

"Copy that. And don't forget the German accent, Charles Douglas of Cleves." At that, I had to laugh. "Our names just roll off the tongue around here, don't they? We owe our parents one for that."

"I'm pretty sure they had zero choice in the matter."

I bowed my head and flushed. "I'm sorry. You're right."

When it came down to it, there was no reason to believe our parents had had much say in anything that concerned us, including our names. Like every other couple at The 48, they'd been matched and approved by the TOD board. Charlie and I, like all children, were raised more or less communally, along with extra Asset trainees who'd been brought into the organization as infants from foster homes all around the world. They helped diversify the bloodlines when they came of age. If and when blood parents died or were terminated—like ours had been—other Assets would step into the role of guardians.

You learned early on never to get too attached, because inevitably, the guardians wouldn't be there one day either. You learned to avoid feeling too much affection for anyone, period.

Not that lust wasn't accepted within The 48. It was actually encouraged, for letting off steam. And no one cared about sexual orientation or gender identity. I never came out as gay because I never had to. But falling in love was seen as a weakness: a loss of control. And The 48 didn't like to have its Assets lose control.

<hr>

A solitary beep echoed around the ground floor of the bell tower. We knew what it signaled. I pulled up the sleeve of my shirt.

Inserted into the underside of my wrist was a tiny rectangular display. It was the same pale color as my skin, and you had to know it was there to really make it out. To anyone looking, especially in daylight, it appeared as if the eight numbers displayed on the minuscule panel were just smudges of dirt.

I thought back to Lady Margaret. I was sure she had spotted the countdown panel on my wrist, but I took comfort in knowing there was no way in a million years she would recognize it for what it was. As far as she was concerned, we were the sons of Cleves.

47 23:59:55

In forty-seven days, twenty-three hours, fifty-nine minutes, and fifty-five seconds, Charlie and I would be somewhere in the palace, standing in front of some artifact that still existed in the twenty-first century, ready and waiting to be drawn back through the cosmic string that had brought us here.

And with a little luck, we'd be leaving secure in the knowledge that Jane Seymour was no longer of any interest to King Henry VIII. I took a deep breath.

This was real. Charlie and I were on our first full assignment.

And our forty-eight days were already grains of sand running through the hourglass.

fifteen

Charles

For obvious reasons, history was an important academic Imperative at The 48. Assets never stopped studying it—from ancient times to modern—and that suited me just fine. I loved history. Reading The 48's archives didn't interest me as much, because they were all about acts of historical manipulation, rather than the real history itself. But studying history as it actually unfolded? It was fascinating. My dream assignment would be to go back to the time of the Trojan War and somehow have a hand in shaping what happened. Or just bear witness to it—to fill the archives with notes that would intrigue the likes of my brother.

I knew it was a futile dream. Given the order from TOD to eradicate religion from the ages, I knew that my short life would now be dedicated to that goal. Even so, knowing that The 48 could shape—and *had* shaped—the course of history was empowering. I might not have been drawn to the archives of our exploits, but I loved being a part of that excitement. Not a single historical figure knew when fate was about to knock on their gilded door, but we did. History was littered with events whose outcomes resulted from our involvement. Not all were assassinations. Sometimes we actually delayed death. Sometimes we helped people to fall in or out of love. Sometimes we gave science a little nudge forward—or backward. Whatever the rich and powerful men and women of TOD demanded.

I was in 1536 now, when no one but Alex and I could know

that in 336 years' time, Queen Victoria would get lucky. An Asset would swap pistols with Arthur O'Connor at the last minute, so that the one he tried to fire was unloaded.

The failed Gunpowder Plot of 1605? It was an Asset who tipped off the authorities to the explosives.

When Assets carried out missions, we did not question them. We didn't look at the bigger picture. We couldn't. Because the bigger picture was being recalibrated all the time by TOD: the collective that funded us with astronomical wealth and operated entirely from the shadows.

My life, my existence, was training. But nothing in my training had taught me how to brace myself for how bad Tudor England smelled. It was almost worse, this second time around. The enclosed brick bell tower had protected us from the worst of it, but as Alex and I walked out into the cool spring air, the smell of open toilets hit me in the face like a sucker punch. It was probably this bad because we were so close to the River Thames, which was basically an open septic tank. The first time we had arrived I had actually thrown up, it was so awful. Ideally, breathing was done through the mouth here.

"Stay close to me, Charles," said Alex, now speaking with a slight Saxon accent. "I don't want to have to spend forty-seven of our remaining forty-eight days looking for you in this rabbit warren of buildings. It's worse than the Louvre."

"The feeling is entirely mutual," I replied. "Now keep your voice down and try to look purposeful. I don't want to be overheard and arrested as a spy before we've even reached the inner walls of Hampton Court." I tried to puff my own chest out and walk taller. "Our instructions include a reminder that there will be plenty of people here who still have no idea who the sons of Cleves are. So our first job is to find Aramis, who can vouch for us. He's probably watching us from some tower right now, seeing how we cope with the return. So look cool."

Alex eyed me up and down and grinned. "Look cool? I'm made of cool."

I ignored that. There was no actually looking cool dressed like sixteenth-century noblemen. Anyway, Alex knew what I meant. We had to project an air of confidence now. We had Aramis—and a king—to impress.

<hr>

Henry VIII was eighteen years old when he ascended the throne—only a year older than an Asset on their inaugural assignment. Henry wasn't supposed to be king, according to the line of succession. He had an older brother named Arthur who died at the age of fifteen. History had Arthur's death written down as a long illness. He was a prince who became sick after his marriage to Catherine of Aragon and never recovered.

The 48 had Arthur's death recorded rather differently. It was noted as Time Assassination AT1502.

Future assassinations were easier to cover up if a psychopath was king.

So after Arthur's death, Prince Henry became the heir instead of the spare. He was ten years old. He was subsequently married to widow Catherine and closeted away for the day when his father, Henry VII, died.

The 48 didn't have a hand, sword, or vial in that one. Some historical deaths *were* natural.

"You look so serious. Aren't you excited? Just a little bit?" asked Alex, nudging me with his elbow.

"*Excited* is the wrong word. We're going to be here now for forty-eight days. The slightest detail could make everything go wrong. We have to do this properly. We *will* do this properly—just as we've trained."

"Breathe, will you? It's an easy assignment, Charles." Alex rolled the *r* in my full name dramatically. "All we have to do is stop Henry from marrying Jane. And you met her. She's nice, but she's not exactly the most captivating person at court. There are plenty of Protestants here for him to choose from who are more likely to catch his eye. We just have to make him see them."

"We can't think like that. There are no easy assignments."

But Alex was infuriatingly right. On paper, manipulating Henry VIII *was* a simple task. Right now, Henry VIII was forty-five years old. Decrepit, paranoid, and desperate for a male heir. He was a monster, driven half mad by pain and disease. As far as the king was concerned, he didn't need a person in his bed; he needed a womb. All TOD asked of us was that we ensure that the womb didn't belong to a Catholic.

"Stop!" a deep voice suddenly cried. "Stop in the name of the king! State your names and business or we will run you through."

I spun around. Three guards stood in a semicircle behind us. They were dressed in tight red pants, black leather boots like ours, and red tabards with golden embroidery on the front. All three were smaller than Alex and I by several inches, but two looked like they had the muscles for a fight. They also had the benefit of spears that were pointed perilously close to our chests. The sun glinted off the metal in sharp beams of light.

If Aramis was watching, he wasn't getting involved. We had to show we could get ourselves out of trouble.

"We are guests, loyal to the Crown and its king," said my brother, who, like me, had his hands raised in supplication. "I am Alexander, son of the Duke of Cleves. This is my brother, Charles. We are already known to the court and to His Grace. You aren't going to declare war on a friend and ally like Cleves, now, are you?"

My brother bowed; I quickly followed suit. Alex had done well; he had jumped straight back into character before I had.

But he stayed stooped. My eyes flicked to the gap between his leg and the black leather of his boot—where I saw he had concealed his knife.

"What is your business in the palace?" asked the guard. "We heard the tolling of the bell. Guests of the king with honorable intent do not take such liberties as to disturb the peace of Hampton Court."

"Forgive us," I replied, raising my body just a few inches. "My brother and I saw the bell tower and could not resist bringing it to song."

I was just as cool as Alex—sometimes.

And I had to make sure he didn't use that knife, not on our first day back.

"We wished to look around the grounds, but we became separated from the Duke of Cleves's party," said Alex. "The area around Hampton Court is truly magnificent, and truly expansive. Much larger than our castle in Cleves."

The three guards looked at one another; one stroked his neatly trimmed goatee with his thumb and forefinger. While they had slightly jaundiced skin and red-rimmed eyes, their unlined faces indicated they were around the same age as Alex and I, and their expressions were a mixture of confusion and fear, indicating they weren't particularly experienced. This meant my brother and I could take the upper hand. We were claiming to be nobility—we were certainly dressed like it. Dare the guards question us? A wrong move in either direction could result in their necks being stretched out from a length of rope on a scaffold. These were dangerous times for all.

"The Duke of Cleves is holding council with the king in the Great Hall," said one of the guards to the others. "As these two are not armed, we should let them be."

"Gentlemen, if you take us to the Great Hall, we can meet with the Duke of Cleves when the king has dismissed him," I said. "I'm afraid the size of this noble palace is as great as the mazes outside it. We are hopelessly lost. The duke will be most grateful for your assistance to his kin."

The guards had lowered their spears. They had stepped back, as if to acquiesce to my request, when a scream sliced through the air. It was so high it made my ears buzz. The three guards pivoted toward the noise.

All five of us immediately sprinted in the direction of the noise. It was coming from the upstairs section of a set of apartments within a cobbled courtyard. The square design amplified the sound.

"Those are Wolsey's old rooms!" shouted one of the guards.

The rooms we were *supposed* to arrive in, I thought. It was just as well we hadn't.

Another scream. We ran through an arched oak door. The smell of incense made my eyes water. It was dark and damp. A bare table was the only piece of furniture I could see, and it was covered in a thick layer of dust.

"Stay here," ordered a guard, throwing back an arm to stop Alex from climbing the stairs. "You are unarmed. I do not desire to have to save your hides as well as a lady's."

"Dickhead," muttered Alex as the three guards charged up the stairs.

"Play nice," I whispered. "You didn't have a problem getting to know yeomen the first time we were here. They could be useful."

Dust cascaded from the eaves as shouts and the sound of furniture being smashed replaced the screams.

"I don't like this," said Alex. "Screw those guards. We could probably take all three of them in a fight anyway. We should get up there. This was our original destination. What if it's connected?"

I always tried to think of everything, but I hadn't thought of that. Taking the steps two at a time, we ran up the stairs and rushed into a room on the right where the noises were coming from. Sweat trickled down my back. Already we were in the thick of the action, and we had been back in time for less than an hour.

We arrived in a bedroom. Thick velvet drapes were pulled back from the single window. There were four spent candles on sconces fixed to the oak-paneled walls, and the centerpiece was a large two-poster bed with a fringed burgundy canopy.

One of the guards had his back to us, but he was holding someone in his arms who was kicking and struggling for all they were worth. Another guard was waving his spear in front of his body as if he were about to skewer a wild animal. The third guard was holding a bloodstained handkerchief to his lip. There were two upturned chairs on the floor, and a pile of books lay scattered across the dusty boards. A silver seal for securing letters rolled past a stained chamber pot.

"This hellcat is about to eat her way through my fingers!" cried the first guard. He clearly had his hand over the mouth of the person who had been screaming, because her screams were now muffled. I looked down and could just make out her white-soled sneakers thrashing between his legs.

White-soled—what?

Then the guard holding her crumpled to the floor. The so-called hellcat had twisted her body around and kneed him between the legs. I winced in sympathy pain...and then felt my stomach drop into my boots.

"Alice!" exclaimed my brother.

Our assignment had just gotten a lot more complicated.

sixteen

Alexander

You know this she-devil?" groaned the felled guard, still clutching his groin.

"Yes," I replied quickly, being sure to keep the accent. "She is...she is a maid from the House of Cleves. She traveled back to His Grace's court with us. We became separated."

I glanced at my brother; his face was taut like a drumskin, slightly vibrating as if it had just been struck.

Stay in character, Charlie, I silently willed.

But I already knew this was a disaster of epic proportions.

Alice had positioned herself in a classic tae kwon do back stance. Her fists were raised and her thigh muscles were taut with energy. Her light brown eyes darted all over the place. I pitied the fool on the floor who had just tried to take her on. Alice was top of the class in every martial art Imperative. She had kicked my ass more times than I could remember. Charlie's, too. She was small, but lightning-fast.

What the hell was she doing *here*?

"Alice—you don't need to be frightened," I said, stretching out my hand, but she was frozen, just like Charlie. I wasn't even sure she recognized me. Her breathing was so rapid I could see she was starting to hyperventilate. Had she already gone through the three stages and the Quickening? I simply couldn't tell.

"You're...you're safe, Alice," stammered my brother, finally realizing that this was actually happening. "We won't...we won't let anyone hurt you. Alexander and I...we'll protect you now."

"And who will protect us?" snapped the guard with the spear. "To attack a guard in the grounds of the palace is regarded as an attack on the king himself. These are not times to be seen as an usurper to the Crown."

"A what?" gasped Alice, finding her voice. "Charlie, Alex, I don't understand why..."

Alice wasn't dressed in sixteenth-century clothes. She was wearing tight black jeans, a crumpled long-sleeved black T-shirt, and red sneakers. Her brown hair was a mass of ringlets, and then I noticed the slick of dried blood congealing in her hairline.

"We'll take responsibility for her," said Charlie quickly, stepping forward to defuse the situation. Alice fell to her knees. She wasn't crying, but she was shaking with shock.

"Did you attack her?" I demanded.

"No," replied the guard who was holding a bloodied handkerchief to his face. "We merely tried to restrain her."

"Then you cannot be surprised if she fought back against you," I snapped. "Alice is a simple maiden from our land. She clearly did not see three honorable guards of the king, but three men rushing to assault her. Would you have accepted your fate, or fought back also?"

"We will take her with us," said Charlie, stepping forward to help Alice up.

"Indeed. Because *we* are taking all *three* of you," replied the guard on the floor. Two skinny black rats scuttled across the bare floorboards. "If the Duke of Cleves does not recognize you, we'll hang you down at Traitor's Gate before the sun sets." He sounded bitter, as if he would like nothing better than to hang us there and then for his humiliation at the hands of Alice.

I stayed back with Alice as the two guards still standing helped their fallen comrade down the stairs. Charlie followed to create a buffer between them and us. He was the better fighter if it all went pear-shaped. I only had a few seconds. Alice's breathing was steadying, but she was still trembling. I quickly scanned her for more injuries, but there was nothing obvious, other than the cut on her head. She was moving okay, so I didn't suspect fractures or broken bones. Concussion would certainly explain her confusion.

"What's happening, Alex?" she whispered. "I don't understand. Why am I here? Grinch..."

"We can't discuss anything here," I hissed back. "Keep quiet until we can find somewhere to talk."

But as Alice steadied herself on the wobbly balustrade and took several long inhalations, I heard a beep and saw a tiny shadow flicker across her wrist. I pulled her hand toward me. Her skin was ice-cold.

A display had been activated.

47 22:39:48

Alice had been sent here, just thirty minutes after we had.

⚊⚊⚊

By the time the six of us had reached the courtyard, the guard Alice had kneed in the groin was walking normally again, although he gave her a wide berth, preferring to guard Charlie, who, understandably, was the quietest of us all.

Having his ex-girlfriend turn up in Tudor England was not part of the assignment.

"Where are we going? What's happening, Alex?" whispered Alice. Her lips were turning blue, and I could see a thin layer of white foam on the inside of her mouth. Severe dehydration. Alice needed water or she was going to start hallucinating.

"Stop talking," I muttered. "We *were* going to the Great Hall, but now we'll have to find somewhere to hide you."

"Why is she here?" whispered Charlie, pulling me to one side as the three guards led the way—single file—down a steep cobbled alleyway that ran between courtyards. "This wasn't her assignment."

"I have no idea," I muttered back. "She started to mention Grinch but I had to shut her up. This isn't right, Charlie. Something's gone seriously wrong here."

"Logical options."

"Sent to spy on us?" I said, keeping an eye on the three guards.

"I doubt it—can't you see how scared she is?" whispered Charlie. "And a spy wouldn't stand out like she clearly does right now. And we aced the reconnaissance. A trainee wouldn't be sent to spy on *us*."

He sounded offended at the mere suggestion.

"So what are your thoughts?" I asked.

"This is an accident—or something more devious," said Charlie through gritted teeth. "Let's just find somewhere to hide her before we go to the Great Hall and make contact with Aramis. Someone will know where he is, and the clock is ticking. We need to push back on everything that isn't the assignment. The assignment is all that matters."

I opened my mouth and then shut it so abruptly my back teeth clacked together. Only minutes ago, forty-eight days had seemed like a lifetime to me. But Alice's appearance had altered my perception. Forty-eight would soon become twenty-four, which would become a week, which would become a day, an hour, a second. Our day one instructions were to meet Aramis and get settled back into court life as if we had never been away—and already we'd gone far astray.

On paper it had sounded easy.

I worried that finding Alice was an indicator of something bigger than all of us—including the assignment.

Our journey through the palace provided a review of sixteenth-century royal living. It was a study in nervous tension. Women in full, heavy gowns and jewels glided around the corridors—and when you looked back, they had disappeared. It was as if they dissolved into the heavy tapestries and drapes. Men looked up from writing desks and then quickly slumped down again, dipping their quills into ink pots to continue scribing.

There was constant noise, but not enough to drown out a conversation. Music played from behind closed doors. Laughter was smothered by coughing. I could sense the paranoia and stress. The whole building vibrated with it.

Which made sense, because Henry VIII's court had a lot to be stressed about. Spain and France were a general threat, but the powerful Catholic Church in Rome, too, was furious with England's ruler. Henry's divorce from Catherine of Aragon had caused the kingdom to split with the Church. Now Henry was raiding the coffers of England's monasteries to pay for his wars and his court's excessive behavior, further infuriating Rome.

Then there were the competing factions within the court itself. Cromwell, for instance, was hungry for greater power, a feeling cultivated by his family's legacy of owning people and land. Another familiar face at court, Edward Seymour, hoped to gain more wealth—and access to the king—via the marriage of his sister to the royal tyrant.

I was getting more and more nervous.

"Do you require a physician, Alexander of Cleves?" asked one of the guards.

It took me a second or two to realize he was talking to me. The guard's bloodshot eyes dropped lazily to my hand. The count-down inserted into my wrist was itching like a healing scab, and I had unconsciously been rubbing it up and down my pants. It was now pink and swollen and drawing attention.

"A physician won't be necessary," replied my brother, pulling down my sleeve. "But food and drink would be most welcome whilst we wait for the duke. Is there a chamber somewhere for the girl to recover her strength?"

I knew Charlie would want to interrogate her. Alice wasn't seventeen yet; her birthday was another few months away. Assets didn't get to go on assignments until they came of age. None of this made sense.

And Alice's modern clothes were starting to draw attention from everyone we passed.

"We are taking you to one of the antechambers off the Great Hall," said the guard. "It is used by the Duke of Suffolk, but I doubt he will return here before sundown. I am not aware of the lodgings given over to the duke whilst he is here. We will find out for you."

<hr>

Hampton Court Palace was a labyrinth of corridors and intercon-necting rooms. Some were familiar to us, thanks to our recon-naissance mission, as well as a modern-day field trip we'd taken to

Hampton Court when we were first given the assignment several months ago. But most rooms were mysteries. Eventually we were shown into the antechamber by the same guard. It was quite small inside, but there were two high-backed chairs next to a long table that took up the full width of the rear of the room. I scanned the tabletop quickly. There were four spent candles stuck in hardened pools of wax, and a round container filled with dark gray, glittering gunpowder. Two blankets had been draped over the arms of the chairs. There was a small fireplace, but it wasn't lit. I could see the soot blowing around the grate as the wind whistled down the chimney. There was another door to the left of it with a set of black keys hanging from the catch.

"I will return with wine and food," said the guard, scratching his face. "Are you quite sure you do not require a physician?"

"Quite sure," I replied. "Thank you for your attention. Could you let the duke know where we are, and if you see a yeoman called Marlon, could you let him know that the sons of Cleves have returned?"

"I will," he replied with a short bow. It looked like we had convinced him, but as he left the room, the door was pulled shut with a solid thump. Everything suddenly felt smaller and cocoonlike. The heavy thud of wood on stone echoed under the gap of the door. I could see shadows outside.

We were being guarded.

I looked down at my wrist. The skin around the small display was inflamed with a pink glow and was already developing a yellow-white crust.

"That doesn't look good," said Charlie, peering at my wrist. "You need to stop scratching it or people are going to notice."

I hadn't told my brother that I was sure Lady Margaret had already seen it.

"I have a countdown too, Charlie," whispered Alice, pulling up the sleeve of her shirt. "I wasn't supposed to have an assignment yet. I don't...I can't..."

Alice's display wasn't inserted into her skin in the neat, almost indistinguishable way displays were usually placed. Her panel was crude and crooked and had not been color-matched to her skin tone.

It had been inserted in a rush.

"What was the last thing you remember, Alice?" asked Charlie. "Who was the last person you recall speaking to? Can you remember anyone attacking you?"

He was still holding on to Alice's wrist, but she shivered and he immediately dropped it. Charlie picked up a blanket from the closest chair. It was olive-colored and made of wool. He wrapped it around Alice's shoulders and scooped her curls away from her neckline. That act of intimacy sent a spike of annoyance through my gut. Charlie wasn't thinking like an Asset. He was thinking like an ex-boyfriend who wanted to be sans the *ex*. Alice had red marks on the nape of her neck shaped like fingerprints. There were several scratches, too, one of which looked rather nasty.

"Anything you remember, however small and inconsequential, can help," prompted Charlie.

"It was Grinch," replied Alice. "She came to see me in my room—it was right after you both left the compound with the other Assets with European assignments. She held a piece of material to my face—it was chloroform, because I recognized the sweetness before it knocked me out. I tried to fight her but I couldn't. When I woke up, I was on a plane—not a commercial jet, it was private, because there were only a few seats. "I guess I passed out again because the next thing I remember is waking up in a car outside the Louvre. Grinch must have been waiting for me to come around, enough so I could walk in with her under my own power...."

"But not enough to realize what was going on, or to fight back," Charlie said, rubbing his temples.

"Yes. And then...then we went in, and she took me to this supply room or something. Right near gallery twelve. It was so weird—it was like we were the only people in the whole place. I went through the door and then she said she was locking me in there. For my protection. And that she'd be back. When she opened the door again I was feeling better, so I started screaming and running—"

"That was *you* we heard?" asked Charlie.

"—But the only way out was through the gallery. Grinch caught me by the Holbein and all of a sudden we were traveling. She went through the time loop with me. And then...here we were. I went through the Quickening and started screaming again and she left me. She *left* me, Charlie."

"This is insane," I said. "You shouldn't be here. What the hell was Grinch doing?"

I swore as Alice let out a frustrated cry. "My head hurts! Everything hurts. I shouldn't be here, Charlie!"

"You need to keep your voice down, Alice!" I ordered. "The door is thick but there's a big gap underneath it. They're going to be listening."

"Don't yell at me!" cried Alice. "This isn't my fault."

"I know!" I yelled. "I know," I repeated. "I'm sorry, okay? I just—none of this makes sense, and I want to try to make sense of it. I need some air. I'll be back soon."

I was pretty sure the guard outside would permit me a brief walk, so I stormed to the door and flung it open.

"The duke is not yet ready to receive you," said the guard.

"I need a walk," I snapped, "and I—"

I noticed that the guard's eyes had drifted away from me. I turned around to see what had captured his attention and saw two young women I recognized immediately.

"Lady Margaret," I said, trying to sound pleased. "Lady Cecily. It is a delight to see you both again so soon."

"Alexander of Cleves," said Lady Margaret. "You have returned."

"And I am delighted to say we are staying this time."

"You departed so...so abruptly," she said, her face turning pink.

"We like to travel at night," I replied. "It means we can sleep during the journey."

"Indeed," said Lady Margaret. Now hives were appearing on her neck.

Her reaction was making me nervous. I needed to know what was going on in her head.

"May I escort you to wherever it was you were going? I have forgotten my way around the palace, and I wish to get reacquainted."

Lady Cecily looked terrified, but she was clearly younger than Lady Margaret and was taking her cue from her.

"It—it would be our pleasure," said Lady Margaret, after a few seconds of awkward silence. "Tell me, Alexander of Cleves, how was your homeland?"

The charming son of Cleves had returned, and he was born for this.

seventeen

Charles

My brother had gone. I heard muffled voices outside, male and female, and then shadows moved. Then it was silent.

"Go after him," whispered Alice. "Leave me."

"Not a chance," I replied.

I swept the curls from her hairline and took a closer look at the cut on her head. It was about two inches long, and the skin around it was already starting to bruise with a pale green swelling. The blood had dried into her hair, and I could smell something like aniseed, which I knew wasn't her shampoo. I remembered burying my nose in her hair and smelling apples, back when we used to lie on my bed and Alice would wonder about life outside The 48, what living it would be like. *Uncertain,* I always replied. For me, that wasn't a good thing.

"Charlie," whispered Alice. "You have to help me. I haven't had the training for this mission. I haven't been formally trained for *any* mission. I'm putting you both in danger. What if Grinch or other Assets from The 48 are looking for me? What if I shouldn't have left that building back there?"

I didn't know what to say to her because I had no idea what was going on.

The events outside our hotel, the screaming at the Louvre, Alice being drugged and dragged into an assignment that wasn't hers—these were all real and present problems that I didn't know how to deal with. They were major deviations from the prescribed order, and I'd been raised to believe nothing should deviate from the prescribed order.

My adherence to that philosophy was why I broke up with Alice in the first place. Because I could feel myself...*deviating*.

Deviations were not the way of The 48. The 48 controlled our time. Our emotions. Our humanity. So again...what the *hell* was going on?

Deep breaths.

Calm the heart rate.

Repeat a Tenet.

Get back on assignment.

We of The 48 consider toxicology a key area of study. Knowledge in this discipline could mean the difference between life and death. All Assets are to become conversant with the naturally occurring toxins and chemical combinations can cause death in humans. Toxicology is to be studied in conjunction with ethnobotany. Trainee Assets will be required to test chemicals on one another to build immunity, and to learn how to create an antidote under pressure.

I repeated it over and over again until I felt my body relaxing. Everything was going to be all right. The 48 might not like deviations, but no institution in the world was better equipped to handle them. And these probably weren't deviations to begin with. Grinch and Aramis would explain everything.

I sent for water. Alice drank and then collapsed into near-unconsciousness. After making sure she was warm, I dozed too.

A while later, I fully woke and was about to go out and start looking for Alex when he walked into the room. There was a strong smell of wine about him, but his eyes were clear. Judging from the large red stain on his sleeve, I guessed he had been drinking with the yeomen, and probably taking mental notes the whole time.

My brother could make friends with a statue and get it spilling secrets.

Alice was still asleep on the floor, wrapped up in the wool blanket.

"Where have you been?" I snapped as Alex flopped onto the floor. "We need to find out where the hell Aramis is."

"Drinking, surveilling, and trying to avoid romantic entanglements with just about every woman at court," replied Alex. "Even the serving girls are *delighted* about the return of the sons of Cleves, and once I confirmed we were unattached…jeez. Marlon was a huge help in distracting them, but he can't be around all the time, and this could start getting in the way of our progress around here."

"Give me strength."

"Marlon thinks you have a gittern stuck up your ass, by the way."

"A gittern…"

"It's like a guitar."

"I know what a gittern is—"

"It's depressing, actually, how obsessed everyone around here is with hooking up, pairing up, getting married, forging alliances, blah blah…"

"Yeah. Agreed. It sucks. Mostly for the women. But we're not here to—"

"I know, I know." Alex held up his hand. "I know what we're

here for." He lay back on the stone floor with his hands linked behind his head. "So have you worked out why Alice is here?"

I shook my head. "No. And Alice doesn't have a clue either. She does have a nasty cut on her head and scratches on the back of her neck, though. If she gets an infection here in this time, it could be deadly. We need to clean her up when she wakes."

"We *need* to find the painting of Henry and send Alice back somehow, Charlie."

"How? She has a timer, set the same as ours, so she's absorbed the radiation of a forty-eight-day trip, not one of the shorter reconnaissance ones. She can't leave until the countdown's at zero. And anyway, what if she's really supposed to be here? What if the reason she's here is to protect her from something bad in the present day? We just don't know enough yet."

Alex growled in frustration. "Why isn't Aramis here yet?"

"For all we know, Henry's chopped his head off."

My sarcasm was meant to mask my worry. We had known Aramis our whole lives. He was thirty-three years old, and when he wasn't time writing, he taught the Imperative of Renaissance history at The 48, which was the time period between the fourteenth and seventeenth centuries. He was a rotund guy—still in excellent shape, but easily the largest of all the Assets—and he was very knowledgeable about all aspects of the Renaissance. Aramis wasn't known for being a fighter, but we wouldn't need that on this assignment. But with Alice here, he would know what to do. He was one of the good guys at the institute.

"So what else were you doing while you were off sulking, other than drinking and avoiding aggressive admirers?" I asked.

"Getting reacquainted with Lady Margaret."

"Lady Margaret?" I wished I was better at remembering

names and faces on the periphery. The name was familiar, but I couldn't place her.

"A maid of honor. You've seen her before, but I don't think you talked to her. She was with Anne Boleyn the first time we met the queen. Lady Margaret could be useful, although there was something about her this time that was...different. But we'll need allies close to Jane Seymour, and they're both waiting on the queen."

"Nice work."

Alex looked rather sheepish. "Yeah, well, I was kind of a jackass earlier when I took off, and I wanted to impress you."

"I'm impressed, but not surprised. You're really good with people, Alex. Much better than me."

We fist-bumped. Alex and I didn't tend to hug it out.

We looked down at Alice. I could see her eyes moving behind her translucent lids. Spidery veins threaded out across the skin.

"It's gonna be okay," I said, putting my hand on my brother's shoulder. "This was probably a surprise training exercise for Alice. We'll confirm with Aramis when he gets here and tell him everything. He'll know what the deal is with Grinch's involvement. Maybe she's taking over the assignment from him. That would explain a lot."

"I'll take your lead on this, brother," said Alex. "I like Alice. A lot. But I'll be happier when it's back to being the two of us."

Alex sat down in one of the high-backed chairs, and immediately his breathing changed, going from short and shallow to deep and sonorous. I couldn't believe it. He was falling asleep—again. I put the spare blanket around his shoulders and settled down on the floor next to Alice. I couldn't take my eyes off her. I'd always thought she looked so interesting when she slept. Alice had the skill of being able to power nap at any time of the day—she was even better at it than my brother. During the previous summer, before I came to my senses and ended our relationship, she and I had taken to meeting in this really nice garden that The 48 had. It wasn't created for Assets' pleasure, really—it was used more regularly as a classroom for botany studies—but no one was ever stopped from strolling in it. Sometimes we would lie under a wooden pergola that was covered in white-and-yellow honeysuckle. Not because it was romantic, but because the scent was amazing. I would read to Alice and she would fall asleep within minutes. She said my voice was soothing; I always thought she was using a euphemism for *boring*. Those times were nice. Just a few moments every now and then when we weren't trainee Assets. I was surprised to find myself looking forward to them more and more.

Then one day Alice started wondering if her parents—both Assets, both dead—had ever lain down in the same spot. She asked if my parents—both Assets, both dead—had done the same. It was weird. It made me think of a future that I knew I couldn't have. I knew it was stupid, but after that one conversation, all I could see was me and Alice and our future kids and then every one of us dead because of The 48.

I had to self-correct. So I told her I wasn't going to see her anymore outside of training and classes. I was going to be seventeen before she was. My training was going to step up. I was going to be too busy. It wasn't her, it was me. I was trying to protect her.

Every dumb-ass excuse for breaking up poured out of my mouth.

Alice didn't cry. She never cried. Even when her mother died on an assignment when Alice was fourteen. She got pulled aside in physics class and told.

Then she was expected to just go back to class and write a paper on kinetic theory.

Which she did.

⁂

The sound of heavy boots thundering up and down the corridor outside startled Alex awake. Alice didn't stir. When the footsteps gave no indication that anyone was coming for us, I made a decision.

"Enough of this waiting. We've been kept too long. We need to find Aramis—now," I whispered.

"But Alice can't wander around the court dressed like that," said Alex. "At the very least, she needs to get rid of the jeans and sneakers."

"I know," I replied. "Which is why you're going to go find her some clothes from this time."

"What! Why me? You go find her clothes. She's your ex-girlfriend."

"I don't want to leave her, Alex," I said sternly. "Now stop effing around, go find that Lady Margaret or whoever, and get Alice some clothes."

"I can't just ask to borrow a woman's dress!"

"Use your imagination, *Alexander*!"

Grumbling, Alex pulled himself off the floor and left the room for the second time.

I unbuttoned my shirt and pulled out the small wad of papers from the kit bag that had been strapped to my chest. It was the full assignment brief. I could still remember the mix of emotions I had felt when Grinch had handed Alex and me the portfolio after the successful reconnaissance. It was still a testament to how well we were graded that we were chosen for an assignment nearly five hundred years in the past. The reputations of new Assets could be made or broken on that first dossier.

Now, with everything that had happened since we'd arrived in Paris, I wanted to look at the dossier again. Was there a clue to what was happening in these papers? What had we missed? I sat down on the floor and started to read, keeping one eye on the small gap between the floor and the door for lurking shadows.

"Is that your dossier?" whispered a voice behind my left ear. Alice was awake and leaning in toward me.

"Hey," I replied softly. "Yeah. I'm just going through it, to see if there's any explanation as to why Grinch would drag you back here."

"My head still hurts," said Alice, touching her temple with her fingertips. "Any chance you have some painkillers?"

"I don't, but I think Alex does in his kit bag," I replied, turning around. Her oval face was inches from mine. I could feel her breath on my skin. Her lips were pale and thick, like half-cut grapes.

"You have your voice back."

"What?"

"Your normal voice," said Alice. "You were speaking with a German accent earlier when those guards were around."

"We've taken on the guise of the sons of the Duke of Cleves," I said. "The story is we've been educated here and in France and so our accents aren't that strong, but we need to be a little Saxon for the cover to be convincing. We've told them you're a maid, so you need to have the accent too while you're here."

"Can I read through it?" she asked, nodding toward the

dossier. "I know it's not my assignment, but I want to be useful. Or at least not screw anything up more than I already have."

"You haven't screwed anything up. None of this is your fault." I passed the file to Alice. Not because I thought she could help, but because I felt important and wanted to show off a little. I had an assignment. I was a real Asset.

The dossier was mainly background stuff. Henry VIII's personnel file in history: height (a towering six feet one inches, which made him far taller than most in his court), weight (at this moment it was an obese 280 pounds—it would get a lot heavier over time), and also his recorded health problems. That last list ran to several pages and included smallpox, malaria, severe migraines, leg ulcers, and a near-death experience while jousting just three months earlier. It was a combination of the pain from these that would turn him into such a psychotic tyrant.

Also listed were close associates (Thomas Cromwell, the Duke of Norfolk, Thomas Cranmer, and Edward Seymour were just a few who would come and go). These were people to be wary of, but also those we needed to get close to.

"And your assignment is to stop him and Jane Seymour from getting married?" asked Alice after she had read through the pages twice.

"Yes. Henry can marry, but his wife needs to be a Protestant. We're part of the team that will end Catholicism in England. The assignment starts under Henry's rule because this was judged to be the best point in time to do it."

"Huh. How are you going to do that?" asked Alice. "Stop him from marrying Jane, I mean."

"What do you mean *how*?" I replied. "We just will."

"That's it? That's your plan? You and Alex *just will?*"

"Yes, Alice," I replied, trying to keep calm because this wasn't her fault. "We're already in the inner circle. I've even played archery with Henry already."

"But there's no information on how you and Alex are actually supposed to do this in the time frame you have."

"What do you mean?"

"I mean, okay, so you're in the inner circle. That's great. But what's it going to cost you, time-wise?"

"What are you saying?"

"I'm saying you can't just make someone fall in or out of love with someone else. Love isn't straightforward. It's complicated. Messing with people's minds and hearts the way you'll need to to accomplish this mission is going to take time. And if you take too much, you might end up killing an innocent woman."

"We're not killing Jane," I said.

"I hope not, Charlie, but that brings us back to the dossier, or rather the lack of one. You don't seem to have been given a lot of information to prevent that outcome. I mean, look at this thing. I would have expected a lot more details. A lot more than the background they gave you. Stuff like recommendations for manipulating personalities, and notes on contingencies, that sort of thing. This dossier is *tiny*."

"Of course it is," I snapped, starting to lose my temper. "I need to keep it hidden on me if we move palaces. I can't go around with a dossier the size of *The Complete Works of Plato* down my pants."

"Well, that's an image I didn't need in my head," she shot back. "My point is, first assignments are supposed to be easy, a gradual easing in for the crap that will come down on us in future years. The 48 haven't made your assignment easy. They couldn't have made it harder if they tried. You do know that you and Alex were the only new Assets chosen for the Religion Eradication operation, don't you?"

"Of course I do," I said hotly. "I'm pretty sure everyone does by now. It's something I'm kind of proud of."

"Well, the others assigned RE missions have years of operational experience, which would probably come in handy right about now. Think about it, Charlie. Look at the background info they *did* give you. Henry the Eighth is a basket case with pain because of the recent jousting accident. He's a ticking time bomb. Anne Boleyn is about to *die*. He *already* has his eye on Jane Seymour. That makes it a pretty complicated mission, don't you think? The 48 have put two untested Assets in huge danger by bringing you guys back to this time."

Alice was making all my worries about deviations resurface. I needed to shut this conversation down.

"You're just pissed that we've got a great first assignment. The 48 think we're exceptional. That we can handle it. And you can't stand that."

"Are you kidding me, Charlie?" cried Alice.

"It's Charles," I replied. "You have to call me Charles. And Alex is Alexander when we're in company."

At that moment, the door opened again and Alex glided through. For someone who was six feet tall, he had amazing grace. He was coordinated in a way I wasn't. I think it was because he truly excelled in the physical activities of the Imperatives. Alex knew how to move without really thinking about it.

I had to think about everything, which was why I had a permanent headache. This argument with Alice was *not* helping.

"Your clothes, milady," said Alex with a theatrical bow. "Do not ask how I got them, for I will never tell. Except to say that people really shouldn't leave their drying laundry unattended."

The tension between Alice and me eased a little.

"Not bad, Alex," said Alice, picking up a pair of gray satin shoes. They were slightly frayed but still in good condition. He had also found a cream-and-pale-gray dress with a high waistline, and a gray fringed wrap. Not a highborn lady's clothes, but those of a chambermaid. A perfect disguise to stop any questions.

"I thought about dressing you as a boy, but you're too pretty," replied Alex. Alice beamed.

"I suppose I can dress like a chambermaid for a few days," she said.

"And a bit of good news for you both," said Alex. "The guard outside appears to have stepped away."

"Seriously?" I asked. "Why?"

"I might've mentioned something about ale down the corridor."

"That'll buy us a couple of minutes," I said. "Alice, you get changed while Alex and I wait outside. Then we're getting out of here to find Aramis."

I didn't wait for an answer.

In the corridor, a distinct chill was setting in as the weak springtime sun dipped lower and lower behind the windows.

"And what were the women's clothes for?" The voice nearly made me jump out of my skin.

"Aramis!" exclaimed Alex.

Our mentor stepped out of the shadows. He looked regal in a pair of burgundy knee-length pants and a belted white-and-gold tunic. His beard had been trimmed into a neat goatee and his deep auburn hair was tied back.

"Good to see you...Father," I said, looking up and down the corridor before adding quietly, "We were getting worried."

"Oh?" asked Aramis.

"We've got a problem. An anomaly. Alice Tanner from The 48 is here. We don't know why, but it appears that Grinch—"

Aramis held up his hand. Two ruby rings glinted like fire as they caught the last of the sun's rays. Aramis's face, which was prematurely lined like those of most older Assets and pockmarked, was creased so much it was in danger of imploding.

"Did you say Alice Tanner?"

"Yes. We found her—"

Aramis suddenly had a wild look about him: wide-eyed and panic-stricken. It was completely at odds with the way older Assets were supposed to behave. It was unnerving.

"No. She can't be."

"Yeah, she is," replied Alex. "We need to send her back somehow. There must have been—"

"Dammit, she's onto us...I thought we had more time," he muttered, pulling a knife from within his tunic.

"This wasn't supposed to happen," he growled. "I'm sorry, Charles, but Alice can't go back. We need to dispose of her. Now."

eighteen

Alexander

Aramis's reply to my brother washed over me. Panicked, I repeated the ethnobotany Tenet of The 48 several times in my head to try to quiet the roar in my ears.

We of The 48 consider ethnobotany a key area of study. Knowledge in this discipline could mean the difference between life and death. Ethnobotany is to be studied in conjunction with toxicology. All Assets are to become conversant in knowing which plants can cause death in humans. Assets will test all trainees without notice. Trainees are hereby given notice that they should inspect all meals at all times for rogue ingredients and be aware of antidotes.

I'm sorry, Charles, but Alice can't go back. We need to dispose of her. Now.

Dispose was a clinical word. It was how you treated trash. You just got rid of it when it wasn't wanted or required anymore.

"Aramis," I said, finding my voice. "I don't understand. You heard us say Alice Tanner, right? Sixteen-year-old Alice—from The 48."

I looked at him. The wide-eyed, crazy appearance had gone. Instead he was staring directly at Charlie with total concentration and clarity. He stepped closer, and his skin took on the menacing orange glow of a recently lit torch above us.

"Did you hear me?" said Aramis. "I'm your superior Asset. Now do as I say and dispose of the girl."

"No."

Charlie's single syllable cut through the air like ice. He looked so calm, so in control. We had been taught to compartmentalize our emotions. We had also been taught to obey at all costs.

But disobeying Aramis wasn't complicated at all—not even for my brother—because Aramis's instructions were absurd.

"This assignment...your work here has...has been compromised," said Aramis; his voice was low and deep. "If you fail on your first assignment, it is unlikely you will receive a second. The 48 and TOD are merciless with failures." He was warning us, and when you received a warning from The 48, you listened.

And I was listening—while also trying to figure out a way to defuse the situation. I didn't want to do anything drastic. Aramis was one of the good ones. But this made no sense.

Like all experienced Assets, Aramis was one step ahead.

"Your brother is looking for a blade hidden in his boot, Charles," he said. "Cease thinking of ways to reach it and just dispose of the girl."

"How do we know *you're* not the one who has compromised the assignment?" I asked. Subterfuge was useless. I had been fumbling around the top of my boot, looking for my knife, but it was gone. "Everything has gone wrong since we came back. For all we know, you're the one screwing it up."

"I am not your enemy," replied Aramis. "But nothing can be left to chance. A third Asset arriving means danger. It is not the prescribed way."

"No kidding!" I cried. "But *Grinch* brought her here. And Grinch is your superior. She's the Deputy Director."

"Get back in that room and dispose of the girl now, or I will do it myself."

"I said no," said Charlie. "And we won't let you hurt her either."

My brother's coolness was heartening to see. But it seemed to fuel Aramis's rage all the more—and his speed, too. With a knife in his right hand, he threw back the door to the antechamber with the other. He was inside before I had time to stop him.

Fortunately, with his back to me, I could disarm him and take the knife myself.

This is how you stab someone with their back to you: You thrust down between the shoulders to reach the spinal cord. Aramis's hair and cloak would act as a barrier to the base of the neck, so I would have to be hard and true. There was no time for debate or fear. *Just do it, Alex.* I could hear Piermont's mocking voice in my head. *Just take the knife from Aramis and do it, Alex. Just do it. Do it.*

Down.

Down.

Down.

"Where's the girl?"

"Alex...Alex." Charlie wrapped his fingers around my arm, which was already raised at head height, readying to grab Aramis in a chokehold. Everything was moving in slow motion. Black amorphous shapes were swimming across my line of sight. Everything was clouding at the edges.

I had been about to kill someone. An Asset. A surge of fear swept upward from my stomach to the back of my throat. I was going to puke.

"Where's the girl?" repeated Aramis, kicking the blanket Alice had used away with his boot. He pulled the table toward him to check behind it. Three candles fell to the floor. The pot of glittering gunpowder wobbled but stayed in place.

The other door. The keys that had been left on the latch were gone.

As was Alice.

"Stay here," growled Aramis. "Do not move until I come back for you both."

With his knife still clasped tightly in his hand, Aramis threw open the small door next to the fireplace, ducked, and disappeared.

"We have to find her," I said. "He'll kill her, Charlie."

"But *why*?" he asked. "Why would he kill her? It doesn't make sense."

"No, it sure as hell doesn't. He's one of us and he's still gone to kill an Asset. This is like what happened back at the hotel in Paris. Something's gone wrong, Charlie. Something major. There's no denying it now. And as far as our assignment goes, Aramis is now as likely to stab us in our sleep as help us with it. And I'm pretty sure we don't want his help, seeing as he wants Alice dead."

"Alice isn't even an Asset," Charlie mused. "She isn't of age."

I stared at my brother, openmouthed. Infuriated by his calm, by his seeming lack of emotion, I kicked out at a chair and then turned to face him with clenched fists.

"Let's *go!* We have to help her! She's one of us, Charlie."

"No, she isn't," he replied. Then he turned to me and gave me a small, sly smile. "She's better than us. She always has been. And I would bet everything I have that Aramis isn't going to find her. Not here. Not in this warren of rooms."

Alice had the brains and training of ten Assets. When she

turned seventeen, she would be a natural. Perhaps the best time writer The 48 would ever know. But Alice had something else, too: a subtle way of creating disorder and distraction.

That had been a problem for some senior Assets at The 48, particularly the directors. There were five of them, led by Asix, who was the boss of them all. The directors were chosen not by TOD, but by virtue of how many successful missions they'd had. They were responsible for a fair amount of trainee education and oversight, in addition to time writing. And Alice questioned them constantly. About everything. Challenged them on their personal philosophies. Pointed out loopholes in the Tenets. Asked for details about TOD's membership. She was shut down left and right. But she occasionally got us thinking outside the box.

Of course, all the senior Asset instructors, and the directors, especially Grinch, hated that. They were always telling Alice that asking the wrong questions would get her killed earlier than her time.

But it was always obvious to me that Alice had instincts and emotions that not even The 48 could snuff out of her. And Grinch truly tried.

"I think you're probably right, that Aramis is going to have a hard time finding her. But we can't leave her out there," I said. "It's getting dark. She doesn't know anyone. She's had no briefing—"

"Alice read my dossier," interrupted Charlie.

"Charles!"

"Alexander, listen to me. If we go looking for Alice, we're just going to draw attention to the fact that she's here. If anyone's going to do that, let it be Aramis. He won't find her. As to her safety, I suspect the reason your knife is missing is because she stole it when you handed her the clothes. She would have known you would be able to find another one without too much trouble."

"You're probably right. But Aramis is still going to be checking in on us."

"Of course he is. He'll probably be back any minute. And he has to be back at the king's side at some point or his cover will be blown. Speaking of which…" He picked up our dossier and waved it in my face. "We still have a job to do. In spite of everything."

" 'In spite of everything,' he says. You are cold sometimes, man," I said, shaking my head. "The 48 would be so proud of you."

Charlie didn't disagree with me, but I could tell from his sharp intake of breath that my comment had hurt. Yet I stood by my words. He was cold. Steely. His goal here was still the mission, and nothing would change that. For me, the goal was making sure Charlie and I came out of this still breathing.

"Let's find Marlon," said Charlie. "Aramis can't drop his guard if others are around us. Safety in numbers. We'll request that Marlon is placed as our watch while we're in the palace."

That was a plan I could agree to. Readily.

⚊⚊⚊

Charlie stayed glued to my side as we walked past doors and flaming torches. Hampton Court was like a little village, with people scurrying on their way. Occasionally a cloud would pass across the moon and plunge the king's court into a Dante-esque inferno scene where the torches cast everything in a red flickering glow. But even though the night was cold, there was something human about the palace. The smell of roasting meat did little to overpower the stench of open sewers, but it was more bearable now.

It was amazing how quickly a person could acclimatize to shit, I thought.

I kept my eyes peeled for Aramis. I knew he'd be angry that we hadn't waited for him, but going after Alice had been *his* deviation from the assignment, not ours. We needed to get to our lodgings, and my new friends in this court were going to be my allies, too. Whether they wanted me or not.

Gittern-up-the-butt notwithstanding.

I heard Marlon before I saw him. There was something unmistakably joyous about his English voice. *It must be nice to live that way,* I thought. In the moment, with no real cares except your next meal and your next fumble in a corner.

"Alexander!" cried Marlon the second he saw us skulking out of the darkness like two cats. "And the brother, Charles of Cleves. Your arrival is most fortunate."

"And why is that?" I called, grinning.

"Wine and song!" cried Marlon, to the cheers of several other guards who were clearly off duty. A crowd of women surrounded them.

"Take one for the team," whispered Charlie. "We need to know where our lodgings are."

"I hate you," I muttered, but soon I was enveloped in a crowd of women who must have been the *loose women* that Lady Margaret had referred to so jealously.

"Do you need rescuing again, Alexander of Cleves?" whispered a voice near my right ear.

I laughed. "You are getting very good at this," I replied, placing my arm across Marlon's shoulder.

It lingered there *just* long enough.

"Is the pretty she-devil not with you?" asked a guard, glancing around.

"No," I replied, hoping beyond anything that Alice was hiding in a cupboard somewhere.

"Then my balls may yet see the dawn," he replied.

It was the yeoman Alice had attacked.

"We started on bad terms," said Charlie. "I would like to rectify that. I am Charles, son of the Duke of Cleves."

"Yes, you said when we first met." He paused, then offered his hand to us both. "Thomas Ladman. The seventeen-year-old bastard son of the Duke of Cambridge. Hence the reason I wear the uniform of the guard and not the jewels of nobility."

I also shook Thomas's hand, which was rough with calluses and as cold as ice.

"You know Lady Margaret," I said.

"Lady Margaret is a rose amongst thorns," replied Thomas. "And destined for a bed that's greater than mine," he added bitterly.

"The duke has procured us lodgings in the palace," I said, changing the subject. "Would either of you know where? We are in danger of becoming hopelessly lost once more."

"I do," replied Thomas. "You are staying in the Base Court. I can take you to your rooms when you are ready."

"Now is as good a time as any. Our journey was...tiring."

"Then let us take you now," said Marlon warmly.

⁓

I followed Marlon and Thomas as they led Charlie and me back past Wolsey's apartments and the empty room where we had first found Alice. We walked across damp cobbles that were slippery underfoot, beneath a portcullis, and out into a larger courtyard. The bell tower where we had arrived was now manned by guards.

The moment we were back inside the palace, we heard angry words being screamed by a woman. It was a mixture of English and French.

"Our beloved queen," muttered Marlon.

"Don't you like her?" I asked.

"There are rumors of witchcraft," replied Marlon. "I would not wish to walk in her shoes."

"Why is she here at all?" asked Thomas. "This wing is for guests of the king. The queen's apartments are in the Clock Court."

"Nighttime wanderings?" whispered Marlon, raising a suggestive eyebrow at me.

"She does nothing to dispel the rumors," said Thomas, shaking his head. "Indeed, she seems to encourage them. I pray that the queen does not take her maids of honor with her to the Tower. It would pain me to see Lady Margaret suffer for her mistress's ill deeds."

"Why should it be the queen's responsibility to stop rumors?" said Charlie. "People shouldn't gossip in the first place."

"Spoken like someone who is already enamored with the French way," said Marlon.

"I wouldn't say that aloud," said Thomas. "The walls have ears in the palace, and Cromwell has spies everywhere."

"Let's just get to our lodgings," said Charlie. "I'm tired."

"They are just along here," said Thomas. "Would you like us to stand watch, as it is your first night in the palace?"

"Yes, we would," my brother and I replied at the same time.

I hoped we wouldn't have need of their protection before the night was out.

nineteen

Charles

We were shown into two separate rooms, connected by a creaking dark oak door that was carved with fleur-de-lis the size of my hand.

Our new lodgings at the palace were certainly a lot grander than the rooms we had stayed in before. A sign, perhaps, of the standing we had already attained with the king. We each had a large four-poster bed and an ornately carved table with a pewter bowl for washing. The fireplaces in both rooms were crackling with orange flames that had a pink tint around the edges. There was a large padded seat beneath each window, and clothes had already been laid out on the beds. Aramis must have arranged all of this, down to the riding boots propped up in the corner.

The juxtaposition of an Asset in control with the man we'd seen earlier was difficult to understand.

"You may wish to wash before the evening meal is served in the Great Hall," said Marlon. He and Thomas both bowed, and the doors closed with a solid thump.

Alex collapsed onto the bed, which immediately sank down several inches.

"Now, this is more like it, Charlie," he said, wriggling into the damask covers. "A comfy bed. An evening meal. Clothes that'll make us look like rejects from clown school."

I walked over to the window. It was latticed into diamond shapes. Each pane showed a distorted view of the courtyard below, giving it an abstract-art appearance, like a Picasso painting.

"Where are you?" I whispered, tracing my fingers down the condensation that was already pooling in the lead lattices. "Where are you, Alice?"

After dinner, which was a subdued affair without the king, even with the strains of plucked instruments, eight rich courses, and plenty of stares, we returned to our rooms. We removed our shirts and placed our kit bags at the bottom of a wooden chest that was set at the end of one of the beds. Alex's chest was pink from where his kit bag had rubbed against his skin.

"What archives did you bring with you?" I asked, leafing through the small bundle of papers he had already placed in the bottom of the chest.

"Just the ones I thought could be important," he replied. "Antidotes, makeshift weapons, that kind of thing. But I had to print them out in a calligraphic font, and really small, so they wouldn't look out of place if someone found them."

"You're going to go blind if you try to read these," I said, holding them up to the light with one hand. With the other, I held my stomach, which was griping after so much rich, greasy food at dinner. I picked up some red grapes that had been left in a bowl, just to try to take off the edge. They were overripe but somehow sour.

The door was flung open and a gust of wind swept through the room. The fire crackled in response.

"I told you both to wait in the antechamber earlier," growled a voice from the door. I recognized it immediately. "It was not a good look to have you both attend dinner without me."

"It wasn't our fault you weren't there," I muttered. Aramis glowered in reply.

"Did you find Alice?" asked Alex.

I was glad my brother asked the question. I didn't tend to ask questions that I didn't want to hear the answer to.

I was a coward sometimes.

"No," snapped Aramis. He slammed the door and sank into an upholstered chair.

"Has this ever happened before?" I asked through gritted teeth. My head was pounding. "Has Grinch ever done something like this before? Alice shouldn't be here—she doesn't *want* to be here. Why won't you help her—help us?"

"I am *your* Asset contact, not hers. And I am aware of Assets turning up unscheduled on assignments before," replied Aramis. "Which is why this deviation must be exterminated. Remember your Imperatives and Tenets, Charles."

"Deviation? Alice isn't a deviation!" cried Alex. "How can you say that? Someone in The 48 is working against us, Aramis. We heard screaming in the Louvre as we started to travel. Grinch had just left the room."

"What? You never said—"

"We haven't...had a chance." I grabbed hold of one of the wooden bedposts. My legs were starting to buckle. I was barely holding myself upright.

"Charlie, what's wrong?"

Pain was stabbing at my insides. Burning spasms pinged around my gut.

"Alex..."

I fell to the ground as my legs gave way. I had no control over them. I had no feeling whatsoever.

"Alexander!" cried Aramis. "Come here, quickly."

I felt hands behind my shoulders, but my sight had clouded over. I couldn't see who was holding me. Liquid was bubbling up inside my throat. It was frying my vocal cords. I was drowning in boiling acid. I knew this sensation, and it filled me with the same fear I had felt when I was testing poisons in my toxicology Imperative.

We of The 48 consider toxicology a key area of study. Knowledge in this discipline could mean the difference between life and death. All Assets are to become conversant with the naturally occurring toxins and chemical combinations can cause death in humans. Toxicology is to be studied in conjunction with ethnobotany. Trainee Assets will be required to test chemicals on one another to build immunity, and to learn how to create an antidote under pressure.

Darkness invaded everything.

twenty

Margaret

Fire could be a friend or a foe. Its tendrils kept away the biting cold in winter; yet it was also a hungry beast that could devour an entire dwelling in moments.

A fire earlier in the year had destroyed a number of the ladies' rooms near the apartments of the queen. Many said it was set deliberately. The queen placed the blame at the door of an unfortunate servant who was not seen again.

But others suspected a more powerful wrongdoer.

One of the rooms that had been destroyed was a chamber I shared with Lady Jane and Lady Cecily. Flames could have been the end of me, but I had been unable to sleep that particular night and had stolen away for fresh air with my two friends. The day after, my own father questioned why I had not been in the room when the fire broke out. Evidently, my reputation was worth more than my life in his eyes. Yet I had been able to satisfy his questions in the furor that followed by being suitably subservient to him and to the irate men around us who sought to root out the arsonist.

To alleviate our distress, my fellow ladies and I had been removed to alternative chambers whilst restorations were calculated.

The calculations were taking a good while. The king was stalling. It was assumed he did not want to spend the money on ladies who served a wife who might not last the year. The only one who mattered, Lady Jane, had already been moved to apartments nearer the king.

Fire could have been my foe that day, but it had inadvertently become my friend. My new chambers were set farther from the queen's than before, ensuring I was guaranteed peace during the night.

Except this one.

I hadn't been able to sleep. I had seen Thomas Ladman earlier in the evening, and the stake had finally been plunged into my heart. My head had, of course, known that we could never now be more than old acquaintances from a childhood long forgotten. Yet the heart does not always align with the head, until it has visual evidence of something that may break it.

We had known each other since I had arrived at the court. He was a bastard son of the Duke of Cambridge, and as such had received an education befitting someone being groomed for higher purposes. Two years after my arrival, the duke's wife successfully delivered not one but two male heirs, and Thomas was abandoned. The king took pity on Thomas and gave him a position of rank in the yeomen guard.

Our hopes for marriage all but disappeared. My father heard of our childish courtship and demanded I stay away from Thomas. A bastard was not worthy of the only daughter of Sir Richard Montague.

Yet Thomas could not stay away from me, and we continued to meet in secret. For more than two years. Our kisses, our secret.

Until I began hearing rumors that I was not the only woman Thomas was kissing. Marlon had the good grace not to speak of it, but the servant girls and other yeomen were not so kind.

Gossip did not feed just the court; it was there to be devoured just as hungrily by those who served.

And then this night I had seen it with my own eyes. He must have known there was a chance I would see him, fumbling and pressing against one of the kitchen wenches, who was clearly delighted by the attention, judging by the moans of longing lingering in her throat.

I felt sickened, despoiled. And, to my shame, above all I felt envious.

Thomas Ladman did not see my tears. He would not have heard my stifled sobs.

Or the hardening of my heart. He would not get another moment of my company.

I was lying awake that night, distressed and distracted, when I heard raised voices; frightened cries. They sounded male.

I knew at once who was making the sound.

I climbed out of bed and wrapped a heavy damask robe around my shoulders.

"Lady Margaret!" exclaimed Lady Cecily. "What in the king's name are you doing?"

"Can you not hear the voices?"

"Of course—I wish I could not," she replied, pulling the bed coverings up to her nose. "Do not venture out there. It is improper."

"Need I remind you that the last time there was a disturbance near our chambers, our lives were almost forfeit?" I said.

Lady Cecily made no reply.

I pulled open the heavy oak door. It creaked a warning as I slipped through; the tie of my robe momentarily pulled me back as it caught on the heavy cast-iron handle.

Alexander of Cleves was staying in the Base Court. An honor indeed. I could hear his and another, deeper, voice. That one had the true accent of the House of Cleves. But Alexander's voice was peculiar. It was elongated and higher, almost as if he had been inflicted with some kind of palsy.

Scurrying like a mouse on the hunt for crumbs, I made my way across the cold flagstones, past flickering candles that were almost spent, until I reached my quarry. I knocked on the door twice, and bravely, without waiting for a reply, I entered.

And gasped.

At first I thought it was Alexander of Cleves writhing on the floor. White spittle was foaming at the corners of his mouth. He was in his brother's arms, and an older gentleman, who I presumed was the Duke of Cleves, was inspecting some grapes.

It was a snatch in time before I realized that it was the brother who had been struck down, and Alexander was the one cradling him.

"Milady!" exclaimed the older man. "We did not mean to rouse you from your sleep."

"What has happened?" I asked, kneeling down beside Alexander.

"My brother...my brother!" cried Alexander. "He's been poisoned."

"Your bag, Alexander," called the duke; he was throwing fruit onto the fire. It blackened and shriveled on contact, causing a rotten stench to rise from the flames.

"I have seen the court physicians use leeches before," I said. "But I fear we do not have time. If it is poison, charcoal will draw it out."

"Charcoal...of course," said Alexander of Cleves. He dropped his brother onto the floor and half staggered, half slid toward the bed.

"Milady, allow me to escort you back to your room," said the duke; his countenance was stern, his tired eyes flecked with red.

"I cannot leave until I know this man will last the night," I replied, taking his head onto my lap. I needed the sons of Cleves alive.

The brothers were the same in almost every way, although Alexander's nose was slightly bent to the left, and his red flaming hair was longer. I saw nothing of the Duke of Cleves in either, from the color of their gray-blue eyes to the shape of their angular faces. If they were both to be acknowledged bastards of the king, the court would welcome them warmly.

Until such a time as they both became a threat.

Alexander of Cleves returned with a pewter goblet filled with black liquid. It was similar to an antidote I had seen used once before. The concoction had been successful on that day. I prayed that history would repeat itself.

"Charlie, drink this . . ."

"Alexander!" rebuked the duke.

"Charles," said Alexander, correcting himself as he started to pour the liquid down his brother's throat. The motionless brother started to cough and splutter.

"He is rousing!" I cried. "Praise to the Lord above and the king."

"You saved him," whispered Alexander. "Thank you, Lady Margaret. Thank you."

The sorcerer-sons of Cleves were now in my debt.

And I intended to call on that favor with haste.

twenty-one

Charles

I could taste bitterness. It coated my tongue, teeth, and throat. I gagged several times. The mixture being poured down my throat was thick and gritty. It rubbed against my gums, filling my mouth with the sensation of drowning once more. I was being force-fed mud. I tried to struggle but stopped when I started to choke. It was going up my nose, it was blocking my throat. I was dying once more.

"He is rousing!" cried a female voice. "Praise to the Lord above and the king."

Whispers followed that I could not understand.

"Don't fight it, Charles," said a voice I did recognize: my brother's. "All the way down. Come on. All the way down."

I could smell Alex. The scent of my brother was soap and sugar. It felt safe. My brother would never hurt me. I could trust him.

The smell of the woman was strange. Not unpleasant, just strange. As if spice and perfume and sweat had been ground together by a mortar and pestle.

I started to relax and accept what was happening. This was just like trying to get over the stages of time travel. The gritty concoction started to soothe my burned throat. I gagged and coughed, but I swallowed it nonetheless. Another body pushed against my side.

"The antidote should start to work soon, Alexander," said

Aramis to my brother. "You did well. We are in your debt, milady, yet you must leave. It would not aid your reputation to be seen alone in the company of three men who are unrelated to you. And you would do well not to speak of this to anyone."

An implied threat that even the stupidest of courtiers would understand.

The cold rim of a metal cup was resting on my chin. The person holding it was trembling. I wanted to speak to my brother, but the paralysis of the poison had affected my voice as well as my eyes. I could manage no more than a groan. I could only see white cloud and black shadow.

"It's fine, Charlie," said Alex. I felt his fingers tenderly comb through my hair. He had never done that before. "You're gonna be fine."

"Alexander!" said Aramis.

I wanted to warn my brother that he was dropping out of character. Alex had to stop calling me Charlie. There was a stranger in the room with us. We were going to be discovered. We'd be hanged or burned or beheaded as sorcerers.

Then I felt a constriction in my stomach, like something nefarious inside was being sucked into a sponge.

Seconds after that, I started throwing up. The more I was sick, the more movement I gained back. Quid pro quo for draining away the poison. By the time my eyesight had started to return, my throat was shredding skin as the activated carbon antidote mixture my brother had given me absorbed not just the poison, but half of my gullet lining as well.

Sweat was pouring off me. It pooled around my neck; I could feel it dripping down my back. Every muscle I possessed ached with pain. Even breathing was uncomfortable. As figures became more than shadow, I concentrated on the one I knew was my brother. He would get me through this—he had before.

I trusted him. He was the only one—other than Alice.

Alex's eyes were red. That was the first color I saw. He was also ringed by a halo of pale yellow light from several candles.

But my brother looked the opposite of ethereal. He looked scared.

"I will leave you now," said the young woman. She had long blond hair that was plaited to the side. Her body was covered in a red damask dressing gown with a burgundy cord.

"May I escort you back, Lady Margaret?" asked Alex.

"No. Your father is quite correct. It is better that I am alone and not seen in company," she replied. "I will see you on the morrow, Alexander of Cleves?"

"I will make sure of it—I am in your debt, milady."

The door opened and closed. A draft ran up my body like a wave. I shuddered.

"Charlie?"

"I'm okay," I groaned, lifting my hand. I tried to touch Alex but merely swatted the night air.

Okay wasn't a word used in the sixteenth century, but I needed Alex to know I was all right. Really all right. That I was myself— whoever that was now. The stranger was gone. I could bend the rules a little.

"You scared the crap out of me," whispered Alex, wiping his red, swollen eyes. "Don't do that again."

"I didn't mean...to do it at all."

"Can you move, Charles?" asked Aramis, pulling me into a sitting position.

"How do you feel?" asked Alex.

"I've felt…worse," I replied. Even my own voice sounded detached, like I was hearing it underwater.

"Good enough," replied Aramis. "Now, on my count, Charles, I want you to stand. One, two…"

On three, he and Alex pulled me to my feet. I wobbled, but more from the head rush than the inability to stand.

"Someone poisoned the grapes," said Aramis bluntly. "It was lucky you only ate one. Lady Margaret has obviously seen this befall someone in the court before, because she knew exactly what to do. You were lucky she alone heard the commotion and no one more important came. Yet be aware she may now be a liability to you. You'll need to watch her like hawks."

"Where are the grapes? We can't leave…them lying… around."

"The remainder of the grapes, and the rest of the fruit, are now burning in the fire," said Aramis. "And from now on I suggest we have someone test your food. There are plenty of servants here who already do it for half of the court."

"Should we abort the assignment?" asked Alex. "Alice, now this. Someone wants us to fail. I would bet anything now that Grinch has gone rogue and is behind all the crap that's been happening."

"You have taken pills for a forty-eight-day assignment," replied Aramis. "And even if I *could* get you back to the institute now, what do you think would happen if you turned up?"

"We wouldn't get…a second assignment?" I said, coughing blood into my open hand.

"Exactly right," replied Aramis, but he spoke too quickly. Something wasn't right. "You cannot—you must not—return to The 48."

The veins in my brother's neck and forehead were bulging, but I was so proud of the way he was restraining himself. It was taking every ounce of control he had, but he was now mastering his emotions, just like Assets were taught.

This was our existence.

"I'm going to get some wine or ale," said Alex, running his fingers through his hair. "Hopefully that's not poisoned too."

Another cold breeze of air wafted across my shivering body as Alex departed the apartment and left me alone with Aramis.

"Did you get my note? Do you still think it wise to have your brother as your Asset partner?" asked Aramis as he helped me to walk into the other bedroom. I didn't want to move, but I was too weak to argue. The poison had sucked the fight out of me.

"I don't trust anyone else as much as I trust Alex."

"One day you might need to put your own welfare ahead of that of your partner," said Aramis quietly. "I have never thought siblings make good Asset partners. There is too much emotion involved. Others disagree, of course, which is why it is permitted. But watching your brother as he mixed the antidote...I don't think he has the capacity to be selfish enough to leave you, and one day he might have to. Could you do it?"

"Why are you suddenly acting like you care?" I asked. "You've been a total shit up until now. I'm pretty sure Alice Tanner would agree."

Aramis sighed. "There are things I cannot tell you right now, Charles. But you will learn soon enough. Now, tell me, what happened as you were waiting to travel in the Louvre?"

"We didn't see whatever happened," I replied. "Alex and I had gone into the designated travel room at the Louvre. We took the radiation pill. And then we heard a scream as we concentrated on the vanishing point."

"So you didn't actually see Grinch, or anyone else, for that matter?"

"No. We saw a black shadow appear in the doorway, but we had already started the time loop conversion...and then we arrived in the bell tower."

"Could it have been Alice Tanner?"

"I couldn't tell if it was male or female, let alone *who* it was, Aramis."

"Grinch was my Asset contact on my first assignment," said Aramis. "I had to keep the Marquis de Sade alive in an insane asylum for thirty-two years. Grinch has always been a stickler for the rules and putting The 48 first. She made me the Asset I am today. And you should be aware that she is known here in the Tudor court. She travels under the guise of Madame du Pont, a French noblewoman. She's been in this era several times."

"Alice said it was Grinch who pulled her through the cosmic string, which makes me wonder if she even took a radiation pill. What is Grinch doing?"

"Time will tell, Charles. But you definitely didn't get a visual on the figure?"

"No. My eyeballs were being stretched out of their sockets."

Aramis shrugged. "It is of little consequence. Grinch is forty-seven."

Aramis didn't need to elaborate as to his thought process.

"How old is Willem?" I asked.

"You know how old Willem is," replied Aramis. "Or you wouldn't be asking."

"What happens to the younger partners of Assets once the old ones aren't...around anymore?"

"They go back to The 48," said Aramis. "You *know* this, Charles."

I decided not to specifically mention Katie. I needed to get back to the assignment. Some desperate part of me wanted to show Aramis that I could concentrate, even after what had happened. And I hated myself for wanting to impress him after he'd threatened Alice's life.

"I heard Anne Boleyn earlier," I said. "She was yelling at someone."

"Her time is almost up too," said Aramis.

"Alex and I end her, Aramis."

"You don't end Anne, Charles," replied Aramis. "But you *will* end Jane Seymour, one way or another. Now I suggest you rest. Tomorrow you will get reacquainted with the king."

I sank down onto the bed and closed my eyes. The pain had transferred from my stomach to my lower back. My poor kidneys were screaming in protest at the poison still filtering through my blood.

"One day you'll be asked to choose a way, Charles," said Aramis. "Choose wisely, and without sentiment. Self-preservation is all that matters in the end."

twenty-two

Margaret

I was heady with excitement as I climbed beneath the bedcovers. Lady Cecily had been awake when I returned to our quarters, but she turned her back to me and refused to talk.

Not that I would have revealed anything of the time I'd spent out of bed. My hands were trembling. I placed them across my chest and felt my heart racing. I was alive, and the sons of Cleves were in my debt. Twice over, now, though they had no knowledge of what I'd witnessed the night they left.

And now I'd saved one of them. I thought of the veiled threats of their father, the duke, and stifled a laugh. He would not tell anyone of my actions. I had saved a Cleves heir from poison. Someone wanted them gone from the court. Cromwell and Edward Seymour were the first names that came to mind. Had they heard something? Was the king perhaps intending to marry two maids of honor to the young men who looked so much like him? Seymour could not have thought Jane at risk for such a match. But these were unpredictable times.

I moved my hand and tucked it under my breast. My heart had slowed.

For the first time in recent memory, I felt no fear. Only clarity of purpose. My good fortune this night was a sign. True, a marital alliance with one of the Cleves brothers, and in a strange land, no less, was terrifying based on what I had seen them do.

But my survival was all that mattered to me. My parents

had other ambitions for their only daughter, yet my prize was clear.

My survival.

And self-preservation was all that truly mattered in the end. Whether my heart was broken or not was irrelevant. As long as it was still beating.

twenty-three

Alexander

A new day dawned. What a surprise—it was raining. How had the English not evolved to possess webbed feet?

I washed and dressed and immediately went to check on Charlie in the next room. He was awake. His eyes were pink and rimmed with dark circles that looked like week-old bruises.

They met mine when I leaned over him. "Thank you for saving my life."

"I'm not sure I can lay claim to saving your life last night. If Lady Margaret hadn't mentioned charcoal, I'd be burying you this morning."

"That Lady Margaret won't cause trouble, will she?" asked my brother.

"We'll find out," I replied. I was aware that I had dropped my Cleves façade in front of her, during the terror of what had happened. There was no point in telling Charlie this; he would only worry. And he had enough to deal with.

I needed to lighten the mood.

I had on a white shirt that looked remarkably similar to the one I had worn yesterday, and a pair of dark brown pants that were too tight around my thighs. One good lunge and the court would be seeing more of me than was decent. At least Charlie wouldn't have to worry. My legs were more muscular than my brother's, so the same clothes would be a perfect fit for him. After struggling for what seemed like an eternity, I had also managed to put on a pair of black riding boots, and to complete the look, slung over a chair with casual elegance was a thick black cloak.

I can do casual elegance, even while looking like a major dumb-ass, I thought.

"Have you heard anything about Alice?" asked Charlie.

"Nothing," I replied. "Which is good news. Now put these clothes on and try not to upstage me. Are you hungry?"

"No," groaned Charlie. "I'm never eating anything again."

"Tough," I replied. "We're in the Tudor court and we will feast and stuff our stomachs—"

"Until we cannot move," interrupted Charlie, recalling the instructions Aramis had given us before our first introduction to the king.

———

With Charlie finally dressed and somewhat washed, we left the apartments. I hoped we wouldn't see anyone important until Charlie had recovered a bit more, but we hadn't gone more than a hundred meters when we walked straight into the queen. Anne's skin was so white she looked like a marble statue cloaked in a burgundy dress. The dress was low-cut, but it wasn't provocative. Her collarbones were extremely pronounced.

Stress and fear were literally eating away at her.

I bowed to the queen and her three ladies, all of whom were older. Charlie followed, but when he brought his head back up, he had gone so green I thought he was going to throw up there and then.

Unfortunately for us, the queen wanted to talk.

"The sons of Cleves have returned," she said. "The court has missed you."

The coldness in her voice didn't match the words.

"And that sentiment is reciprocated," I replied, hoping my brother wouldn't faint. "We are very much looking forward to staying here now."

"And have positions been granted to you?" asked the queen.

She clearly didn't know what was going on in her own court. This was something we could use to our advantage.

"Not as yet, Your Grace," I replied. "We are servants to the king."

"And Cromwell, no doubt," muttered the queen. One of her ladies smirked and looked the other way. Down the corridor, an approaching servant girl spotted Her Majesty and disappeared into a nearby room. To avoid any royal abuse, no doubt.

"You're very quiet, Charles," the queen said. "Has the cat got your tongue?"

"Traveling does not agree with me, Your Grace," replied my brother, looking more like Grinch with every passing second.

Would the poison have triggered something in the radiation toxins? I tried to recall the pharmacology Tenet.

We of The 48 will utilize the Imperative of pharmacology in order to save an Asset partner if necessary. However, discretion is permissible. One's own life, in the name of mission success, outweighs that of a partner.

No. Dammit. I needed a radiation-specific Tenet. What was written about radiation and pharmaceuticals?

I realized that the queen was staring at us both like we were imbeciles. "I am looking for wit and merriment today," she said spitefully. "Not witless wonders. You will visit me when you have *recovered.*"

She glided away, her three ladies following her in lockstep.

Charlie swore and pushed his back against the wall. Sweat was starting to bud around his top lip and in his hairline.

"She terrifies me more than the king," he whispered. "There's something about her eyes. They're so black. They're almost alien."

Anne was a divisive figure in history: hated by the Catholics who saw her as the destroyer of the faith in England, but pitied by historians who saw her as a woman who was simply too strong-willed for a misogynistic king.

She had been Queen of England for three years. It was easy—too easy—to look at the peripheral details in an assignment dossier when it was written down in black and white.

Anne Boleyn was only thirty-five years old. History wouldn't record her as reaching thirty-six.

"You look like death, Charlie," I said. "Go back to the room. I'll make excuses at breakfast if anyone asks."

"Thank you," replied my brother. "I'll find you as soon as I'm feeling a bit better."

"And don't eat any grapes," I called after him.

He looked around to make sure we were alone, and then, most uncharacteristically, gave me the finger.

I smiled, taking one split second to push the thought out of my mind that someone had tried to kill my brother.

Or were those grapes meant for me? The sons of Cleves were already marked men.

twenty-four

Charles

It took me ages to find my room. And I couldn't get the queen out of my head. I didn't understand why, but there was something so *alive* about her. It was disorienting. I hadn't felt this with Henry, but perhaps that was because I knew that Anne was only weeks away from dying.

When I finally reached our apartments, I was pleased to see a tin bath already waiting, filled with water that was so hot, swirls of steam were dancing around the room. I didn't know at first who had ordered it, but then I noticed the other thing waiting for me.

Alice was sitting on my bed.

"What the—"

"Shhh," replied Alice, putting her fingers to her lips.

"What are you doing here?" I cried. "If Aramis finds you—"

"Are you going to tell him?" asked Alice, launching herself off the bed. She pushed a dark wooden seat, curved like an upended letter *C*, in front of the door. One of the spindles blocked the latch perfectly.

"No, of course not," I replied. "But Aramis has a habit of walking into this room unannounced."

"I've blocked the door, and Aramis was walking toward the armory the last time I saw him," said Alice. "I won't be found unless I want to be, and I don't want to be. So keep your voice down. Now, I understand you were almost poisoned last night, and you didn't have time to have a bath this morning, which is why I ordered some squires to prepare you one. Need help scrubbing your back?"

"What…how…have you been *following* us? Knowing that Aramis is after you? Alice, you're insane."

"And you stink. Seriously, you need a bath, Charlie. I'll turn my back if you want."

Grabbing Alice was out of the question, but that didn't stop the rising urge to shake her by the shoulders to wake her up. What was she doing? She was taking a huge risk being in this room, where Aramis could walk in at any second.

"I'm serious, Alice." I gently took hold of her hand. Her fingers immediately linked with mine. They were long and slim. Her skin was much warmer than it had been the day before. I took that as a good sign that she was recovering from the effects of chloroform and time travel.

"I know you're being serious," said Alice. "You always are. But I can't sit back and play servant girl and *wait* for whatever comes next. I need to figure out what's going on. And I wanted to see you. To—to see if you've learned anything."

"Nothing. I don't have any ideas about anything, Alice, except that Grinch going rogue just isn't Grinch. And Aramis attempting to assassinate a trainee Asset is just as mad. If it were Piermont, then I would understand, because he treats The 48 like a military camp—"

"It *is* military, Charlie," said Alice quietly. I noticed then that she had changed her clothes from the ones Alex had found her—she was now wearing a simple dark gray cotton dress, and her corkscrew curls were tied back beneath a white cotton headdress. Her face was serious.

She was so pretty.

"Your water's getting cold," she said, pointing to the tub. "You need to get in, especially if you're taking the king on at archery after dinner. You want to be presentable."

"How did you know that? Even *I* didn't know that."

Alice tapped the side of her freckled nose. "I'm quite the spy."

I didn't want her to leave, but she wasn't safe with me. It wasn't that I didn't trust Alice to take care of herself. I did. I just didn't trust myself to be able to complete the assignment if I was constantly worrying about where she was. The faster we handled our mission, the faster I could focus on helping her. If she wanted my help.

I didn't own Alice.

"Have you seen Queen Anne?" I asked as she removed the chair from the door.

"I just saw you turn into a gibbering idiot in front of Queen Anne," replied Alice a little caustically. "Does that count?"

"And just how in the hell do you know *that*?"

"Chance, actually. I was on my way here and I nearly ran into you all along the way. So I ducked into an antechamber and waited out your wreck of a conversation."

"I wasn't a gibbering *idiot*. I was poisoned last night and I feel like crap. I thought I was going to throw up out there."

"Yes. As I said, I'm aware you were poisoned."

"Who told you?"

"I heard Lady Margaret in the chapel this morning," said Alice. "She was talking to herself. Confession, I think."

"She saved my life. She knew about charcoal absorbing poison."

"I don't trust her," said Alice.

"You don't even know her."

"She's a living, breathing member of the court of Henry the Eighth," said Alice. "You shouldn't trust her or anyone here. I certainly won't until I work out why I'm here."

"You're probably right."

"You need to keep an eye on her. And the queen. And the rest of her ladies."

The idea hit me like a ton of bricks.

"You do it."

"Do what?"

"Spy for me."

"On what?" asked Alice.

"The queen."

"Spy on the queen?" asked Alice, turning to face me. She looked intrigued.

"I don't know how I'll arrange this, but what if you were to go and act as a servant to the queen? She doesn't trust her ladies. You could keep an eye on all of them and tell me what they're talking about. Jane Seymour is one of them. You would be able to get into places I couldn't."

"What about Aramis?"

"He might burst into *my* bedroom, but even *he* wouldn't accost the queen. You'd be safer near her than anywhere else in this palace while you're trying to figure out why you were brought here."

"Arrange it, and I'll do it," said Alice, nudging me with her arm. "Maybe it's fate that I'm here."

"There's no such thing as fate. And you should know that a hell of a lot has gone down since we left Toronto, not just your arrival here. When we were in Paris, Alex and I saw Willem being dragged into an unmarked van. Katie, too. In the middle of the afternoon, in public."

"What? Did they hurt her?"

"I didn't see much, although from what I did see, The 48 weren't being gentle."

"How old is Willem?"

"Old enough to be decommissioned permanently," I replied. "But it's always covert, right? I've never heard of an aging Asset being taken away in broad daylight—and especially not their partner as well."

Alice nodded thoughtfully. Then she opened the door. "I'll be back later," she whispered, peeking out.

"Alice," I called.

"What?"

"Did you take a radiation pill before you traveled here with Grinch?"

Alice didn't miss a beat. "I have no idea, Charlie," she replied. "I guess we'll find out when my countdown gets to zero. If I absorbed the full dose of radiation, then I'll be pulled forward through the cosmic string, and I had just better be standing in front of a painting that checks all the right boxes when I do." She smiled. "And if I don't, well, then, I guess I'm stuck here for good if there's no one to take me back with them."

"Alex and I will take you back before you reach zero."

"If you're successful—and still alive," she replied.

Then she slipped silently back into the corridor.

⚊⚊

Alice was right about the bathwater. By the time I had removed my clothes and slipped into the tub, it was no longer swirling with steam. It was tepid at best. A thin, oily film had settled on top and gave it a rainbow sheen. A bar of rough yellow soap that didn't lather had been left for my use, along with strips of cloth that I assumed were towels. I washed my hair with the soap and dried myself in front of the fire. I didn't feel any cleaner.

Two servants came in as I was standing butt naked by the flames; they didn't bat an eye. Then a third servant came into my room and started pulling clothes from a dresser. I spent the next few minutes being manipulated like a doll until I was fully outfitted in clothes that smelled vaguely of sandalwood. The process afforded me time to think. About Alice, about Alex, and about Anne.

The three As.

"I see you've finally had a bath." The familiar voice made the hair on my arms stand on end. "What were you thinking, allowing yourself to be taken ill in front of the queen? Sickness is a sign of weakness, Charles. Especially in a court where news of affliction strikes fear in His Majesty."

The fourth A had arrived.

"Where's my brother, *Father*?" I asked, glancing around the room to make sure Alice hadn't left anything.

"He's walking around the grounds with a couple of the yeomen."

"But it's pouring outside."

"Alexander didn't seem to mind," replied Aramis, settling into a chair and dismissing the servants. "I've shown him the armory and given him a guide to Henry's favorite haunts around the palace. There are more secret passageways here than in The 48."

"I didn't realize there were *any* at The 48."

Aramis ignored me. "It's time for you to step up your game. What happened last night was unfortunate, but you must not allow it to cloud your thoughts. You have an assignment. Get it done. Remember not to be too sycophantic with the king. And one of you boys needs to get in with Cromwell. He's a powerful ally. Do it soon. I'll only be here another day."

"You're going back? Why? What happened to supervising us? And what about your little manhunt for Alice Tanner?"

"Have you seen her?" Aramis asked dryly.

"No. Have *you*?"

I wasn't stupid, but neither was Aramis. We looked at each other for a long moment before he spoke. "Certain developments require me to set the issue of Alice Tanner aside for the moment. I'm needed back in the present."

"I see."

"No, Charles, you most certainly do not." He straightened the ruby rings on his fingers and got to his feet. "I'll see you at dinner tonight."

After he left, I grabbed a fur-lined gilet and slipped it on, securing it with a thick brown belt. It was incredibly warm. A ceremonial knife had been left for me on the dresser, and that went into the boots I had brought with me.

I was furious with Aramis, but he was right about one thing: I had to start being proactive. It was time for another audience with the queen.

This time, I would be coherent.

It took a while to track her down, but I eventually managed it when I was nearly mowed down by two of her giggling maids of honor who'd been running hand in hand along a corridor. Looking contrite, they showed me to a drawing room that overlooked the gardens.

I went in and found Queen Anne staring out of a window. "Your Majesty," I said, feigning surprise at meeting her. "I did not realize this room was occupied."

She didn't turn.

"What is the weather like in Cleves?" she asked. "I have never been there."

I took a few tentative steps forward, impressed that she recognized my voice. "The weather in Cleves is much the same as it is here, Your Grace," I replied. "Cold in winter, warm in summer. And rain on the days in between."

"I do not believe anywhere on God's earth could have so much rain as this place," said Anne. "There are times when I wish..."

"You were back in France?"

Anne turned around; her black eyes flashed. "My place is with my husband," she said haughtily.

"Forgive me, Your Grace," I said, bowing. "I did not mean to imply that you wished to be anywhere other than here."

"I simply wish for the sun."

"Then I will wish it for you," I said.

"I wish for many things," said Anne. "They are rarely granted."

That was the opening I needed.

"Could—could I ask a wish of you, Your Grace? If it is not too bold a request?"

Anne's face remained impassive. I had nothing to lose and everything to gain. I was an Asset. I had to be bold when the occasion demanded. Alex would just ask.

"There is a young woman in the palace, Your Grace. She came with us from Cleves and is extremely able. Tending to the whims of my father isn't pleasant work, if you understand my meaning. I have taken pity on her. If you should require a serving maid—"

"What I *require* is for my ladies-in-waiting to know their place," said Anne under her breath. "Every last one of the Catholic's simpering courtiers should have been sent to Kimbolton with her. She wore a hair shirt, you know. Penance for her crimes as a liar."

Catherine of Aragon had died a few months earlier. Despite Anne's derision, Catherine had been very popular and had ruled for twenty-four years. There were rumors that Henry and Anne had poisoned her, but in fact it was The 48 who had hastened her demise as part of the Religion Eradication operation. An assignment that had taken just twelve days. Her daughter, Mary, would be next.

"The Spanish witch is dead, and yet I am still not free of her treacherous whispers," continued the queen.

I didn't reply because I didn't want to interrupt her train of thought. Patience was a virtue I had in spades. If she felt she could unburden herself to me, then I would gain her confidence.

"A serving maid, you say?" she said eventually.

"Very hardworking. Loyal. Discreet."

I whispered the last word, leaning in slightly toward Anne. She turned her head toward mine and I saw her nostrils flare slightly, as if she were sniffing me out.

"Bring her to my rooms, Charles of Cleves. After dinner. I would like you to regale me with news of the outcome of your archery games with my husband."

Another one who knew I was playing archery with the king, even though no one had actually told me, since I'd missed breakfast.

It was almost as if I were being set up for a fall.

twenty-five

Margaret

I could have you arrested for speaking to me," I whispered. "You dare—"

"Of course I dare," he whispered back. "I love you, Margaret. Yet you will no longer even look me in the eye. It is tearing at my very being."

He had accosted me in the rose gardens. A rare occasion when I was alone. I was becoming reckless, and for a moment that realization had chilled my heart. I knew better. I had seen the bruises that appeared on some of the younger ladies of the court after they had been foolish enough to travel without a companion. Men of this court could do what they liked, when they liked.

And I was no better than any of them now, slipping away like this. But I needed to *think*. And I could hardly think in the anxiety-ridden din of Queen Anne's apartments.

My stomach had knotted at the sight of Thomas Ladman, but I clenched my teeth together and pulled my shoulders back. My heart did not belong to me; I was not even sure I had one anymore. I was playing the game of survival now.

In a different time, in a different land, perchance Thomas and I could have raised a family and been happy.

Yet *this* was our land. And our time was now. And both were cruel.

I could smell wine and smoke and cheap perfume on Thomas's uniform of the guard. A sickness rose in my throat, which I pushed down. It deepened my resolve.

Thomas Ladman was below me in every way. It had been a foolish, childish dream to believe we could be together. He was a bastard son of a duke, all but forsaken by his family.

"Never speak to me again, Thomas," I hissed. "Or I will go to the king and claim you've been stealing from the courtiers."

"You would never—"

"I would. I would without a second thought. You would lose your head and your entrails..."

"What has happened to you? Where has the woman I loved gone?"

"I have seen things here that would make your hair turn white," I replied. "Go back to your kitchen girls and beggar women. It's all you're good for."

<hr>

My father had been right after all. I was highborn. I deserved better.

I would *have* better.

twenty-six

Charles

The following week passed in a blur of rain, boring council meetings with an increasingly overwrought king who liked to yell in Latin when he was humiliating certain overseas envoys, indoor archery, and even more rain. I was wet from the moment I woke to the moment I fell asleep. The dampness aided the foul mood that had started to creep into daily life around the palace.

The only people who didn't seem foul-tempered were my brother, Lady Margaret, and Jane Seymour. After the dramatic first twenty-four hours, Alex had quickly fallen back in love with court life and spent nearly every available moment dragging me off to see some new part of the palace. The one time I saw him annoyed was when we were shown the maze by the young sons of two dukes. The boys were affable but barely eleven years old. We got hopelessly lost, were caught up in another shower, and ended up bedraggled and on the verge of hypothermia before dinner.

Alliances were already being sought for the two of us, and because Aramis had left us and gone back to the future, Alex and I had to navigate everything by ourselves without causing offense. Thankfully, Lady Margaret was proving to be very helpful in this regard. We welcomed her friendship not only because she had saved my life, but also because she was close to Jane. And Alice was right; Alex and I also needed to keep an eye on her and make sure she didn't talk about my poisoning. The sons of Cleves shouldn't be on anyone's watch list.

Rain and gloom aside, the court would have been wholly

fascinating if it hadn't also been so inherently depressing. Young women who had barely reached adolescence were being farmed out like cattle by their relatives. Boys and girls who couldn't have been older than six or seven were in the service of the palace, and the work they did was such intense labor it was a wonder their little bodies didn't break. The highborn were also very free with the backs of their hands, slapping the children if something wasn't cleared away quickly enough. It was so wrong it made me feel ill. And it wasn't lost on me that, in a way, we were actively participating in all this. Our orders were to find a Protestant partner for the king. TOD would be perfectly happy with anyone we found, but the king wouldn't be interested in someone his own age, who'd be less likely to give him an heir.

The more I thought about this assignment in those terms, the more it troubled me. Because choices were part of what made people human, whether it was a choice of love or religion, or anything else. When I really thought about it, it seemed to me that love and religion could bring a lot of happiness and peace and joy to humankind. And artistic inspiration. And acts of kindness. When it came right down to it, choices breathed a lot of the humanness into the humanity TOD claimed to want to preserve.

But then, I told myself, I was one of The 48. It wasn't as if we were allowed choices either. Our lives were dictated to us as much as anyone else's.

It wasn't a nicer frame of mind.

But it was easier.

———

Jane Seymour was being manipulated by relatives too, but the more I observed her in action, the more I wondered whether a match with the king was actually something she *wanted*. Jane

155

was subtle, the complete opposite of Anne Boleyn, who swept through the palace like a tornado. Jane had a soft, soothing voice, and when she offered an opinion, it was measured and sensible. I found myself seeking her out at court because I found her attitude refreshing. Maybe it helped that Jane was at least a decade older than some of the other girls, some of whom would have been in seventh grade back in the twenty-first century.

Jane and I routinely came across each other in the Great Hall. Taking inventory of the paintings there was becoming part of my daily routine, to ensure that I knew where they were at all times.

"It is an impressive piece, don't you think, Charles?" said Jane quietly. She was already there one morning, as if waiting for me— although there were others in the room, including her brother, who was whispering in a corner to a heavyset man with body odor I could smell from twenty feet away.

Jane was staring at the Hans Holbein painting of the king. The hairs on my arms prickled when I got close to it. I suspected that my body, so recently assaulted by radiation and time travel, was responding to the radiation of the artwork. It was reassuring. It meant the energy loop was still there.

"Master Holbein is very talented," I replied.

"I would very much like him to paint me one day, yet, alas, I am too inconsequential."

"You are anything but, milady," I replied.

"You are kind, Charles of Cleves. And you have a pleasing influence on the king. He talks fondly of you."

"I am honored the king pays any attention at all to me."

"We are all in his service, so to be especially noticed is a great honor." She looked hard at the painting. "Yet those in his favor must also have caution. If you would take some advice from a mere woman, I would counsel you to listen more than you speak."

"Do not belittle yourself, milady," I replied. "And your counsel is most welcome. All of your words are. You are the wisest of all the queen's ladies and maids of honor."

Jane smiled, curtsied, and glided away as if she were floating. Her words stayed with me long after she was gone. But the truth was, I didn't have the luxury of listening more than I spoke. The clock was ticking, and Alex and I had a lot to convince Henry of before our time expired.

<hr />

Alice kept me up to date with reports every evening on Anne. She would sneak into my room and we would huddle under blankets that had been warmed in front of the fire. The 48 wouldn't approve, but Aramis wasn't around to stop us. And I kind of liked how it was a hold on reality—*my* reality.

"The queen is so unhappy, I think I heard her vomiting in her bedroom," reported Alice one night.

"Could she be pregnant?" I asked.

Alice shook her head and wiggled to take more of the blanket.

"Not a chance. The king won't have her anywhere near him. And now Cromwell is also refusing to see her. She was raging because he always used to be on her side and now she can't get an audience with the king's advisors, let alone Henry. Everyone is deserting her. Her ladies-in-waiting and maids of honor are terrified. Except Lady Rochford. She hates Anne with a passion that is almost psychotic. I wish you could see her, Charlie. I swear she sits there just smiling as the queen screams at everyone."

I actually wanted to help the queen. I wanted to tell her to get on a ship with her young daughter, Elizabeth, and sail to France. Her life in the palace was only going to get worse—and then it would end.

And then there was Alice's situation. If Grinch really had dragged Alice back here, where was she?

"Any sign of our favorite green Asset?" I asked.

Alice closed her eyes. "No."

I left it at that. Forty-eight days had become thirty-eight on the countdown in my wrist, and I was becoming less and less confident about the time we had left to succeed at anything.

<hr>

The next morning I was awakened by a harsh knock at my door. I opened it to find Edward Seymour waiting for me. He strode right in, not bothering to address me by my name or follow basic formalities like bowing.

"I tried your brother's room, but he appears to be out and about," he said sharply. "He is to accompany me to Wulfhall. I have neither the time nor the inclination to wait for him, so *you* will pass the message on. We leave tomorrow. A two-day ride. I take it he can ride?"

"Y-yes, he can, but my brother is not going anywhere," I said, my stomach twisting.

Seymour moved toward me. I was taller, and yet his arrogance made him seem larger than life.

"The king has decreed it."

And I knew that was all he had to say. Stone-faced, I closed the door, dressed, and left to eat, attend court, be on the lookout for a Protestant prospect for Henry, and, with any luck, find my brother along the way.

It wasn't until afternoon that I finally caught up with Alex near the Base Court.

"I've been trying to find you all day," I said furiously. "Where have you been? Because *I've* been at court since breakfast enduring too much food and kiss-ass, two-faced courtiers. And the company of a bombastic king who wouldn't let me out of his sight and asked for constitutional advice about the Duchy of Cornwall. For all I know, I've declared war against Wales and increased the taxes on sausages. Speaking Tudor English all day with a German accent is exhausting, but finding you when I need you is *impossible*. My brain is fried."

"Finished ranting?" replied Alex. "Because I've been collecting information."

"With Marlon?"

"With Marlon, yes. We talked, and I talked with his friends, too. The yeomen know every nook in this palace, Charlie," replied Alex evenly. "They're better informed than anyone. You should use them more as allies instead of hanging out with the two-faced courtiers. The guards listen in on every council meeting and stand outside every door. They know more about what goes on here than the king. Yeomen might have the weapons to stab you in the back, but the courtiers are the ones who would actually do it. And the yeomen are good for a laugh. Most of them are our age. We're not that different, really."

I sighed and looked down at my wrist.

38 22:18:01

"What's up?" asked Alex. "You're very quiet, especially seeing as practically every single person in the palace has told me you were looking for me."

My neck was stiff with tension. "Let's go for a walk," I said.

I waited until we were in a long, empty corridor before I told my brother the bad news.

"You're being sent away," I whispered.

"What?" said Alex with a laugh. "No one can send me away."

"Edward Seymour has demanded that you accompany him on a trip to Wulfhall. The king has decreed it. A two-day ride."

Alex made a strange noise through his nose.

"Why me?"

"No idea," I replied. The truth was, I had several thoughts, from Seymour wanting to make a Cleves alliance, to Seymour wanting to kill a Cleves and make it look like an accident.

An image of grapes swam into my mind.

"We can try to get you out of it," I said.

"Unlikely, if the king has decreed it."

A heavy silence surrounded us. Two brains working as one, trying to see a way out of a real test to the assignment.

"We could use this to our advantage," said Alex eventually. "Seymour is promoting his sister as an alternative queen. With him gone, you can really step it up around here."

"But we shouldn't be apart; we haven't even formed a strategy beyond information-gathering—"

"Charles," interrupted Alex. "You're better off here. Alice needs you, even if she would never admit it. If wherever we're going is a two-day ride, I'll be away for four days, five at the most. Edward Seymour won't want to stay away longer. And this could be the push we need to actually make a more strategic movement. We have plenty of time before the assignment goes critical."

I wasn't so sure I agreed. An assignment entered the critical countdown at day fourteen. From that time until the second our wrists displayed zeros was the period when assignments succeeded or failed. When Assets returned to the present day as heroes or failures.

It was when Alex and I would have to decide whether to assassinate Jane Seymour or not. And time seemed to be moving faster every time I looked at my wrist.

"You're taking this better than I did," I said. "I thought I was going to throw up when I heard."

"Aw, that's sweet," said Alex, smirking. "Don't worry. You just work on the king while I'm gone. You've had some nice conversations with Jane Seymour. I know you're asking Henry about other women to feel him out. Did you know Henry was seen going into someone else's bedroom last night? That's one piece of info I got from the yeomen earlier."

"The clan of Wulfhall are no better than pimps," I muttered.

"I hate to break it to you, brother," said Alex. "But you and I aren't much better, doing this assignment."

"I know. I've been thinking a lot about that."

"I've been trying not to. Because honestly, it makes me nauseous." He rubbed his wrist absentmindedly. "You know what I've been thinking? I've been thinking Senior Assets didn't get so cold from years of training. I think it's psychological. From years of playing with people's lives."

"You know if Jane doesn't marry the king and have his son, she'll probably live longer," I said. "This assignment could end up *saving* her, if we don't have to...you know." I couldn't quite say the words aloud.

"You're starting to like Jane, aren't you?"

"She's just not what I was expecting," I replied.

"I'd better come back to find you with your head still attached."

"Just come back, Alex," I said.

Two doors suddenly slammed in quick succession. Alex and I had our knives drawn within a second. It was reflex.

Two ladies-in-waiting walked slowly into the corridor where Alex and I had been talking. I recognized one as Lady Rochford, the sister-in-law of the queen. The other was no more than thirteen years old. She looked like a child playing dress-up.

The ladies dipped into small curtsies and we bowed. No wonder people stopped doing that a few centuries later. My back hurt from all the stretching and bending.

"The queen has commanded your presence, Charles of Cleves," said Lady Rochford stiffly. She seemed to talk without moving her mouth. "It's getting late. I wouldn't keep her waiting."

She gave a sly glance to her companion, dipped again, and glided away past two servants who were starting to light the multitude of candles that lined every corridor.

"Watch your back around that one," I muttered. "Alice was filling me in on the women in the court. Lady Rochford hates the queen more than Cromwell does. She's planning something."

My brother hugged me. It was fleeting.

"I'd better start packing," he said.

"I want you back in five days," I said.

I wanted to hug my brother back. For longer than a fleeting connection.

Instead, I let him leave.

twenty-seven

Alexander

Should I have left Charlie? Did I have a choice? Edward Seymour and two others had business away and had requested I accompany them. The king had said yes.

No one argued with the king and stayed out of the Tower.

<hr>

We were heading for Wulfhall: the ancestral seat of the Seymour family. I knew about the manor house because I had researched it. Charlie was worried about our being separated, but I saw this as quite the stroke of luck. This would give me the chance to ingratiate myself even more with the Seymours. And the more information Charlie and I had on them, the quicker we could use it to our advantage to get Jane away from the king.

It took two days to ride to Wiltshire from Hampton Court. We spent our first night at an inn, where I was kept awake for the first couple of hours by the fleas in the straw mattress. There wasn't an inch of skin that they didn't find delicious at first, but then they just left me alone. Maybe twenty-first-century blood was too weird for them.

Edward barely spoke to me at first; I wasn't even sure why he had asked me to come along.

But I wasn't anyone's man—yet. And here, alliances were everything.

<hr>

Wulfhall was a shabby-looking timber manor house, with a thatched barn, a clock tower, and a tiny chapel in the grounds.

Not the grand house I was expecting, and Seymour seemed almost embarrassed by it. I didn't get a tour. I was just shown to a small bedroom with a little window overlooking a large, tree-lined gravel path.

Dinner that evening was taken in a long hall that had roaring fires at both ends. An older man, the spitting image of Edward with narrow, mud-colored eyes, a long face, and a long black beard, was sitting at the head of the table, drinking deeply from a pewter goblet. He gave me the briefest of looks as I walked in, but other than that, he didn't register my existence until Edward introduced us.

"Father, this is Charles, son of the Duke of Cleves from the Rhinelands," said Edward. "My father, Sir John Seymour. And this is my mother, Margery Wentworth, daughter of Sir Henry Wentworth."

A beautiful woman walked across the floor and stood at her husband's side. She had flaming red hair that was pinned in ornate waves on top of her head. I bowed; she nodded her head.

"Are you favored by the king, boy?" asked the older Seymour.

"He is," said Edward, answering for me. "The resemblance is remarkable, wouldn't you say, Father?"

Idiot, I thought. Edward Seymour had Charlie and me mixed up. It was my brother the king liked better. I had just been introduced as Charles. Edward had asked for the wrong twin to accompany him.

"The resemblance is clear," replied Sir John. "And what does our queen think of you, Cleves?"

"I have barely spoken to Her Grace," I said.

"Has Cromwell gotten to him yet?" asked Sir John.

164

"No," replied Edward, his mouth twisting into a sly smile.

"Good," replied Sir John. He pushed his chair back and stumbled. Serving staff rushed forward, as did his wife, but the old man yelled at them to leave him alone.

"I'm not hungry," he said, gripping the table. "You can eat without me."

"He doesn't appear well," I said quietly as he walked slowly from the long hall. The old man looked as if he was in pain.

"My father is as strong as an ox and will outlive us all," retorted Edward. "And you would do well to say nothing to the contrary at court."

"What did he mean when he asked if Cromwell had gotten to me yet?" I asked.

Edward walked around the table and sat in the velvet padded seat his father had just vacated. It was probably still warm, I thought. He grabbed a chicken leg and tore into it with yellow teeth.

"Cromwell has eyes and ears everywhere," replied Edward. "There is a certain...sense to an alliance with him, as he is influential, to be sure. But the Seymour family is on the rise. We reward loyalty—and destroy those who work against us."

"And you brought me here to get me on—on your side?"

"You have eyes, Cleves. You will have seen the way the king acts around Lady Jane. Their union is only a matter of time. And when she produces a son—the world will belong to the family she represents."

"And what does Lady Jane say about this arrangement?"

Edward threw down the chicken leg and thumped the table.

"She does what she's told," he snarled. "And you would do well to do the same. Stay away from Lady Jane. She is not destined for a marriage bed in foreign lands."

He really *did* have me mixed up with Charlie.

"I serve and obey the king," I replied.

"His Grace looks to you for advice. You have been in the court for barely a whisper in time and yet he's looking to *you* for your counsel—on matters like the Duchy of Cornwall! So while you have his ear, *tell him to marry Lady Jane.*"

"The king is married to Queen Anne," I replied coolly.

"Are you defying me in my own home?"

"Not at all," I replied, with a deferential nod. "I am honored to be a guest. All I am saying is that I have no sway over the king. I am barely in his thoughts. My brother, Charles, is the one the king converses with more freely. I am Alexander. I did not correct you in front of your father, as I did not wish to embarrass you. It is an easy mistake, but a mistake nonetheless."

"I thought...I asked—" said Edward, his eyes widening.

"We look very similar," I replied. "Many people mistake us."

Edward's mouth curled. "Then perhaps it should be your brother who gets the warning. The king *will* marry Lady Jane. And I will kill anyone who gets in the way."

twenty-eight

Margaret

I read the letter thrice over. I could hardly bear the finality of the last few words:

> *This letter must do us both well, dear Margaret. The duty you undertake now as my daughter will be your greatest achievement until such day as you provide your husband a son and heir. The king's permission will be sought forthwith. I see no reason unbidden that His Majesty will refuse this request, as it will further secure ties between the Scottish lords and those in this kingdom who already benefit from his magnificent grace.*
>
> *It is your duty. Do not forget that. Or forsake me.*
>
> *Your loving Father*

I threw it on the fire.

Even so, the amber flames could not burn my father's words from my mind. The rumors were true after all. He intended to seek the king's permission for my marriage to the Earl of Moray forthwith. Negotiations were done. A settlement had been agreed upon. All without my knowledge or assent. My opinion was worth less than the charred embers curling in the grate.

Like my friend Lady Jane, I was the chattel of men.

Lady Jane believed she had no choice in her future. I believed differently. My choice was to adhere to the path laid down by my father, or to at least try to change the course of my future.

To turn against my father was akin to treason. I would be abandoned at best, arrested at worst.

Yet the more I struggled with accepting my father's decree, the more resolved I became. I simply had to move faster.

And pray for courage.

twenty-nine

Charles

"You have a woman?" asked the king.

"I do not, sire," I replied.

"Why? What is wrong with you?"

I didn't know Henry well enough to tell whether there was humor in his question. The king had summoned several young and old courtiers to take a walk with him around the gardens of Hampton Court, which were filled with mint.

We of The 48 understand the symbiotic value of herbalism. Mint is the herb of choice to camouflage distinguishable poisons, or odors about one's person. It is useful, for example, to mask the sulfuric buildup exhibited by many Assets with considerable time travel experience.

It felt good to recite to myself a Tenet excerpt in the silence that followed Henry's question. Thinking about how older Assets smelled wasn't pleasant, but it gave me a few seconds to think of something other than Alex.

The king was in a foul mood, despite the sunny day. Cromwell was at the king's right side as always, and looked unperturbed. Looking more worried was the ludicrously named Richard Rich, who was the king's solicitor. I knew he was looking into the legality of the king's marriage to Anne, though that had not been explained to me here.

"I asked you a question, Cleves," snapped the king. "Answer me."

169

"I do not believe a man should rush into any relationship," I replied, trying to keep the nerves out of my voice.

"You do *prefer* women?"

I knew *now* what the king was asking. The Buggery Act had been passed by Parliament only three years earlier, and it would be hundreds of years before it was repealed.

Only the day before, five men had been hanged for crimes in defiance of the act at Tower Hill in the heart of London. A messenger had arrived that morning to tell the king.

"I enjoy the company of women very much," I said, silently cursing him for his cruelty.

"Then I will make a match for you that will benefit Cleves and England," said the king. His shoes were squelching into the dark mud, which was getting thicker as we walked farther from the palace. I tried to steer him back onto the flagstone paving, but he didn't seem to realize where he was treading, or he just didn't care. After all, it wasn't as if the king cleaned his own shoes. He didn't even wipe his own ass. The Groom of the Stool did that.

"I would be honored, Your Grace, by such a match. The joining of Cleves and England would delight my father and my homeland," I replied.

And I will be long gone by the time it comes to any wedding service, I thought.

"Do you enjoy poetry, Cleves?"

"When created by someone who knows the written word better than I, yes," I said, not sure where this conversation was going.

"I write poetry," said Henry, and there was a humble tone to his voice that I hadn't heard before. Henry was such a strange man. The smallest thing could move him, and yet his temper was horrible. He was like two different people in one enormous body.

And now here he was, apparently confiding in me. While my head was pounding with tension, I had been training for such a moment for years. I had to continue to engage the king. I had to make him trust me.

"Do you write often?" I asked.

"When the occasion befits," replied the king quietly. He was staring ahead, but not really seeing.

"For a lady?"

"Always."

It was a pretty safe bet that these days, he wasn't writing poetry for the queen. I smiled casually. "May I inquire as to the name of the lady who was fortunate enough to receive your words of admiration?" I asked.

The king suddenly stopped walking. A cold drenching of fear gushed through my insides. I had moved too quickly—gone too far by being too intimate.

"It was the Lady Jane," said the king slowly. "I gave her a purse of money. And a few verses, sealed in a letter. She did not open it."

Because she's smart, I thought.

"Walk with me further, Cleves," ordered the king. "Only you."

Cromwell's sallow face twisted as he and Rich removed their hats, bowed, and were left standing with the rest of our confused little group as the king and I continued to walk along the saturated gardens.

"She kissed the *seal* of the letter," said the king. "What am I to make of that, Cleves? Lady Jane refused my gift and yet kissed the seal of a letter she did not even read."

"Lady Jane does not strike me as a woman who teases," I replied. "She is also virtuous. Lady Jane sees the landscape, not just the portrait, and does not wish to be tainted by even the hint of scandal. It is the same in Cleves with women who...who understand their place. Perchance another lady would give you the outcome you desire? Lady Margaret is spirited and yet penitent."

"It is the queen's doing, isn't it? She is the bringer of misfortune. She has cursed me."

"Your solicitors can advise you in that regard better than I, Your Grace."

"You are uncorrupted by the court, Cleves," said Henry. "You have not been here long enough to build alliances, nor to have made enemies. I see so much of my younger self in you. Tell me, if you were to walk in my shoes, what would you do?"

I took a deep breath. *I am from The 48,* I thought quickly. *This is the moment. My moment. To change history and set things right as best I can.* Anne's time as queen was nearly over, but I could try to negotiate a good settlement for her and Elizabeth. I was a time writer, after all. I could change things already recorded if they didn't directly impact the assignment.

"Have your solicitors draw up the papers declaring your marriage to Anne illegal," I said confidently. "Have her and the Princess Elizabeth safely removed from the court. You could set her up in her own house like the Dowager Princess of Wales. Then you would be free to seek a more suitable queen of the Protestant faith. Someone still chaste and virtuous."

"Jane is chaste and virtuous," replied the king wistfully, completely ignoring my comment about looking for a Protestant. "She is queenly."

No, not Jane, you imbecile! I thought. *That's not who I meant!*

"The people—and God—will love her and reward me for that choice," continued Henry. "You are right. Your counsel is received

172

with gratitude, Cleves. An English education has been for your betterment. I am of a mind to create a high position for you."

"I would be honored with a position in your court, Your Grace," I replied, wanting to punch him in the face.

"I'll speak with Rich. He can take you on in the legal chambers."

The king made no offer for Alex—he hadn't even mentioned him—and my worry for my brother intensified.

But I did what I was supposed to do and bowed.

As we rejoined our party and headed back to the palace, the king seemed much cheered. He remarked on the grass, lush and long after so much rain. And the gardens, which were ablaze with color from across the spectrums.

"Come to my rooms at sundown," said Cromwell, sidling up to me. He didn't take his eyes off the king, who was also now walking with a pronounced limp. "We can take supper together."

"I would be happy to," I lied.

"You're favored by the king, Cleves," said Cromwell. "It's time to take sides."

Inside, I headed to the library, where I could eavesdrop under the pretense of having my nose buried in a book. And be spared the pressure of conversation, at least for a little while. Except—

"Charles of Cleves. What a joy to see you."

I looked up from my reading to see Jane Seymour. I couldn't help grinning at her. She looked...happy. Probably because she wasn't being suffocated by the overbearing presence of her brother.

"Lady Jane—you look radiant."

She really was glowing. Her skin was colored a slight shade of pink, as if she had sat out in the sun for just the right amount of time. She was wearing a dark green velvet dress with a high neck. Her pale red hair was swept back tightly under a small pearl-edged hood.

I rose and bowed, trying not to catch the eye of other courtiers who were clearly listening in.

"Shall we walk?"

Jane beamed and offered her hand. "To the chapel?" she suggested.

She was a smart one. No one could say that a walk to the chapel was untoward, and it was just down the hall.

We passed a couple of yeomen, one of whom was Marlon; he raised an eyebrow at me. I resisted the urge to thump him. I was just walking with Lady Jane. Nothing more.

Like every room in the palace, the chapel was a spectacle of gross wealth at work. There were so many variations of gold in the room, from the floor to the high, star-speckled ceilings, that my eyes hurt. I almost didn't see Lady Margaret there, deep in prayer. But she must have heard us enter, because she quickly crossed herself and stood to face us. She nodded to Jane, curtsied to me. Her face was streaked with the drying tracks of tears.

Jane Seymour dropped to her knees in front of the altar and crossed herself.

"The queen told us this morning that the king is moving the court to Windsor," said Lady Margaret, quickly composing herself. "Will you be making the journey, Charles of Cleves?"

Great. Alex and I needed a change of setting right now like we needed the Black Death. "If I am asked," I replied. "Although I am expecting my brother to return soon. He is with yours, Lady Jane. What was their business away from court?"

"You do me the honor of pretending to believe I know," replied Jane with more than a hint of sarcasm.

"It would trouble me not to be here when he returns," I said.

"You and your brother are very close," observed Jane.

"Yes. He is my dearest friend and ally."

"I have seen you laugh together," said Jane. "It is a glorious sight."

"Do you have someone like that, to laugh with?" I asked.

"Not yet," replied Jane. She crossed herself and stood.

"Do you, Lady Margaret?" I asked. "Do you have a confidant you trust beyond all others?" If she did, then I would make it my business to befriend them, just to find out what Margaret was really like.

"I will have such a person...one day," replied Lady Margaret carefully.

"Your father knew what he was doing, bringing you and your brother to court, Charles of Cleves," said Jane, taking a step toward me. Her eyes glistened like pools of pale water, catching the ethereal reflection of the candles lit behind me.

"Does the king desire a match for you?" asked Lady Margaret. "You were walking alone with him just now."

I tried to conceal my shock. It had been a half hour, at most, since my conversation with Henry. News traveled faster here than in the twenty-first century.

"I have neither the time nor the inclination for marriage."

"Inclination and time are irrelevant," said Lady Margaret. "We all serve His Grace."

"Then it is not a subject I give much thought to," I replied.

175

"It is unusual to see someone new to the court keep their counsel as you do," said Jane.

She stepped even closer to me. She smelled of rose water.

"Do not close your eyes for a moment, Charles of Cleves," she whispered. "Watch and listen to everything. Very little in this court is what it seems."

Jane's warning wasn't malicious. The kindness in her face was so endearing it made me want to hug her. Then she and Lady Margaret curtsied and left the chapel. I counted to twenty to give them a decent head start so no one would think worse of them if they saw me leaving too.

Damn, this was tiring. And now I had my upcoming conversation with Cromwell to think about.

I made my way back to our rooms, where I discovered my door was open. Maybe a servant was inside, stoking the fire for the evening. I wasn't taking any chances, though. I pulled out my knife and slipped the cuff of my shirt over my fingers to conceal it as I stepped into the room.

"What the—"

Bile rose in my throat at the sight before me. I had seen a lot of death in my seventeen years of training, but this was something else.

Blood was smeared all over the floor, wet and glistening. My pulse pounded in my ears.

Alice. Where was she? Had she been here waiting for me? I started to see amorphous black shapes across my line of sight. My fingertips were cold but soaked with sweat as I fumbled at the wood paneling to keep my balance.

The crimson trail led from my room to my brother's, but there were small lumps in the blood, like skin, on the floor too.

Whatever had happened had taken place in this room. I could barely breathe as I reached the connecting door between the rooms.

The blankets and sheets had been dragged onto the floor, but I couldn't see the bed because curtains had been pulled around it.

"Alex?" My voice cracked. "Alice?"

There was no movement from the bed. Blood had soaked through the under-sheets and was dripping onto the floor.

"Alex?"

I dragged back one of the drapes and gagged at the sight in front of me. A large, bloody mass of muscle and flesh was lying in the center of Alex's bed. The throat had been cut and a deep black gorge opened up in the flayed skin of the body. Both eyes had been removed from the sockets and placed on the blood-smeared pillows.

I gagged again. My eyes watered and my throat burned as I fell back into a large wooden cabinet. The door splintered from its hinges as I fell to the floor. Blood oozed through the gaps between my fingers. My boots were sliding in it.

"*Charlie!*"

Alice was there then—grabbing my arms and pulling and sliding my body across the floor. Once I had managed to stand, I threw off the cloak I had been wearing. The metallic stench of blood and guts was overpowering. We both vomited into a copper container filled with kindling.

"What the...what the hell is that?" cried Alice, covering her mouth with her hand. "Oh, Charlie...who would...why..."

The animal carcass was impossible to identify, although I wasn't looking too carefully. It had four legs and was the size of a large wolfhound. Every last bit of fur had been skinned from the body. From the amount of blood over the two rooms, it was clear the blood had been drained from its body—probably from the slash across the throat.

"It's a warning," I gasped. "We need to clean this up before someone sees it. I—I don't even know where to start—"

"Charlie, what if this was done by the same person who tried to poison you?"

"It doesn't matter! I'm hanging on by a thread here, Alice. I'm trying to stay on track with this assignment, trying to keep a psychotic king happy, I'm worried sick about my brother, and on top of that, I've got to deal with a river of blood in my lodgings."

I sank to my knees as the room started to sway. I couldn't lose it. I was better than this. I had been trained for this.

"Charlie, control your breathing," whispered Alice. "Don't freak out. If you freak out, then I'll freak out. And if I freak out—then I'll really freak out!"

I laughed, sounding hysterical. "Why is this happening to us?" I whispered. "You being dragged here, me being poisoned, this—"

"I don't know. But we'll make them pay when we find them."

"How?"

"Forget time writing. We've been trained to be time assassins, Charlie," replied Alice flatly. "We can use time for our own devices. Someone is after us. So we get to them first. That's how we make them pay. For everything."

thirty

Charles

Alice left for a short time and then reappeared with scrub brushes, a pile of old rags, and a bucket full of steaming water. "I'll bring fresh linens after I get this cleaned up."

"What? You're not doing this alone."

"No, I'm not. There are a couple of chambermaids who I bet will help me. They've been friendly, and I think they're used to drama. A son of Cleves shouldn't be caught near a mess like this, so you need to leave."

"Friendly doesn't equal trustworthy, Alice. And there's no way I'm leaving you alone in this room." I got on my knees and started scrubbing. It actually helped calm the maelstrom churning in my head.

Somebody was after us. I should never have let Alex go away alone with Edward Seymour.

We should have stayed together.

⸻

The bed was stripped. The carcass was removed. The scene had been enough to put me off meat for life. Which reminded me...

"Cromwell has asked me to take supper in his rooms with him," I said to Alice.

"You can't, not looking like that. You're covered in blood."

My voice caught in my throat. I didn't want to cry, but I could feel the end of my nose prickling.

"It reminds me of growing up, Alice. The blood. I have so

many memories of training growing up, and nearly all of them are triggered by the smell of puke and blood."

"It's pretty screwed up, isn't it?"

I pulled Alice into me. I just held her. I thought the smell of her shampoo would remind me of something nice, something I wanted, but Alice was just as contaminated by death as I was.

"Isn't there anything else?" I whispered. "Anything that's normal in our memories?"

"The smell of honeysuckle is normal," she replied, slipping her warm hands around my waist. Bare skin on bare skin. I wanted to touch her back. I wanted to move my fingers down the nape of her neck, which was soft with babylike hair.

"Your turn, Charlie."

"I can't remember..."

"Try," said Alice, gazing into my eyes. "Think of something—anything."

"Skinny-dipping in the lake."

"Finding blackberries and gorging on them until we were sick," she said, nodding enthusiastically. "Give me another normal."

"Watching the sun set and being glad you're alive."

"Yes," whispered Alice. "And being loved."

I dropped my arms and took a step back. "Love isn't normal. Not for us. Love makes you hurt."

"It is normal. Tell me you didn't love *me*, Charlie. I dare you to say what we had wasn't love."

"I *can't* love you."

"That's not what I'm asking. And not loving and not being *able* to love aren't the same."

"We're different from other people, Alice."

"Why? Because we've been told to *be* different?"

"We *are* different. Look at us. We're talking about love and we're covered in blood. Our lives, our existences, are not normal."

I wasn't prepared for Alice to kiss me. Her warm mouth parting against my cold lips, her soft skin sliding against my five-day stubble, her breath mixing with mine and not knowing who was inhaling and who was exhaling…it caught me off guard. But I didn't stop her.

I want to love you, I thought. I wanted *this* to be normal.

But it wasn't. And Alice knew it.

She knew everything.

I could still taste her kiss long after she had run from the room. Long after I'd bathed and dressed in presentable clothes and made my way through the maze of corridors. Right up till the moment I knocked on the door of Thomas Cromwell's apartments.

When a servant opened the door, I saw that the interior beyond was large and dark. There was a single lead-latticed window behind his cluttered desk, but it let in little light. My eyes started to ache within seconds of being shown in. I rubbed them but quickly withdrew my hand. Despite my bath, dark traces of animal blood were still trapped under my nails and caught between my ragged cuticles. Would Cromwell be able to smell it, or was I just being paranoid? My stomach was churning. I didn't know whether I was ill, hungry, or just tired.

"Sit, Cleves," instructed Cromwell. His tone wasn't unkind or rude, just perfunctory.

He was sitting in a large wooden chair with a high square back. It didn't look comfortable. I was offered a smaller chair with a padded tapestry seat. Cromwell's office space was filled with books and scrolls. I could see the melted wax from his seal glistening red in the light from a large sconce filled with candles. The seal had been recently used.

"How are you finding life in the court?" asked Cromwell, passing me a plate filled with bread and cheese. "Different from Cleves, no doubt."

"Yes. Life here is…different."

Cromwell chuckled. It was the first time I had heard him truly laugh. It was disarming.

"Your father was playing either an interesting game or a foolish one, introducing his two sons to the court now," said Cromwell.

I didn't reply. Putting a big chunk of cheese in my mouth helped. I had decided my churning stomach was hungry.

"What do you think of Seymour?" he asked.

"Which one?"

"Lady Jane Seymour."

"She is very pleasant."

"It has been noted that she and Lady Margaret are spending an increasing amount of time with you and your brother," said Cromwell.

"Courts are sociable places."

"Lady Jane was overheard singing your particular praises," said Cromwell. "What would you make of that?"

"Perhaps she was complimenting my brother," I replied. "People often mistake us for each other, but if one of us is receiving a kind word from people, it's usually Alexander."

"And yet your brother is no longer here. So perhaps your father's game is neither interesting nor foolish. Perhaps it is wise…and cruel."

"Cruel?"

"What sort of man leaves one son to the whims of Edward Seymour, and the other alone at court in such uncertain times?"

"My brother will be returning to the court soon," I replied.

"By which time we will be at Windsor, and then on to Greenwich."

"I go wherever I'm asked—so will my brother."

"Then you should fare well. Especially if you are in the service of my office. For I reward loyalty, Charles of Cleves," said Cromwell, nonchalantly spreading lumpy gray paste onto a thin slice of toast.

"Don't we all serve the king?"

"We do—but there are ways of serving the common people as well as the great amongst us," replied Cromwell. He hadn't once looked me in the eye during the exchange. Instead, he was concentrating on the plates of bread, cheese, and fruit. Liars usually maintain eye contact, because they incorrectly believe it's what truth-tellers do.

I didn't mark Cromwell down as a liar, but he was as strategic as a commander going into battle.

"If I were to serve your office, what would you wish me to do for you?" I asked.

"Three simple things. Watch, listen, and report only to me."

"You want me to spy for you?"

Cromwell exhaled through his nose. It was almost disdainful.

"*Spy* is a crude word," he said, throwing me an apple. I caught it with one hand. The chief minister nodded to show his respect, looking directly at me for the first time. "And your mother tongue makes all words sounds cruel, Charles of Cleves. The Rhinelands have such harsh languages. No, my boy, I do not wish you to *spy*.

I only want you to tell me what the queen is doing. Let's say I am looking out for her welfare."

"You are referring to Anne?"

"Is there any other queen?" asked Cromwell sarcastically.

Working for Cromwell was exactly the sort of liaising Aramis wanted me to do. But I didn't have time to run around after Anne Boleyn. That was what Alice was doing....

Alice. Of course. Fate was finally working in my favor. Brilliant, resourceful Alice was already my link in the queen's chambers. I wouldn't have to spend time finding out information for Cromwell at all because Alice would already have it. Between her and Lady Margaret, I would have all bases covered.

Which meant I could continue steering Henry away from Jane, while also having direct access to the king's chief minister. The setup was perfect.

"When do you wish me to speak with you? Daily?"

Cromwell smiled to himself. He saw me as a pawn in a bigger game, I knew that, but chess was a game for two players, and I had been training for it just as long as he had.

"I will send for you," he replied. "Do not let anyone else know that you're now my man, not even your brother—should he return. Or your father."

"My brother *will* return," I said. "Seymour has only taken him for a visit to know him better outside of court. But Seymour won't be away from court a moment longer than necessary."

"You are learning, Cleves," said Cromwell. "And what about your father, the duke? Will he return?"

Two candles on Cromwell's desk had burned down to nothing; his face was bathed in darkness.

"If the king sends for the Duke of Cleves, then the Duke of Cleves will attend," I replied. "But otherwise, I do not believe my father has plans to return to the court."

"And yet he remains in England."

A sudden prickle on my neck made me shudder. "N-no, my father is departed for Cleves."

"I have eyes at every port," said Cromwell, leaning forward slightly. "The Duke of Cleves did not board a ship. If he did not board a ship, then he remains in England."

My mouth was running dry. I desperately wanted some water, but all Cromwell had was wine.

"They who profess to be your eyes must be seeing in a dim light," I said. "Much like the light in here."

At that, Cromwell leaned back and a young boy in a dark green doublet and knee-length breeches scurried in. He started clearing Cromwell's desk of plates. The casket of wine was left. I took the cleanup as a hint and rose from my chair.

"You're my man now, Cleves. Don't forget that."

Cromwell didn't say another word. I nodded and made my way to the door.

Outside, the night sky was littered with stars. I rubbed the back of my neck, where Cromwell's words about Aramis had made me shiver, and looked down at the countdown in my wrist.

37 19:01:38

I wanted Alex back. We had never been separated before. Even in The 48 we took Imperatives together. Being apart from him felt wrong, like part of my DNA had been extracted without permission. And after everything that had happened today, being apart from him felt dangerous.

We didn't talk about it, but my brother and I had a bond.

Alice would call our bond *love*.

Grinch and Asix would call it weakness.

Piermont would simply exterminate it, given the chance.

I looked up at the night sky again and found the biggest star. It had a pinkish tinge.

"Bring my brother back to me," I whispered. I stared at it for so long that the imprint of the star was burned into my retinas.

⚊

The star was the last thing I saw from my window as I fell asleep.

But Alex didn't return the next day.

Or the day after that, when I received the king's invitation to join the court at Windsor Castle.

⚊

A week later, there was still no sign of my brother as the court moved from Hampton Palace to Windsor Castle. Windsor was a cold, drafty, lifeless palace that had none of Hampton Court's warmth or color. But I noticed immediately that it *did* have Edward Seymour.

I pounced on him the second I spotted him alone.

"Edward, you've returned!" I tried to make my voice jovial. "How was your visit to Wulfhall?"

"Your brother has not already told you, Charles of Cleves?" he asked testily.

"He has not. Indeed, I was hoping you could tell me of his whereabouts. I've not seen him since he left with you."

"Pity," said Edward. "He had a message to give you concerning my sister."

"Which is . . . ?"

186

"Only that I expect you to keep your distance from her."

"I see. And why has my brother not delivered the message himself?"

"You cannot expect me to know that. I am not your brother's manservant. We returned to Hampton Court together, but I departed for Windsor before he did."

My heart sank. I nodded and walked away as fast as I could.

"Charles of Cleves!" Edward called to my back. "Do not forget what I said."

I was too preoccupied to turn and acknowledge his tacit warning.

Alex was missing. The queen's court had not yet arrived, so Alice and I were separated. Speaking to Lady Jane was going to be difficult. She had traveled with the king's court, but as Edward had just made plain, she was now under his watchful eye once more.

Where was my brother?

Days passed. Without the queen to report on for Cromwell, I mostly spent my time walking with the king and filling his head with thoughts of ladies of the court. He was openly flirting with a number of women in the court, including Jane Seymour, while the aura of the absent queen hung like a toxic cloud over everything.

After what seemed a lifetime, half of the queen's court, some of her ladies-in-waiting, and, more importantly, Alice, arrived at Windsor. On the eighth day, the queen herself arrived with her remaining entourage, having made a detour to the house of one Lord Robert of Bray, presumably to try to drum up support for her position as the king's wife.

I tried to engage the king with the suggestion of a tennis match that day, but he was in such a foul mood over the queen's presence that I was glad he sent me—and everyone else—from the court. There was a rumor, whispered behind hands, that the king had taken a woman to his bed and had been unable to perform.

"Not as homey as Hampton Court, is it?" said Alice. She was walking around my new lodgings with her hands behind her back.

"I don't care." I was sitting at a rickety table with my head in my hands. My stomach was cramping so much with worry and fear that I wanted to tear my own guts out with a knife.

"Alex will be okay," said Alice. "He'll be back soon. He's probably just doing some more reconnaissance work."

"You don't know that."

"And you don't know he's in danger. It's not like people can text here. And he's too smart to send a written message. It could be intercepted."

"No, he's too smart to send a written message with dangerous information in it. There's no danger in sending a message with a simple *I'm fine, see you in a few days* in it."

This was a disaster. Anything could have happened to him. *Grinch* could have gotten to him. Why hadn't I insisted on going to Wulfhall with him?

There was a knock—three quick raps from a blunt instrument. Alice gave me a panicked look and ran to the hinged side of the solid oak door. Her back was flush against the wall. I had not been given connecting lodgings at Windsor Castle because Alex had not traveled with us. I had only my brother's belongings—most of them borrowed—to remind me he had been here in this time at all.

A young squire was standing nervously in the hall. He handed me a sealed note, bowed, and stared at the floor, making no attempt to leave. I opened the heavy parchment and scanned the looping script inside the note.

By Lady Seymour
I greet you with yll tydyngs. Come wyth express readyness to Horseshoe Cloyster at the West End of the Lower Ward.

"Is there a reply, milord?" asked the squire.

"Who gave this to you?" I demanded.

"The lady, milord."

"I'm not a lord," I said. "Did the lady hand it to you personally?"

"She did, milord. Is there a reply?"

"Was she alone?" I asked. I casually reached around the side of the door and handed the note to Alice, who was still hiding quietly behind it.

"No, milord," replied the squire. "There was a surgeon there. For the injured man."

"What injured man?"

"The—the one who looks like milord, milord."

"The one who looks like—"

No!

I started running.

thirty-one

Alexander

The pain was so great I couldn't recall the Imperatives. I searched around in my fever for excerpts from the Tenets. Something— anything—that would remind me of what I was. Who I was.

But my mind was lost to agony.

Pain meant I was alive.

But I wanted to die.

thirty-two

Margaret

Lady Jane wished to take food to the poor. It was a fool's errand. The poor spread the summer sickness, every great house knew that. I wanted to get away from this court, but I did not wish to do it in a casket lined with lead.

Yet my friend was determined, and the thought of being free of the constraints of the castle, just for a while, made me reckless.

As I gazed upon my reflection in the polished mirror in our shared bedchamber, I barely recognized myself. My long, fair hair was brushed to perfection, tied up, and hidden beneath the hood of a black cape. My blue eyes were as pale as the dress that for so long had kept me hidden from view. It was a familiar sight, and yet on the inside, I was changed.

The highborn lady who had been happy to exist in the shadows was gone. She had to be, if I was going to defy my father by not marrying the man chosen for me. I should have been horrified by my actions—consorting with sorcerers, envisioning a life abroad with them.

But all I could think about was my anxiety for the return of Alexander of Cleves to court. I would have to confront him, tell him that I knew his dark secret. But also that I was trustworthy, and that if he assisted me, then I would be forever loyal to him.

Why hadn't he come?

Lady Jane and I had left the castle by the sally door: an opening that was supposed to be a secret, but one which the men at the castle, highborn or not, used regularly to visit the local taverns and brothels. How Lady Jane knew of its whereabouts, I did not ask. I had enough secrets to keep for now.

We carried baskets of bread and cured meat. Too stale for the court, but a feast for those who had nothing.

I kept my face covered at all times. I did not wish to be recognized, and I did not wish to inhale the air that surrounded the desperate. It was a foul-smelling, invisible fog with groping fingers that lingered and brushed against my skin. It seemed to be an omen of the path I was now choosing to walk.

———

It was on the way back through Horseshoe Cloister that evening that we heard Bewsey, a yeoman, calling for help. He was older than Thomas Ladman and the head of his guard.

Not that I cared for the Ladman bastard anymore.

"Quick, we must hurry inside," I whispered to Lady Jane. "No one must see us."

"But he sounds alarmed. What if someone is hurt?"

I tugged at her arm. "We cannot tarry. Someone else will come along."

"We have done nothing wrong today, Lady Margaret. The king will not punish us for taking care of his subjects beyond the walls of Windsor Castle."

"The king will not punish *you*," I snapped. "*My* good name will be ruined."

"Then leave."

"I cannot leave you."

"Then stay. The choice is yours," said Lady Jane. "See, over there. That is Fiennes, one of the surgeons. I was right. Someone is hurt."

"Fiennes is a butcher!" I cried. "Please, it will just be a prisoner who has—"

Then Lady Jane and I gasped to see the body of a young man illuminated by torchlight as Bewsey and Fiennes carried him into a cottage.

It was Alexander of Cleves.

He was dead.

thirty-three

Charles

We of The 48 regard the civilizations of the Greeks and the Romans as the genesis for time writing and time assassinations. Neither civilization showed weakness in the face of death. Assets are expected to learn such fortitude when faced with death.

There was another sentence to the Tenet.

And I couldn't remember it.

Windsor Castle consisted of a palace, a small town built around that palace, and a brick fortification surrounding everything. The private apartments where I had been given lodgings were at the back of the town—to the east of the State Apartments used by Henry.

It couldn't have been farther from Horseshoe Cloister if it had tried.

I left the squire in my dust. Alice and the letter, too. I ran down to the quadrangle, which was a large rectangular courtyard behind the famous Round Tower. Momentum and gravity became my allies as the downward descent aided my speed.

It was Alex. It could only be Alex.

Jane's handwriting flashed in front of my eyes as I continued to run.

yll tydyngs . . . yll tydyngs . . . yll tydyngs . . .

The squire had said that a surgeon was there. Why? What for? If anyone had hurt my brother, I would kill them.

I would kill them all.

<hr>

The Gothic castle seemed to loom up on all sides like a steepled tsunami as I ran into the Lower Ward. My chest burned as the cold night air pumped in and out of my lungs. Windsor wasn't as large as Hampton Court, and it was much easier to navigate. Once I had passed St. George's Chapel, with its tall windows and ornate façade, I took a slight right and ran straight into the first open door I saw.

"Alex!" I cried. *"Alex!"*

"Charles!" called a female voice.

The voice was delicate and soft, the complete antithesis of the screams that were pulsing out of my burning chest.

"Where is my brother? Where the hell is my brother?"

"Calm yourself, lad." Muscular arms wrapped around my chest. Immediately my Imperative martial arts training kicked in. I threw my captor over my shoulder. He landed with a heavy thud.

Jane Seymour immediately stepped in front of me.

"Are you going to attack me, too, Charles?" she asked, putting her hands up in supplication.

"Where's my brother?"

"He's through there," replied Jane, sweeping her left arm back. "Please, Charles. Do not let him see your worry. You must remain strong."

My head was spinning. I felt so light I wasn't sure I was walking. My entire body was floating. All of my training had disappeared.

The countenance, the language, the accent, all gone. All that mattered was my brother.

Jane led me into a warm room, heated by a roaring fireplace that crackled and spat orange embers onto a gray stone floor. My brother was lying on a long table. Another man, in a bloodstained apron, was standing by his head. Lady Margaret was at Alex's side, holding his right hand in hers. She was praying in Latin.

Alex's clothes were lying on the floor. He had been stripped of everything except a simple white shirt and his underwear. Thick wadding had been wrapped around his thigh, but even as I watched, a patch of blood on the cloth was growing larger and larger.

"I have been unable to contain the bleeding," said the man in the apron. "And we have to roll him over so I can deal with the wounds on his back."

"His back?" My voice was detached. An echo.

I floated over to Alex. His eyes were moving beneath his translucent lids. Beads of sweat were popping into life all over his unshaven face.

"Alex...it's Charlie...can you hear me?"

Nothing.

I bent down and stroked his face. His skin was hot.

"Alex...I'm here, Alex. I won't leave you. I promise."

"He has not spoken once in the time we have been here," whispered Lady Margaret. "Yet there is life in him still. Prayer and the Lord's favor will see Alexander through this. Have faith, Charles of Cleves. Hope is not lost."

"I'll require assistance in turning him over and holding him steady," said the surgeon. "Where's the rosemary water?"

It was Jane who placed a shallow bowl of steaming water on the table. The man I had thrown over my shoulder joined her. He didn't look angry.

"Bewsey, you take the legs." The surgeon turned to me. "Cleves, is it?" I nodded. "You hold your brother's shoulders. Lady Seymour, Lady Margaret, you should both remove yourself from these quarters. This is no place for highborn ladies of the court."

"I'm not leaving," said Lady Margaret.

"Your concern is noted, Master Fiennes," replied Jane Seymour. "Now, what can we do to help?"

The surgeon named Fiennes sighed. "The lad's back needs to be cleansed with the water, and I will apply the balm. On my say...now."

Bewsey, Fiennes, and I rolled Alex onto his left side. My brother groaned, and then his tongue fell out of his mouth. Lady Margaret stifled a gasp.

I didn't know how I stayed standing.

Alex's bloodstained shirt was slashed as if he had been mauled by a lion. Fiennes tore the remnants off with a few tugs to reveal Alex's mutilated skin, which was crisscrossed with slashes. Some were deep, with exposed purple flesh that pulsed with bubbles of blood. Others were shorter and more like scratches.

"What devilry did this?" cried Lady Margaret.

"Nasty," said the surgeon, so matter-of-factly he could have been commenting on the weather. Then he and Jane got to work. She carefully dabbed at each wound with a soaked cloth. Fiennes then placed a clean piece of muslin, dressed with a balm, against each slash. The larger ones had to be done several times before Fiennes was satisfied.

The smells of rosemary and lemon permeated the stifling heat. I could see that the long hem of Jane's dress was wet with water and tainted with my brother's blood.

"*Alex!* What happened to him?"

Alice rushed into the room; she still had Jane's letter in her hand.

"I found him down by the sally door," said Bewsey. "I was doing a sweep of the fortifications."

"Did he say who attacked him?" asked Alice.

"He hasn't said a word since I brought him here," replied Bewsey. "Fiennes was dealing with a prisoner in the dungeon. I called for help because the lad here is of the nobility. Lady Jane and Lady Margaret...well, I'm not right sure what miladies were doing there..." Bewsey trailed off as I continued to whisper words of encouragement to my brother. His breathing was labored but steady.

Lady Margaret had backed into a wall. Her round, pale face was aghast, and several locks of blond hair had fallen down to frame her face. She looked like a terrified cherub witnessing Hell.

"Please do not reveal my presence here to my brother," said Jane, and her calm nature was betrayed by a quiver in her voice. "Lady Margaret and I were outside the castle walls, taking food to the poor. We also came in and out via the sally door. We saw and heard no one."

"What's a sally door?" asked Alice.

"It's an opening in the fortification around a castle," I replied. "A way of getting in and out without disrupting the integrity of the main structure. Would one of the yeomen guards have done this?"

Bewsey shook his head, but it was Fiennes the surgeon who replied.

"Nay. Whoever did this took great delight in ripping up the boy's back. Your brother has been whipped and stabbed. A yeoman would not do this. This was done by someone who likes torture."

Stabbed. I had been so busy concentrating on Alex's back, I had forgotten the wound to his thigh.

I didn't need to move him to look. Blood was dripping from the table and was pooling by my feet.

"He's still bleeding!" I cried. "Please help him."

"Charlie, he needs a tourniquet," said Alice. "We need to cut off the blood to his leg or he's going to bleed to death."

"We may need to amputate," said Bewsey.

"*No!*"

Jane Seymour was trying her best to remain composed as I screamed and yelled, but she was starting to sway. Her skin now had a jaundiced tinge, just visible in the flickering light of the fire. Lady Margaret was sliding down the wall.

"We could cauterize without removing the limb," said Fiennes. "I have seen it done on the French mainland."

"Char...Charlie..." Alex groaned and swatted at air as he tried to grab me.

"I'm here." I held his hand, which was cold and clammy. "You hold on."

"A...A..."

Each letter was costing Alex dearly. His head fell back onto the table with a thud.

"He is losing too much blood," said Fiennes. "It's amputation or cauterization—you must decide."

I wasn't religious—the only higher power that The 48 were instructed to believe in was the Termination Order Directorate—but I started to beg something greater than me to help save my brother.

Fiennes took that as acceptance for his experiment.

"Bewsey, hold a poker in the flames until it burns with a white light."

"Alice, get Lady Jane and Lady Margaret out of here," I said.

"I will stay," replied Jane.

"As...as will I," stammered Lady Margaret. She crossed herself as she pulled herself up.

"Your brother, the queen, even the king could be looking for you both," I said. "You shouldn't be here."

Jane arched her back and stared up at me.

"The king? You think because it is night that the king would be looking for me to warm his bed?"

"That's not what I meant—"

"Can you get over yourselves and start thinking about Alex?" snapped Alice. "Now, is there any alcohol in this place?"

"There's probably wine," replied Bewsey.

"No. It needs to be pure. We'll need it for disinfecting and anesthetic."

"Anesthetic?" asked Jane.

Alice nodded to Bewsey, who was holding a long iron poker in the heart of the fire.

"Alex is about to have a burning poker placed on his leg. We need to knock him out or his screams will raise every single person in the castle."

Bile rose in my throat.

"Cleves, you place your arm across his shoulders and hold him down," said Fiennes, taking a small bottle from a tatty black leather pouch around his waist. "Miss, you be ready to pour this whiskey onto the leg—but have a care to jump back before he starts kicking. Pour some into his mouth now." He handed the brown glass bottle to Alice. "Bewsey, you hold the leg. I'll cauterize."

"And what of me?" asked Jane.

"We should pray, Lady Jane," said Lady Margaret. "Pray that whatever wickedness has fallen on this place is forsaken. The Devil needs to be driven out of Alexander of Cleves. Driven from us all."

"Religion," muttered Alice. "Your God isn't going to save anyone."

Then Alex made a noise like someone choking to death and the division in the room evaporated. Whatever our reasons, we were all united in wanting this to be done, and quickly.

"Lady Jane, Lady Margaret, could you both stand by the door and make sure no one comes in?" suggested Alice. "If that's all right with you, miladies?"

Jane smiled at Alice, deliberately ignoring me. I hadn't meant to offend her, but Alex was all that mattered to me now.

"I will make myself useful there," replied Jane.

Lady Margaret went to stroke my brother's forehead and then pulled away, as if she was worried about catching the pain.

"Be quick, Fiennes," said Bewsey. The poker was glowing white in his hand. Sweat was dripping down his face. "This is not some traitorous scullion being racked. This is the son of the Duke of Cleves. Your head is on the block if harm comes to him."

"Harm's already come to him!" I cried. "Just do it."

Alice opened Alex's mouth and poured the whiskey into it. He coughed, spluttered, and tried to shake us off, but Bewsey and I now had a tight grip on him. Fiennes passed Alice a wooden block, which she immediately placed between Alex's teeth. The surgeon had the poker gripped tightly in his right hand. He pulled back the bloodstained wadding...

Alex arched his body and cried a primal scream of pain that was only slightly muffled by the wooden block. The sickly sweet smell of burning flesh filled the room.

I hated this time.

I hated time travel.

I hated The 48.

"I'll stay with him, Charlie," said Alice. She looked at Alex, who had fallen into a pain- and whiskey-induced unconsciousness. "The queen won't notice if I'm not there to put a warming pan between her sheets. You go clean yourself up."

"I wouldn't count on the queen not noticing you aren't there," said Bewsey. "And if she does, the queen will see it as a personal affront. I need to be gone too. I've more rounds to complete, and the chief yeoman will have my entrails on a plate if I'm any later."

"Thank you for your help," I said, shaking the surprised guard's hand. "If I can do anything for you..."

"Aye, well, try not throwing me next time," replied Bewsey. "I'll have a fair bruise on my arse..." He stopped suddenly and gasped. "Miladies, humblest apologies for my language."

Lady Margaret scowled and slipped out of the door into the still night air. Jane dipped her head and smiled.

"Alice, if you stay with Alex, just until I get back, then I'll escort Lady Jane and Lady Margaret back to their lodgings," I said.

Jane didn't protest, but I knew she still hadn't forgiven me for my earlier comment. I wished she hadn't misconstrued my meaning.

"Have a care," said Fiennes the surgeon, grabbing my arm. "Even in the dead of night, this castle has many eyes."

"Thank you for saving my brother tonight," I replied. "I won't forget."

"I'll check on him tomorrow in the morn to change his dressings. If he takes a fever, send a yeoman to find me."

The motley crew of saviors dispersed into the darkness. Alice was left alone with Alex. I knew she wouldn't fall asleep. Alice had stayed awake for three days and nights straight before.

"Please accept my apologies, Lady Jane," I said as the three of us walked back up the Lower Ward toward the imposing Round Tower. "It was not my intention to imply any impropriety in your behavior."

Jane had her hand placed on mine for balance. The urge to stroke her skin was overwhelming. I wanted her to forgive me. I wanted to show her that I respected her very much. Lady Margaret was four steps ahead of us; I could hear her muttering, but it was so rapid, I couldn't catch it. She seemed to be asking for forgiveness.

Jane and I continued walking in silence for several minutes. My apology hung in the air, a heavy weight on my shoulders that was adding to the horrendous grief I felt for putting my twin brother in danger.

"The serving girl called Alice," said Jane. "You have a peculiar manner of speaking when you converse."

"I know her very well," I replied, flashing back to twenty-first-century words I might have said in my blind panic. "She arrived in England with my brother and father also."

"You seem very familiar with her," said Jane. "There was tenderness in your eyes when you spoke to her."

"It was probably the heat from the fire making my eyes water," I mumbled. "And my upset at my brother's condition."

"I may not be a woman of the world, Charles of Cleves. Yet I know when a man is in love."

"I do not love Alice," I lied. "She is...she is like a sister to me. No more."

"Do you love another?" asked Jane as we passed through the twin-turreted Norman Gate.

"I do not seek love," I replied.

"That is not what I asked," replied Jane. I could feel her fingers trembling.

"I do not love," I lied again. "But what of you? You are an exceptional woman."

"I am a possession of the men of Wulfhall," replied Jane quietly. "I will love whomever they require me to love."

"The king?"

"The king is married. And to speak otherwise would be treasonous."

We had reached the Quadrangle of the Upper Ward. To my left, the State Apartments. Straight ahead were the private lodgings, including my own. It suddenly occurred to me that I had offered to walk Jane Seymour back without knowing where she was staying.

Lady Margaret continued up a set of steps and disappeared from view without so much as a backward glance, quickly slipping into the shadows with her black cloak wrapped around her body and the hood lowered over half of her face.

"I will leave you now, Charles of Cleves," said Jane. "If we part now, in the open, then no harm may be done to either of our reputations."

She curtsied; I bowed. Jane entered the apartments via the same set of steps as Lady Margaret. I followed her movements, wanting to ensure her safety, but as my eyes traveled up the Gothic building and away from Jane, I saw a huge figure illuminated by a large candelabra.

Henry VIII had been watching us.

thirty-four

Margaret

I had been overjoyed to be reunited with Lady Jane in our bed-chamber after the decampment to Windsor, yet I could barely bring myself to speak with her as we undressed and climbed into the large bed we now shared. We should not have been out this night. My dearest friend had made her decision; was she now going to cause turmoil for me as I tried to make my choice?

Our chambers in Windsor Castle were west-facing, and even though it was well into the night, our room was still stifling hot and oppressive.

My entire existence was suffocating. I had to remind myself to breathe.

The king had seen us. Seen me.

Tomorrow would come the questions.

Questions to which I had no answers.

thirty-five

Charles

By the time I got back to the shabby lodgings where Alex had been treated by the surgeon Fiennes, he had been moved from the table onto a pallet. Alex was so tall his feet hung over the edge.

Fiennes and Bewsey were gone and Alice was now alone, sitting on a threadbare rug with her legs crossed. My brother's sleeping face loomed just over her right shoulder. She was leafing through a leather-bound book.

"If he pukes, you know it's going all over your head," I said.

"Trying to defuse a stressful situation with ill-timed humor is merely situation avoidance," she replied imperiously, not bothering to look up.

"When I find out who did this to my brother, it won't be situation avoidance," I replied. "It'll be situation contained and exterminated." I exhaled slowly, trying to release the tension in my chest. I was so relieved to have Alex back, even if he was battered and broken. But my relief ended there. I had been poisoned, a bloody carcass had been left as a warning on Alex's bed, and now someone had done their best to make Alex resemble it.

"Did he say anything while I was gone?" I asked.

"He's mumbled, but it's been incoherent."

"Alex was trying to say something, before his leg was..."

Alice finally looked up. She closed the book and placed it on her lap.

"Why did you let him go with Seymour?" she asked.

"I had no choice—and neither did he. The king ordered it."

"Alex would follow you to the ends of the world and beyond," said Alice quietly. "He would have found a way to stay with you if you asked it. And you should have found a way. You've been a mess without him."

I knew Alice was right.

"Do you trust Lady Jane?" she asked.

"Yes."

"Do you trust Lady Margaret?"

The reply came just as easily.

"No."

She cocked an eyebrow at me. Just as with Alex and me, there were times when Alice and I didn't need words.

"She's scared for her life, you know." Alice looked sad. "Practically all the maids of honor and ladies-in-waiting in Anne's court are. And frightened people make mistakes, get desperate. I don't know exactly what her deal is, but she does seem to be trying to lie low, which is hard in a toxic court. I admire her for it, but I have a feeling you, and especially Alex, might be collateral damage if she loses whatever tenuous control she has on her life."

I tried to pour myself some water from a silver pitcher, but my hands were shaking so badly, I couldn't fill the goblet. Two fat tears dripped down each side of my nose. I put down the pitcher and wiped up the spilled water with my sleeve.

"It's not your fault, Charlie," said Alice. I felt one of her hands flat against my back. The crook of her finger wiped away a tear that was clinging to my eyelashes. The tears were starting to blind me. The world was swimming in them. I was so tired, it was beyond exhaustion. I wanted to close my eyes and sleep back to the future before any of this had happened.

"What if we can't complete this assignment?" The words were choking me. "We're already halfway through our time. What will happen to us—to Alex? To you?"

I sat down on the carpet. A freezing fear was draining my entire body, and the only thing that moved was the tears.

I had nothing left.

In the nightmare that followed, I saw my brother kneeling on a wooden stage. A bloodstained block was positioned in front of him. He bent forward and placed his neck on the curved base. Piermont was there. He wasn't dressed in Tudor clothes; he was wearing gray sweatpants and a black T-shirt. Piermont's head was shaved to the scalp, and a pale pink scar ran from his ear to his throat.

He was blindfolded. My brother wasn't.

But Piermont was the one with the sword.

I woke to the sound of Alex crying out.

"Alex. It's okay . . . you're safe . . ."

Alice had jerked awake too. She was on her feet with the poker that had cauterized Alex's leg wound raised high above her head.

"Charlie . . . Charlie . . ."

"I'm here."

"I'm on fire!" yelled Alex, arching his back.

"Alex, you need to calm down," I said. "I know it's hard, I know you're in a world of hurt, but if you don't calm down you're going to reopen your wounds."

Alex was panting through the pain, but at the sound of my voice he stopped twitching and instead screwed up his face with a suffering grimace.

"You've been badly hurt," I said. "Can you remember anything? Can you remember who did this to you?"

Alex bit down on his knuckles and attempted to muffle a guttural cry. "Damn, what I wouldn't give...for the Quickening now," he said, gasping. "I stayed...stayed at Seymour's place for two nights. Then we heard...heard that the court...had moved on to Windsor. Seymour freaked out because...because he didn't want his sister left to her own devices with the king...but then... but then we heard the queen was still in residence...at Hampton..." Alex trailed off, arching his back in pain. His hand was rubbing at the skin above the wound to his thigh. "I hurt, Charlie...please help me."

Useless was the only word adequate to describe how I felt. If I could have absorbed his pain, I would have done so in a second. I grabbed his hand.

"Squeeze it," I said. "As hard as you can. Break my fingers if you have to. Channel your pain into me."

"The surgeon said he would be back this morning," said Alice. She handed Alex the remnants of the whiskey from the night before. "This will have to do for now. It'll take the edge off."

Alex took three swigs, made a face like a baby sucking lemons for the first time, and grabbed my hand in a viselike grip.

"We went back to Hampton Court." His face was screwed up in a mixture of pain and concentration as he spoke. "And then Seymour left me. I traveled with the remainder of the queen's court yesterday...or the day before...I can't remember now. We stopped overnight at a house belonging to some nobleman . . . Sir . . . Sir Robert of something. He was having a banquet in honor of the queen . . . but it was pathetic. No one wanted her there. Everyone is distancing themselves. I felt sorry for her. Anne was crying one minute . . . enraged the next. Some of her . . . ladies-in-waiting were trying to calm her down . . . tell her that all is well . . . but they have no real importance or influence over what's happening. I was walking through the house . . . when I heard someone call my name. And it was . . . Aramis."

"Aramis?" Alice and I cried.

"I know!" said Alex, his breathing starting to steady as the whiskey kicked in. "Aramis was shocked out of his mind to see me, because he called me . . . Alex instead of Alexander. Everyone thought it was just a term of . . . endearment from a father to a son, but I could tell he was seriously pissed."

"Are you saying it was Aramis who attacked you?" I asked.

"I think it was," replied Alex. "I didn't see him, but I'm sure it was. Aramis has that mint smell that a lot of the older Assets have, you know? To cover up the sulfur odor from so many years of taking radiation pills?"

"So you smelled the mint on him," I said. My heart was pounding at this news.

"And there were others, too."

"Did you see them?" asked Alice.

Alex shook his head. "No. I didn't see any of the attackers because someone put a cloth bag over my head. I had my knife, and I think I got a couple of them in the struggle, but I got myself, too." He gingerly pointed to his thigh.

"You did that to *yourself*?" I cried.

"I didn't mean to! I was fighting for my life, Charlie."

Alice stood up and walked over to the large fireplace. She placed her hands on the stone surround and lowered her head, resting it against her forearms.

"I was strung up and whipped," continued Alex. "I lost consciousness several times. They would throw water over me. I kept being told that I was involved in the Rewriting."

"What's the Rewriting?" I asked. "That doesn't sound like a Tudor saying."

"I know," replied Alex. "I swear, Charlie. The people who did this to me weren't sixteenth-century people. And even if it wasn't Aramis, they were from our time."

My mind was starting to get fuzzy. It was like I had a head cold. But Alex was starting to fade fast. The color was draining from his face. Sharing his story had taken every last piece of him.

thirty-six

Alexander

I was trying so hard to manage the pain, but I was losing the battle. My hands were gripping the fabric of the chaise so tightly it was starting to tear beneath my nails. My back had been torn to shreds. I had a knife wound that had been cauterized to seal the bleeding, and nothing more than rosemary water and balm had apparently been used to treat it all.

"I'm going to find Fiennes. I won't be long, Alex." Charlie was trying so hard not to panic, but I could see it in his eyes.

"Charlie, before you go, we need a plan," said Alice. "This is now completely out of control. People from The 48 attacked Alex—"

"We don't know that, not for sure, and right now, my brother needs proper treatment!" cried Charlie. "And the best I can do for him is find him a butcher from a time where the average person is dead before middle age!"

"Will you listen to yourself?" shouted Alice. "What do you care about *dead before middle age*? The 48 are *all* dead before middle age!"

But Charlie had already run from the room.

thirty-seven

Charles

I sprinted from the room and back out into Horseshoe Cloister. The castle grounds were bustling. The sun was already beating down from a cloudless, cornflower-blue sky. Yeomen guards were walking in twos, their boots stomping on the cobbles in time with their spears, which were being slammed into the ground like walking staffs. A thickset man with a stained apron was jangling a set of keys, trying to find the correct one to open a large door to my right. The smell of freshly baked bread lingered momentarily in the air before being completely displaced as a strong gust of wind brought the rancid smell of the Thames into the courtyard. Flags with Henry's coat of arms flapped furiously, seeming desperate to fly away over the battlements and beyond.

I didn't know where to even begin searching for Fiennes, or the apothecaries of the court. Would I even be allowed to request the use of one?

Blue pills.

The Death Tenet screamed in my head. Every voice of every Asset was with me. Death was drilled into us.

For it comes to all in the end!

And yet it was only now that I truly appreciated how utterly final it was.

"Charles," called a man's voice. "Charles of Cleves. You are ailing. Come, sit down."

It was Marlon. I grabbed the shoulder of his red-and-gold doublet.

"I need to find the surgeon called Fiennes, or one of the king's apothecaries if he isn't around. It's my brother. He has returned to the court and he's been gravely hurt, Marlon. You have to help me."

"Where is he?" asked Marlon quickly.

"In one of the rooms down in Horseshoe Cloister. It's through the second door on your left as you enter the courtyard. Alexander was brought there last night."

"Fiennes is not a surgeon to trust," replied Marlon. "His methods are not those of the king's surgeon."

"I don't care who we bring, as long as they have something to stop his pain," I begged. "Please, Marlon. My brother was stabbed and whipped."

Marlon's throat bobbed like a snake swallowing an egg.

"Come," said Marlon. "The apothecaries may not listen to me, but they will listen to a nobleman of Cleves."

Cleves! I had completely forgotten again that I was supposed to be speaking with a Saxon accent. Had Marlon noticed? If he had, would he say anything? I had already slipped in front of Lady Margaret and Jane. Now I would have to be wary about the king's own guard.

This was so much harder than anything my training as an Asset had ever prepared me for.

Marlon and I ran through the Norman Gate and straight into the first entrance to the State Apartments. We took the stairs three at a time.

"Where are we going?" I asked, panting as we reached the top.

"I am seeking Tom Claremont, a barber," replied Marlon. "He will assist Alexander. He is highly regarded."

"A barber!" I exclaimed. "Alex needs something for the pain and his dressings changed. He doesn't need a shave."

Then I remembered. Barbers were the ones who did the cleansing, the bloodletting, the lancing...and basically anything that involved a knife.

I pulled Marlon back.

"No," I said forcefully, remembering the accent this time. "Alexander doesn't need surgery. He needs something for the pain. Fiennes cauterized the knife wound to stop the bleeding."

Marlon crossed himself. Then his gaze flickered to something or someone over my shoulder. He bowed.

"I cannot seem to be rid of you Cleves brothers," said Queen Anne. She had crept up on us like a ghost. "Alexander at Sir Robert's; you skulking in the corridors of Windsor Palace."

I bowed. "Alas, you will be rid of my company soon, Your Grace. I am seeking an apothecary."

"Why, are you ailing? You certainly seem to wilt in my presence." The queen laughed at her own joke, but her two ladies-in-waiting, Lady Margaret and the one I recognized as Lady Rochford, weren't amused. Lady Margaret couldn't seem to raise her eyes off the ground, and Rochford's mouth was twisted into such a severe pout that my own facial muscles ached in sympathy.

"I am always left breathless in your presence, Your Grace," I replied. "But I must beg your leave. I need to find—"

"Nonsense," snapped the queen. "I demand you walk with me on such a fine day. You will read to me."

"I cannot."

Lady Margaret looked as if she wanted to run the other way, but Lady Rochford clearly couldn't believe her luck at witnessing such an exchange in the middle of the State Apartments. I was past caring about my defiance. The only thing that mattered was Alex.

"I will find the apothecary, my lord," whispered Marlon. "Walk with the queen."

"But—"

"Walk with the queen," urged Marlon. "I will go."

I was struck by the depth of Marlon's kindness as he snapped back against a long, colorful tapestry depicting the Virgin Mary feeding peasants in the countryside. He was standing at attention with a straight back, staring at the wall opposite. The yeomen knew exactly what to do and when to do it. I knew that the longer I delayed the inevitable, the longer it would take Marlon to find help for my brother.

I bowed in submission to the queen. She smirked. I didn't bother checking to see what the two ladies-in-waiting were doing. They would follow like little lapdogs. Watching, listening. Ready to exaggerate anything that could be construed as gossip.

If Lady Margaret said a word against my brother, or revealed what she knew of the night of my poisoning, I would end her.

"Do you read poetry, Charles of Cleves?" asked the queen as we descended the stairs.

"No, I do not, Your Grace," I replied sullenly.

"I am not surprised. You have the wrong style of voice. Poetry needs to be read by the English or French, where there is melody in the voice. It is the same for song. Tell me, do you sing? Play music?"

"I am proficient, Your Grace."

"You and Smeaton will play for me. A duet," she said.

"I will do my best," I replied.

"Tell me, Cleves. Have you seen Cromwell recently?"

"I have not, Your Grace."

The queen tutted. "You expect me to believe that?" she said. "My ladies tell me Cromwell has taken you into his office."

At least Lady Margaret had the decency to look abashed, but Lady Rochford was starting to resemble a shriveled prune. Her lined face was imploding in on itself as she scowled at everything that moved, including me.

I hadn't been summoned to Cromwell's rooms for two days. I had nothing to report anyway, but if he had sent a messenger to my rooms the previous evening, they would have been out of luck because I'd spent the night on a drafty floor next to Alex. This was another loose thread I would have to be prepared to tie up, if asked about it.

"Your ladies-in-waiting should stick to what they're good at," I replied. I didn't elaborate on what I thought that was, and I didn't turn around to catch their attention. My mind was racing. So many batons to juggle, and each was lit with fire.

Where was Lady Jane? Had she gotten back to her room safely? Would the king have been annoyed to see me with her? If so, would he shun her or bring her closer to the fold? In the midst of this chaos I still had an assignment ticking away—except that Alex's situation was far more urgent. How long had it been since I'd parted ways with Marlon? Had he found someone who could help Alex? If so, who? I comforted myself with the knowledge that Alice was still there. She would stop anything too medieval from being done to my brother. At the same time, she was a young woman existing in a time in which her opinion didn't matter. Any men present who disagreed with her would overrule her, by force, if necessary. She could almost certainly handle herself, but I wouldn't want her to get hurt in the process, and the mission was still my priority... after Alex.

An image of Alex led to my next trail of thought: what he had recounted about his ordeal. His calmness in the face of pain had astonished me. My brother was physically strong, but I had always thought he was weaker than me because he had never shown total clarity of focus in our Imperatives before. When it came right down to it, though, Alex had proved himself braver than I could ever be. I was so proud of him. And I would get him home again, about that I was resolute. Alice, too.

I heard Alice's voice in my head. Alice had questioned aspects of the training at The 48 before. She'd pissed off all the senior Asset instructors growing up, but probably Grinch more than any of them. Alice had said that Grinch was responsible for her being here. Was that why Grinch had brought her to Tudor England? To *expel* her from The 48?

Except that didn't make sense. Assets didn't get expelled. If an Asset was a problem, they were simply... disposed of.

<hr />

"Charles... Charles..."

Anne Boleyn's sharp voice brought me out of my reverie just as Aramis and Piermont had started to swim into my thoughts.

"My apologies, Your Grace," I said. "I was miles away."

"You are frightful company this morn, Charles."

"Again, my apologies, Your Grace."

"Come to my chambers later and be prepared to entertain me," replied the queen. "That is not a request."

No, indeed, it was a command. From a queen who desperately needed to be made to feel important in a court that was openly humiliating her.

"Charles of Cleves!" The high voice of a young servant carried across the manicured grass of the Upper Ward. He ran down several steps and bowed to the queen, who ignored him.

"A message, sir," said the servant, handing a small scroll to me. I opened it and quickly scanned the script.

Presence requested wyth much haste. The boy wyll
show you the way.
Your benyfactor Thomas Crumwell

"I must take my leave," I said to the queen. "Your servant, as always."

I didn't give her the chance to command me to stay. Shingle stone crunched beneath my feet as I followed the servant across the courtyard.

"What's going on?" I asked him.

"Follow me, sir," was the reply, and the little imp shot off up the stairs. I was quick, but it was all I could do to keep up.

He came to a halt near a door with a tall, freestanding candleholder burning away outside it. Nine candles were dripping white wax onto the floor.

The servant knocked, and Cromwell's familiar voice bid us enter.

"Go in, sir," urged the boy. The door creaked as I pushed past it.

"Cleves," said Thomas Cromwell. "Where were you last night? I called for you."

Lies bred more lies, but could I trust Cromwell while Alex was in such a fragile state? Unless Fiennes, Bewsey, or Lady Margaret told anyone, Alex's being here could easily be my secret for now.

"I was enjoying the charms of a lady whose name I can't quite remember," I lied.

"You can't remember? Then you would not be referring to Lady Seymour?"

My breath caught in my throat. The king might have told him that he saw Jane and me together from the window of his apartments.

Or Cromwell's spies were watching me. I had to be careful here.

"I escorted Lady Seymour back to her quarters last eve after meeting her by chance near the chapel," I replied. "There was no impropriety on either part."

"Yours are but two of the *many* eyes I have in this court," said Cromwell, and there was a hint of menace in his voice. "Remember that."

"I can hardly forget it," I replied. "You remind me often enough."

Cromwell chuckled. "Indeed. There are some who need reminding more than others. Still, you are here in my sight now, and I am advising you that the court is leaving Windsor for Greenwich tomorrow."

"Greenwich? We've only just arrived at Windsor."

Cromwell sealed a letter with a knob of wax. "The court rarely spends more than a week in one palace. With the fine weather, the king wishes to watch the joust, and Greenwich serves him well in that regard."

"Is that why you called me here? To tell me we're leaving for Greenwich?"

Cromwell looked up from his papers. His bloodshot eyes were crowned with deep black circles that looked like bruises.

"Whom do you serve?" he asked, sitting back in his chair, appraising me thoughtfully.

"You," I replied swiftly.

"Then you must travel with me to Greenwich," said Cromwell. "Do not leave my side for any woman or any man, even kin." He lowered his chin to his chest; his eyes remained fixed on me.

I had no choice. I had to tell Cromwell about Alex. There was no way I was going to leave him behind.

"Sir, my brother is here, being tended to by apothecaries down in Horseshoe Cloister. He has been badly hurt. We will need to bring him with us, but in secret."

"Why the need for secrecy?" asked Cromwell. He seemed neither shocked nor upset at the news of a nobleman from overseas being hurt.

"Because someone is out to get him. And I don't know who, or why."

"It is a treasonous offense to attack a nobleman," replied Cromwell. "And to attack nobility from overseas...I have seen wars started for less."

"Can you help get my brother to Greenwich?" I asked. "I will do anything you want of me, but he needs care—and discretion."

"It would be prudent to keep this from the king for the present time," said Cromwell thoughtfully. "His mind is elsewhere at the present. Is your father aware of your brother's injury?"

"N-no, I have not had time to send word to Cleves."

Cromwell's thick eyebrows rose toward the creases in his forehead. He knew I wasn't telling the truth, and there was every chance that his spies had seen Aramis at the same house where Anne had stayed, but I had to stick to my original story. As far as the sons of Cleves were concerned, their father *had* left England. Fathers didn't tell their sons anything that didn't concern them.

"If you'd been in your chamber when I sent for you, you'd already know that the king left for Greenwich late last night," said Cromwell after several awkward seconds of silence. "He will arrive there today. I will assist you and your brother, and the king's absence from Windsor will aid our subterfuge. Yet be warned, Charles of Cleves: I will deny all knowledge of your brother's injuries if asked."

"Agreed."

"Are the injuries to his leg and back enough to stop him from riding a horse?" asked Cromwell.

"He can't ride," I said, a lump forming in my throat. "He can't even stand."

"Very well. I will have transport readied for him. Be prepared to depart on my word, Charles. And remember, you serve me. Speak to no one. Especially the queen."

"Thank you," I said. "I will go to my brother now, if you will allow me?"

Cromwell threw a couple of gold coins at me and waved a hand. His bulbous nose was back in his books before I reached the door.

But my senses were scratching. Something wasn't right.

I figured it out as I reached Horseshoe Cloister.

Cromwell had asked if the injuries to my brother's leg and back were bad enough to stop him from riding a horse.

I had never told Cromwell what my brother's injuries were.

thirty-eight

Margaret

"You are loyal to me, aren't you, my sweet Margaret?"

"Yes, Your Grace."

"And you would tell me if anything...*untoward* were concerning the young men from Cleves?"

"I would tell you anything, Your Grace."

"You have been in my household for two years now, dearest Margaret. Do you know the anguish that would befall my heart if anything were to happen to you? If there were to be... accusations—however false?"

My blood had turned to ice. Queen Anne's words were anything but sweet and caring. The threat to my well-being was not just being implied.

It was a promise. If she went to the Tower, I would too.

"I am yours to command, Your Grace."

"Mm. Until you are married off to Moray," she said with a twisted smile.

The queen knew about the Earl of Moray. So my father had done the evil deed. Permission for the marriage had already been sought. I had little time left to make Alexander of Cleves see that a union would be for the betterment of both of us.

I said nothing in response. I did not trust myself not to lash out.

"Dear Margaret, I have no faith anymore in Lady Rochford or any of the others. As you are aware, the Seymour girl is as good as dead to me. But I need eyes and ears on the brothers of Cleves. Did you not see Charles of Cleves's face when we walked today? I can practically smell the stench of ill deeds around him. Find out what is consuming him, my Margaret. Get into their beds if you have to. I will ensure that the king provides a good marriage for you. Someone more worthy than that decrepit old toad from Scotland. A handsome young man with wealth. Would you like that?"

The queen had as much influence over the king as I did now, but I had to play the game. Or at least be seen to be playing it.

Dear God, I was tired of playing the pawn.

Perchance it was time to play the queen.

thirty-nine

Alexander

My lord Cleves." A pause and the voice became gentler, less officious. "Alexander. It is I, Marlon Chancery. I am here to care for you."

I looked up at the vision in front of me. Marlon's short beard was flecked with gold that glistened in the flicker of the candles Alice had painstakingly lit in the dark and dingy room.

He looked like an angel.

"I'm afraid I won't be up for walking around the grounds for quite some time, Marlon my good friend," I said, grimacing as I tried to move. My leg and back were competing violently against each other to be the body part that pained me more. My back was winning—just.

"What happened?" asked Marlon, kneeling down beside me. I saw him move to take my hand, but then he looked up and saw we weren't alone. "I will find who did this—"

"You will do nothing of the sort," snapped Alice. "Alexander needs discretion as well as relief from the pain. I take it Charles sent you to provide both?"

I grinned at the look of shock on Marlon's face. Alice was fierce in any moment in time, but in this one...

"I have brought milk of the poppy..." he started to say indignantly, as if offended that anyone would doubt his reason for being here.

"That isn't strong enough," said a man whose voice I recognized. "Now, out of my way."

"This is Fiennes, Alexander," said Alice. "He saved your life last night."

"Thank you," I said to the haggard-looking man who was now standing behind Marlon. He carried a scruffy leather pouch bulging with metal implements that weren't shining in the way newly sterilized medical tools should be. His apron might have been white in a previous life but was now stained with streaks of various shades of red and brown and black.

If Marlon looked an angel, this guy was the opposite. But I knew he was my best hope.

"Don't thank me, you aren't free from danger yet," replied the surgeon. "We'll need to change the dressings on your leg and back and clean them out again."

"Do what you have to do," I said. "I'm just very grateful."

"I must object to this man's being here," said Marlon. "Let me find one of the healers—"

"Miss Alice, pour some of that wine into a goblet and stir this in," interrupted the surgeon, passing Alice a small, cloudy-looking vial.

"What is it?" asked Alice.

"Opium. It's not as diluted as milk of the poppy, although they come from the same plant. And we'll need that block of wood from last night. It seemed to fit his mouth just right. It's rare to find a person, even a highborn lord, with such strong teeth."

"What are you doing?" demanded Marlon. "I am a yeoman of the king's guard—"

"Yes, yes, you look very fancy in your doublet and hat," retorted Fiennes. "Now, as I said earlier, get out of my way."

I liked blunt people. I liked people who clearly knew what they were doing. And if the Devil could stop the pain...

"Where do you want me, Fiennes?" I asked.

"There will do," replied Fiennes. "Now, drink this, bite down on this, and if you stay still, it'll be over sooner rather than later."

I drank. I bit down. But I couldn't stay still. There is only so much pain a person can stand from the Devil without going through an exorcism.

"Have this, it's milk of the poppy," whispered Marlon, bending down next to the chaise I had been carried to. He and Alice had dressed me in clean clothes, taken from the laundry by her.

I took the goblet from Marlon and sipped an amount that would have filled a thimble. It was different from the opium drink I'd just taken. It tasted bitter, and the glutinous white liquid stuck to the back of my throat, causing me to cough. I could feel it on my top lip, too, which had immediately become cold and numb.

My head became heavier, or my neck weaker. One of the two. I couldn't keep my head upright. Clouds appeared on the ceiling. Fluffy white pillows of smoke.

Alice was deep in conversation with Fiennes about stab wounds, and which artery would cause the most blood loss.

It was the aorta. Alice should have known that.

The biggest were usually the quickest to fail.

forty

Charles

I arrived back at Horseshoe Cloister to find my brother sitting up in fresh bandages and clean clothes.

He was also as high as a kite.

Alice was there, as was Marlon. Fiennes was hastily packing up to leave the shabby lodgings—which I suspected had less to do with my arrival and more with the fact that Marlon, who was armed, was throwing eye daggers at the surgeon. Thankfully, Alice had taken control and was talking animatedly to Fiennes about blood loss and ways of restricting—and encouraging—it.

When she moved on to the subject of garroting, Marlon started to stare at Alice with clear unease.

My brother was sitting on the chaise with a bronze goblet held—none too tightly—between his hands. Whatever had been in it had left a milklike white residue around his top lip. It glistened on top of his golden-red stubble. Alex's eyes weren't closed, but they weren't fixed on anything, either. A dumb smile was spread across his face, which was slightly puffy and bruised.

I was so thankful not to see him in pain anymore that the worry that had beached itself on my shoulders over the course of the last day lifted just a little. The gold coins from Cromwell—money for services rendered, and those still to come—were still in my hand, and I passed one over to Fiennes as payment for his help—and silence. He nodded and pocketed it quickly. A wordless understanding.

"Miss Alice," the surgeon said, "it has been a pleasure. I hope to converse with you more, perhaps once the patient is fully recovered." Fiennes turned to me. "Keep the wounds clean. My methods are not to everyone's liking, but I save more than I kill."

Once Fiennes had left, Marlon started to voice his opposition.

"That man is dangerous! He should not be allowed near nobility. He is given the scum in the dungeons for a reason."

"And what reason would that be?" asked Alice.

"No one cares if they die," replied Marlon flatly.

"Fiennes speaks more sense than you realize," said Alice. "And his methods may be unorthodox now, but in the future..."

Alice trailed off, looking aghast at her slipup. She reverted to character; meekly, passively, she curtsied and edged back to the side of the room. For the briefest second our eyes met. We were all utterly drained.

The remaining gold coins slipped from my fingers as I collapsed into the nearest chair and ran my fingers through my hair. It felt greasy. I smelled like I had slept with pigs. Granted, half of the royal court smelled like they had never seen a bar of soap, but that hardly made me feel cleaner. The relief I'd felt at seeing Alex drugged up and pain-free was being diluted by fear and worry again. And old questions, mixed with new.

Why had Grinch dragged Alice here?

Who had nearly poisoned me?

Who had left the carcass in our rooms?

Who had attacked Alex? Would Aramis have attacked one of his own? My mind drifted to a Paris backstreet and what had happened to Willem and Katie.

The 48 Assets were capable of anything.

Questions, questions, more damn questions.

How did Cromwell know about my brother's injuries?

What was the Rewriting?

What was Aramis doing?

Did the success of our Religion Eradication assignment even matter now? The answer to that came quickly, but it wasn't in my voice. It was the combined voice of every Asset at The 48.

Of course it mattered—or at least, it was the only thing that was supposed to.

I shook my head. "Alice, Cromwell is going to get Alexander and me to Greenwich today. The king is already there," I said quietly.

"The king has left?" questioned Marlon. "When?"

"Last night," I replied. "I think this is it. The beginning of the end."

"The end of what?" asked Marlon, but I couldn't—and didn't—answer him. The queen's fate would be known to all soon.

"Marlon, you've become a good friend to Alexander," I said. "When the time comes to move him, I'm going to need your help."

"Of course," replied the yeoman. "I would do anything for Alexander...for both of you, of course. I am here to serve nobility."

I saw my brother smile. I couldn't remember the last time I'd seen him look that genuinely happy.

"What do you want me to do?" asked Alice.

"Go back to the queen. Stay with her. I'm pretty sure they'll move her to Greenwich too."

Alice had looked down at her wrist. So did I.

27 08:43:22

Deep breaths.

"Are you all right, milord?" Alice asked.

"Are you?" I asked.

"I'm fine, in case anyone's wondering," drawled Alex, raising his cup. He smacked his lips together.

Alice shuddered. "You are gross, Alexander."

"You're high, Alexander," I said.

"I feel like I could climb the walls of the castle and touch the clouds," called Alex.

"You already are."

But Marlon was looking worried.

"What did you do?" I asked. His cheeks flamed and he refused to meet my eye. I recognized guilt when I saw it. *Marlon?*"

"I could not bear to see him in so much distress!" replied Marlon. "Yet I fear it may have been too much."

I swore. "You mean you gave him something in addition to what Fiennes gave him?"

"I told you not to trust that man."

"That man saved my brother's leg last night," I retorted. "No wonder Alexander is...not himself." I turned to Alice. "What did your new friend Fiennes give him?"

"Ground opium. In wine."

"And what did *you* give him?" I asked Marlon.

"Milk of the poppy from one of the apothecaries."

Alex had been given an extra double dose of morphine. No wonder he was high; I was amazed he wasn't unconscious.

"Someone needs to stay with him," I said.

"Well, I can't," said Alice. "I need to go back to the queen."

"And I need to get changed and await word from Cromwell."

"I would be happy to remain by Alexander's side," said Marlon. He said this to me, but he and Alex had locked eyes.

"I choose *him*," slurred Alex. "He's armed. And he has two arms." He snorted at his own joke. Even high and in excruciating pain, my brother had more humor in him than I did on a good day. Marlon was smiling.

I felt a lot less worried about leaving my brother in the hands of someone who genuinely seemed to care for him.

"I'm going back to our rooms, Alexander," I said quietly, crouching down at his side. "I'll make sure everything is ready to go and then we'll wait for Cromwell's order."

"Cromwell is going to lose his head," laughed Alex. "Me too."

"Those are not statements to make even in jest," said Marlon.

"Pay him no heed," I said to Marlon. "Alexander wouldn't recognize our own mother right now."

And neither would I, I thought as Alice and I shut the door and walked back out into Horseshoe Cloister.

***

"It stinks out here," remarked Alice, wrinkling up her nose. "It's even worse than Hampton Court."

"That's probably because we're neck-high in crap," I replied.

"Metaphorically."

"I wouldn't be too sure about that."

"You need to walk ahead of me now," said Alice, giving me a subtle push.

"I know. But I'm not sure when we're going to get to talk again, and I've been thinking a little bit about Grinch. I want to hash out why she might have brought you here when you aren't even a proper Asset."

"What do you mean by that?" she demanded. "I'm just as good as you and Alexander."

"Right, but you aren't—"

"I'm not what?"

"You're just a trainee, Alice. You haven't passed—"

"Oh, screw you, Charlie," snapped Alice. "You think you're so amazing because you're older than me? Look at yourself. You've done nothing but stumble from one crisis to the next on this mission. I wouldn't have believed you were so hopeless if I hadn't seen it with my own eyes."

She curtsied and fled—down the path, past a woman carrying a huge bundle of washing under her left arm, and into a doorway that had tendrils of steam curling out of it.

Slamming my head into a stone pillar was not an option, although it was probably the only way I was going to release the tension now strung through my entire body. I needed a release or I was going to punch the first duke I came across.

I am Charles Douglas of The 48.

Of age and of willing mind.

I accept this assignment and affirm that I will faithfully execute the instructions within.

And will, to the best of my ability, preserve, protect, and defend the Tenets of The 48 from now until my end. They are all that matter.

But Alex mattered. Alice mattered. I mattered.

Jane mattered, dammit.

⚊⚊⚊

It was clear that the king had left. People were bustling in and out of rooms, preparing to leave too. I saw Edward Seymour and three other men dressed in velvet doublets the color of plums talking animatedly by a large window that overlooked the grassy Upper Ward. The feathers in their pearl-studded hats flapped imperiously as they gesticulated and spoke over one another.

"Cleves," called Edward Seymour. "A word."

His thin face twisted into a look of barely concealed disgust at my appearance and smell as he got closer to me.

"Good God, man," said Seymour. "Have you been sleeping with cows?"

"What can I do for you, Seymour?" I replied wearily.

Combing his gloved fingers through his long black beard, Seymour leaned in and whispered in my ear.

"I told you before, Lady Jane is spoken for. Any more late-night strolls, and I will personally ensure that you are mistaken for an intruder and dealt with accordingly."

"Are you threatening me?"

"I don't threaten—I promise," replied Seymour menacingly. His hot breath lingered on my neck. He was one to talk about cows—his breath stank.

"I assure you, sir. I have no romantic intentions toward Lady Jane whatsoever."

"Good. Because romance is for fools. As is love. And this is about power. Now go and take a bath. You smell of shit."

I was dismissed like a fool. Edward Seymour had managed to do what even the king hadn't done, which was to make me feel like a six-year-old child again. With shame burning in my chest, I walked quickly away to my lodgings. The high-pitched laughter of Seymour and his men tolled like bells in my wake.

I was an idiot to walk Jane back to her rooms. Jane's disappearance from the castle for such a long period of time would have been noted by anyone watching her—and of those, there were plenty.

It took a while to accost a couple of servants, but eventually I managed to find two squires to fill a bath with hot water and find me a few sets of clean clothes. I wrapped one set into a bundle for Alex and hid it under a cloak. Then I looked around the room. I wouldn't miss it. With any luck I would never be back at Windsor Castle again.

A warm bath and soap didn't work miracles, but they were enough to make me feel human again. And with that feeling came a shred of confidence that I could get a grip on myself—and the assignment. It was all on me now. Alex needed to recuperate.

The next two weeks would decide what would become of Jane. I would need an audience with the king as soon as we arrived at Greenwich. All of my concentration and words now had to be focused on making Jane the most unattractive option for him to replace Anne.

Even if all else unraveled, I would save Jane, and she would thank me in the end.

forty-one

Margaret

The trip to Greenwich had been long and uncomfortable, yet I would have given anything to be back on that wooden barge, traveling up the foul-smelling river, if it meant I could escape this moment.

"Did you not hear me, Lady Margaret?"

Slowly, I lifted my eyes to meet the king's. He was looking at me oddly.

"You should be pleased, Lady Margaret," he said. "Your marriage to the Earl of Moray will benefit your father's house. Strengthen ties between England and Scotland. You should be beyond happiness." His face had turned a light shade of pink.

"I—I am happy, Your Grace," I replied, digging my nails into my thumb to distract my mind from the horror of what had been finally confirmed.

"You do not look it. You serve me, don't you?" The pink shade had deepened, and I felt my knees weaken.

"Gladly, with every breath I take, Your Grace. Indeed, I—"

"Enough," replied the king, clicking his bejeweled fingers. Now he was smiling. "I have neither the time nor the desire for grateful weeping. The marriage will take place within the month, once your father has paid the dowry the earl has demanded. You do have the means?"

The king turned to my father, who had joined us at Greenwich, not to visit his only legitimate child, but to bargain her life away.

"It will be done with immediate effect, Your Grace," replied my father. He was beaming, as if he had just sold a prize stallion for a grand sum.

I was dismissed. I had served my purpose. My father stayed behind to loiter with the king. My father would say and do anything for the king's favor.

But I was more intelligent than he was. I was more intelligent than all of them. I was going to play the game and win.

I took a deep breath, smoothed the skirt of my pale blue gown, and went to knock on Cromwell's door.

forty-two

Charles

Cromwell's instructions came from a squire, who led me to the gates of the Lower Ward during the changing of the guard. *Smart,* I thought. This was a grand spectacle—and noisy—and would be a good distraction for anyone curious about what he had to tell me.

"Lord Cromwell departed for Greenwich many hours ago," the squire said. "But he told me to tell you a barge awaits you." He gave me directions to the meeting point and then disappeared into the crowd.

I was relieved and somewhat surprised at the promptness of the squire's message. But true to his word, the king's chief minister had arranged to help me move Alex quietly away from Windsor Castle.

We would be taking a private barge up the river to Greenwich, separate from everyone else. It was perfect. No potholed roads to ride on that would cause Alex instant pain. Instead, a leisurely boat trip in nice weather, with nothing but ducks and swans for company.

I knew that I now owed Cromwell big—and he wouldn't let me forget it.

Alex was looking pale and clammy by the time I got back to him, which I put down to the double dose of morphine withdrawal. Marlon and I got him to the barge with no real problems, but

Alex started puking within seconds of the oarsmen punting off, even though the river was perfectly calm and the sun pleasantly warm.

Marlon went to speak to the captain of the small barge, and I seized my chance to talk to Alex alone.

I sidled up to him and flipped his wrist over.

26 23:59:59

I looked down at mine. It read the same. I took a wet cloth, wiped his sweating forehead, and opened my mouth to speak.

At which point, Alex needed to puke again. There was nothing left in his stomach, but his dry-retching still made me go through the replicate motions. It wasn't a twin thing. I just hated the sound of violent heaving.

"My tongue . . . feels like it licked . . . a badger's ass," he croaked.

"Got much experience with that?" I replied.

"Ha," said Alex. Groaning, he eased himself down, front-first, onto his bed of cushions. I wiped his mouth with the cloth. His lips were a pale blue color and very chapped. I lifted his shirt to inspect his back and winced at the sight. The sheer brutality was more evident than ever.

I heard Marlon's footsteps hurrying toward us.

"He needs to be under cover. The sun will roast him alive," Marlon said worriedly.

I placed my hand on Alex's forehead. He was definitely feeling much warmer than before.

"As soon as we get to Greenwich, we'll need to dress the bandages around his leg again," I said. "But I'm really concerned about the cuts on his back."

"You are concerned they will cause him to take a fever?"

I nodded. "I know you have other duties, Marlon, but could you—"

"I will not leave his side, Charles of Cleves," replied the yeoman. "I have friends in the guard. Thomas Ladman, for one. He will cover for me. Sir, if it is not too forward of me...I know you wish to keep Alexander's malady a secret, but is it not time that your father, the duke, was told of his son's ill health?"

"I have sent word," I lied. That was the second time I'd told that lie. The first was to Cromwell, who hadn't believed me for a second.

I thought again to Alex's description of his attack. Who he thought he'd seen and heard. What he'd smelled. I looked again at his back, and then, suddenly—

Piermont.

The name chimed like an alarm bell in my head.

Alex thought it was Aramis who'd been in the room with him as he was whipped, but his wounds, and the torturous element of the attack, had Piermont written all over them.

How old had I been when I saw Jack McConnell struck through the eye with an arrow at The 48?

Nine. I was nine years old when it happened, because I remembered showing Alice where Alex and my new rooms were before the lesson. We were on the archery grounds outside the ten-story dormitory, and I was pointing to my window on the ninth floor. *Nine, just like me,* I'd told her. That was the last time either of us smiled for weeks.

We were told it was Jack's fault. He moved during Piermont's demonstration. He'd been shaking with fear. We all knew not to show fear in front of Piermont.

I could still remember Piermont pulling the arrow out of Jack's face, eyeball and all. There was a sucking sound like a wet kiss. I remember thinking his eyeball was big—way bigger than the eyeball of a nine-year-old should be. It took up a quarter of his face.

Or at least, that was what I remembered in my nightmares in the weeks that followed. It was hard to separate them from reality.

The night of Jack's death, the entire class had to attend an Extraordinary Imperative: a one-off because of what had transpired earlier that day. It wasn't a game. Imperatives were statutory. Everything at The 48 was.

The exam was a single question. A memory test. We had to remember the color of Jack's iris. Despite the horror, what information had we remembered about the "little details"? This was important, Piermont explained, because it was the little details that would keep us alive as Assets.

Jack's eyes were blue with black flecks. Anyone who failed to recall that had to stand outside in the pitch dark while Piermont shot an arrow through an orange placed on their head.

I got it right.

Alex got it wrong.

When he came back inside, with orange pulp dripping down his ashen face, the first thing he did was go shower.

He didn't speak for twenty-four hours.

<hr />

"What are you thinking about?" asked Alex. His voice was lower, almost as if he were forcing the words out from deeper inside. I looked up and I realized Marlon had left us.

"Jack McConnell," I said.

"Jack McConnell, or Piermont?"

"They're inextricably linked," I replied quietly.

"Well, that's the damned truth."

"Alex," I whispered. "You said someone smelled like mint. What if it was him? Piermont?"

"Did I say that?"

"You can't remember?"

"I can't remember anything about the attack anymore. Just people yelling about rewriting or . . . something."

"Do you remember them asking you questions? I'm thinking about your injuries. And what you said about being strung up. The bag over your head. It's so brutal, Alex, what happened to you. I admit, it's not hugely creative, but if an Asset *was* involved . . . well, Piermont would be the first to resort to torture to try to get what he wanted."

Across the deck, Marlon was loosening a coil of thick rope and singing to himself. The oarsmen were laughing and calling across the water. I peered over the side of the barge. We were moving toward a small wooden jetty on the bank.

"I think we're here," I said.

Alex grabbed at my leg. It was the nearest body part to him.

"We'll talk more when we're in our lodgings," I replied, kneeling down by my brother's pale, sweating face.

"We're running out of time," groaned my brother.

"That's not your concern. You just concentrate on getting well. You know the signs of infection. You have to tell me right away. I'll get you the best help possible while we're here, I promise."

⌐┅

But by the time we got Alex to our new lodgings in the palace at Greenwich, he was starting to lose consciousness.

26 20:42:18

　　Ticktock.

26 17:02:41

　　Ticktock.

26 08:31:29

　　Ticktock.

In the end, I didn't have to request an audience with the king. I was summoned to see him the next day. It was the twenty-third of April, 1536.

I hadn't slept and had barely eaten. The thought of leaving Alex's side made me feel ill. I had stripped his back of bandages to get air to the wounds, but the deepest cut, which was at least six inches long, was weeping with pus, and the flayed edges were red and inflamed. And now, without a doubt, he was running a fever.

Marlon and Thomas Ladman, who'd been taking turns to help me look after him, had to team up to force me to wash and put on clean clothes.

"You cannot refuse a summons from the king," said Thomas. "Charles, go to him, and I will send word if Alexander's condition worsens."

"I cannot leave my brother."

"You cannot refuse the king."

"I'm *not* leaving my brother."

"You have no influence over your brother's health whether you are here or not," replied Thomas harshly. "Yet if you displease the king, and refuse to attend him when commanded, it will result in a worse state of affairs for *your* health than that of your brother."

"He is beloved by you, I understand that," said Marlon gently. "But you do Lord Alexander no good by weeping over him. I have been in the guard almost half of my life. No one says no to the king and lives to tell the tale."

It occurred to me just then that I had spent my entire life saying yes to people. I was conditioned to do what I was told. I didn't know any other way. And even with my brother hovering on the precipice of death, I could feel myself being pulled in the direction of obedience.

And I hated myself for it.

"Do not allow anyone other than Alice—if she ever arrives here—into this room," I said. "And if you see my father, the Duke of Cleves, or another man—a large man with many scars— anywhere near this room . . . you do whatever it takes to keep them away from Alexander."

"You wish to keep the duke away?" asked Thomas.

"Everyone who isn't me, you, or Alice stays away from my brother," I reiterated.

"We understand," replied Thomas, and he pulled out an ivory-handled knife and placed it on the table next to the bed. "I too have a father who has failed me."

I leaned down and kissed my brother on the crown of his head. His face was half buried in his pillow. I couldn't remember ever doing that before, but it felt oddly natural.

"Don't you leave me," I whispered. "Don't you leave me ever again."

But I wasn't sure he heard me.

Greenwich reminded me of Hampton Court, only bigger. No wonder each palace had its own staff and resources. The frequency with which Henry bounced from one court to another would have made it impossible for a single staff to continually pack and unpack. This time, the king had moved to Greenwich because he wanted to joust. It would soon be May Day, and that was the tradition.

The poor starved while the rich played their games, I thought grimly. *That* was the timeline that needed to be rewritten.

I hurried through the corridors, hoping I was heading in the right direction. How was anyone supposed to find anything in a palace that was the size of a city? When I spotted Anne Boleyn walking with two male courtiers, I veered outside and across a courtyard, making a mental note that Alice was likely here now. And that was when I heard Henry's booming voice tearing apart some poor soul. I stepped back inside and followed the vibrations that were juddering the frail windowpanes around me until I reached a sitting room where the king was perched, looking furious.

"Cleves, damn you!" yelled the king the second he saw me. "I called for you hours ago."

"My apologies, Your Grace," I said, bowing. "I was—"

"Your excuses bore me," boomed the king, and I saw several courtiers wince, although not Cromwell, who was as still as a statue next to him. "When I want you, you bloody well appear."

"Yes, Your Grace." I moved to the king's side, next to Cromwell.

The king was red in the face, and his left leg, which was clad in white stockings, was severely swollen. There was an unpleasant stench, like rotting food, coming from his body, and not even the very obvious smell of lavender from an open pot could disguise it.

Several other courtiers approached the king with matters of state, but from the way the king was fidgeting in his chair, he didn't want to sit and listen anymore.

Someone clapped their hands and several musicians entered the room. I shifted my position and exhaled loudly. Was this why I had been dragged away from my brother—to listen to music? I realized, just then, that I hadn't given a single thought to Jane Seymour—and why I'd needed an audience in the first place.

"When we are dismissed, you will come with me," whispered Cromwell, barely moving his lips.

"Why?" I asked, my stomach filling with dread.

But Cromwell merely folded his hands in front of his body and began relaying to the king various details of the joust that would be taking place the next day.

Eventually the music stopped and the roomful of people was dismissed. No one remained with the king except for several older men who I suspected were healers of the court.

"What are they doing?" I asked Cromwell as we made it into the corridor.

"A very noble occupation" was Cromwell's reply.

"What was that smell?"

"Something you would be wise never to mention again."

He didn't have to tell me. I already knew but was curious whether Cromwell would speak of it.

The king was quite literally rotting on the throne of England.

Cromwell led me to his chambers, which were larger and

grander than the ones at Hampton Court and Windsor Castle. There were large paintings on the wall—and to my delight, I recognized one of Cromwell himself by Hans Holbein that also hung in the Louvre. If the court stayed in Greenwich for the remainder of our assignment, then Holbein's painting of Cromwell was another way we could get back home.

Grinch would enjoy this room, I thought, gazing around— seeing history being painted as a true landscape instead of just being written—but then, Grinch had probably seen works of art actually being created during her life as a time assassin.

"You seem distracted," said Cromwell, moving a thick pile of parchment from his desk to a shelf filled with books.

"I'm just thinking."

"You do a great deal of that."

"Is it a crime?" I asked.

"It is inadvisable to allow others to realize you're thinking," said Cromwell, handing me a small scroll. "Always remain impassive, even when planning. Your face betrays you, Charles of Cleves."

I tried to relax my facial muscles.

"What's this?" I asked, casually waving the scroll.

"I am trusting you, Charles," replied Cromwell. "Yet know that the reason for that trust is not because I like you. It is because you have not been at the court long enough to be in a position to betray me. And your brother's confinement is extra surety."

"Did you attack my brother?" I asked suddenly.

"I did not."

"Do you know who did?"

"Your brother was found outside the castle walls at Windsor. It was my men who brought him inside."

"And they left him?"

"Your brother's fate is not my primary concern at present," replied Cromwell.

"And what is?" I snapped.

"That scroll in your hand," said Cromwell, breaking the seal so that it unrolled. "You see a list of names?"

I nodded, trying to decipher Cromwell's slanting prose.

Mark Smeaton
Henry Norrys
Francys Weston
Wyllyam Brereton
Thomas Wyatt
Rychard Page
George Boleyn
Charles Cleves

The first seven names, I knew from my history Imperatives, were men who would soon be accused of having committed treason by having sexual relations with the wife of the king.

But my studies had not prepared me to see my name on that list too.

forty-three

Margaret

"Lady Margaret. You are alone!"

"Yes, milord. May I come in?"

"Of course, child." Cromwell held the door for me himself and waved away his attending squire. "I beg you sit, Lady Margaret. You seem troubled. Would you like some wine?"

I didn't drink wine; even the slightest amount pained my head. Yet I needed courage. I was in the lair of the beast.

"A drop, milord. Thank you."

"How are you faring, Lady Margaret? I understand that your union with the Earl of Moray is imminent. My congratulations would be forthcoming, and yet I see unhappiness in your countenance. You can tell me anything, you know that. With your father often away from the court...I am the eyes, ears, and even the voice of His Grace. If I can assist in any way, I am more than happy to do so for one as fair as yourself."

Perhaps Lord Cromwell was going to make this easy for me.

"It is the queen, milord," I said. "I am so very fearful."

"Fearful for the queen?"

"For myself. Of condemnation. For perceived...perceived deviations from the righteous path He leads us down."

"You fear for the queen's soul?"

"No, milord. Again, for mine. I cannot..."

"Speak to me, child. You should not be burdened with another's devilry."

"I have seen things…heard things."

"You can give me names?"

"Yes. For a price."

"And what is that?"

"Could a different match be made for me? One that would still strengthen ties between His Grace's court and another? Perchance with a house abroad? Alexander of Cleves…"

"Consider it done."

"You do not wish to know why?"

"Child, do you think you are the first lady of the court to desire a life away? I have made it happen. And I have undone a life secured as well."

A piece of parchment slid across the table. The quill scratched at the surface as my trembling hands wrote down name after name, pausing only briefly before writing down the last.

"The last name…it is insurance only," I explained.

"I understand."

"I will not get Alexander of Cleves without the will of the brother, you see. But his name is to be used as leverage only."

"For both of us."

"When will you be able to guarantee my future?"

"Soon. You are under my protection now, and I will not forget your assistance, Lady Margaret."

I played the conversation with Cromwell over and over in my head for the rest of the day. But I gave little thought to what I'd actually done. I was a player in the biggest game of all now, and I could not lose.

Charles

What is this?" I demanded. "Tell me who wrote this list!"

"The first joust of the May Day celebrations will take place tomorrow, Charles," replied Cromwell. "The king will be told of the queen's treasonous dalliances during this time. Your name is on this list to ensure your obedience."

"You're going to offer me up as a sacrifice? Why? I've done nothing wrong. I barely speak to the queen."

"You are hiding something. I want to know what."

I could hear the echo of my heart in my ears: pushing, pulsing, pressing.

"I'm not hiding anything."

"Where is your father, the Duke of Cleves? What is the maid to you—I have seen her in your company more than is proper. What are your true intentions as to Lady Jane—you are in *her* company far too often too. Those are just a few of the many questions I want answers to."

"What is any of this to you?" I cried. "What I do in my own time—"

"Your time?" replied Cromwell coolly. "Your time? Your time is the king's time, and by rights, my time. Save His Majesty, I am the most powerful man in this court. And for a reason, Cleves. I make everyone's business my business. Now, where is your father? Is he planning a rebellion?"

"That's nonsense. No, of course not."

"Then where is he?" demanded Cromwell.

"I don't know."

"And what of your feelings for the maid?"

"Alice is a girl I have had relations with before. I care for her."

"Is she with child?"

"No!"

"And your intentions as to Lady Jane?"

"She is a lady of the court. I speak to many in the court."

"You do not wish her for yourself?"

"No!"

"Is your brother spying for the Seymours?"

"No!" I cried. "Sir, this is madness."

"You will no longer speak to Lady Jane," ordered Cromwell. "I have both you and your brother under my thumb. I can make you or destroy you, Cleves. Greater men have gone to the block for less than what this paper implies."

"What do you want me to do?" The blood was still rushing in my ears. "I told you that I was your man in the court—I still am."

"I want you to go to the queen's chamber," replied Cromwell. The steady measure of his voice was unnerving. It reminded me so much of Grinch, Asix, and Piermont, and the other Assets who managed to survive into their forties. Self-preservation was all that mattered to Cromwell.

"I will," I replied obediently.

"You are to continue to watch her movements as you have done thus far," continued the chief minister. "I now want to know *every* person who enters and leaves her rooms. I want a record of *every* conversation. Every flutter of the eyelashes. Every heaving of the breast. Every mannerism, every whisper, and every touch. Do you understand?"

"Yes." The word came out as more of a gasp.

"Leave now."

With my legs buckling at the knees, I made my way to the door of Cromwell's grand rooms.

"One last word, Cleves," called Cromwell. I turned around, steadying myself by placing my hand on the doorframe.

"Yes?"

"If your brother survives, he would do well not to take any more late-night strolls with the yeomen of the guard, especially with the one named Marlon Chancery. It is extraordinary how well my eyes see in the dark."

"What are you—"

"Alexander would do well to make a match with Lady Margaret. She is keen…and willing to do *anything* it takes to find a match abroad."

A shadow crossed Cromwell's face, but I could see the smirk.

The scroll was still in my hand as I lurched into the corridor. I held the thick parchment to the nearest candle and watched it take the flame. Cromwell would have another copy—probably several. I was under no illusion that I was protecting myself by destroying the scroll with my name written on it. But I had to get rid of it still.

Cromwell had said that Lady Margaret was willing to do anything to find a match abroad. Had she given my name to Cromwell? Why? To see that she was married to my brother, just to escape this court of blood and ashes?

I heard a cough behind me and I jumped.

"I didn't mean to startle you, Charles," said Jane Seymour. She was with another lady, much younger than herself, who must have been a maid of honor. She looked no older than twelve.

"Lady…"

"Charles, what is wrong?"

"Nothing…I…"

"I wanted to inquire as to your brother's health," said Jane, concern painted across her pale face. "I have not seen you since that night…"

"I can't…I can't speak…" My hands were shaking

"Charles, you are ailing. What is wrong? What has happened? Is it your brother?"

"No…yes…"

"Charles, you are frightening me. What has happened? You must tell me."

"Not here," I gasped.

"Then let us go where we will not be heard," whispered Jane, glancing at Cromwell's door. She held out her hand for me to take. The other lady was as still as a marble statue. Could I trust her to keep my meeting with Jane secret? Could I trust anyone?

Why wasn't I running as far away from Jane Seymour as I could get? My brother and I had just been threatened with death by the king's chief minister. If it came to it, it would be Lady Margaret's word against mine. Accusations of spying, rebellion, homosexuality, and treason would surface. They would cut off our heads where we stood if I didn't do what Cromwell wanted.

But keeping Jane away from Henry was my assignment from The 48, and that took precedence over everything…didn't it?

"How…how are you, mil…milady?" I asked, slipping my hand underneath Jane's to escort her away.

"I am well, Charles," replied Jane. "Which, alas, is more than can be said of you. You look as if you have seen a ghost."

I stole a deep breath and held it. *Be calm,* I demanded of myself.

This is Jane.

Your objective.

Your assignment.

But she was also my friend now.

And I was not a coward. I would not run from Cromwell like a little boy. He had no right to try to control me like this. I had allowed my body and mind to betray me for a moment, but I was a trained Asset. I could handle worse than Cromwell.

"I have not seen a ghost, milady…but I am aware that I look and smell like death," I said slowly. Jane gave a nervous giggle. It was a lovely sound.

I looked behind us. The young maid had fallen back at least five steps in deference to our higher standing.

"You do yourself an injustice," said Jane. "I would not go so far as to say *death.* Perhaps scrofula?"

I shouldn't be playing this game. Not here. Not anywhere. But Jane was doing a wonderful job of calming me down. I could actually feel my heartbeat slowing inside my chest.

"Perchance the plague?" I said, dangerously continuing the game. The feeling was empowering—a sensation I hadn't felt since that first game of archery with the king.

"No, not the plague—the sweats?" suggested Jane.

"Puerperal fever?" I added, and Jane giggled again.

We continued on in a comfortable silence, passing tapestries and a large painting of a castle.

"Are you attending the joust tomorrow?" asked Jane.

"Will you be there?" I asked quietly.

"I will. The queen has asked for all her ladies to attend to her on the royal dais."

"Then as I will be in service of the king, I will see you there also," I replied, dropping Jane's hand as we reached the end of the corridor. I turned and bowed to both ladies.

"But you've not yet told me how your brother fares," said Jane.

"He is healing, milady," I lied.

"Please send him my regards," said Jane. "His smile and witticisms are much missed in the court."

"I will," I said. We stood there, looking at each other. Her skin was so pale, it was almost translucent. She had freckles dotted around her nose. I had done her such an injustice when I first saw her. She was lovely inside—and out.

The bang of a door brought me to my senses. It wasn't in the direction of Cromwell's lodgings, but it was enough to cause my stomach to lurch and the hairs on the back of my neck to prickle.

I bowed to the two ladies again and left without another word.

The sound of Jane's laugh stayed with me until I reached the gardens of Greenwich.

Cromwell had ordered me to go to the queen's rooms. But before I made my way there, I had to check on my brother. I opened the door a crack and saw Alice at his side.

She barely glanced at me as I entered the room. She was too busy watching an elderly man with a long white beard. The aroma from three open bowls of sweet-smelling liquid permeated the room. The man was leaning over my brother's back. At first I thought he was dabbing small white buds of cotton onto the wounds, but then I saw one of them wriggle between the old man's fingertips.

"What are you doing?" I gasped, and then I realized.

Maggots. Amazing little creatures. Place a maggot in a wound and it would eat the damaged flesh and leave the good flesh alone.

"Was this your idea?" I asked Alice.

"Well, it wasn't yours."

"It's brilliant," I said softly.

"I try."

The old man placed a few more maggots on my brother's back and then stood. "I don't think he requires more," he said. Alice and I nodded our thanks.

When he had left, I turned to Alice. "Welcome to Greenwich. Are you still pissed at me?"

"Nice to be here, and I'm always pissed at you," she replied. She picked up a maggot and held it in a pincerlike grip.

"Stop…flirting…over…maggots," groaned Alex. He flapped his right hand, feebly trying to get my attention.

"How are you doing?" I asked, pressing my hand against his forehead. My hands were still sweaty after the meetings with Cromwell and Jane Seymour, and Alex's skin was slick with perspiration.

"Not dead…yet," replied my brother, his voice half muffled by a pillow.

"I've been ordered to up the spying on the queen, but I'll come back as often as I can to check on you."

"What about...Jane?" said Alex; his voice crackled like sandpaper against brick. "You can't...do...this...assignment...by yourself."

"Yes, I can," I replied. I decided there and then not to tell him about Lady Margaret's intentions toward him, or the list of names that Cromwell was threatening me with. "So you just lie here and accept that you're maggot bait for a day or two. You'll be fighting fit by the time we go critical."

"How many days...until that stage?"

"Twelve." My heart hurt at the realization that my brother was too weak to look at his own wrist.

"Stay safe," moaned Alex.

"I'm not the one who needs to be told," I replied.

"Is it done?"

Marlon had entered the room, looking rather green around the edges. Without a guard's hardened exterior fixed in place, he actually looked younger than my brother.

"Where have you been?" I asked. "I asked that Alexander not be left alone."

"Blood I can cope with, but debridement..." Marlon shuddered. "Maggots are difficult to tolerate when you have accidentally eaten a mouthful of them in your broth."

"Go, Charles," said Alex feebly. "I'm going...to drink myself into...a twelve-day...sleep..."

There was a goblet of creamy white liquid on a table. Alex was being given more opium.

Alice caught up with me as I reached the door.

"I'll walk with you," she said.

"How is Anne's mood right now?" I whispered as we walked down the corridor toward Anne's court. I could hear raised voices in the distance. One was female. Accented English. Angry. The other was male. Native English. Pleading.

"It's hard to say. She seems hell-bent on acting normally. Earlier she demanded lace so she and her ladies-in-waiting can make favors for the knights." She showed me her pockets, which were stuffed with lace scraps.

"The queen would be better off packing and getting herself away. Everything's about to go down, Alice. And there's something you should know."

"What?"

"Cromwell has his list of traitors—and I'm on it if I don't do his bidding. He doesn't actually suspect me of sleeping with Anne—but he knows the Cleves family is keeping something from him."

"We could run away," suggested Alice. "Just until your countdown is due to reach zero. And then we could just keep on running when we get back to the future. Away from The 48, away from everything."

"And what would we do then?" I didn't expect the sarcasm in my voice, but it was there. Dripping down the stone walls, making the flames on the candles flicker.

The raised voices in Anne's court were getting louder.

"We would be together. We'll take Alex and settle abroad where it's safer."

"Nowhere is safe from The 48, Alice. Whatever is happening there at the moment, they'd find us."

"We could at least try."

"Listen, you'd better get the queen her lace. I need to think of an excuse to go in there, and it's better if we don't show up together anyway. Cromwell already thinks we spend too much time together. He asked if you were pregnant."

Alice swore. I couldn't help but smile at the indignant look on her face. It felt good to smile.

We reached the door leading to the queen's rooms. A few yards away, a tall woman in a moss-green dress was gazing out of the window in the hallway. Alice took a couple of seconds to compose herself, and then, with her body hunched and subservient, she disappeared into Anne's court.

I leaned back against the stone wall, thinking I should probably just improvise. Which seemed fitting, seeing how nothing was going according to plan on this assignment. It hadn't from the moment we had met Grinch in the Louvre.

I walked over to the window. I just wanted to press my head against the cool glass for a moment before—

"*Bonjour, Charles.*"

The feeling of déjà vu swept over me as the woman in green turned around.

It was Grinch.

forty-five

Alexander

The door.

I heard it creak.

Felt the cool breeze of air brush my skin.

I had been dreaming. About Jane Seymour and the assignment to eradicate religion.

"Lady Jane." I had said her name while dreaming.

No. Not dreaming. I had been in a nightmare.

I couldn't breathe. White, fluffy clouds had been replaced by dark shadows. A storm. Lightning flashed across my retinas. Brilliant white light.

I couldn't breathe. The pressure was building up behind my eyes. I shook my head. Something was pressing down on my face. A heavy mass.

I wanted to cry for help, but sleep paralysis had me in its grip.

No, not sleep paralysis. I could feel pain. In my back and my leg.

Not dark shadows. A pillow. Being held over my face.

Even now, a Tenet sprang to mind.

Asphyxia, from the ancient Greek for without *and* sphyxis, *meaning* squeeze, *is an ideal route for disposal if the subject is already incapacitated and the Asset has the luxury of time. It is not the lack of oxygen that kills. It is the buildup of* CO_2*. Coma and death can be achieved in less than three minutes.*

Charlie!

forty-six

Charles

A time-traveling Grinch had not lost the sickly green tinge to her skin that everyone at The 48 had come to associate with this Asset. The smell of mint permeated the corridor.

And then I saw the swollen purple scar that ran in a curve from Grinch's left ear to her throat.

Grinch must have noticed my eyes trailing downward, because she pulled up a green silk cowl that was attached to the neckline of her dress.

"What are you doing here?" I gasped.

"I am here to see you and your brother," replied Grinch. Her voice was even deeper than before, but it also had an artificial twang to it, like a synthesizer.

"Why?"

Alice's name was on the tip of my tongue. It stayed there. I no longer trusted Assets. The realization was terrifying and liberating in equal measure.

"You need protection and guidance, as events are now unfolding at The 48 that I had not foreseen," replied Grinch. "We are under attack, Charles. From forces outside The 48, and from within its own walls. I will not explain further here. I wanted to make contact with you, and I will do the same with your brother, although Alexander will follow your lead, which is why I am approaching you first."

"Is this to do with something called the Rewriting? Alex—"

The sound of footsteps reached our ears as a pair of yeomen rounded the corner ahead. I silently cursed them.

"I will make contact again, Charles," said Grinch. "When we have more time and are unlikely to be interrupted. I am known in this court. Unlike others, I have freedom to move around here."

"What's the Rewriting? Alex has been badly hurt, and those who beat him kept saying that word."

"Be on your guard, Charles," whispered Grinch, ignoring my question. "Trust no one. From this time, or your own."

The yeomen were closer.

"Why did you drag Alice back here?" I asked urgently.

"Stay in the shadows, Charles. Do not forget your assignment. The 48 is all that matters."

Her voice was starting to break. Spit was pooling in her gums and hanging in gauzy drips across her teeth. She swallowed, but it was hard work. The grimace on her face couldn't be hidden by the cowl, and a slight pink tinge mixed with the jaundiced color on her cheeks. Without another word, she limped past the next few windows and disappeared around the corner, just as the yeomen took positions outside the queen's apartments.

It only occurred to me once Grinch was out of sight that perhaps I should have asked her how she was. Because it was very obvious to me that someone had tried to slit her throat.

"Charles of Cleves deigns to grace us with his presence," called the queen as I was shown into her rooms. "Aren't we fortunate?"

Anne was sitting on a dais with four ladies-in-waiting sewing at her feet, Lady Rochford among them. I took a quick inventory of the other people in the room. Alice wasn't there.

Neither was Jane, or Lady Margaret.

"Make yourself useful before you start gathering dust. Perhaps you'd like to sing for me? And if so, what words would you have, Cleves? You and Smeaton together would make a pretty pair of cooing doves." At that, the queen laughed. No one else did.

"I would be happy to read for you, Your Grace," I said stiffly. "Or walk with you outside should you require a steadying hand."

"And now we arrive at Charles's real reason for entering my rooms," said the queen, her voice high with nerves. "He wishes to read me words of love."

"No," I replied quickly.

The queen's face darkened.

"You do not love me? All men love me. Why, don't they, Weston?"

The queen's attention turned to a young man who was wearing a navy-and-red doublet. As he spoke of his devotion, I swapped looks with Lady Rochford. Her husband, Anne's brother, was on the list that Cromwell had given me. She wouldn't care if he died; it was well known that she despised her husband.

What a wretched existence, I thought. *To live with such hate in your heart.*

I spent the rest of the afternoon as the queen's object of ridicule. I sucked it up like a sponge. Cromwell wanted every conversation, every glance. He was going to get it.

That night I told him of everything and everyone I had seen and heard in Anne's apartments. He seemed satisfied.

"Tomorrow is going to be a long day, Charles," he said ominously when I hastened to the door. "Be ready."

forty-seven

Margaret

Madness had overtaken me.

I hadn't meant Alexander of Cleves harm. I had simply wanted to see him—to hear him say he had agreed to marry me. That he was as happy with the news as I was. Cromwell had told me to consider it done. I needed to know that the union had been sought. That I would have a new, happier life abroad.

But Alexander of Cleves had not said my name when I'd slipped into his room. He had called for Lady Jane.

My thoughts raced. If Alexander loved another—Lady Jane or otherwise—it mattered not. Charles of Cleves was my insurance. Cromwell had his name. If Alexander knew that, ill thoughts of other unions would instantly flee his mind. It was cold, and calculating, but if that was what I had to be, so be it.

I gripped the bedpost. Would that I could simply disappear, as he and his brother had that night, so many weeks ago.

The question hit me like thunder.

Would Alexander do it again, if he were under duress? Would he take me with him?

I scarcely recalled reaching for the pillow. Or asking God's forgiveness.

But I did recall the feeling of fear that fell upon me as he struggled, and struggled, that he was not going anywhere.

forty-eight

Alexander

I was afraid to sleep. I knew someone had tried to smother me. Someone stronger and with more evil intent would have carried it all the way through.

Well, if they had come back to finish the job they had started on the way to Windsor, they had done a pretty poor job of it. I was still in Tudor England, in body, if not spirit.

I was finding there was something strangely empowering about surviving assassination attempts. It would have been interesting to discuss this with Charlie, but he had too much else running through his head. I didn't even tell him about the suffocation attempt when he came back to the room, even when he mentioned the burst blood vessels in my eyes. He could hardly talk—he looked like death himself.

Charlie was hiding something from me. I was hiding something from him. We were twins. We both knew it.

But instead of talking with him, I downed several goblets of wine. Then I lost the battle to stay awake.

⁂

No nightmares, but I woke up feeling wretched, with a hangover from Hell. I had only wanted to numb the pain for a few hours.

Charlie had obviously done the same.

"You. Look. Terrible." I was standing by the end of Charlie's bed, hanging on to the post for dear life because I was still unable to put any weight on my cauterized leg.

"You shouldn't be out of bed," replied Charlie, wincing. "And I shouldn't have had any of that wine."

"I need to be out of bed because I should be at the opening joust," I replied. "People are going to talk. And I think the wine was fermented through the open pores of plague victims. It's the only explanation for how I feel."

"People are not going to talk about you not being at the joust," said Charlie, getting out of bed and taking my arm. We both lurched as I tried to turn around. I was going to either puke on him, or puke on my bandages.

My brother would have to take one for the team this time. I didn't need vomit-soaked bandages.

"The only people who know you're back here are me, Alice, Marlon, Thomas, and the doctors who have treated you," said Charlie, wiping himself off. "No one will be gossiping because no one will know."

He felt my forehead and smiled. "I think your fever's broken. But you still need to rest."

"You said there was another guard too, at one point. Didn't you?"

"Yeah. An older yeoman called Bewsey," replied Charlie, helping me back into the bed. "But he seemed decent. He won't say anything. So promise me you won't try to leave this room today."

"You have that look on your face," I said, turning my head to look at him.

"What look?"

"The one where I think you're either constipated or planning to kill someone."

"Might be both."

"Concentrate on the assignment, Charlie. If you get hurt because you're trying to get back at someone, we're screwed. Lady Jane is all that matters."

Charlie knelt down by my head and ran his fingers through my hair.

"This mop has grown twice as fast as mine in the weeks we've spent back in time. If you had a wet suit you'd be the perfect surfer."

"Get me a board and watch me," I murmured.

"Nothing will go wrong from now on," he whispered. "And I'm going to get you back to the twenty-first century, I promise."

But the only sound I heard in reply in the darkness was my own snore.

forty-nine

Margaret

The first joust of the May Day holiday was important. I had bathed and dressed in a gold-and-cream dress for the occasion. Small pearls lined my French hood, and a single string of the same, a wooing gift from an earl several months earlier, pressed down on my throat. My head was pounding as if my heart had been placed there. Alternate mouthfuls of milk and honey-covered bread did nothing to settle my stomach, which had been churning since I'd fled Alexander of Cleves's room the night before.

The ladies-in-waiting and maids of honor in the queen's court waited for her to finish dressing. We would follow her procession. I took no joy in the knowledge that her fate was about to be sealed. I had enough humanity left in me to feel sorry for Queen Anne.

At the same time, I could not stop thinking about the Cleves brothers, whose lives I held in my hands. And the feeling of power that brought me.

At the earliest opportunity, I would speak with Cromwell to discover where things stood. One way or another, things were coming to an end.

fifty

Charles

The first joust of the May Day holiday was important. I had bathed and dressed in a gold-and-cream doublet for the occasion. I looked like an idiot, but I had to blend in and yet still stand out enough for the king to call on me. My wine-induced headache was still pounding away, but alternate mouthfuls of milk and honey-covered bread that servants kept circulating kept the puke down. It was what everyone here ate when they felt ill.

It wasn't just the hangover that was causing my stomach to waltz across my intestines. It was that list of names that Cromwell was intending to present to the king. Anne's fate was about to be sealed. I had enough humanity left in me to feel sorry for her, but the queen's timeline wasn't the one I had to work on. It was Henry and Jane's.

But yet again, as I walked down to the grand tents and stables erected for the tournament, I couldn't stop myself from thinking that I shouldn't be doing this. Jane's life choices should be up to her, not some Termination Order Directorate from five hundred years in the future.

Thinking about choices. Daring to doubt what I had been told to do. Alice's questions had been a bigger influence on me than I cared to admit.

⁂

I arrived at the large field; the king wasn't there. That was good. I wasn't in the mood for his cantankerous yelling, with my sore

271

head. I glanced around at the laughing faces—while trying to avoid eye contact with all of them—for people I recognized.

There was no Cromwell, but that wasn't a surprise. I didn't think for a moment he would actually be the one to deliver the list of names to the king. Assuming it went down according to the history I knew, the men—including Anne's own brother—were going to be accused of having sexual relations with her. They would all be arrested with the queen. All would be found guilty. And if history wasn't changed, all would be executed.

<hr>

Anne Boleyn was already at the jousting field, sitting under a silver fabric canopy decorated with the letters *A* and *H* entwined. Her ladies-in-waiting were perched on chairs just below her dais. Lady Margaret was wearing a dress made from the same ridiculous gold fabric as my doublet. She looked different. She wasn't trying to disappear into the crowd. Margaret wanted people to see her. Even the angle of her head was higher. Prouder.

She gave me a sideways glance; I swore I saw a smile play out on her pale lips. Was she mocking me?

I decided there and then that Hell would freeze over before I let her get near my brother.

Jane was to the queen's left, and my chest tightened, just enough for me to catch my breath. She was wearing a caramel-colored gown with a simple string of pearls around her neck. Her hair was pulled back under a matching French hood, but the sun was beating down on her face, making her hair look more golden than red. I didn't catch her eye, but I couldn't avoid the gaze of her brother, Edward Seymour. He was standing next to the empty dais of the king, glaring at me. His face was even thinner and more pinched than normal. In fact, he didn't look well at all.

Good. Maybe he'd caught something horrible that would result in gangrene or pus-filled boils.

I recognized Marlon Chancery and Thomas Ladman next, standing tall among the yeomen guard. Their being here meant that Alex was unguarded for the day, unless Alice was able to slip away from whatever duties she'd been assigned. I understood— even if I didn't like the situation. The two yeomen's obligations were to the king before the sons of Cleves, and Marlon had already risked so much to help Alex.

A dull ache formed in my chest as I thought of Marlon and my brother. I wished like hell that Marlon came from our time. He and my brother had no chance together here. They belonged in different worlds. Would they end up having the same depressing conversation Alice and I had had? Would they wonder if it had been friendship, lust, or something more?

Then again, even if Marlon *did* come from our time, it's not like he and Alex would have any future together. He wasn't raised within The 48. And even if he were, if anything beyond friendship or lust developed between them, the culture around The 48 would stop it eventually. Because that's how things worked there.

The takeaway, I decided, was that love sucked. The 48 had the right idea there.

And then my eyes landed on Anne Boleyn, and my heart broke. She had been watching me, and when her stunning black eyes caught mine, she smiled. Not a toothy smile, but not a fake one, either. There was something innocent about it. Like she was just saying hello to a friend, and I knew she had very few of those.

The king arrived then, to a great trumpet fanfare and flanked by minions. He was wearing a golden brocade doublet and white stockings and shoes. Sweating already, he looked like a cooked goose. As the knights were introduced by their heralds, I began to make my way over to the king's dais. By the time I reached him, the ground was thundering with hooves as the first two horses charged toward each other. I turned around in time to see the splintering of a lance against the silver armor of a knight who was falling through the air. The crowd cheered and booed in equal measure. The king roared with laughter, and I took my place near him and his other courtiers.

"Your first May Day joust, Cleves?" called the king. "They don't have this in the Rhineland."

"Indeed, Your Grace," I replied with a short bow. "I have much been looking forward to it."

"I would have liked to have seen you and your brother face each other," said Henry. "What a sight that would have been."

"Not as great as seeing you joust," I said sycophantically. I edged a few steps closer to the king. "Will you be taking part this week, Your Grace?"

"I may yet," replied Henry, glaring at an older man in black robes. "And I defy anyone to tell me I should not."

The sun was beating down on my head. The hat I was wearing was much plainer than the hats of other men of the court—it had no feathers, for a start—but it was made of thick black fabric and was acting as the perfect heat conductor. I could feel the nausea rising in my stomach again. The queen and her ladies were all covered by shade, but on the gentlemen's side, only the king was protected.

If I puked now in sight of Henry, it would be game over. My

head would be on a spike at the Tower of London before the heaving had finished. I grabbed the back of a nearby chair.

"What's wrong with you, Cleves?" demanded Henry.

"My apologies, Your Grace. I do not have your healthy constitution. I am afraid I ate something last eve that has disagreed with my gut."

"Get the man some wine," ordered the king to one of his squires. "And where are the next horses?"

"Not wine," I whispered to the squire, grabbing his arm as he made to run off. "Water."

I spent the next hour sipping tepid liquid that tasted like someone had washed their clothes in it. The king got louder and more obnoxious as the tournament progressed. A constant supply of food and wine meant he only moved once, and that was to take a piss. That act was completed behind his canopy, which displayed his silhouette for all to see.

The king never engaged the queen, even though they were only a few feet away from each other. Several times Anne attempted conversation, only to have her words dismissed with a contemptuous flick of the king's hand. What also couldn't be missed was the way Henry looked at Jane and, bizarrely, Lady Margaret. It was beyond gazing, it was leering. His mouth was set in a smirk and his eyes were narrowed and covetous.

⚊⚊

And then it happened.

⚊⚊

A young squire, whom I immediately recognized as one of Cromwell's messenger boys, approached the dais. I held my breath as a piece of paper was passed to a courtier and then the king.

What was on that paper?

Was my name written there?

Every muscle I possessed was clenched. I could feel the sweat dripping down my back. Even my top lip was budding with per-spiration. My stomach turned in on itself as I waited for my name to be called out as a traitor. I had a knife in my boot, but it wasn't my own safety that was running through my head. It was the well-being of Alex and Alice.

The king read the parchment twice. No one seemed to notice he had even been approached. Cheers went up from the crowd as another rider was unseated.

Only Anne seemed to be aware that something was happen-ing. Her dark eyes flicked several times from the joust to the king. She shifted nervously in her seat. Then Lady Margaret glanced over. She kept her eyes lowered, but her chest was rising and fall-ing rapidly.

Quietly, with no fanfare or fuss whatsoever, the king rose from his throne on the dais and stepped down.

And he walked away without a word.

Several courtiers ran after him. Others looked around in con-fusion. The queen asked where the king was going, but no one answered.

Because no one knew.

I decided to take my chance while everyone was distracted. Crossing the grass, I made my way toward Jane Seymour. In a moment of sentimental madness, I stopped to pick a few daisies along the way.

When I reached her, I dropped them in her lap. "Stay safe," I said softly.

"My favorite. How did you know?" she whispered back.

We smiled at each other. And then I took off running after the king.

I would deny everything.

There was no proof, and if it was Lady Margaret's voice against mine, I would shout the loudest.

I caught up with Henry just beyond the line of brightly colored tents that had been set up to house those jousting in the tournament. There were several courtiers with him, but no one was speaking. No one dared. Edward Seymour was there. For once he didn't glare in my direction. He raised a wiry black eyebrow at me, as if to say *What the hell is going on?* I shrugged. My head was still attached to my neck for now, but I was utterly convinced that Cromwell had made his final move to end the marriage of Henry and Anne.

The king bounded up the short flight of steps into one of the entrances to Greenwich Palace. He took a left into a long corridor, a right, and another left. He knew exactly where he was going.

We entered a large room with tall windows made from warped glass that went from waist height to the ceiling. There were several chairs lined up against the wood-paneled walls.

And in the center of the room stood Thomas Cromwell. His long black hair was greasy and lank and his small beady eyes looked bloodshot.

The king strode forward and hugged him.

"You have saved me," said the king. "You have saved us all."

"Do you wish to know the names?" asked Cromwell.

"No," replied the king at once. Bile rose in my throat. So I wasn't safe yet. "Gather the council. I want it expedited."

He turned triumphantly to his courtiers, his hands spread wide in exultation. Edward Seymour was older than the rest of us by at least twenty years and he remained calm, but two of the younger courtiers standing on either side of me were fidgeting nervously. One was biting his nails; the other had sunk his nails so far into his thumbs I could see the crescent shape already forming.

"Tennis, Cleves," said the king. "To the courts."

Adrenaline seemed to be working wonders for the king. He was like a new man. The bad leg that had plagued him ever since I arrived wasn't troubling him at all.

"Your Majesty," called Cromwell. "May I borrow Cleves's ear, just for a moment?"

"Have the whole of him if you wish," replied the king, roaring with laughter.

"What do you want?" I asked.

"I wanted to tell you that I was sorry," replied Cromwell quietly.

"So my name *is* going to be on the list you give the king?"

A bubble of anger in my chest was rising and thickening. I could feel my head shaking with suppressed rage. I had done everything that had been asked of me, by everyone.

And I was still going to die.

"You're not taking me," I snarled, getting right into Cromwell's face. "I will slit your throat before you say another word."

"*Your* position in the court is safe for now," replied Cromwell.

But it was the way he emphasized *your* that made my legs buckle. And I knew instantly what he meant.

Alex!

fifty-one

Alexander

Cromwell shouldn't smile, ever, I thought as he loomed over my bed. His teeth were like little yellow headstones.

But it wasn't that which turned my stomach. It was that when he smiled, his mouth opened.

His breath was poisonous.

He was a basilisk. Ready to strike with his eyes, his mouth, his entire toxic being.

—————

Cromwell had knocked on the door and allowed himself into the chamber without a response from me.

"If you are looking for my brother," I said feebly, trying to maintain the accent that had become second nature to me when the assignment first commenced, "he isn't here. He's gone to the joust."

"I am aware," replied Cromwell, peering around the room. "It is you I have come to call upon, Alexander of Cleves."

"I'm afraid I am not entertaining company at this moment. Indeed, I am not capable of much at all."

"That is good to hear," said Cromwell. He looked over his shoulder and beckoned in two hulking men who were dressed in stained brown pants and gray tunics.

"Take him."

fifty-two

Charles

22 23:18:59

The investigation into Anne Boleyn's treasonous behavior was now official. It was April 26, 1536. She hadn't been arrested—no one had—but the behavior of the king at the first day of the May joust had sent the entire court into an uproar. The wise ones were finding reasons to leave for their country homes.

With the exception of the Seymour family, who were now so many in number it was as if they were breeding in front of my eyes. They knew their time was coming.

Alex was gone. Taken to Cromwell's home in Stepney.

Alice had been dispatched to the Tower of London. Not as a prisoner, but to "make preparations for the queen."

Lady Margaret had gone to the Tower too, with several other maids of honor and ladies-in-waiting. Rumor was that she fainted when told. She wasn't under suspicion, but the queen would still need attending to, even in prison, when she went.

Jane Seymour remained at court. She was no longer referred to as an attendant to the queen and was now barred from seeing anyone without the presence of her brother.

Grinch's and Aramis's whereabouts were unknown to me. And I strongly suspected no one else at The 48 was coming to help me.

***

"Why are you doing this to me?" I asked Cromwell furiously.

"Because I need you more than the king does," replied

Cromwell with utter indifference. He was writing more instructions, which I was to deliver around the court. I had become his carrier pigeon. Nothing more than vermin with broken wings.

"If I do this, will you take me to my brother?"

It was a question I now asked constantly, ever since I had run back to my lodgings to find my brother gone and a pile of blood-stained sheets left in his place.

"In good time" was Cromwell's standard response. "Take this to Rich. He will then have a job for you. Do it quickly and report back to me."

"I want to see my brother. If I report this to my father—"

Cromwell held up his hand. He was not going to listen to that bluff again. I was powerless, and he knew it.

Outside, I kicked a stone pillar until my toes throbbed with pain. Then I slammed my open palm again and again and again until shards of stone started to crumble away. I took no comfort in knowing that Cromwell would eventually meet his end on the block too, just like Anne Boleyn. I wanted him dead now.

Richard Rich was possibly the only man in the court who was surrounded by more paper than Thomas Cromwell. As the king's solicitor, his rooms were not as large as those of the chief minister, but they were filled with manuscripts and leather-bound books. The floor was covered in pieces of string and discarded quills. It was a mess.

Rich opened the letter and read Cromwell's words. A thin smile played out across his mouth. It was a smile of respect.

"Do you know what is in this letter, Cleves?" he asked.

I shook my head.

"You see those ledgers over there?" Rich pointed with a long-nailed finger to a pile of large accountancy books. "Those are the bookkeeping ledgers for the queen's expenses. The smaller green book on top is the one we have procured from Mark Smeaton."

"The queen's musician?"

"And more besides," replied Rich with a sneer. "Go through them, match them up, and report back to Cromwell."

"Match what up?"

"Gifts of money from one, with expenses paid in the other."

It was obvious what they were looking for in the ledgers: payment in kind from the queen.

"And what if they don't match up?" I asked.

"They will—because you will make it so."

There was a finality to his words that made me realize that even if I didn't find corresponding accounts, it wouldn't matter. Cromwell made Wall Street financiers look like missionaries. But he had my brother, and his power over the queen's situation meant he controlled Alice's whereabouts too.

The threat was clear. I *had* to find something to incriminate the queen.

<hr>

I pored over the ledgers until my eyes were seeing numbers and Tudor script in triplicate. Mark Smeaton was paid one hundred pounds a year from the king's purse, but he had also managed to purchase horses and expensive clothes that were way beyond his means. Someone was paying him extra, but I had found no evidence it was the queen.

I wasn't the only person in this poisonous court who was being set up.

Rich eventually left the room as the sun set. My entire body had seized up and my ass was numb from sitting on it most of the afternoon and early evening, but the moment I heard his footsteps fade, I seized my chance. I went straight to his desk and started looking for an address.

Cromwell's house in Stepney.

I had found a map of London on the large table where I was working. It was archaic, but I had been given a copy of this map in my dossier. I had memorized palace names and knew how to trace a route from Greenwich to Stepney. It was about five miles. I was fit. I could run it in half an hour; it would take even less on horseback.

Cromwell was smart, though. He probably knew that I would eventually track down my brother. The chief manipulator would also know that I stood a good chance of getting to Alex before anyone realized I was missing. And so he had deployed another round in the arsenal of weapons I had inadvertently given him.

Alice.

By separating the three of us, Cromwell had ensured that if I made a choice to save one, it would immediately condemn the other.

The candle in front of me was almost burned out. I pulled it from its waxy foundations and held it over the parchment I had been writing on. The corner took flame and the oily paper was quickly engulfed. The heat pressed against my face, making my eyes water. The orange flames threatened to burn my fingers. I knew it wasn't normal to crave pain, but it was such a release. I just couldn't cope anymore with making decisions about my life, and the lives of those I loved and cared about.

I could burn down this whole palace, I thought. Every room was a mass of kindling just waiting to be ignited. I could start a fire in every corner, and the court would be so preoccupied with saving itself that I might have time to save Alex *and* Alice.

"Put the flames out, Charles," said a voice from the door. "Playing with fire will only get you burned."

Grinch was standing in front of the closed door. I hadn't even heard it open.

"What are you doing here?" I gasped. "I was starting to think you hadn't happened."

"Your assignment is crumbling around you," she replied. "I expected more."

"Cromwell has taken Alex to his house in Stepney. A...Aramis isn't here. I don't know if either is alive."

I had been about to say *Alice,* but there was a ringing in my head. I chose to take it as a warning sign. None of us knew why Grinch had dragged Alice back in time to an assignment that wasn't hers, and Grinch hadn't been prepared to offer up the reason when I last saw her.

"Alexander is alive," replied Grinch impassively. Her scarred face wasn't moving. She wasn't even blinking. "But you have disappointed me, Charles. Director Asix and I gave you an assignment instruction and you have deviated from that task. With your tunnel vision, you have placed valued Assets in mortal danger—"

"That wasn't me!" I cried. "Don't you dare blame me for what's happening to Alex right now."

"I am speaking of more than just Alexander. I, for one, am

in a timeline where I should not be. You care too much. Love is weakness—you know this."

"Then *why are you here, dammit?*"

Although what I really meant was, why was Alice here?

"To remind you of your failings," said Grinch. "I have been monitoring the timeline from the institute, and the timeline you were supposed to be writing has gone dark. You know what that means, don't you?"

Gone dark? Yeah, I knew what that meant. Assignments were always based on either success or failure. Going dark meant failure. Ultimately, failure wasn't an option, so other Assets would be sent back to correct the failing of original Assets who had reached the line of zeros without success.

The latter were punished by The 48, and if they were newer Assets, and disposable...

Was Grinch here to kill me because I was failing? Was Grinch here to assassinate—dispose of—me?

I had often wondered how I would react when faced with my own mortality. And yet the fear I'd thought would consume me at the end wasn't there, not really. Not for myself. It was Alex who was my main concern now. If I could protect him, get him safely back to the twenty-first century, then I would submit myself to whatever fate Grinch had in store for me.

"I'm not here to dispose of you, Charles," replied Grinch, as if reading my mind.

"If you touch my brother—"

"I'm not here to remove Alexander, either," she added. "You asked earlier about Aramis. Well, I am now your Asset contact on this assignment."

"Why? What happened to him?"

"Aramis is dead," replied Grinch, as calmly as if she were telling me what the weather was doing.

"What...how?"

"Let's just say it was his time."

Grinch was cold at the best of times, but there was a strange gleam in her eye as she spoke. Her jaundiced skin flushed, and the long scar flared as if illuminated as the blood rushed to her face.

Grinch was *happy* that Aramis was dead.

"So. What is your plan?" she asked, slowly limping across the room toward me. I started to back away. I didn't trust her. Even hurt, she was still almost certainly lethal.

"I'm going to get my brother."

"Wrong answer. What's your plan, Charles?"

"I'm going to get my brother," I repeated, more forcefully.

"Wrong answer."

"We can play this game all you want," I snapped. "But you aren't going to make me—"

"Your assignment timeline has gone dark," repeated Grinch. "Remember your training, Charles. There is no escape."

Grinch wasn't just throwing words at me—that wasn't her way. She was repeating a line from a section of The 48 Tenets.

Do not fear death. But do not make death your friend. Death is your master and your servant. There is no escape. For it comes to all in the end.

I didn't want to die.

"How can I get the assignment back on track?"

"What have you done wrong?" asked Grinch. "Think hard, because in less than ten days this assignment will go critical."

"But I don't know what to do," I replied. "I can't get Henry to consider other Protestant women. He wants Jane."

"You must think."

"What's the Rewriting? I asked you about it when I first saw you back here. You went a strange…a strange color."

Grinch stopped limping toward me. Her cheeks pulled in slightly as her nostrils flared. I had embarrassed her.

"*Rewriting* is the term used for deliberate sabotage during an assignment."

"But Alex and I aren't sabotaging anything," I replied.

"The Assets on the official assignment are rarely the Rewriters," Grinch responded. "The saboteurs may not have even shown themselves to you."

"People attacked Alex—in this time. They mentioned the Rewriting, and they wanted it to continue. Which means there are other Assets here. Was Aramis a saboteur?"

"You have set things in motion that have to be undone," said Grinch. "Loyal Assets are scared—it is not a state they are accustomed to. Your assignment was to ensure that Jane Seymour and Henry the Eighth do not become betrothed. I am now ordering you to kill her."

"I will not!"

Grinch inhaled and didn't seem to stop. She tipped her head back as her chest expanded like a balloon.

"Love is a weakness, Charles."

"I know. I've been told often enough."

"Do you?" snapped Grinch. "Then could you please explain to me why this important timeline in the Religion Eradication program has gone dark?"

"I don't know. And I don't know why you're not talking about our countdowns. We're still in the flatline stage. We have time. I think you need to show more patience. You've called it dark too early."

"The reason we have called this assignment dark," cried Grinch, "is because the target, and the Asset sent to remove her, care too much for each other. Now, what do you have to say to that, Charles Douglas?"

fifty-three

Margaret

I sobbed into the abyss of my own making.

Yet there was no one to hear me.

No one other than the maid who came with the brothers from Cleves.

I had trusted Cromwell.

I was a fool.

Alexander of Cleves had been spirited away. And the look his brother gave me at the joust told me that he knew. He knew I'd betrayed him.

I had betrayed him—risked his life in order to save myself. I had tried to manipulate his brother's future by putting myself in it.

Charles of Cleves could have been my ally, yet I had made of him an enemy more dangerous than Cromwell.

For the king's man dealt with matters of the head.

I had wounded Charles's heart.

<hr />

I screamed into the abyss.

What had I done?

The maid from Cleves came to me, but she had little time or empathy for a woman far higher in rank than she.

"Are the queen's rooms to your satisfaction?" she asked. "I have asked another lady-in-waiting, but all she can do is cry too."

"You will refer to me as milady," I snapped, desperate to take my anger out on someone who by birthright deserved to be suffering more than I.

The impudent creature just shrugged. "A yes or no will suffice," she said. Then she bent down close to hiss in my ear. "You're going to be sharing those rooms when the queen arrives. And if I find out you betrayed the brothers of Cleves, I will do everything I can to make sure you share the scaffold, too."

fifty-four

Charles

Grinch's words had frozen me in place.

"What are you talking about?" My voice sounded tight. "I don't *care* for her—we barely know each other."

"I've seen the future, Charles. I live it. Do you think you are the first to develop feelings for an assignment target and have those feelings reciprocated?" replied Grinch, not unkindly. "The history of The 48 is littered with Assets who struggled with their emotions. They are deemed casualties of war. You and your brother are unlike other Assets of your age. I have watched you both and I know you could be the future. But your inability to rein in your emotions will be your downfall if you don't get it together."

"I'm an Asset. My downfall is already written. As is yours."

Grinch straightened. There was something imposing about her figure that added to her height. It was the stiff way she held her head, almost like an animal sensing danger. Her neck was several inches longer than most people's, and with the newly added scar across it, she looked ferocious, almost wild.

"Get the assignment back on track, Charles," said Grinch slowly. "My order to kill Jane Seymour stands. Keep the royal line in England Protestant. TOD is already putting the pieces in place for Protestantism to fade naturally in the twenty-first century. So if you fail now, Charles, your very first assignment, then you will have no one to blame but yourself for what happens next."

"You're threatening me?"

"I see promise in you, so I'm giving you a chance to rectify the anomaly," replied Grinch. "The 48 has invested seventeen years in you and your brother. Other senior Assets would not hesitate to kill you and Jane now and be done with it."

"How do I know The 48 is even active anymore? You said yourself that The 48 was under attack—from forces inside and out."

Grinch pulled a cowl around her neck to cover the scar and tucked it neatly into her dress.

"There will always be The 48, Charles," she replied. "Because there will always be a Termination Order Directorate. The power is too immense to stop. It's only the personnel that will change."

"And Aramis was part of that change?"

"Aramis and his coconspirators were not the first to seek change at The 48," replied Grinch. "And they will not be the last. But they were fools for thinking they could take on Director Asix...or me."

"Where are you staying in the palace?" I asked.

"In the shadows, where we should *all* work from," replied Grinch. She was preparing to leave, but I still had so many questions. It was pathetic the way I was ready to cling to a person from my other life, but it was the only existence I knew.

"Did *you* kill Aramis?" The words blurted out of my mouth like an unstoppable force. Grinch faltered by the door. Her hand was on the cast-iron latch. For a moment I thought I saw it trembling, but then Grinch pulled her shoulders back so tightly the blades were almost touching.

"Yes, I did," she replied. "And I will kill them all if I have to in order to preserve the true order."

Grinch was totally institutionalized. She was getting close to the age of disposal, and yet she was still prepared to do the absolute bidding of TOD and The 48.

I had to get away from this. I had to get my brother away. And Alice. But could we make it on our own in a world—the so-called *real* world—in which we'd never actually lived?

I had perfect control over my feelings about Jane Seymour, I told myself that evening. I was just getting close to her to get her away from Henry.

So why couldn't I stop looking over at her?

The court was dining together in Greenwich's Great Hall. The queen was absent, which meant Henry was in a good mood. She still wasn't under arrest, but it was only a matter of time now. The king ordered the musicians to play long and loud as eleven courses of food were delivered from the kitchens. The smell was suffocating. Roast boar competed with chicken. Hams with glistening fat took on the smell from huge beef joints still dripping in blood. I couldn't stomach any of it. My nerves were being shredded like the meat being pulled apart by the king's rotting teeth.

Jane was three seats away from the king. As the evening wore on, I saw her forced to move up the table until eventually his frame was almost smothering her. That made me sickest of all.

"You barely picked at your plate, Charles of Cleves," said Lady Rochford as the court began to disband for the night. "It is not good for one's constitution to have the appetite of a sparrow."

"Perhaps instead of mocking me, you should be looking for your husband," I replied. "I noticed George Boleyn wasn't at dinner, but then, I suppose he's probably with the queen, seeing as he clearly prefers the company of his sister to the company of his wife."

Lady Rochford's cheeks blazed. I had embarrassed her and I was glad.

"Good eve to you, sir," she said, dipping into a barely there curtsy. I didn't reciprocate with the formalities.

Then I saw Edward Seymour being called to the side of another duke, and I couldn't resist. I knew where Jane's lodgings were.

I waited in her bedchamber, half hidden behind a folding screen in case someone came in.

Hiding.

What the hell was wrong with me? I was hiding in a woman's bedroom. Had I completely lost my mind? Forget if anyone else discovered me closeted away like a stalker—what if Jane came in and found me? This was inappropriate in *any* time in history.

I was absolutely losing my mind, and it was all because of Alex. When he was with me, I had a purpose—which was usually to protect him. But when he wasn't there, it was like I was missing part of my sensibility. I couldn't make decisions; I could barely function. Back at The 48, I was one of the top trainees in the Imperatives, but out on an assignment by myself I was a mess. Aramis had thought teaming us up was a mistake. He clearly couldn't have been more wrong.

And now he was dead, too.

"Charles!"

Jane's exclamation at finding me in her room was loud. A slim hand flew to her mouth as she quickly pushed the door closed with the other hand. She should have screamed. It was what I deserved.

"I'm so sorry." I put my hands out in supplication. "I shouldn't be here. I'll leave now. Please forgive me, Lady Seymour. I...I missed you."

"Wait," replied Jane, placing a hand on my arm as I went to pass her. She smelled like lavender, but there was something else, something unpleasant.

It was the king. The image of him pressing against her during dinner surfaced in my brain. I tried to push down any feelings of revulsion. Grinch was wrong. I could control my emotions. Jane was the only friend I had here anymore.

"I just wanted to see you," I said, "and when I saw your brother called away..."

"If my brother discovers you here—"

"I know. They'll kill me. But you're the only one in the court who doesn't judge me. I like speaking to you."

"I have wished to converse with you, too, yet my brother is now at my side like a second skin."

"I wish *my* brother were."

"Where is Alexander? I have been so worried for him."

I slumped into a chair. The weight was already starting to lift, not just physically but mentally. Screw the Seymours. I just wanted to talk. They couldn't take friendship away from me.

"Cromwell has Alexander. As surety."

"Surety against what?" asked Jane, taking a seat in an ornate armchair across the room. Her hands automatically crossed on her lap. The distance was crushing.

"I am one of those investigating the queen's *improper* behavior," I replied. Jane wasn't stupid. She was one of the queen's maids of honor and the front-runner now for the transference of the king's affections. Jane knew exactly what was happening.

"So Cromwell has taken your brother to ensure your compliance and silence?"

I nodded. "I don't know what to do. I want to save him, but the thought of doing so at another's expense is sickening."

"Then why not ride to Stepney and flee? You don't have to stay in this court, Charles. Return to your homeland. Others are doing the same, albeit in silence."

"I can't. There's Alice...you remember Alice?" Jane's lips tightened as she nodded. "Alice has been moved to the Tower. To make preparations for the imminent arrival of the queen. So if I flee with Alexander, I won't have time to get to Alice too."

"I am aware; Lady Margaret was called away too. The queen will be permitted her ladies with her."

"Will they die too?"

"Die? Do they expect to find the queen guilty?"

"They *will* find her guilty," I replied. "And it's hateful to say, but it's you I'm more concerned about."

Jane smiled. "Your concern is touching, yet unwarranted."

"How can you stand being near the king?"

"For the same reason you walk by his side, play tennis and archery with him, counsel him, and bear his rages," replied Jane. "Do not labor under the pretense that I am unaware of what the men at court say and do. There are those who attempt to turn the king's head one way; my brother and kin have the king pointed in my direction. I am a possession of more than just Edward."

Jane was right. The 48 had marked her down as a possession of time, and by delegation of an assignment, that was exactly what

I had done. Jane would never know the truth, but she already knew the strategy behind it.

"Come with me." I stood up, and the chair I was sitting in squealed back with a noise that set my teeth on edge.

"Where?" replied Jane, tilting her head to the side.

"Away from this place, this court. We'll get my brother and Alice and—"

"Charles, you jest, surely?"

I slid down onto my knees in front of Jane; she didn't recoil. I could swear she moved closer to me. Her hands were still clasped together on her lap. All I had to do was reach out and touch her.

"Run away with us, Lady Jane. Bad things will happen to you if you stay here."

"Bad things? What do you mean? Charles, what do you know? The queen—"

"I'm not going to incriminate the queen. I've raised this with the king before and I'll do it again—I'll push for her to be given the same settlement as Queen Catherine. This time it will work. I can save everyone. I know I can. The king is mad, but I can stop him."

But Jane Seymour was looking at me as if I had gone completely crazy. Her hands separated, but instead of reaching for me, her fingers pressed into the chair arms with so much effort, they started to turn purple.

"Please leave, Charles," she whispered. "These are words of treason, and with them you are frightening me."

"I didn't mean to, I just—"

"I admire you very much," she interrupted. "But I know my place in the court, and my future—"

"You don't!" I cried. "You don't know your future. I do."

"Leave now, or I will call for the guard," said Jane. Her eyes were glistening. I felt sick. I had screwed up my chance to save her.

"Lady Jane—"

"Leave now...I beg thee."

"I'm sorry, milady," I said, standing up. "I will go. Do not think ill of me for my behavior tonight."

"Do not think I don't care, Charles," called Jane. "For I do—so very much."

If Jane thought that would make me feel better, she was wrong.

For the next three days, I spent every waking hour near Henry, if not engaging directly with him. I was as jovial as possible. If Henry found me diverting, then he would not allow Cromwell and Rich to enlist me in their campaign against Anne.

But it didn't matter. On the fourth day, Anne appealed directly to Henry in front of the entire court.

It was April thirtieth.

---

18 21:51:02

In four days' time, our assignment would be critical. I hadn't seen or heard anything of my brother in nearly a week.

Then Alice returned from the Tower of London.

She looked a shell of her former self. It was early in the evening and I was heading to dinner when I saw two maids carrying buckets of water to an outhouse. One stumbled, and her pail dropped to the ground with a heavy clang before soapy water cascaded over the gravel. The other maid didn't stop to help or even ask if the other was okay; she just scuttled away. The fallen girl was holding her left side as if her ribs were hurting. Then she looked at the sky.

That was when I realized it was Alice. Her curly hair had been cropped short and I could see sores around her mouth. I ran toward her and helped her stand.

"Alice...Alice..."

"Charlie!" cried Alice. She threw her arms around my neck. I had never been so happy or relieved to see anyone in my life. I squeezed her tightly, but she gasped in pain.

"What happened? Are you hurt?" I put her down on the ground but didn't release my arms from her waist.

Alice nodded. "My ribs...let's just say I got into a bit of a fight at the Tower."

"Guards?"

"Yeah."

"What did they do to you?" Anger was rising up in my chest again, and I didn't fight it. Tudor England had undone seventeen years of Asset training in the space of a month.

"Charles, really? I handled them." Alice winced as she arched her back. "That's not to say they didn't give me a good beating in the process. And that Lady Margaret didn't lift a finger when one of them dragged me out of the queen's rooms by my hair. It's thanks to her that I nearly got scalped. She told them I was infected with lice."

"Why did Lady Margaret turn on you?"

"Probably because she's terrified and she didn't like the fact that a maid had the audacity not to care about her status or her life."

"I'll find out from Marlon who the yeomen were," I replied. "Two guards who can't walk straight should be easy enough to find. I'll take great delight in throwing them in the Thames with rocks tied to their necks."

"Your chivalry is touching," said Alice, using her thumb to rub my chin as if she were erasing something. "But as I said, I don't need it. And you don't look well, Charlie. How's Alex? I've been trying to keep an ear out for news, but he wasn't mentioned. Even Lady Margaret was trying to get word of him, for her own benefit, obviously, but all the talk from everyone is about the queen. They've already tried her in their heads."

"Everything's a mess, Alice," I replied. "Alex has been taken to Cromwell's house in Stepney as a bargaining tool to make sure I do whatever Cromwell wants. I haven't seen Alex for nearly a week. I don't even know if he's..."

I couldn't say the word *alive*. Simply uttering it with a negative was too prophetic for someone who was supposed to write time.

"He is. You're twins. You would know otherwise," said Alice resolutely.

"I've seen Grinch, though."

"Grinch is here?" Alice went pale.

"Yeah. She claimed to know that Alex is alive, but I don't know how much I can trust her."

"What else did she say? Did she tell you why she brought me here?"

I shook my head. "I spoke to her, but I said nothing about you. Grinch has gone mad. She killed Aramis."

"Aramis is *dead*? But does that affect the assignment, the future, our future?"

"There isn't a paradox. Aramis's life timeline wasn't compromised. But Grinch was going off about The 48 being under attack and something about loyal Assets being scared."

"The 48 is finished?"

"Not according to Grinch. Grinch said it would always be there because TOD would always be around. It was just the personnel at The 48 that would ever change. But Alice, from the sound of it, I think there's something major going down."

Alice's mouth dropped into a perfect oval. I could see her tongue, which was coated in an unhealthy white layer, making it look like she'd licked chalk.

"I don't want this anymore," I said quietly. "I want out."

"We just have to stay alive for the next two weeks."

"Grinch has now ordered me to kill Jane."

"You knew there was always a chance you would have to assassinate her."

"I won't do it."

"If you don't, Grinch will."

"Then I'll kill Grinch."

"Would you?" asked Alice. "Could you?"

And I knew that I could.

Everything I had been taught, everything that had been forced upon me since I was old enough to remember my own name, was wrong. I understood that now.

But I was still a trained assassin. And that knowledge was finally going to be used.

fifty-five

Alexander

Everything about Cromwell's house terrified me: a creak on the stairs; the tapping of a tree branch on the window; and the voices—especially the voices.

Even the food left in my shabby room was an enemy. It was only after I allowed a mouse to nibble at it, and saw it still scurrying a half hour later, that I decided to take a mouthful.

In retrospect, I should have eaten the mouse. It probably would have tasted better than the pig's slop that Cromwell's cook had concocted.

And all the while I thought of my brother. A single player in the most dangerous court the English monarchy would ever know. Forced to navigate an assignment by himself.

He needed me, and I needed him.

Where was he? Why hadn't he come for me?

In the morning, I was awakened by screams. At first I thought they were mine, but I came to and realized they were coming from elsewhere in the house. The noise seemed to go on for hours: heavy boots on the floorboards. Shouts. Begging. More screams.

But it was the pleading that was the worst. I tried to block the noise out, but it burrowed into my bones.

And then, just as abruptly as it had started, it stopped.

I didn't want this anymore. I wanted out.

Out of this house, out of this assignment, out of The 48 altogether.

fifty-six

Charles

Alice was back. That meant I could make a plan to get the hell out of this mess. For good. Time was running out, but I was calm. I wouldn't get a second chance. I started formulating a mental list of what we needed.

Number one was obviously my brother—I wasn't going anywhere without him. Number two was a place for me, Alex, and Alice to hide out until our forty-eight days were up. Number three was the painting of Cromwell by Hans Holbein, which would ensure that the three of us *would* return to the twenty-first century and the Louvre.

And number four was securing Jane's safety.

All four priorities were achievable. I knew Alex was at Cromwell's house in Stepney, and thanks to my snooping, I knew where the house was. Once I had my brother, I knew we would be able to find a safe house. Marlon could help with that. The painting by Holbein was in Cromwell's lodgings in Greenwich Palace, and because the old fool was far vainer than his appearance indicated, it traveled everywhere with him. The painting was also the easiest requirement to keep an eye on, because it wasn't as if anyone else in the palace court were going to take it. So unless Cromwell moved about, it would stay where it was.

The biggest challenge was going to be trying to save Jane, and it was her fate that weighed heavily on my mind. I hadn't been able to convince her in person to run away with us. I needed another way. My concern was exacerbated by another discussion I had with Henry, who had risen early on the first day of May to inspect his horses for more jousting and demanded that I accompany him to the stables after breakfast.

"Tell me, Cleves," said the king, running his fingers down the neck of a glossy chestnut horse. "What is Cromwell waiting for? I keep expecting to see the papers for the French woman's arrest any day, but they are never forthcoming. I am getting impatient."

Anne wasn't even called the queen anymore.

"Cromwell is not a man to be rushed, Your Grace. Better a job done properly than quickly with the risk of failure."

"But it will be done soon?" inquired the king.

Oh, yes, I thought. *My* job will be completed very soon. And I'll be away from you and your madhouse court of murderers and schemers before you can arrest *me.*

"Of that I am certain, Your Grace," I replied diligently.

"She is beautiful, is she not!" exclaimed the king, tugging on the lead of his horse.

"A very impressive horse, Your Grace. She should win you many tournaments this summer."

"I wasn't talking of the horse, man," snapped the king. He slapped the horse's back. It shuffled its hind legs nervously and then went back to eating from a hessian bag that was being held over its nose by a groom.

"Forgive me, Your Grace. Whom did you mean?"

"I know you have whispered about other ladies since you have been in my court, Cleves. Yet I am enamored of one alone. You cannot have failed to notice my words of love and adoration."

"You mean Lady Seymour?"

Stay away from her, you murdering bastard, I thought.

"I am moving her into even finer lodgings," replied the king. "You were right in your opinion, Cleves. Jane is indeed queenly, and she will be mine."

"If that is what Lady Seymour desires, then I pray for your happiness," I lied, my stomach gripping with pain.

"Go back and tell Cromwell that," said the king. "I have decided. Jane is mine."

But I knew that the words were not for Cromwell's benefit. They were for mine.

<hr/>

"You studied the horses with the king this morn," said Cromwell. "How was his mood?"

I was back in Cromwell's dark and dingy chambers. Being in this room was suffocating.

"Why don't you ask him yourself?" I asked. "You're his favorite person in all of Christendom. Why do you need me as your conduit?"

"I am not avoiding anyone," replied Cromwell. "I am choosing my moments to be in his presence. Choice of one's own actions is the greatest freedom we have in this life."

Choices? Funny, I thought, coming from a man who controlled everyone like puppets.

"The king's mood was fine. He said he was moving Lady Seymour into better lodgings."

"So he has chosen?" said Cromwell quietly.

"Yes."

"You do not approve?" asked Cromwell.

"My approval counts for nothing."

"On that we can both agree." Cromwell stood up and coughed. He stumbled as he reached for a white handkerchief. "I have been in this room for too long. Charles, we will leave within the hour."

"Leave for where?"

"Stepney."

My stomach lurched with a sensation I had not felt in a long time. It was excitement and...hope.

"Will I be permitted to see my brother?"

"Of course."

Forget the Quickening. This was the best high in the world. Being apart from Alex had felt like something deep inside was stretching away from me and I had no way of reeling it back in. Just Cromwell's words were enough to feel that pull again.

And I was never going to let Alex out of my sight again. I would tie us together if I had to.

"Thank you."

I had never said two small words with such sincerity before.

Cromwell smiled with one side of his mouth.

"You are still my man?"

"I'll do anything."

"Go and pack. You'll need a change of clothes...and bring something to wear that you aren't fond of. Clothing that can be... disposed of."

I wasn't fond of anything I wore in this time. Alex and Alice and I were going to look like complete idiots once we traveled back to the Louvre in Tudor clothing, but we would cross that bridge when we came to it.

I had an hour. I needed Alice. She was sitting on my bed when I got to my room. It was like the fates were finally aligning.

"Cromwell is actually taking you to Alex?" she exclaimed. "But that's wonderful."

"I know." I was grinning like an idiot, I couldn't help it.

"And you're serious about getting away?" asked Alice. "You aren't going to get Alex and then change your mind and go all serious and culty on me?"

"*Culty* isn't a word, Alice."

"You know what I mean. Promise me that this is the beginning of the end of our time in The 48."

"It is," I replied, throwing clothes into a chest that one of Cromwell's men had brought up to my lodgings. "There will be a few more things still to do."

"Like what?"

"I can't leave the existing history to take its toll on Jane's or Anne's life."

"We're not responsible for them."

"I am," I replied. "If Jane marries that monster and has Prince Edward, she's going to die. I won't let that happen. And I can't allow Anne to be beheaded, either. She hasn't done what she's accused of."

"Anne is vile, Charlie. She's responsible for as many executions as Henry is."

"I'm running away from The 48, Alice. And I'm leaving without having become an assassin. Do you understand how big a deal this is for me? I've been conditioned in death since I could remember."

"You like her, don't you?"

"Who—the queen?" I replied, knowing full well who Alice was referring to.

Alice's demeanor changed. Even though she was wearing a voluminous maid's dress, I could see that her whole physicality had become stiff. She was putting up an invisible wall in front of her.

"Alice, please don't…"

"Just get Alex and bring him back here," said Alice, and her tone confirmed my thoughts. Warmth had been replaced by ice. "Then we can work out a plan to go into hiding before our countdowns reach zero."

"Alice…"

"What?"

I found I suddenly had no words, and Alice's eyes filled with tears.

"I've done more things I've regretted than I'm proud of, Charlie," she said softly. "But I swear the worst thing I ever did was fall in love with you."

"Alice, please." I tried to put my arm around her, but she pushed me away, hard.

"Don't. Ever. Touch. Me. Again."

"Alice—"

"I'll find you when you're back from Stepney." And then she was gone.

My argument with Alice played over and over in my mind as Cromwell and I rode to his house. I was expecting the simple black carriage—a mode of transport only used by the nobility—to take us through built-up tenements and rickety wooden streets smelling of human waste, but the journey took us into the countryside.

We passed a large church with a long nave and a white stone bell tower.

"We won't be alone at Great Place," said Cromwell. "I expect discretion, Charles."

"Of course."

The carriage pulled up outside a country mansion. Pink-and-white blossoms covered scores of fruit trees, as far as the eye could see, and every time the wind blew, the blossoms would fall to the earth like confetti.

A small, squat woman opened the door, and I followed Cromwell inside. It was dark and gloomy, the antithesis of the riot of color outside. A shiver rippled through my body.

"Where's Alexander?" I demanded.

"Madelaine?" responded Cromwell.

"This way, sir," replied the woman. She couldn't have been more than four and a half feet tall in her shoes, and I towered over her as she led me along a dimly lit wood-paneled corridor and up two small flights of steps that were uneven, with loose boards.

The house smelled like wet dogs, and I could hear a repetitive thudding like something being continually dropped on the floorboards. As I reached the last stair, I pulled my knife from my boot.

. . . I'm leaving without having become an assassin.

The words I had said to Alice suddenly rang hollow.

The woman pushed a door, which swung open with ease. And there he was. Alex was sitting in a chair; his chin was resting on his chest. A gray woolen blanket was wrapped around his shoulders.

I tried to say his name, but the words got stuck in my throat.

Instead, I flew across the room and slid on my knees, ending up by his legs. Alex flinched before he had even opened his eyes. Dark circles, like week-old bruises, surrounded his eyes like thick frames on a pair of spectacles.

"If I'm dead, you weren't the first person I expected to see in the afterlife," he croaked.

"You aren't dead," I whispered, taking his hands in mine. "You're very much alive."

"Not for the want of people trying to kill me."

"I'm never leaving your side again."

"I appreciate the sentiment, but no offense, being with you twenty-four/seven for the rest of my life would be a horrible existence."

I made a *shush* noise and looked behind me to the squat woman, but she was either gone or listening on the other side of the door.

"I'm going to get you back to Greenwich and Alice. And then—"

But Alex was shaking his head. He was looking at someone over my shoulder.

"You have seen your brother, as promised," said Cromwell. He was standing by the door, his face bathed in darkness so that I couldn't see his eyes. "Now you must come with me."

Alex was furiously pawing at me, trying to grip my arm, but he had little strength. His mouth was in a flat line, his lips pursed together.

"Where are we going?" I asked, rising to my feet.

"We have arrested Mark Smeaton for treason," replied Cromwell. "And it will be your job to witness the *confession*."

fifty-seven

Margaret

I hardly recognized the fabric of my own existence anymore. One moment I was quiet and subservient, wearing the skin of the girl who didn't want to be seen around a court that was heady with the stench of treachery and blood. The next I was conniving, doing all I could to halt a marriage the king himself had decreed for me, in order to secure a better future for myself abroad. And now I was acting the part of a proud, highborn daughter trying to do her duty as a maid of honor in this hope-forsaken place. Giving orders for nothing but the finest of furniture and fabrics for the queen's apartments in the Tower. It was ridiculous. Everything was a sham.

The Lieutenant had ordered one of the jailers—a rough-looking man built like a Shire horse—to escort me around the Tower. *For mine own protection,* the Lieutenant had stated. The jailer talked at me of Queen Anne.

He talked at me of a future Queen Jane.

And he also talked at me of Charles and Alexander of Cleves.

He seemed to know them. Truly know them.

If indeed they were men of Cleves at all.

This man had a brutish nature. He spoke strangely of pain and death; almost fondly. He reveled in the screams and cries of those in the Tower. He called it his own personal symphony.

The truth was, he scared me.

But now, everything in this wretched world scared me.

fifty-eight

Charles

I stayed at Cromwell's country house in Stepney for less than an hour. By nightfall I was in the Tower of London, some two miles to the east. Not under arrest physically, but certainly I was a hostage psychologically. My role was clear: to witness the torture of the court musician, Mark Smeaton, and the confession that would be inevitable under the circumstances.

If I didn't, then Alex would suffer.

I now understood why Aramis had been so wary about Alex and me being paired as partners for this assignment. Just as I was starting to know my own mind, just as I was starting to break free, I had been brought back into the fold again. And it was the threat of something happening to my brother that was the spark. Aramis had even seen this coming.

Grinch had killed Aramis, and she had me exactly where she wanted. Cromwell, too. Two different times were combining to steal from me the tiny amount of self I had found, because whether I wanted to or not, I was about to become a time assassin. People were going to die because of me and my failures.

The rack was a fairly innocuous contraption on its own. It was a rectangular wooden frame with a thick roller at either end, and a number of pulleys and ropes were connected to the frame at both ends. By itself it looked like the frame of a bed.

But tie the naked body of a terrified young man to it.

312

Rotate the rollers in opposing directions.

And then listen to the screams and the sucking sounds and the popping noises as ligaments are snapped and bones are dislocated.

In seventeen years of experiencing death, I had never witnessed anything as barbaric as the rack. I wanted to end Smeaton's life, just to save him from what the jailers were doing to him.

<hr />

Mark Smeaton confessed to being the queen's lover before the night was through. It was I who untied his broken body and carried him, as gently as I could, to a cell in the Tower. I wrote my witness statement, and another of Cromwell's men took the news to the king's chief minister. Jailers slammed his dislocated joints back into place while I held Mark, and I felt no shame in crying with him.

As Mark sobbed, he told me he loved her. I didn't ask who he was talking about. I wasn't convinced he was really conscious, and I didn't want him to say any more than he already had.

<hr />

I didn't sleep that night as I sat by Mark's side. I was too scared of what nightmares my subconscious would bring to me.

<hr />

The next day, May second, Anne Boleyn was arrested. I overheard yeomen mockingly avowing that she had collapsed screaming and wailing at Greenwich Palace. How would they know? They hadn't witnessed it. The urge to take my anger out on other people was rising again. I ended up punching one of them so hard I knocked out three of his rotting teeth. The 48 had given me the skills for violence; the Tower had now given me a reputation for it.

Anne Boleyn arrived at the Tower of London on a decorated barge that sailed up the River Thames. From one of the towers I watched her calm demeanor as she walked through the Court Gate instead of the Traitor's Gate. There was no screaming or wailing—at least not while a single subject was witness. She was met by Lady Margaret and another young woman. Both were dressed in black and had white lace pinned to their hair.

I swear Lady Margaret knew I was watching. She looked up, straight into the window where I stood. I didn't move. Let her see me. I knew what she had done by adding my name to the list of alleged lovers of the queen. She wanted Alex; Cromwell wanted me as his man—body and soul.

I could see what Margaret saw in Alex. Obviously. But putting *me* at risk like that made my blood boil.

As for Cromwell, I hated him with every fiber of my being.

***

Anne Boleyn looked regal. Her head was held high; she even smiled and acknowledged the guards. *Queenly* was the word Henry had used to describe Jane. Yet his wife about to die was finally being exactly that.

But as soon as Anne was taken to her rooms—the ones that Alice had helped prepare—she collapsed. This time I could hear it. She was crying for her father and brother.

She did not yet know that her family had forsaken her too.

***

Alice arrived in the next barge, as did another four ladies-in-waiting who were shaking and crying with terror themselves. Watching from afar, I couldn't cry out to Alice from the small window, so she had no idea I was already at the Tower. I assumed she would have been forced to come back here after the beating she took before, or perhaps she had perversely agreed to come to prove she wasn't scared of anyone. I didn't know, but I would get her away as soon as I could.

—

16 17:49:13

Sixteen days left. In just over two weeks' time our countdowns would reveal a line of zeros and we would be dragged forward in time. If we weren't near that painting, then we would disintegrate.

I left the broken musician and went to find Alice. My assignment would go critical—according to The 48 Tenets—in two days.

As far as I was concerned, we were already there.

—

Windsor Castle had been a dank Gothic place, but the dungeons of the Tower of London were even worse. They were so claustrophobic it was as if the architects were trying to suffocate the prisoners before their execution. The stone steps were steep and circular, and the windowless corridors were narrow and oppressive. The queen was being kept in the far more luxurious royal apartment between two of the towers. They had been renovated just a few years earlier, so Anne's prison was a fine one. Alice had assisted in preparing them for the queen, and she would know her way around. Our getaway had to be quick.

—

I came across two yeomen near the lodgings of the Lieutenant of the Tower. They seemed scared of me and flinched back as I approached them.

I was Cromwell's man, as far as they were concerned.

"There is a serving girl with the queen. Her name is Alice," I said. "I want her."

The yeomen swapped looks, and without a word, one of them

went into the royal apartment. It was starting to spit with rain, but it was also humid and stuffy. Looking up into the dark sky, I could feel the weight of the storm clouds starting to gather.

"And I will require a litter back to Stepney," I said to the yeoman still waiting. "Make sure it is done—Cromwell's orders."

The yeoman nodded. "Aye, milord."

So this was how people got things done in this world, I thought. Get a reputation for brutality—or serving brutal people—and others will acquiesce without question.

"Charles!"

Alice came running down the steps, her short hair covered by a white bonnet that was untied.

I stepped back as she moved to hug me. She let her arms drop to her sides as her face fell for a split second. She curtsied.

"What is it, milord?" she asked.

"Come with me." My voice was detached, soulless. Utterly cold. I turned to the yeoman. "The litter—now."

"This way, milord," he replied. And he led me and Alice away from the queen's prison.

The rain was falling a little harder, and the first rumble of thunder growled in the distance.

"Come with me to Stepney," I said in a low voice. "We'll get Alex, get the painting, and go into hiding until this is over."

I could hear how dead my voice was. I barely had the stomach for living anymore.

"What's wrong with you, Charles?" asked Alice. She knew something was wrong—Alice always knew.

But I shook my head. I couldn't tell Alice what I had witnessed on Cromwell's behalf last night. If I gave my actions a voice, then I would have to own them. My entire existence felt contaminated.

I just kept hearing the screams.

"Have you seen Alexander?" asked Alice.

"Yes."

"We're going to him now?"

"Yes."

I wasn't being deliberately obtuse in my replies. I just couldn't find the will to speak. My throat was stinging.

Why wouldn't the screaming in my head stop?

The guard had led us to a gate where a small black litter was waiting. It was an enclosed black box that would be carried by four people. We weren't far from Cromwell's Great Place. I was finished here, and I wanted to be back with Alex before nightfall.

If he hadn't been moved.

Alice and I squished together on the seat, which had a red velvet cushion, stained and frayed. I wrapped my traveling cloak around her shoulders.

"I'm sorry for what I said to you at Greenwich," she whispered. "And for pushing you. I was so angry."

"It's forgotten. I'm sorry, too."

"Is Alex okay?"

I nodded, swallowing painfully. My sore throat was getting worse.

"What's happened, Charlie?"

"I did something terrible. I had no choice."

"It's okay." Alice slipped her fingers through mine, but I pulled them away. I wanted to hold her hand so badly, but my hands weren't objects to be comforted. They were instruments of torture as much as the ties and pulleys of the rack. They had written the death sentence for a court musician whose only mistake had been to love a queen.

"I can't…I just…"

"They threatened to hurt Alex again, didn't they?"

"Aramis warned me this could happen," I replied, pushing my head back against the wood and closing my eyes. We were jiggling left to right to left. We were on the move.

"Warned you what would happen?" asked Alice.

"That Alex and I being paired up was a bad idea. That we were too close and others would take advantage of that."

"Don't let what Aramis said would happen define what's actually going on here," said Alice. "Don't let them have that control over you, too. You are the only one who can resolve this. For you and Alex. I believe in you."

I opened my eyes and looked at Alice. "How can you still have hope, after everything we've seen and done?"

"Because once you've lost hope, you have nothing," she whispered. "And I'm not going to let them leave me with nothing."

Alice allowed me to trace a line down her face with my fingers, from her hairline to her jaw. Her skin was cold and dry. Her lips parted enough to let me see her tongue resting behind her teeth. She had the longest eyelashes of anyone I had ever met.

"I'm not going to let you play me, Charlie," replied Alice. "You need to make a choice."

"I'm not playing you."

"I still love you—you know I do."

"Don't use that word."

"Love, love, love," mocked Alice, and she crossed her arms in front of her chest.

"What do you want from me?"

"I want you to man up and start owning your feelings," snapped Alice. "And finish this. Ask yourself, Charlie, do you have what it's gonna take to get out of this mess?"

"Keep your voice down, Alice."

"You don't, do you?"

"In case you haven't been paying attention, I've been trying to keep you, Alex, and myself alive. So yeah, I'd say I have what it takes!" To make my point, I flung my arm wide out the litter window—and with such force that the curtain went flying out with it.

Alice burst out laughing and then quickly stuffed her knuckles into her mouth as the litter rocked.

"You're hopeless," I muttered, straining my eyes to see through the small vertical gap to the outside world.

"I'm sorry, Charlie," replied Alice. "It's just so good to see you smile."

Her words immediately sobered me.

"You didn't kill that boy, Charlie."

So Alice already knew what I had done to Mark Smeaton.

"No—but I've set him up to be killed," I replied.

"If the need came, could you do worse than what you've done?"

"Worse than torture someone? The only thing that's worse is to kill someone."

"And could you?"

I inhaled through my nostrils. We were traveling adjacent to the Thames, east toward Stepney. The wind was picking up, and with it, the stench of the sewage-filled river. The smell made my eyes water.

"If Alex or you were threatened, then yes, I could do worse."

"Really? Look me in the eyes and tell me you could be the assassin you've been trained to be."

I could see myself reflected in Alice's dark irises, which reminded me of Anne Boleyn's eyes. The reflection was a tired, haggard face I no longer recognized.

"I could do worse."

Alice's thumb dragged against my bottom lip, pulling it down.

"I want to kiss you," I said.

"Then do it," she whispered.

I murmured something incomprehensible as her lips met mine with an urgency that was hard and fast. Her hair was so short now my fingers couldn't wind into it, but that made the contact between us even more frantic. I loved kissing Alice.

I loved Alice.

fifty-nine

Charles

We stayed wrapped around each other in silence for the rest of the journey back to Cromwell's house. Adrenaline and nerves about my brother's fate combined again to create a maelstrom of rushing thoughts through my head. I played out dozens of scenarios, from finding him gone to finding him well.

All of them ended up with Cromwell dead.

I hated him. I hated him for what he had done to Alex, and I hated him for having so much power over me that he had turned me into the person The 48 always thought I could be. Cromwell had sped up the process like a professional.

It ended now. Ownership of my life and death was mine—no one else's. And even if I couldn't see a way out, I would go down fighting for what I now truly believed in.

<hr />

I ran into Cromwell's house and up the stairs. I couldn't remember the location of the room that Alex had been kept in, so I threw open every door until I came to the one I recognized.

My brother wasn't there.

sixty

Alexander

Charles, what has that box ever done to you?"

My brother was kicking seven hells out of a wooden box that was starting to chip and splinter. Alice was leaning over him, trying to calm him down. When he heard my voice and turned, he practically tackled me.

"Alexander! I thought—I thought...I couldn't find you," he said, holding me tight.

"Back still hurts, man," I groaned, but I didn't let Charlie go. Physical affection was actually starting to feel natural.

But Charlie pulled away and ruffled my hair, sending droplets of water cascading over my shoulders onto the clothes I had been given: a long nightshirt and black slippers.

"You look like an idiot," he said.

"I'm channeling my inner Ebenezer Scrooge," I replied, clapping my hand over my mouth in mock horror. "Don't tell The 48 I mentioned a work of...fiction for enjoyment purposes. I might get flogged...again."

"Don't even joke about it," replied Charlie.

"They've actually taken pretty good care of me here," I said, and it wasn't a lie. "I think a couple of Cromwell's housemaids are starting to get all maternal over me. Too bad their cooking sucks."

"Speaking of that bastard, do you know where Cromwell is?" asked Charlie.

"I haven't seen him since yesterday," I replied. "He disappeared not long after you did. Where did you go? What were you doing? No one would tell me anything."

Charlie led me over to the chair by the window and sat me down in it like I was a child.

"You deserve the truth—all of it. Keeping information from you and Alice in order to protect you both hasn't worked. Just don't think less of me after I've finished. Knowledge is power, and we're going to reclaim it from those who have taken it away from us."

"Uh-huh." Sometimes Charlie got a little lofty on me. It was best to just hear him out. So I did. I listened intently as Charlie told me everything. I knew it was everything. There was stuff that no one would willingly claim ownership of unless they were consumed with guilt. What he had done for Cromwell since I had been taken from Greenwich: the first joust; the arrest of the queen; Jane; and even witnessing the torture of Mark Smeaton. Charlie held nothing back. It was almost confessional. Once he started speaking, it was as if he couldn't stop. I could physically see the weight of the words lifting from his shoulders. It was perversely cathartic.

And then he got to Grinch, and my stomach lurched as if ice-cold stalactites had started to grow inside my soul.

"She's here? But does that mean other Assets are?" By *other Assets* I meant the one who really scared me.

Like Piermont.

"I don't know," replied Charlie.

"And do we know yet why Alice was brought back here?"

Alice shook her head. "If I knew, I would tell you, Alex. She told me it was for my protection, but we all know she puts The 48 above all else. Which means the objective of your mission will still take precedence in her mind. Over me, over any of us.

323

That means she's crazy dangerous. Everybody outside this little trio is."

"Well, Charlie," I said. "If we're going to get back to Greenwich, it seems we ought to leave now."

<hr />

I stretched out and tried to stand. I had lost a lot of weight, and my muscle definition was nonexistent.

Charlie's jaw was set rigid as he watched me struggle. "Can you stay on a horse long enough to get back to Greenwich?" he asked.

"Alex can ride with me," said Alice. "I could pass for a boy with this haircut now. Just find me some different clothes."

"What happened to your hair, by the way?" I asked.

"Lice," replied Alice flatly. "And don't look at me like that, Charlie. They're gone. You aren't going to catch them from kissing me. God, it's as if I had girl-cooties or something."

"Look like what?" he exclaimed. "I didn't do anything."

"I wasn't aware cooties discriminated against the sex of the individual they were cootying on," I said wearily. Charlie gave me a weak smile. It was pretty pathetic, to be honest. Watching him watching me trying to joke, trying to reclaim my identity in the only way I knew how.

"When you two have quite finished," said Alice. "We were getting on horses and that was as far as the plan went."

"Right. So, Alex. Can you ride with Alice?" asked Charlie.

"Yes," I replied. "Let's go."

<hr />

The servants in Cromwell's house didn't try to stop us from leaving. Maybe they were used to people coming and going at all hours. Maybe they simply didn't care enough to try. Maybe, as far as they were concerned, we were dead men riding.

sixty-one

Margaret

The knife pressed down on my throat. The blade was as cold as winter; it made a sound, like mice scratching behind the walls, as it scraped down my neck. If the thick arm had not been holding me tightly around the waist, my legs would have given way beneath me.

"I have told you, sir," I begged. "I know nothing."

The jailer replied with five harsh words, spat with venom, that I had never heard before, but I knew they were not of foreign European lands. It reminded me of something, though. A voice, or voices, raised in alarm.

"Where is Charles of Cleves?"

"I know not, sir," I pleaded, my belly paining not just with fear, but at the large fist that was pressing into it, as if this beast were attempting to push out my very soul from within.

"He's taken his brother. And the girl. Where are they? I've been watching you for weeks. You've been in their inner circle since day one."

"Please, you are hurting me. I'll scream. I'll—"

The monster just laughed, a mirthless sound that chilled my very bones as he tightened his grip.

"Cry out, then," he snarled. Spittle landed on my neck. "But you should know by now, no one comes to rescue those who scream in the Tower. They never have, and they never will."

Fear such as I had never felt before was coursing through my body like a sickness. I was going to die in the Tower. I was going to die this very day.

"I dreamt of being close to one of the men from Cleves once," I replied, my breath ragged and short. "It was a fool's dream. They are..."

"They are what?"

The jailer spun me around so I was facing him. He was tall and bald, and his face and bare chest were covered in welts and scars.

He was the Devil—the stuff of nightmares.

Then his fist connected with my belly. Gasping for breath, I fell to the hard stone floor. Hot tears fell between my splayed fingers.

"They are what?" repeated the Devil. "What have you seen?"

"I...cannot—"

A boot connected with my shoulder. I screamed.

"What have you seen?" cried the monster once more.

"They are...they are sorcerers."

"Tell me. What have you seen?" My hood fell from my head as the Devil twisted his grip into my hair.

"Alexander of Cleves...he disappeared. Before the painting by Master Holbein!" I cried.

The Devil let go. Fear had sapped the last drop of courage I had. I collapsed onto the floor, sobbing. My chest pained with the effort. I could not breathe. I was too frightened to try.

How long I stayed there, I do not know, for when the Lieutenant found me, I was alone.

The Devil's voice stayed with me, though. Haunting my waking moments and the snatched occasions of fitful slumber.

And in the morn, with my gut and shoulder aching where he'd struck me, I recalled where and when I had heard that strange intonation before.

It was during a most desperate conversation between the brothers of Cleves.

The night I found Charles of Cleves close to death, foaming at the mouth like a poisoned, possessed dog.

sixty-two

Alexander

I sat in front of Alice, who had dressed in men's clothes, stolen from one of the many bedrooms in Cromwell's house. Even with a cap pulled down over her eyebrows, there was no way anyone looking closely was going to believe she was a boy, but from a distance we might just get away with the subterfuge.

I knew Charlie was allowing the fate of the queen to preoccupy him on the sunset ride back to Greenwich.

I could have used the quiet to recite the Tenets. Calm my nerves. But I could no longer remember a single one.

It was perversely freeing.

It was only once we arrived back and stabled the horses that I realized just how bad things were. A groom informed Charlie that Cromwell had decided Mark Smeaton's written confession wasn't enough to convict Anne, and had arrested courtiers Henry Norris, Francis Weston, William Brereton, Thomas Wyatt, and Richard Page—who, along with Weston and Brereton, was a knight—and George Boleyn, too.

Every name on the list that Cromwell had shown him—with the exception of his own.

"You can't go into the palace, Charlie," I said, groaning. My injured leg that had been cauterized was giving me a world of pain. "They might be looking for you. You'll be arrested on the spot. You have to hide now."

"We have to hide *you*," he replied. "I wouldn't put anything past Cromwell now. He'd have you in the Tower on the pretense of being me by midnight. But *I* have to risk it. We need to find Grinch and then find that painting. *Then* we hide."

"There's no need to look anymore."

Alice had already ducked out of view with such speed that I was left wondering if she had gotten off the horse at all, as the figure of a tall groomsman stepped from the shadows.

"Grinch," I gasped. I stumbled over a hay bale as I stepped back. Even the horses were whinnying at the appearance of the Deputy Director of The 48. She looked strange. Larger and unnatural. She was wearing men's clothes.

"I expected so much of you two," said Grinch. "Yet how little it took to throw you off track. Charles, what is wrong with you? I instructed you to carry out a very simple assassination when we last spoke. You are not as special as I thought, or hoped."

Charlie had told me of Grinch's injury, but the sound of her voice still shocked me into stillness. Charlie already had a knife in his hand, however. His eyes were flicking up and down Grinch's body. Through the eyes or in the neck? Which would be the easiest kill? That was what he was now thinking. Grinch was no longer an Asset in our minds, she was a target.

"Why are you here, Grinch?" he asked calmly. "These stables are never left unmanned. A groomsman will see you threatening men of the court and your head will be on the block before you can say another word."

Grinch made a noise of contempt. Her boots had a stacked heel, which aided the impression of height. Charlie and I were six feet tall, but she wasn't far off us. But there was something else about Grinch. More than the sickly green tinge to her skin. It was her eyes. Normally hazel, they were now almost as black as Anne's. But while the queen's eyes were mesmerizing, Grinch's made her look reptilian. She pulled out a long, thin piece of metal, like a tapered screwdriver. Even though the sun was almost gone, I could still make out the blood dripping from the pointed end.

"There *was* a groomsman here—and he isn't listening now," said Grinch.

"What do you want from us?" I asked, trying to buy Charlie some time to formulate a plan to get us the hell out of here. Alice was still completely hidden in the shadows.

"I am *demanding* your complete, unwavering loyalty."

"Yeah, yeah. Self-preservation and the assignment are all that matter," I said.

Grinch smiled grimly. "And that's only the small picture."

"What do you mean?"

"You see, Alexander, before I slit his throat, Aramis had been helping Piermont recruit Assets for a splinter group from The 48. A faction dedicated to profit and warmongering, rather than to the betterment of history. I knew Aramis was going to recruit you both, but I thought your seventeen years of training would have conditioned you to do what I said. I forced Alice Tanner back to this time to protect her from the treacherous words of Aramis; I believed you would both be a loyal and true influence on her, but clearly I was wrong. So it's time to get as dirty as the traitors. And if that means you die—then that's what will happen. Religion must be eradicated once and for all. That is the instruction from TOD, and I will see that it is done. But this assignment will succeed, with or without you, now."

sixty-three

Charles

Grinch's words hit me like a bucket of ice water. "What do you mean?" I demanded. "What the hell are you saying?"

"Aramis and Piermont were breaking away from The 48," replied Grinch slowly, as if she were speaking to a small child. "They saw religion as a military objective. They didn't want it eradicated, they wanted it radicalized. Piermont was leading the recruitment of several other traitors, and Aramis had a number of trainees marked down as recruits—including you and Alexander. Alice Tanner was another one. She had quite the aptitude for subtle insubordination back at The 48, which appealed to them. As I said, I believed, with the correct influence, she could be kept in line. You too."

Alice was slowly inching around the back of the stalls, unseen by Grinch. I knew that her best chance of getting away was for me and Alex to keep Grinch distracted.

"Piermont and Aramis didn't count on anyone discovering their deviance as I did," continued Grinch. "But after my partner was murdered, I developed tunnel vision. I cared for nothing but the well-being of The 48, and I knew deviations when I spotted them—no matter how well disguised."

"Murdered?" said Alex, his voice far higher than usual. "Assets don't talk about murder. That's criminal. *Assassination* is the word we've always been told to use for ending a life. Or *termination*."

Alex's breathing had hitched up to a whole new level. He was already in so much physical pain, I could only imagine what being near an elder of The 48 was doing to his psychological well-being. Alex was nowhere near full fitness. If it was fight or flight, Alex wouldn't have a chance at either.

Grinch snorted again.

"I don't mean my Asset partner for any given assignment. I mean my life partner. He wasn't an Asset. I fell in love with an Outsider who lived near the institute. I was lucky that Director Asix thought highly of me, or I would have been disposed of when he found out. It is that ability to sense weakness in others that has kept The 48 thriving. And I learned from my mistake. The rules were then tightened to ensure that Outsiders and Assets did not have cause to meet around the institute."

The fact that Grinch had once fallen in love with an Outsider came as a shock. If her partner had been murdered, it went a long way toward explaining her control of her emotions now.

"Who murdered him?" I asked. "Who killed the Outsider?"

"Take a guess," replied Grinch. She held up the bloody thin blade and twisted it from side to side, as if admiring the slick new coating. "But I have to give Piermont credit where credit is due. Even as a trainee, he could put more experienced Assets to shame with the clinical way he disposed of a target."

A movement between the far stables caught my eye; Alice was almost there.

"You didn't need to come back here, Grinch. You should have had more faith in us. Alex and I know we have to complete the assignment," I lied. "And we will. We will assassinate Jane Seymour to ensure the continuation of the Protestant faith for the time being—and then we'll return to The 48 to continue the

Religion Eradication program. We aren't on Piermont's side. Nobody has ever tried to recruit us to anything outside of The 48. This infighting has nothing to do with us."

"You need to listen very carefully, Charles," replied Grinch, taking several steps toward us. "Piermont intends to be a power ruler. He needs you to fail this assignment. Piermont wants religion to endure because throughout history, it has been a root of war, right alongside territory and natural resources and personal ambition and the desire to conquer. He wants those roots to thrive too. Do you have any idea how much *money* there is in war, Charles? And Piermont is hungry for the power. For the mental challenge of pitting people against one another through time. So again, he *wants* you to fail. Aramis wanted to recruit you, but Piermont did not. And make no mistake, Piermont *will* find you."

"Was Piermont responsible for the attack on Alex?" I asked, gritting my teeth and clenching my fists at the thought of the damage done to my brother.

"No," replied Grinch. "That was Aramis."

"I knew it!" exclaimed my brother.

"Aramis and two traitor Assets who had already been recruited attacked you to distract you both from the assignment, but he watched over it to ensure you were not killed. It was Piermont who left the bloody calling card on your bed."

"What about poisoning me?" I asked. "Aramis or Piermont?"

"That was Piermont too," said Grinch. "But he is a wanted man in this time and had to be quick, which meant he was sloppy. I have no doubt he is lying low somewhere. Aramis has been lying to you both from day one, but he allowed you to be saved from the poisoning because he wanted the Douglas twins to join the

new faction. Aramis had a twin too—once. He was rather sentimental in the end—and a fool."

"They found out you knew what they were doing, didn't they?"
I asked. "Which one tried to slit your throat?"

"Neither," replied Grinch. "That was Willem. He was recruited,
albeit under duress apparently, and told to kill me. He failed. I did
not."

I thought back to Paris and what we had witnessed from the
hotel room. Did that mean Katie was now under Piermont's own
brand of leadership now? Was she even alive? The possible truth
of either was too awful to comprehend.

"You killed Willem?"

"I will kill every traitor if I have to."

"You're insane."

"Charlie, shut up," hissed Alex.

"Charlie's right—you are insane."

Grinch looked confused for a split second. Then a spade made
contact with her head with a metallic thud that made my ears
ring. I don't think Grinch even saw it coming. She slumped to the
ground. A small cut just above her right eyebrow was bleeding
slightly, and her eyes were open. Had Alice killed her? I couldn't
tell, and I wasn't about to attempt resuscitation.

"*Run!*" cried Alice. She was still gripping the spade like a base-
ball player about to swing at a pitch.

We didn't need to be told twice.

Alice and I made it out of the stables, but by the time we reached
the first of the many fruit orchards, Alex was lagging behind. I
stopped and ran back to him, but he urged me on.

"Leave me," he commanded.

"Never again," I replied. "Get on my back."

"You can't carry me," said Alex, limping badly with one hand on his injured leg.

"Get on my back," I repeated, bending over.

"I'm a hundred and fifty pounds, Charlie."

"Correction, you were," I replied, grabbing his arm. Alex acquiesced and slipped his arms around my neck. The exhalation of relief pushed into my back. I tucked my arms under his knees and carried him piggyback through the orchard. It was dark, but the lights were blazing in every window of the palace, lighting the way.

"Where are we going?" I called. "We can't go back to my lodgings in case Cromwell and his men are waiting to arrest me. And I'm not convinced Grinch is dead, and she'll know where the lodgings are."

"Shhh," hissed Alice. She had stopped running and was crouching down by the thick trunk of a plum tree. I came to a halt next to her. Alex slipped from my back and held on to the trunk.

I mulled over everything Grinch had said as I watched a changing of the yeomen guard by a large set of double doors. But remarkably, it wasn't my own destiny that was troubling me. It was the fate of Mark, Anne, and Jane that weighed most heavily on my mind. Maybe it was the darkness amplifying the noises in my head, but I could hear Mark screaming, Anne crying, and Jane...

Jane was laughing.

I shook my head. After everything Grinch had just told us, I needed to try one last time. "Okay," I said urgently. "We need the painting of Cromwell, and then a place to hide. Then you two can stay out of sight and I'll try one last time to get Jane away."

"I suppose there is no point in arguing with you, is there?" asked Alex.

"Stubborn idiot," said Alice.

"You can call me all the names under the sun when we're away," I replied. "But at this point, I want Piermont's grand plan to fail just as much as I want to save Jane."

The three of us sprinted across the gravel. I slipped and stumbled in the three-inch-thick covering of stones.

We reached the doors. My eyes were so accustomed to the darkness that they immediately watered from the blaze of light that greeted us.

"Down this way," said Alice. "I know a back route to the kitchens."

She led us down stone staircases and up again. I could hear the noise of clanging pots and smell the wood burning before we reached the main arched entrance to the kitchens.

"They'll be cooking for dinner," said Alice. "In here."

The three of us bundled into a small antechamber. It was freezing cold and was filled with dead birds hanging by their feet from the ceiling on one side, and cuts of meat tied with string on the other side. A lone torch at the far end illuminated the storeroom.

Alex turned over a wooden bucket and sat on it. His eyes and nose were running.

"Now I know why Assets are decommissioned at age forty-eight," he groaned, wiping his face. "Can you imagine having to do this when you're old? And what your blood pressure would be like, knowing time is running out?" He looked at his wrist pointedly. I noticed it was shaking, and I looked at him questioningly.

"Withdrawal. And you have no idea the willpower it is taking for me not to overturn this bucket and use it as a toilet."

"Listen," said Alice urgently. "We divide up our plan. I can find Marlon and ask him to hide us. Charlie, you can go and get Cromwell's painting, get it back to us, and then do whatever you're going to do to save Jane. Alex, you'll need to stay here, hidden until Marlon can get you out."

"What about Piermont?" asked Alex.

"We know he's here—but he isn't going to show his face around a court that treats him as a wanted man," said Alice. "Grinch can get away with that because she's known from previous assignments, but the one thing Piermont needs right now is to lie low. That means if we stay in the palace, we're unlikely to run into him. It's worked so far."

"Hidden in plain sight?" said Alex. "What do you think, Charlie?"

"I think this will work," I replied.

"Do you think Grinch survived being a piñata?" asked Alex.

"She survived," said Alice. "I'm strong, but that spade rebounded through my shoulders like I was absorbing the whack."

"Charlie," said Alex quietly. "What if you can't persuade Jane to leave? We will have to leave her—and she will die."

"I won't fail," I replied. "We have a plan. Let's make it work."

I ran out of the cold storeroom. The route to Cromwell's lodgings was clear. Any member of the court with common sense was sticking to their rooms at this point.

I kept going over the timeline that I was trying to write.

If Jane turned down Henry and ran from him, her life here would be over if they ever caught her. If she did marry him, she would die in childbirth.

What would saving her really mean, then? Could I take her back to the twenty-first century with me? Could she hold on to me and travel into the future? It was an idea that I was mulling over in my mind because of Alice. Her countdown was behind ours— and we were planning to take her back with us. If Alex held on to Alice, I could hold on to Jane.

I was so preoccupied with that thought that I didn't hear the ragged breathing in the room until it was too late. I hadn't even reached the large wooden desk with all of Cromwell's papers. One paper in particular, a list of names, was the one I wanted, as well as the painting.

A black bag was quickly placed over my head, and as one thick pair of arms held mine behind my back, a heavy, blunt object was smacked into my stomach four times. It was then brought down twice on the back of my neck.

The assignment and my existence went dark.

The bag was wrenched off and the cold water was such a rude awakening that my back teeth bit into my tongue. Another drenching. I took a mouthful and gagged. It was vile and smelled like the water of the Thames. I was tied to a rack.

I was in the Tower of London. In the same room where I had managed the torture of Mark Smeaton. My feeling of poetic justice and redemption lasted a second before the terror set in.

"Don't do this," I begged.

"The king has ordered your arrest," said Cromwell, his face haggard and swollen. Edward Seymour stood behind him, smiling with thin lips that almost disappeared into his red gums. "You are charged with high treason against His Majesty and with fornication with Queen Anne."

"You know I didn't!" I cried, pulling my bound wrists down. The rope simply tightened.

"This isn't my doing," said Cromwell. "I did not show him the list. I implore you, Charles. Confess."

"I didn't do anything. You know I didn't."

Cromwell nodded to a hooded man who was waiting patiently by the door. The king's chief minister did not stay to watch.

The hooded man took the wheel, and my screams matched those of Mark Smeaton.

sixty-four

Charles

Day became night became day. If it were not for the countdown in my wrist, I would have had no idea whether a day or a year had passed. My existence had become a blanket of pain.

---

14 00:00:00

   Assignment—critical.

   My existence—critical.

   Fate of Alex and Alice—unknown.

   Whereabouts of Grinch and Piermont—unknown.

   Screaming in the Tower of London—incessant.

---

13 23:59:59

   Food was brought into my cell by a yeoman. So far I had been given hard bread, broth that looked like puke, and some fatty slabs of meat. I hadn't touched any of it. The hunger pains in my stomach were a constant companion that joined the rest of the hurt done to my body.

   "Where's Cromwell?" I asked every yeoman.

   They never replied.

---

12 23:59:59

   I wasn't chained, but I could barely lift my arms. One had gotten close to dislocation, and I feared that any sudden movement would pop the ball joint out of the socket. My wrists and ankles were grazed and bloody from where the ropes had worn away layer after layer of skin. My ribs and stomach pulsed with pain— courtesy of the beating I'd taken in Cromwell's lodgings.

But it was my sense of self that had taken the biggest punishment. Who the hell was I? I just didn't know anymore.

***

11 23:59:59

I started eating the broth. The hunger pains had won. I found two live maggots floating in the greasy brown liquid. I picked them out, flicked them onto the ground, and watched them writhe. I was so delirious they multiplied before my eyes until the floor of my cell became a white, squirming mass.

***

The hooded man came back. He was alone. I couldn't fight him as he picked me up and tied my arms and legs to the rack again. I screamed until I started choking on my own vomit. My left shoulder dislocated with a rush of pain that felt like fire.

"Where is your brother?"

Snot and tears combined down my face. I didn't have the will to breathe anymore, but I would not admit to treason or give them my brother.

The masked man left. I could hear him laughing.

***

10 09:02:14

I had stopped watching the countdown at the precise moment the days changed. The numbers were starting to fade away, just like my life.

Where were Alex and Alice? Had they gotten to safety in time? They had a couple of allies in the palace in Marlon and Thomas.

It was the hope that they hadn't been taken by the king's guards that kept me from going completely insane.

Even when the hooded man returned and beat the soles of my bare feet with a stick.

"Where is your brother?" he repeated.

They definitely didn't have Alex.

He was safe.

Nothing else—not even my own life—mattered more.

---

9 22:42:03

I continued to add to the symphony of screams in the Tower of London until I was dragged out of the cell and placed in a bath of tepid water. Two elderly women in black smocks scrubbed me with a wire brush until my skin was raw.

I was taken to a different cell, more like a sparsely furnished room. It had a bed with blankets, a writing table and chair, and a scenic view over a courtyard.

A scaffold was being built. I was too weak to stand and watch, but the banging of nails into wood became a repetitive death drum.

Dinner was on a plate—that was a first. Potatoes, pink meat that tasted like ham, a yellow lump of something that had the bitter taste of undercooked root vegetables, and bread that was warm.

I ate it all so quickly that I threw up. Yet the effect a couple of almost-nutritious meals had on me was remarkable. My head started to feel less fuzzy; my arms still ached, but I could lift one now almost to my head, although full rotation of my shoulders was out of the question; and the cramps only came in bursts.

So when a yeoman unlocked the door to my cell, I actually had thoughts of attempting to overpower him.

"Charles, it is I, Marlon," whispered the guard who had been our friend since day one. He placed a tray of food on the writing desk and put his finger to his lips. "I don't have long, but you have friends, and we are working to free you."

"Oh Marlon, thank you, thank you," I cried, stumbling across the cell on bloody, blistered feet. "How is my brother? And Alice?" Have you seen them?"

"Alexander and Alice are in hiding outside the palace walls. They are both safe and with someone I would trust with my life."

"Tell them...tell them I am not afraid," I said. "Tell them I *will* get to them."

Gripping my shoulder, Marlon grimaced and shook me gently to show his support. The damaged tendons in my shoulder throbbed with heat-filled pain.

"I will return after sundown, and will try to bring more food."

Once Marlon had turned the key and locked me in my cage, I ate my meal slowly, staring out of the narrow window at the scaffold below. It was almost finished. One person, dressed in a black cloak, was staring up at it. He took off his feathered hat and scratched his graying hair.

It was the Lord Steward, the Duke of Norfolk. He was the queen's uncle. Probably here to pay his niece a visit. The Duke of Norfolk put his feathered hat back on his head and hurried away. The workmen were almost finished. Two men half dragged, half carried a bale of straw across the grass and dropped it next to the short steps that led to the main platform.

It was straw for soaking up blood.

The duke was followed minutes later by a woman. She crossed the grass quickly, as if she didn't want to be seen. A ghostly shadow in black. Then she stopped and looked directly up toward my cell window.

It was Lady Margaret. Even at a distance, I could see fear etched across her face, once plump and pink, now pinched and pale.

I removed myself from her line of sight and pressed my forehead against the cold stone of the cell. The sun was starting to dip beyond the battlements, splaying orange fire across the city beyond. It was the year 1536. In just over one hundred years' time, this city would burn to the ground in the Great Fire of London.

I should never have made a friend of Jane Seymour. Friendships were discouraged in the Tenets of The 48. If I had ignored her and just concentrated on the king, which was exactly the plan Alex and I had decided upon that first day in the court, then I wouldn't have had any problems in letting her go.

Mark Smeaton
Henry Norrys
Francys Weston
Wyllyam Brereton
Thomas Wyatt
Rychard Page
George Boleyn
Charles Cleves

There was one more name to add to Cromwell's list.

Anne Boleyn

I could hear Alex's sick sense of humor invading my head.

They're gonna need more straw.

I started to laugh. I continued to howl long after the sun had set and the sky had turned from orange to indigo to black.

---

3 18:03:19

Hope. What did that word even mean anymore? I couldn't remember. Those four little letters seemed so important, and the exhausted frustration I felt at not being able to recall the definition was the straw that broke my back.

My defeat was aided by the hooded man who had reappeared with a flaming torch after sundown. The torch wasn't to light the gloomy room. It was prodded and poked at me until I was cowering naked in a corner, having removed my rags for fear they would catch on fire and I would burn alive.

This wasn't just torture, this was a sick game.

"Where is your brother?"

Same question. Same cadence. Did they really think I would hand over my brother?

"I don't know, you freak!" I screamed. "So just kill me. Go on—do it. *Just do it!*"

I was shaking, mouth frothing. My anger had drained what little strength I had.

The hooded man just laughed. It was cold and heartless. He had none of the crushing guilt I had felt after torturing Mark Smeaton. Which meant he enjoyed it.

"Thought you might like to know, the queen refused to confess," said the man. "She was found guilty anyway. She'll die. And once she's gone, I'll go after the other one. The one you've been trying to save."

It was the most he had said to me in several visits.

And in that moment I knew him.

I stumbled back, landing in a heap on the ground.

"Finally worked it out, haven't you," said Piermont, pulling off his mask. He leered at it, as if it were his most prized possession. "I do love the Tudor court, even if it doesn't love me. But it's amazing what you can get away with when you're masked."

"You said... you said she's been found guilty..."

"The queen, idiot," replied Piermont. "That timeline is already written. Pity the other one isn't as pretty, I could have had some fun before—"

"You stay away from Jane."

Piermont sniggered. "You're in no position to dictate anything. Anne Boleyn will be executed, and then you're going to die as well, along with the other traitors. By the blade of an executioner on the block out there, or by my hand, it makes no difference to me."

"Grinch said—"

"What Grinch said is of no consequence. She's a high-and-mighty, sorry excuse for an Asset with no imagination and no sense of a grander picture. She looks like a toad but she has the brain of a sheep. Blindly following The 48's orders, and they blindly follow the TOD initiative. Not me. Religion isn't going anywhere, and I intend to profit from that fact where I can. So you and your weak-minded brother had to fail. I wanted to kill you right away—but Aramis thought you could be persuaded to join us. Now he's dead and I'm calling the shots. You will fail in this assignment, the other Assets will fail in theirs, and I'll be free to move ahead with my own agenda."

Rather than explain just what his agenda was, Piermont lunged forward, grabbed my hair, and shoved a rag into my mouth. I could only move one arm, and I was no match for his size and strength as he dragged me out of the cell, down two flights of cold stone steps, and into another room that had manacles bolted into the stone wall.

My arms were wrenched upward and my hands strapped in. I stayed conscious just long enough to feel the agony of my shoulder dislocating again.

***

When I regained consciousness, I was on the floor and naked, save for a pair of stained baggy briefs. There was little relief in my shoulder, the ball of which I had to push back into the socket by myself.

But the most pain now came from my wrist, which was bandaged crudely with a blood-soaked piece of cloth.

I untied it, wincing as dried blood pulled away from the raw skin, instantly setting off the bleeding again.

***

Piermont had cut out my countdown, for no other reason than to terrorize me with the thought of having no idea when the end was here.

sixty-five

Margaret

He will send for me."

No, he will not, I thought, but I kept my counsel. The walls in the Tower had keener ears than the court.

"His Grace will send for me and pardon me. Once I have knelt at his feet and begged his forgiveness."

You are a dead queen walking, I thought.

And despite my best efforts, I was once again a person of no consequence who might or might not keep her head, depending on the whim of a madman who sat upon a golden throne with a replacement, my compliant friend, waiting in the wings.

⟶

"He *will* send for me," insisted Queen Anne a third time, turning her head away from the open window, which had a perfect view of the block that was waiting patiently for her slim, pale neck to rest upon it.

The crowds were already starting to gather for those who would die today. I could hear the excitement in their voices. Bloodlust was the Tudor way, and the court embraced it with relief that it was not their blood being spilled.

"What will become of us?" whispered Lady Cecily. She was on her knees, praying. Every waking moment was spent begging His mercy.

The king had none. We all knew that.

Except for the queen, who was keeping her composure even now.

In complete denial that she had been cast aside for another, in the same way the loyal and beloved wife before her had been removed with the ruthless efficiency that only the Tudors could provide.

"When I am forgiven, I will take you all with me to the country. My daughter and I will still require attendants. Elizabeth is of royal blood. The rightful heir. We will have a court to rival—"

"There will be no court. There will be no forgiveness," said a voice. Dull and without accent. As if the life had been sucked out of it.

The voice was mine. I could keep my own counsel no more.

"How dare you—"

"We are all going to die in here, and you will be the first," I said. "The king will not forgive a wife he believed cast a spell on him and bedded half his court."

The goblet of wine missed my head by a short distance. The red wine left a trail across the floor like...

...like blood. What else.

"Get out...get out...*get out!*" screamed the queen. "You treacherous snake. I will see your head roll before mine."

I was not with Her Grace when the heads did start to roll. I still had some freedom of movement granted to me as a lady of the court who was not yet under suspicion or arrest. But if I was to leave this world for His Kingdom, then I had to cleanse my soul of the evil that had seeped into it.

One final chance at redemption for my ill deeds.

It was Thomas Ladman, of all people, who aided my request for absolution. He had been moved to guard those in the Tower in readiness for the horror of what was to come. Whom or what he was guarding was of no consequence to me. I simply needed him to bring me what I needed.

I stole out of the Tower on the eve of the sixteenth day. The air was tempered with the threat of rain. I pulled my hood over my headdress as the first spits of precipitation fell onto my face.

"I have brought them to you," whispered Thomas. "As a sign of my unwavering loyalty."

"I do not need your loyalty," I replied. "And these will be the last requests I ever make of thee."

"Margaret..."

"Take me to them."

Thomas sighed. He was resigned to letting go. A wooden door to the left opened with a creak. I was outside the Tower walls and had unbarred myself to every danger known to a highborn woman in this time. Yet I had to finish this.

I entered into darkness. A single candle was illuminated.

"What do you want?" asked the chambermaid from Cleves. "And know this before you speak: I don't trust you. Betray us, and I will not think twice about slitting your throat."

"I wish to help you to free your brother and return to your homeland—wherever that may truly be."

"Why?" asked Alexander of Cleves. His face was illuminated by the candle, and it showed all too well how badly he had been treated in the court of the king. His eyes were sunken and his skin looked mottled.

"I have done you both ill. And I am truly sorry. I merely wish for the chance to put it right."

"Why did you do what you did?" asked Alexander. "Why did you betray my brother?"

"I was frightened. I saw a chance of a better life. One free from fear and tyranny. I am a woman in a court…in a world of powerful men with bloodlust in their souls. I simply wanted to…"

"Survive," said the chambermaid.

I nodded.

"What do you propose?" asked Alexander.

sixty-six

Charles

It was over. I would never get back to the painting before my forty-eight days were up.

I was going to die. The radiation would tear apart every atom in my body as it searched for the time passage home.

Would it be painful? Would it be quick?

Did it matter?

⸻

The next time food was delivered by a yeoman, the yeoman wasn't Marlon. The meal was a bowl of broth, steaming hot and filled with vegetables. But every jangle of keys in the Tower corridors sent a surge of fearful adrenaline into my system that immediately killed my appetite.

⸻

It was May 17, 1536. I knew this because one by one, the men found guilty of improper conduct with the queen were sent out to die. They were all allowed to speak. I didn't watch from my window, but I heard them. There were only two voices I recognized. Mark Smeaton showed more bravery with his few words than I had ever done. He certainly didn't deserve death, even though he said he did.

George Boleyn was astonishing. His long speech was eloquent, and the crowd paid their respect to what was clearly a fabricated charge of incest with his sister by staying quiet. That meant I heard the whistle of the blade all too clearly as it made its way through the air. There was a crunch as it sliced through muscle and bone. It was a more brutal sound than I could ever have imagined.

When I wasn't dragged out to the platform to join them, I knew I would never face a trial. Never hear the jeers of the crowd, baying for noble blood. My death would come to me here, in this cell. I would die alone. In secret. I would never see my brother again. There was no afterlife, no Heaven. I would rot down to nothing. My skin would become atoms in the air and my blood would sink into the foundations of the Tower to mix for eternity with the blood of countless others.

It was May 19, 1536. I knew this because the queen was sent out to die. It was early morning. I watched this one. The queen deserved my attention, and I deserved the haunting in my final hours. Her ladies-in-waiting were crying. Jane wasn't there; neither was Lady Margaret. I could see Cromwell in the crowd. I wanted the swordsman to fall off the scaffold and take his head off instead. Anne spoke, but her voice was so quiet I couldn't hear the words. She kept looking to her left. I think she believed up until the end that someone would stop her execution.

No one came. With a blindfold hiding the angle of the French sword from her sight, it sang through the air and the queen was dead.

The queen was dead. Long live the next queen.

How long did I have now? Piermont hadn't been back, but he had shown that he liked me to heal for a couple of days before inflicting more pain.

353

But seeing how brave the queen was in facing her death had lit a fuse in my stomach that was burning through my veins. I would fight back, one last time. I was going to die anyway. It might as well be now.

<hr />

The jangle of keys was my alarm. I wasn't allowed cutlery, presumably because it could be used as a weapon, but I had been trained by The 48 to improvise. After tying a musty-smelling cloth around my mouth to muffle my cries of pain, I had pulled on a wooden slat in the bed frame until it came free. The tendons in my shoulder sockets were on fire, but at least I had a weapon.

"Come on, you bastard," I whispered, holding the wooden slat like a bat. "Come and get me. One last time."

But it was Marlon at the door.

Lady Margaret was with him.

And Jane Seymour, too. I dropped the wooden slat.

"Jane!"

"Charles!"

"Lady Jane, Lady Margaret, you can only have a moment. If you are discovered—" Marlon spoke in a hurried whisper, the words running into one another as they escaped his mouth.

"Thank you, Master Chancery," interrupted Jane. "Could you leave us, please?"

Jane was wearing a black cloak, and underneath was a gold dress, threaded in thick blue cotton. Even in the flickering light of the torch she was holding, I could see she did not look well. Lady Margaret looked even worse. Her face was so drawn and thin, it was as if someone had stretched wax over a skull.

"Get her out of here!" I cried. "She's the reason I'm in here in the first place."

"It is because of Lady Margaret's bravery that I am here at all," whispered Jane. "Please, Charles. Listen to us."

"I am sorry, Charles of Cleves," choked Lady Margaret. "I saw an escape. I believed I saw it with you and your brother. I have come to realize that I am not strong enough to play at these games. If this is my last act, then please do not think ill of me."

"I—I don't think ill of your reasons, Lady Margaret. But you have been playing with our lives." As soon as I said the words, I hated myself for my hypocrisy.

"I know," she sobbed. "I will spend the rest of my life praying to our Lord for your forgiveness. If it is of any comfort to you, I am to be married to a Scottish earl, and it will not be a union of love or happiness."

"Of course that's no comfort!" I cried. The desperation on her face was hurting my stomach. I couldn't deal with this. I turned to Jane.

"What are you doing here? If anyone were to see you—"

"I couldn't bear it, Charles," said Jane quietly. "I had to see for myself. What have they done to you?"

Her long fingers caressed my face and wrists.

"You shouldn't be here."

"Your brother is waiting for you by the docks. So is the girl, Alice. Lady Margaret has put herself at great risk to help you."

"What if it's a trap? How can I trust anything she does or says?"

"They had a message for you," said Lady Margaret. "They said 'The painting has not been moved.' These are not words I could conjure on my own. They said you would know the intent."

"You have friends, Charles," said Lady Jane. "And whilst you may not be who you claimed, you have been a friend to me. I will not forget that... once I am queen."

355

"Don't do it," I whispered.

"He is my king," Jane whispered back. "It is an honor. And for the first time in my life, I will be more powerful than anyone else in Wulfhall."

"Look out my window," I replied through gritted teeth. *"That's the honor of being queen in this time. Blood-soaked straw. You're not safe here."*

"Who is safe anywhere?" replied Jane. "At least here, I will rule. I am to be the next Queen of England and I will be cherished above all others. And I can assure safety for you."

"I don't want you to do this. I will find another way out of here."

"Nowhere is safe in this court. Those who endure know what they must do. This is what I must do. I am not here to negotiate with you, Charles. His Grace and I are to be betrothed in the morn. I am here to say goodbye."

"We must go," interrupted Lady Margaret, pulling on Jane's arm. "We have done what we came to do. We need to return. You will already be missed."

"The king will be the death of you," I said.

"Not if I give him a son."

Especially if you give him a son, I wanted to scream. There must be a way out of this for all of us, but I just couldn't see it. Jane bit her bottom lip and looked down at the floor. I was suddenly conscious of how dreadful I looked and smelled. One pitiful excuse for a bath in days was not enough to wipe away the grime, pain, and shame of the Tower of London.

"I will remember you always in my prayers, Charles," said Jane.

"Don't marry him," I begged.

"Lady Jane, please!" cried Lady Margaret. "Someone is coming."

The door to my cell opened. Marlon was holding another torch, which illuminated him in an orange glow.

"Miladies, you must leave," he said.

Jane stepped forward and pressed something into my hands. "I will be forever grateful for your concern and confidence. And your friendship."

Lady Margaret said not another word before she scuttled out; Jane was out of the door with her smaller torch before I had drawn a breath.

I looked down at what Jane had placed in my bloodied hands. Crushed daisies, the same flowers I had given her at the joust.

<hr>

It wasn't Marlon or even Thomas Ladman from the yeomen guard who came to take me to the docks. Instead, it was three other men who didn't look older than me. I was quickly escorted out of my furnished cell in the Tower of London toward Traitor's Gate. Two bodies, blackened by the decay of death, were swinging from ropes. Two crows were snatching at the rotting flesh.

From there I was bundled onto a smaller barge and into the custody of two older men who had weathered, tanned skin that made them look like the carved wooden figureheads on a boat. They rowed away with me sitting between them, the small barge gliding gracefully through the water, which lapped at the sides with a gentle plopping noise.

I didn't believe for a second that I was being taken to my brother and Alice, even though I trusted Jane completely. Our track record for luck didn't allow me to. So I said nothing. I was just watching, listening, and thinking. I knew I could get away.

The only question was when.

The opportunity arose once we reached the shipping docks.

It was dark but cloudless. The moon cast a silver light over everything, making the men and women who worked the evening appear as ghosts. Crates were being hauled onto ships, and drunken laughter and shouts were punctuated by the odd scream that no one paid attention to.

I wasn't bound, but I had feigned frailty. I wanted my watchers to believe I was weaker than I really was. A couple of days earlier I had been a wretched creature, but adrenaline remained the best anesthetic for pain there was, and my release had given me the boost for one last battle.

I was escorted off the barge and led through the dock. There was a tavern on my left, and men were spilling from the doors and onto the damp cobbles. One sailor with no front teeth grabbed hold of one of my watchers to steady himself. He then promptly vomited over his boots. It was the chance I needed. As fists started to be thrown around, with no thought as to what they were hitting or missing, I made a run for it. It didn't matter where. I just needed to get away.

But days of being incapacitated, tortured, and underfed had left me seriously weak. I ran into a side alley and took a left, staying parallel with the river to keep my bearings, but I was gasping for breath within a couple of minutes. Pain wrenched at my side as my lungs burned. My legs alternated between feeling as heavy as concrete and so light I wasn't sure if I was putting my feet down at all.

But the darkness and the crowds were my allies as I stayed hidden. In my court finery I would have been robbed on the spot, but dressed in black pants and a filthy white shirt, I was one of them.

The echoes of shouting were following me, but they were diluted by other cries and objects being thrown. Even a few dogs were adding to the symphony. But I had done it. I had escaped from the malevolence of the Tudor court.

The thrill of my success was short-lived. I would die if I couldn't get back in front of the painting, and with the count-down gone, I had no idea of time.

I slumped against a wall and slid down. Defeated and alone.

The shouting was getting closer. *Let them take me,* I thought wearily. *Throw me in the Thames and drown me in crap. What a perfect metaphor for my life.*

And then I heard my name.

"Charles!"

"Charles!"

"Where the hell is he?"

"Charles!"

"Alexander, stop yelling and running around like a madman."

"Charlie!"

"Alex!"

I didn't have the energy to stand. Instead, I crawled on my hands and knees in filth toward Alex and Alice, who were sprinting toward me.

"Jane did it...she did it!" cried Alex, throwing himself down into the muck with me. I must have yelped like a wounded dog, because he immediately rolled off me. "Charles, holy crap. What happened to you?"

"We'll compare scars later," I groaned. "I think we have less than a day left."

"I wasn't happy about trusting Lady Margaret at all," said

Alex, hugging me again, despite our dual pain. "But let's be honest. She was dealt a really crappy hand. And I feel sorry for her."

I sighed and nodded. "She was hoping for a better life."

"Like we are," Alice said quietly. "And unlike Lady Margaret, we still have a chance at it."

"Okay. So where to now?" I asked.

"Greenwich isn't far from here," said Alice. "We have time."

We all knew we didn't, not really. But it felt good to hear.

<hr>

We slept under a tree after walking for what seemed like forever. It was only when I collapsed for the fifth time that Alex refused to go on until I had rested. When I woke up, two red squirrels were nibbling at the frayed leather of my boots. They scampered off as I jerked awake, my legs and arms twitching like a marionette's. Dew from the grass had soaked into my pants and shirt. I sucked on my sleeve and took in a little moisture. It wasn't enough to quench my thirst, but it was enough to line my gums, which were swollen and sore from neglect.

"It's supposed to be the end of spring," said my brother, stretching in a way I couldn't because of my damaged shoulder. "You wouldn't have thought it by looking at the gray sky. English weather is weird."

"That's what's weird?" exclaimed Alice. "We've time traveled, each been used as a pugil stick and worse, but it's the weather that's weird."

"I swear it's going to start raining—again," said Alex, putting his hand out as if to catch imaginary raindrops.

"Alex," said Alice incredulously. "Sometimes you can be a real idiot."

"But I'm handsome, and, unlike my brother, I can move my shoulders," he replied, climbing to his feet before gently helping me to stand. "So not everything is lost."

I didn't know what else to do, so I hugged him.

"If today's our last day, then I'm glad I'm with you," he whispered.

I just nodded and let my tears answer for me.

<hr />

We had traveled farther along the river than I had thought possible. Greenwich Palace was in the distance. And twenty minutes later, we finally reached the stables. Almost immediately we heard voices, so we slipped into one of the stalls and waited for the grooms' chatter to diminish.

As silence fell once more, I thought of Jane. She would be betrothed to the king today, and she would die after giving Henry a son. And then Jane Seymour would be a symbol of Catholicism for years. Some would even regard her as a saint.

"What are you thinking about?" asked Alice. "You have that look of deep concentration on your face."

"Jane. Grinch. Life. Death. Take your pick."

Alice kissed my shoulder. The one I still couldn't move.

"I've been thinking about Jane too," said Alex. "She dies in childbirth, doesn't she? Well, what if there was a way to save her? We'd never have got you out of the Tower if it hadn't been for her and Margaret. So that surgeon—the one who saved me. He was called Fiennes, wasn't he? What if we told him what was going to happen? He understood that we were different—even though he didn't ask questions. What if we gave him the idea that women die from infection? He knew about keeping wounds clean, anyway."

"He's considered an outcast. A physician for the prisoners because they're disposable. They'll never let him near Jane when she eventually gives birth..."

"Jane knows what she's doing," said Alex.

"She has no choice."

"You're very sweet, Charlie," said Alice, standing up in a fluid movement that was almost balletic. "But sometimes I think you were better off when you were fully indoctrinated by The 48."

"Are you saying I'm weak?"

"I'm saying you need to find the middle ground. You swing one way and then another. Life outside The 48 will be made of tough choices too."

"We aren't outside it yet."

"Then let's make our final hours mean something," said Alex. "And we don't split up. If we're going to die today, we die together."

He put his hand out; Alice placed hers on top. I went last, gingerly cradling both of their hands in mine with every ounce of strength I had.

sixty-seven

Alexander

We didn't have the luxury of waiting for nightfall. We had to get to Cromwell's rooms and the painting, and we had to set aside time for Grinch, whom we fully anticipated having to dispatch. Charlie's countdown had been butchered out of him, but mine was working.

———

0 0:59:35

Anne Boleyn had been dead for less than twenty-four hours, but I knew that, according to the history ledgers, the king would be betrothed to Jane today. That meant that the palace would be busy. Even so, we'd need to blend better than ever.

"I think we need yeoman clothes," I said. "It's our best hope of getting through the palace unnoticed. And we don't have time to ask politely."

Charlie nodded; Alice looked fierce. This was what we had trained for. It was perverse, knowing that we would be leaving The 48 forever after this, but that our final actions in another time would be exactly what they had shown us we would have to do in order to succeed and survive.

We had no choice.

The three of us made our way from the stables to the orchards. It was early in the day, so few people were around.

The first yeoman we came across was easy pickings. His clothes were too small for Charlie or me to fit into—once I had rendered him unconscious—but they fit Alice perfectly, and the hat was large enough to cover her short hair and most of her face.

We made it into the armory, and Alice and I teamed up to take out another guard. Charlie was only there for moral support. He could barely lift his arms, and his feet were still so badly blistered he was hobbling like an old man. I saw Alice wince more than once at the burns on his body.

It was my turn to look after my twin.

And anyone who got in my way would have hell to pay.

Charlie took the second guard's clothes. The pants were too short, but they would suffice. My clothes were stolen from a yeoman who came to check on the guard we had just disabled. Our success was fueling my adrenaline. In fact, I felt like I was on fire. No one would ever have thought that I had been near death myself just a few weeks earlier. I was totally owning life.

Which meant that it wasn't adrenaline at all. The reverse Quickening was starting.

"Charlie, can you feel your fingers?" I asked, feeling the grin spread across my face.

"Yeah," he replied, giggling. "It tickles."

Alice swore. "You can't do anything stupid now. Either of you."

Stupid? Stupid was this dumbass assignment that had used me and my brother as punching bags. When I got hold of Grinch . . .

Grinch. The green-skinned creature who had dragged Alice here, who had killed our contact, and who was going to kill us if we didn't get to her first.

I was going to find her, and end her.

"Charlie, Alex, listen to me," said Alice, blocking the exit from the armory. "You cannot go all Godlike on me right now."

"Where is Grinch's room?" I replied. "We're cool, aren't we, Charlie-boy?"

"I'm cooler than you."

"Never in a million—Marlon!" I suddenly exclaimed.

A third yeoman had appeared behind Alice.

"What are you doing?" asked Marlon, looking down at the bare legs of the two yeomen we had already undressed.

"We're—we're leaving," I said. Even with the Reverse Quickening flooding my bloodstream, I could feel my throat constrict.

This really wasn't fair. Any of it. I wanted more time with him. At least enough to tell him how *grateful* I was.

Before anyone could say anything stupid, I crossed the floor and kissed him.

It was a blissful state, just for a couple of seconds. When we parted, his eyes were wide with surprise.

"Sorry," I said. "I should have asked."

"Yes, Alexander of Cleves." Marlon was grinning. "And a lot sooner."

"Thank you, Marlon. For saving us all." I embraced him swiftly once more, then rejoined Charlie and Alice and the three of us headed for the door.

"Will I see you again, Alexander of Cleves?" called Marlon.

I didn't have the heart to tell him the truth. I wasn't sure I had a heart left.

The Reverse Quickening had steadied. We ducked through arches and hid in doorways as Alice led us to Grinch's room, the location of which she had found out from another chambermaid who had been cleaning it.

Grinch wasn't there.

"We don't have time to wait," said Alice. "It was a long shot anyway. We need to get to Cromwell's rooms now."

"She'll come after us," I said. "In the future."

"I know," said Charlie.

"We don't have time!" cried Alice. "If we don't get to that painting, then the fact that Grinch is still alive to get to us will be irrelevant, because there will be no *us* left."

Both Charlie and I were happy to let Alice lead now, so we kept in the shadows as we made our way to Cromwell's rooms. The place was deserted—no doubt everyone was getting ready for the imminent betrothal of Henry and Jane.

The radiation had already moved into the next stage, which was a feeling of intense nausea. Charlie was the first one to retch; my stomach ached so much I couldn't even manage that. Bile moved up and down freely in my throat.

"How much time do we have?" asked Charlie as we reached Cromwell's door.

"Less than ten minutes," I replied, herding us all through the entryway.

When we got inside, we all gasped—even though I had half expected the sight before me. Or, expected half the sight.

Grinch was there, waiting for us.

"I knew you would come here," she whispered. "And now you are going to see a real Asset carry out what you should have done the moment this assignment went dark."

"You know the sons of Cleves, Madame du Pont? What a small world we exist in."

It was the king's chief minister and master of death, I *hadn't* thought I'd see—and he was standing right behind her.

I reacted first. I grabbed Grinch around the throat and dragged her into a corner. Alice went for Cromwell and pointed a knife she had taken from the armory just below his Adam's apple, which was bobbing furiously.

Cromwell's hands were already raised in surrender, but Grinch was fighting back. Then Charlie joined me, and despite the obvious agony it was causing him, he and I combined to tackle Grinch to the ground. I placed my knee in the center of her spine to incapacitate her.

"Don't say a word," I commanded. "Because I swear I won't need a rack to reciprocate what you and your Asset friends did to us. I don't even mean here. I mean back home. To all of us. For our whole lives."

Grinch was coughing and shaking her head.

Grinch, Piermont, Aramis, Asix…they were all the same. Evil. The lot of them. And those who weren't evil were just liars.

"You were prepared to sacrifice Charlie and Alex for The 48. Now it's time you were *disposed* of, Grinch. Charlie, pass me those tongs from the fireplace."

But Charlie had staggered back.

"Charlie, we have to finish her," said Alice urgently.

Grinch groaned as Alice wrapped her hands through her hair, exposing her already wounded neck.

"No!"

"Charlie—"

"We aren't assassins. We aren't like them. We're not—we're not monsters, Alice."

"Alex?" Alice said. Tears were streaming down her face. I realized my cheeks were wet too.

"Okay," she whispered.

"Okay," I repeated. "Charlie, toss me some of that drapery cord." He did as I asked. I tied up Cromwell, and then Grinch. Then I got down in Cromwell's face. "This woman is here to assassinate Jane Seymour. When help arrives for you, you need to make sure she never gets near the next queen. Do you understand?"

"You'll never get away from this court," croaked Cromwell.

"Watch us," I replied. "We're not from Cleves, and you damn well know it. We're from a world that would make your head spin if you knew a fraction of what we know, and—"

"If you are not of Cleves, where are you from?" said another voice quietly.

And the whole world stopped moving.

Jane Seymour had stepped out of the darkness. Her gown was golden and edged in pearls. A necklace of rubies lay against her pale skin. It clashed with the peak of red hair just visible under a cream-colored hood.

"Jane! What are you doing here?" cried Charlie.

"My life changes today," replied Jane. "I wanted the privilege of being Lady Jane of Wulfhall one last time. I met Master Cromwell, and he asked me here to sign some papers. Madame du Pont was already here, and she asked me to wait. I never thought I would see you again, Charles...if that is indeed your name?"

"It is Charles. Charles Douglas."

"You're Scottish?"

Charlie smiled. It looked strange. Like he was saying goodbye to a character in a play whom he wanted so desperately to be real.

"No. No, milady. I'm a time traveler," he replied. "I'm from many years in the future. And I know yours. And I want to help you."

"I don't understand."

"I don't expect you to," he said. "But I'm serious when I say I know your future."

"My future, or my fate?" replied Jane. "This sounds like witch-craft, Charles Douglas."

"Charlie," I whispered, burning rising in my chest as I looked at the countdown. "We don't have long."

"We're leaving," said Charlie, taking a step toward Jane, and then another, and another when she didn't flinch away. "You saved me, Jane. Let me save you."

"You've saved me in more ways than you can imagine," said Jane, smiling with her eyes as well as her mouth. "Your love for your brother touched my heart, as did his love for you. When I am the king's wife, I will reunify his daughters. And then, God willing, I will provide him with a son."

"Charlie!" screamed Alice. "The countdown... I'm warning you."

"You *will* have a son," said Charlie, taking Jane's hands in his. "But you need to listen to me. Your son will become king, but you will become ill after his birth. There is a surgeon called Fiennes at Windsor Castle. You know him. He helped Alex. Fiennes will keep you well and free of infection in the days after. You have to call for him, even though the king's physicians will not want it. Do you understand me? You need to make sure Fiennes is allowed to tend to you."

"I will have a son?" whispered Jane.

"Yes, but you have to understand about the sickness that will follow—"

"Charlie!" screamed Alice again.

"Jane, promise me..."

But Jane was a picture of contentment. Her face was serene as she closed her eyes and smiled. She believed she was safe. That by giving Henry a son she would endure.

<hr />

I strode across the floor to the painting of Cromwell by Hans Holbein. Alice dragged Charlie away from Jane Seymour and twisted his face to look at the portrait.

"I can't wait here for my countdown to get to zero!" she cried. "Hold on to me and I'll travel through with you. Just don't let go of me."

My chest was contracting. I couldn't breathe.

"Vanishing point...vanishing point," Alice whispered. "Don't let me go, Alex."

My body was stretching through time. Cromwell's lodgings became a swirling whirlpool of color. I wrapped my left arm around Alice.

"Fiennes...Fiennes..." Charlie kept saying the same word until it just became a garbled noise. Jane held out her hand. I could see into my brother's head, as if we had become one entity moving through time. If he stretched far enough, he could take her with him. She would be safe with him.

<hr />

The floor was cold against my skin, freezing, biting. I was being flayed alive by Aramis again. It had all been a nightmare, and I was back in the clutches of Aramis and Piermont as they recruited for their own breakaway unit from The 48 and TOD.

I was dying.

"Don't...fight...it...Alex."

Hands were on my face. Callused fingertips.

"We...need...to...get...away...before...anyone...from...
The...48...finds...us."

I wasn't dying.

I was Alexander Douglas.

A time writer.

A time assassin.

And this was the beginning of my new life.

I was back in my own time.

And Jane and Margaret were dead.

sixty-eight

Margaret

Six seasons had passed since Lady Jane's betrothal when my dear friend and I at last heard the words the entire kingdom had been hoping to hear.

"You have a son, Your Grace."

The excitement in their voices was like warm sunlight flooding through the darkened room. I could have sworn to God that the physicians had actually torn down the heavy drapes that had covered every window during my dear friend's confinement.

She had done her queenly duty. She had given the king a son.

"Is he healthy? Will he endure?" she asked.

"He is a bonny boy, pink and princely."

Princely. I liked the sound of that word. It was musical. I could already imagine the bells that would peal across the kingdom, announcing that a son had been born to the king.

"His name is Edward," she whispered. "Prince Edward."

"Prince Edward," voiced a chorus. Their approval was obvious.

"You will be beloved and cherished above all others," I whispered, pressing a damp cloth across Queen Jane's forehead. "You have saved yourself and all of us. You are a saint."

Dampness was spreading across her thighs as the physician pushed down on her swollen belly.

This would soon be my ordeal and duty.

"I will be beloved above all others," whispered Jane, closing her eyes. "Above all others..."

It had taken three torturous nights for my dearest Jane—the Queen of Christendom—to bring her healthy son into the world.

Twelve torturous nights later, my dearest Jane—the queen who had sacrificed everything for duty—passed into His loving arms. At one point she had asked me to bring forth the surgeon called Fiennes, but he was not allowed near her quarters, despite her request.

The king went into the deepest mourning. A court that had been restored to order and serenity wore black and cried a river of true tears.

I was one of the twenty-nine official mourners who followed the king's eldest daughter Lady Mary during the queen's funeral at Windsor Castle. Queen Jane would be evermore thought of as a saint of her people and their Catholic faith.

I missed my friend. And I also mourned for the life that I, too, would never have. Felt guilt for the gambles I'd taken with other people's lives.

Once Jane was interred, I went back to my home in Scotland to await the birth of my own child. My husband, the Earl of Moray of the clan Douglas, was a distant man, aware that his obligation—like mine—was to serve.

I just did not know with whom his loyalties lay. Men on horses came and went at all hours of the day, and I knew that if Scotland went to war, my marriage was not enough to secure fealty to Henry.

I would always live in fear.

My son Charles was born on Christmas morn. His brother, Alexander, followed two years later. An heir and a spare.

I had done my duty to my husband and king.

Three years later, my daughter arrived. I called her Jane for my beloved friend. And I vowed that my daughter would know love and learning. My Jane would never be a possession of men. And while she would never hold a sword, she'd have a more powerful weapon at hand: her own mind.

Teaching her to brandish it would be my duty to her.

sixty-nine

Charles

The money we had stashed in the French hotel room got the three of us to England. We traveled by boat and paid dearly for the privilege to avoid customs. We didn't need The 48 knowing when our passports had been used.

Alice had traveled through the cosmic string thirty minutes before her time expired by holding fast to my brother. Thirty minutes after we arrived back in Paris, her retching and subsequent Quickening had been so severe we had to hold her until she recovered.

Even now she wasn't fully back to her old self. She slept a lot.

———

When I first proposed the idea, Alex wasn't happy at all about going back to Windsor, even several hundred years in the future. But I insisted. I had to see this first and last assignment through to the very end.

I had to say goodbye.

———

Windsor Castle was bustling with tourists. It looked brighter than I remembered it. And people weren't scared.

"Do you want us to come with you?" asked Alice. Her hair was growing back into its wild mass of curls, and to my delight, she had developed a liking for an English snack called a Jaffa Cake, which meant her face no longer had a pinched, unhealthy look to it.

Healthy was a look that suited Alice.

"No, it's okay. You two stay here," I replied. We were outside St. George's Chapel. The sun was shining and the grass was like a bright green carpet. "That way you can keep an eye out for…"

I didn't need to finish the sentence. We weren't safe. We would never be safe, not as long as Grinch and The 48 survived on one side, and Piermont and his breakaway order survived on the other. We had every reason to believe that both would be coming after us.

The Quire was in the eastern part of the chapel, near the cloisters. A helpful yeoman had handed me a map.

Under a black marble slab, surrounded by black-and-white tiles, I found what I was looking for. It had been a month since she saved my life.

But I had been unable to save hers.

IN A VAULT
BENEATH THIS MARBLE SLAB
ARE DEPOSITED THE REMAINS
OF
JANE SEYMOUR QUEEN OF KING HENRY VIII
1537
KING HENRY VIII
1547
KING CHARLES I
1648
AND
AN INFANT CHILD OF QUEEN ANNE.
THIS MEMORIAL WAS PLACED HERE
BY COMMAND OF
KING WILLIAM IV 1837.

I had picked a couple of daisies from the grass outside. They were crushed in my hand, but I thought Jane might appreciate the irony.

"She was his favorite," said a woman beside me. She had an overtanned face and platinum blond hair that was teased and sprayed to within an inch of its life.

She was my favorite too, I thought.

I left the daisies on a stone ledge. I didn't pray. I had no religion. But I was very, very glad our assignment's failure had meant that the Catholic religion endured. People should have choice. They should know their own minds and be able to act on their thoughts.

Jane had taught me that.

—————

"You okay?" asked Alex when I rejoined him and Alice. My brother was looking healthier too, although his back was a Metro map of scar tissue. He was fiddling with the bandage on his wrist. Alice had one too. We had cut out their timers—just in case.

I shrugged and slipped my hands into my pockets.

"So what's next?" asked Alice. She stared at me, as if goading me into saying that we should split up.

She knew me better than I knew myself. Alex and I were inseparable. But it might be that one day soon, it would be safer for us all if my brother and I went one way and Alice went another.

I wasn't going to say that today, though. Instead, I put my hand on my heart and closed my eyes. "Well, you see, Alice...I don't know what's next. Because really, death is the only constant in life. The majority of lives end without notice or legacy. Memories fade into the same dust as bones. Existences are words forged to be forgotten. We of The 48 are charged with ensuring that the chosen few take the path of historical importance and remembrance. Do not fear death. But do not make death your friend. Death is your master and your servant. There is no escape. For it comes to all in the end."

"Uh, Charlie," whispered Alex. I opened my eyes and discovered a couple of tourists in I LOVE LONDON T-shirts giving me funny looks.

"Heh," I croaked. "Sorry about that."

"Let's not say those words anymore, okay?" Alex said. "In fact, I'd like to erase that Tenet from my brain forever."

"I'm not going to forget it," I replied. "Because it's wrong. *Living* is the only constant in life. And we have the freedom to make our lives mean something now. On our own terms."

"Sounds good to me," said Alice. "Now...I'm sure I saw a supermarket just outside the walls. I'm hungry."

"For Jaffa Cakes, no doubt," said Alex. "I don't know where you put them."

"In my mouth," replied Alice, opening wide. "See?"

"Gross," said Alex, shaking his head, but the two of them walked off arm in arm. They instinctively knew I needed more time—for everything.

Was this a new normal? The choir started to sing the morning service in the chapel, and I couldn't help but shudder as the hairs on my arms stood to attention.

Someone had just walked over my grave, as they would say in England. And if Piermont was still out there somewhere, I would bet the world it was him.

Waiting. Watching.

The time thread in which Jane married Henry and gave him

a son was a fixed point now. Nothing could stop the events that immediately followed. By failing in the assignment, we had inadvertently helped Piermont. But it also meant we hadn't done anything to harm people's choices and beliefs.

I gave St. George's Chapel once last look and put my hand on my heart for Jane. I could hear her laughing in my head. Her ghost was my memory.

And despite my best efforts, I had become a time assassin in the end.

"I'm sorry, Jane," I whispered.

I couldn't decide for Alex or Alice, but I wouldn't let Jane's sacrifice mean nothing. My new life *would* mean something.

I hustled after the two people I loved most in this world.

It was time to get that life started.

Author's Note

Research is a key component of writing any novel, but especially one that has its fictional heart based in reality. The Tudor time line in *The 48* is real, and, aside from Anne Boleyn's actual execution, I think nothing reflects the brutality of her demise more than the speed at which the king, the Tudor court, and even Anne's own uncle, set her aside for the sake of a new queen, who they hoped would produce a male heir.

The House of Tudor has always intrigued me because of its cultural, political, and religious legacies that still dictate much of British life even now. It only consisted of five monarchs (Henry VII, Henry VIII, Edward VI, Mary I, and Elizabeth I) and it's a period in time that is disturbingly fascinating. Of course, for me, understanding life in the Tudor court meant more than just reviewing dates along a time line, and that is one of the reasons writing *The 48* was so challenging. I also wanted the reader to be able to see, taste, and even smell what Charlie, Alex, and Alice were experiencing. I borrowed heavily from every resource I could find, including actual letters written by Jane Seymour, which I pored over to ensure some degree of tonal accuracy in the fictional note she writes to Charlie.

I am particularly indebted to the staff of Historical Royal Palaces, who are responsible for the preservation of the Tower of London, Hampton Court, and other royal homes in the United Kingdom. These custodians of the past are also dedicated historians who make their valuable work available to the public. It's amazing how many stately homes in the UK have their own piece of Tudor history in the HRP archives, and it was in those archives that I often found informational gems outside of the other museums and libraries I consulted.

The majority of the Tudor characters in this novel actually lived, though Lady Margaret did not. I wanted a character from that time line who could narrate for me, and so I created one. Any historical inaccuracies are my burden to bear.

The Historical Royal Palaces' website (hpr.org.uk) is a terrific resource for familiarizing yourself with the Tudor court and its dwellings—but if you are ever in the UK, I strongly recommend a real-life visit to both Hampton Court Palace and Windsor Castle: Henry's home in life, and his tomb in death. (I first visited Hampton Court Palace as a child, so you could say this book has been forty years in the making!) I lived close to Windsor for several years and it is a beautiful, almost peaceful place—certainly a world away from the terror that Henry's tyrannical reign inflicted.